RAVE REVIEWS FOR
LOVE A REBEL,
LOVE A ROGUE

"A fascinating slice of history and equally fascinating characters. Enjoy!"

—Catherine Coulter

AND FOR SHIRL HENKE'S OTHER HISTORICAL ROMANCES

"Fast paced, sizzling, adventurous. *A Fire In The Blood* is a true Western with a strong-spirited heroine and a provocative, hot-blooded hero who will set you on fire!"

—Roseanne Bittner

"*White Apache's Woman* is a fascinating book, rich in history, wonderful. I enjoyed it thoroughly."

—Heather Graham

Terms of Surrender is "a romantic romp of a Western. I loved it!"

—Georgina Gentry

"*Terms of Love* is a sexy, sensual romp. Without a doubt, Shirl Henke at her best!"

—Katherine Sutcliffe

"Strong characters, exotic settings, and a wealth of historical detail....*Return to Paradise* swept me away!"

—Virginia Henley

"A riveting story about a fascinating period. I highly recommend *Paradise & More.*"

—Karen Robards

HANDS OF A REBEL, HEART OF A ROGUE

Quintin dropped the book and clasped Madelyne to him. His breath was labored and his whole body rigid with lust. He could feel her squirming against him as soft little mewling protests formed on her lips.

"Damn, don't you have anything on but this transparent stuff? 'Tis less than mosquito netting!"

"Let me go. You're drunk! I'll scream the house down," she gasped.

His grip was so strong that it squeezed the breath from her. "So, scream and bring my father and all the servants to see you half naked, roaming alone through the corridors."

"You are despicable! First you insult me and make it plain you are loath to wed me; then you attack me. You are no gentleman, sir!"

"And you are....What are you, Madelyne?"

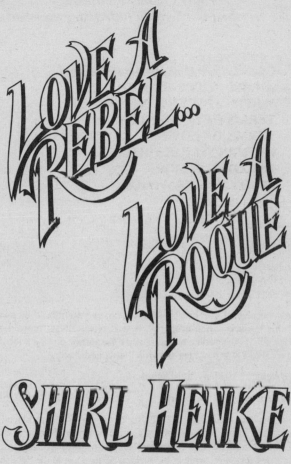

LOVE A REBEL...
LOVE A ROGUE

SHIRL HENKE

LEISURE BOOKS **NEW YORK CITY**

For Roy Charles Nehrt Sr.,
the very best brother any little sister ever had.

A LEISURE BOOK®

October 1994

Published by

Dorchester Publishing Co., Inc.
276 Fifth Avenue
New York, NY 10001

Printed in the United States of America.

"There never was a good war or a bad peace."

"I cannot but lament...the impending Calamities Britain and her Colonies are about to suffer, from great Imprudences on both Sides—Passion governs, and she never governs wisely."

—B. Franklin, February 5, 1775

ACKNOWLEDGMENT

The South during the era of the American Revolution was virgin territory to my associate Carol J. Reynard and me when we began the story of the Blackthorne family, set in the Georgia Colony of the 1780s. As usual Carol read up on Georgia's plant and animal life in the late eighteenth century, while I began researching the general historical background of the colony. Along the way we received a great deal of help from a wide variety of people whom we wish to thank.

Two fellow authors guided me to invaluable information about the Colonial South: Sharon Bills sent me a wealth of material on furniture and architecture, and Janelle Taylor provided me with a whole reading list on dress and social customs. You gals are the greatest.

Eileen A. Ielmini, archivist for the Georgia Historical Society Library's Savannah branch, provided me with an excellent bibliography, which yielded rich resources on Georgia life and history. I am particularly grateful to the Savannah Area Convention and Visitors Bureau and Jenny Stacy, media relations, for sending me printed materials about the city and its dramatic past.

Mrs. Hildegard Schnuttgen, director of reference for the Maag Library of Youngstown State University, and her superb staff have again come through for me with dozens of interlibrary-loan books, journals, and unpublished doctoral theses on Southern Colonial life. The Public Library of Youngstown and Mahoning Counties was also an excellent resource for my research.

Love A Rebel, Love A Rogue is our first manuscript to be printed on our new laser printer. We also have a whole new data-storage program in place, thanks to the work of Dr. Walt Magee. Mr. Mark Hayford saved us from the dreaded Michelangelo virus and gave our computer a clean bill of health. Since the wizardry of computers is Carol's domain, she especially wishes to thank them for their considerable assistance.

As always, my husband Jim has edited our rough copy, choreographed fight scenes, and even searched out books from the library for me. We are also indebted to our weapons expert, Dr. Carmen V. DelliQuadri Jr., D.O., for the assembly of rifles, muskets, pistols, and knives for the characters in *Love A Rebel, Love A Rogue*.

Prologue

He huddled in the stall, crouching in quivering silence amid the itchy straw and trying very hard not to cry, not even to breathe. The shadows engulfed his small, thin figure, concealing him from his father, who had come in search of him.

"Quintin, I know you're here. Show yourself at once." Robert Blackthorne's voice cut like the riding crop he flicked angrily against his thigh. His agitation grew as the boy continued to defy him. He scanned the dark interior of the stable. Damnation, the child was so small and thin that he could fair squeeze between the cracks in the walls!

Just then Robert heard a small hiccup in the musty silence. He cursed Obediah for saying the boy was not in here. The slave had lied for Quintin. So did all the servants. He stepped into a stall and found his quarry. "There you are. Come out before it goes harder on you."

Quintin forced down the sour bile gathering in his throat and stood up. For a seven-year-old, he was tall, if reed-thin. He held his chin up defiantly, swallowed once, then clenched his teeth lest his jaw betray him by trembling. Small, grimy fists were clenched tightly at his sides as he stepped into a shaft of yellow light filtering in from the open door. His black hair was matted with straw, and an angry bruise discolored one side of his face. He did not feel the pain as he looked up into Robert's cold blue eyes.

Robert Blackthorne saw the flash of defiance in the boy's bright green eyes before Quintin averted his gaze. "Look at you, the heir to Blackthorne Hill, filthy as a stableboy!" He cracked the quirt smartly against the oak post by the boy's head and was rewarded by a slight flinch. Good.

"You were forbidden to ride King's Pride. You could have injured a valuable breeding animal. Fortunately, he threw you before you broke his neck."

"I would never harm the colt! I halter-broke him myself. I've been riding him bareback all spring," Quintin said in a sudden rush of pride.

Robert's quirt did strike home this time, cutting through the linen of the boy's shirt, leaving a thin red line on his arm. "You ride like one of those damned savages! I know you were with that Indian trash of Alastair's!"

"Devon is my cousin. He's not trash."

"His mother is a Creek Indian and a disgrace to my brother's name. I've forbidden you ever to speak with Alastair or his mongrel get."

Now certain that his cousin Dev had escaped while Robert searched for him, Quintin felt goaded beyond endurance. "Uncle Alastair and Cousin Dev are my family. They care about me. You don't. Why don't you let me go live with them?"

"Go to your room at once," Robert said, following his curt command with a swift slash of the quirt against the boy's leg.

Ignoring the sharp pain, Quintin slipped by the towering giant and ran to the house, seeking refuge. His solace was not in his cold, beautiful room, however. It was in the attic.

Several months ago, he had overheard two servants whispering about the Lady Anne's pretties, all packed away in the dusty confines of the third floor of the mansion. He had searched through a maze of crates, barrels, and boxes stacked far higher than his scant four feet. After a dozen or more forays, he had found the treasure—his mother's beautiful gowns, jewels and paintings. One cedar chest held the best keepsakes, at least from the viewpoint of a seven-year-old boy. So now he sat surrounded with her memories, clutching a bundle of old letters from his father to her.

"If only you were here, Mother, things would be better. Father wouldn't be so angry all the time. Why did you have to go and die?" He stroked the satin ribbons holding the packet of letters, deeply absorbed in an imaginary world where a golden-haired lady held a small, dark-haired boy in her arms.

"Mistress Ogilve told me this is where I'd find you expressly where I've forbidden you to trespass."

"These are my mother's things. Why must they be hidden?" Quintin noticed that his father's manner had shifted. He was not shouting, but the unholy gleam in his eyes made the boy even more wary.

Calmly, Robert walked over to Quintin and took the packet of letters from him, replacing them carefully in the cedar chest. He took a small key from inside the chest and turned the lock on the lid. Fixing a hard stare on the boy, he said, "We're due for a talk. I think this is the best time. Yes, a most opportune time for you to understand your position. You are my only heir, and all the considerable wealth of Blackthorne Hill will one day come to you."

"I don't want anything that's yours," Quintin said, suddenly terrified by Robert's deadly quiet. He had grown used to being beaten, even being locked in the dark dressing closet in his room, but this icy calm was something new, and he had no defense against it.

"We're going down to my study, just you and I, Quintin. I have something to tell you, something of great moment that no other living being must ever hear. Do you mark me, boy?"

With a growing sense of dread, Quintin Blackthorne replied, "Yes, Father."

1767, Ravenal Hall, Outside Charles Town

"Oh, Aunt Isolde, he's quite the prettiest thing I've ever seen!" The little girl's silky hair bounced in shiny ringlets as she jumped up and down with delight in front of a sleek white pony.

Isolde Ravanal looked down into her niece's sparkling amber eyes, so like Marie's. She patted Madelyne's mahogany curls and laughed. "I thought you would fancy such a pony. Now let us see, what shall we name him?"

"Pegasus! For the winged horse in those wonderful Greek myths."

Isolde readily agreed, thinking delightedly of how her brother-in-law Theo would disapprove of his daughter reading Greek classics. She could hear his voice now: *Filling the gel's head with rubbish, that's what, Isolde.* With a wicked smile, she thought, *And so I shall!*

"Madelyne, how would you like to take a ride? Pegasus is quite well trained. Of course, we should change into riding clothes while the grooms saddle your Pegasus and my Wild Star." She watched as the girl's face rose, then fell.

"Must we go to such bother? Father will arrive for tea this afternoon. It was nearly noon before we were able to get Aunt Claud to leave, and we have only a couple of hours." Her voice took on a pleading tone that usually worked on her soft-hearted favorite aunt.

Isolde tapped her cheek with long, slender fingers and appeared to debate. "Well . . . no one is about to saddle the horses . . . and changing *would* take time."

"We've ridden bareback before, only you held me on Wild Star. Now that I have a pony of my very own, I can manage him without a silly old saddle. I promise not to race."

Laughing, Isolde scooped Madelyne into her arms and hugged the small girl fiercely. "I know your penchant for riding all too fast. I fear you shall take a tumble or two from Pegasus just as you have from other horses, but that is part of learning to ride. There is no greater freedom than feeling a horse beneath you while the wind blows in your unbound hair."

"Then let us ride like the wind, Aunt Isolde. Let us fly!"

And off they rode, two pairs of bare brown legs clinging to the sides of their horses, their skirts rucked up and their hair flying freely behind them like gleaming mahogany banners in the warm Carolina breeze.

Chapter One

May, 1780, twenty miles south of Charles Town

"Either you turn to scrubbing that floor or I'll have Will shoot that mongrel of yours, and there's an end to it!"

Madelyne Marie Deveaux knelt with her arms about a brown dog of no particular distinction except for his imposing size. She glared up at the prim, cold face of her aunt as the dog began to growl low in his throat.

Claud Deveaux pursed lips as thin as her emaciated body but did not yield an inch. With a wave of her hand, she silently summoned Will, a large, surly indentured servant who appeared from inside the house with an ancient fowling piece in his hands. "If that dumb brute moves, he'll die and you'll live to regret it; that I promise you," Claud threatened.

Madelyne felt the sting of tears. Helpless frustration welled up in her as she looked from the icy, unruffled demeanor of her father's sister to the leering servant with his weapon at the ready. "Tis Will Tarant who's the dumb brute, not Gulliver," she replied in a choked voice. "How can you be so heartless? All I did—"

"I am a God-fearing woman filled with Christian charity to take in a hoyden who disobeys her elders," Claud interrupted in her thin, precise voice. "Well, Madelyne, what will it be?" She eyed the dog with distaste.

Madelyne patted Gulliver and commanded him to remain sitting as she rose to face her tormentors. "I shall go to the kitchens straightaway and fetch bucket and mop."

Claud allowed a mere whisper of a smile to touch her lips. "That is sensible of you, Madelyne. I shall teach you gentle courtesy yet. This is suitable punishment for taking the coach horse and riding without escort, bare-back and astride like a common trollop." She looked at the dog with her cold pewter eyes and added, "Take that beast and tie him in the stable. I'll not have him running loose anymore . . . if you value his life."

Madelyne hid her clenched fists in the folds of her coarse gray cotton skirts. "I will see to him— if Will Tarant will put down his weapon. I fear lest he shoot one of us by accident!"

Claud nodded and Will silently shambled back into the house. She then turned with a swish of gray silk and followed him. Madelyne watched them vanish into the gray frame structure that was as plain and drab as its owner. "Merciful heavens, how I hate it here. Everything is gray. Even the weather," she muttered, glancing up at the sky massed with low hanging clouds. It was unseasonably warm for spring and the swampy air hung thick as tree moss. She turned toward the stable and began to trudge listlessly, the dog trotting obediently behind her.

As she tied him with a crude length of rope, Madelyne sighed. "I may reap a fearful penance before the day is done, but the ride was worth it, was it not, old friend?" She patted his head and he nuzzled her hand as if in agreement.

Early that morning, Madelyne had slipped from the house and taken the carriage horse from her aunt's stable. Both horse and girl had loved the freedom of her impetuous excursion. So had Gulliver, tagging along behind them. It had been almost as if she were back in Charles Town, on an early morning ride with Aunt Isolde.

Memories of her previous life again assaulted her with bittersweet poignancy. She left the dog and headed resolutely toward the kitchen. If Claud caught her dallying, her aunt would only prolong her penance. Madelyne had come to live with her father's spinster sister last winter when her Aunt Isolde died. Since her arrival, she had been engaged in a contest of wills with Claud Deveaux, a contest which the iron-willed old woman was slowly winning. How many nights without supper? How many days confined to her drab room? And now, the threat to kill Gulliver, her only remaining tie to her past life. After all manner of corporal punishment had failed to curb Madelyne's impetuous conduct, the shrewd old lady had finally hit upon her one weakness, her only friend.

By early afternoon, the gathered clouds had dispersed and thin yellow rays of sunlight broke through, making the low-lying swampy plantation even hotter and more pestilent. Every breath was an effort as Madelyne and the black slave Essie beat the sitting-room carpet. The rug was regularly cleaned and turned, but not replaced even though the dark blue wool was faded from the sun. Although a wealthy heiress, Claud Deveaux did not believe in frivolous displays.

Madelyne paused after one fierce swat and coughed, then resumed her strokes with methodical precision.

Essie, a thin, wiry young woman, let out a low chuckle. "You be dreamin' dat rug is Miz Claud."

Madelyne stopped and grinned conspiratorially at her companion. "Tis not as good as using the beater on her, but I suppose it does serve," she said, rubbing one grimy hand across her forehead and shoving back masses of sweat-darkened red hair. "A pox on this mop of mine. I shall fix it." She reached into the large pocket of her skirt and extracted a calico kerchief, knotting her hair behind her head and binding it fast with the cloth. "There, that is much cooler," she said, picking up the beater once more.

Essie giggled. "You look like one of Massah Mose's high yeller wenches with yo' hair tied up." An uncomfortable look swept across her face then. "Miz Claud got no right to work you like dis. You her blood kin."

Madelyne grimaced. "Don't remind me. I take after the Ravenal side of the family, not the Deveaux side."

Just then the sound of hoofbeats drumming up the front drive caused both women to stop and peer from their partial concealment at the side of the house. Mistress Deveaux had few visitors except for Madelyne's father, who was not expected.

"Lawdy, Glory, look at dat one," Essie said with awe in her voice.

Madelyne peeked around the corner, clutching the rug beater with both hands, as transfixed as Essie with the elegantly dressed rider astride his magnificent black stallion. His boots gleamed as brightly as the raven locks of his blue-black hair. His bottle-green coat was faultlessly cut across wide shoulders, and he wore a plain buff waistcoat. He reined in the black and dismounted in one smooth motion. His pants hugged his long, slim legs indecently, Madelyne thought.

Then her eyes traveled up his broad chest, above

the stark white silk of his stock, to fasten on the most arresting face she had ever seen. Harsh and hawkish it was, and unfashionably darkened by the sun—the face of a fallen angel. The purity of its lines were in classic proportion—firm jaw, straight nose, high forehead, with heavy angular eyebrows framing dark eyes that keenly swept the front of the squat, ugly house. Madelyne squinted, trying to decide the color of those piercing eyes, but the distance was too far. His lips were sculpted as if by the hand of Michelangelo, but he did not smile.

Until Essie inadvertently poked her in the ribs with her rug beater, Madelyne forgot to breathe. Both women watched as he tied the stallion to the post and strode grimly to the front door, vanishing from their sight.

"Who is dat debil? Sho is a pretty 'un. Think he be kin to you?"

"He's certainly no relation to Aunt Claud. I'd bet my last good ball gown on that—especially since she'll never let me wear it again. It's been packed away for so long it's probably molded by now."

"Miz Claud don't hold wid dancin', ner ladies showin' what God give 'em in low-cut dresses neither. Bet you looked like a real princess in one of them gowns, Miz Madelyne."

Madelyne sighed, then turned back to the rug with resignation. "Tis no matter, Essie. I'll never dance again—or have a beau to ask me, if Aunt Claud has her way. We'd best get this rug cleaned and rolled so Abram can replace it before evening or I'll spend another night without dinner—and I'm starved!"

"Mr. Blackthorne, what a delightful surprise. My brother Theodore said you would not arrive for another week," Claud said, making a stiff little curtsy in front of her tall visitor.

"My apologies, Mistress Deveaux, but I was able to

complete my business in Charles Town more quickly than I anticipated, since his majesty's forces have retaken the capital. I must be on my way home to Georgia and could not dally longer." He sketched a bow, his face as unsmiling as hers.

"Of course. I understand. You're here to see the girl." Claud paused, struggling to conceal her agitation. "If you would but take some refreshment, I will prepare her."

"No need. I only require a few words with her and tricking her out in finery will interest me not in the least. I must be back in Charles Town before dark."

"I would offer you the hospitality of my home, Mr. Blackthorne. You need not ride back tonight."

"I think it best if I do," Blackthorne replied dryly. Her hospitality was probably as cold and thin as yesterday's porridge. But if her aloof Calvinist manner was any indication, she had raised the chit to know her place, and to obey.

"If you're certain, I shall summon her. She has been set at tasks outdoors all afternoon. Please forgive her appearance. Madelyne is a hard worker."

"I am gratified to hear it. Have no fear for her appearance. You and I both know virtue is internal." He smiled as she nodded in fierce agreement. Now *that* had struck a familiar chord in her Huguenot soul.

"I will fetch her directly." Claud swished from the room.

She found Madelyne in the yard and was appalled. The girl was filthy! "Come with me," she said imperiously. "And none of your sass. We have an important visitor, who would have a few words with you."

Madelyne's mind raced. Surely the beautiful dark stranger could not want to meet her? Before she could gather her scattered thoughts, Claud's bony fingers clamped on her shoulder with surprising strength.

"You listen to me, niece, and you heed me well. Mr. Blackthorne's father is an old friend of your father's. You will be meek and polite before him. One word of hoydenish sass from you, and I promise you will not eat for a week—and you will never again see that filthy mongrel. I will have him destroyed! Now take that disgraceful kerchief from your hair and—"

"Mistress Deveaux, the gentleman says he must be gone soon." The maid Leta burst into the back sitting room and curtsied breathlessly. "He would not take tea but sent me to ask after Miss Madelyne."

Claud watched as Madelyne pulled her hair free of the sweat-stained red kerchief. It fell in damp, tangled clumps about her shoulders and down her back. "Take off your cap," she commanded the servant. "Let Madelyne at least confine her hair decently beneath it."

Madelyne did as she was bidden, still wondering what on earth was happening. Dumbly she followed Claud down the hall to the front sitting room.

Blackthorne took one look at the filthy urchin and nearly burst into bitter laughter. Restraining himself, he bowed and smiled perfunctorily. "Your aunt said you were a hard worker. It would seem she did not exaggerate." God, her hair, some undefinable dark shade, was confined beneath a mobcap that suspiciously resembled the one the indentured maid had been wearing. A few straggling tendrils fell across her forehead and more stuck damply to her nape. She was small and thin like her aunt. Beyond that he could tell little, for her dress was loosely cut of a coarse gray cotton and hung like sacking on her.

He had steeled himself for her to be plain, even prayed for it, but he would have no half-wit in the bargain! He studied her wide set eyes, an odd shade of pale golden amber. "Can you speak, mistress? I am Quintin Blackthorne. Your father and mine campaigned against the French in the late wars."

Her tongue cleaved to the roof of her mouth as she stared at the cold, beautiful stranger. *He is rude, no matter his blinding looks*. Yet she knew Claud watched her with a pinched expression on her face, ready to pounce if she misspoke herself. "I—I am Madelyne Marie Deveaux, Mr. Blackthorne. My father has never mentioned the Blackthorne family to me."

"Of course not, child. Fathers do not speak of that beastly war against the Papists with their children," Claud chided her.

"Have you any skills with sums?" he asked, ignoring Claud.

Madelyne's chin went up a notch. Aunt Isolde had seen to a thorough if highly unorthodox education for her. "Yes, I can do sums and read. Even write a passable hand. I have read the classics in Latin and—"

"Enough of such vainglory," Claud interrupted. "The important thing is that you can read your Bible and know the Heidleburg Catechism."

"Yes, of course, Aunt Claud," Madelyne said, struggling not to show her anger. She searched Blackthorne's chiseled features, which revealed nothing except for the startling dark green color of his eyes. *At least that much of my curiosity is satisfied*.

He nodded. "She will do. Have her ready to travel in a fortnight." With that abrupt announcement, he turned and swept up his hat. "With your permission, ladies, I must ride for Charles Town at once."

As Madelyne stood at the window watching him ride away, a shiver of premonition ran down her spine. "Whatever did he mean?" she asked Claud.

"Your father will arrive tomorrow. Tis for him to explain," was all the old woman would answer.

"He is *what!*" Madelyne dropped her spoon, which fell with a clatter into her bowl, staining the white linen tablecloth with a fine spray of soup. Claud started to reprimand her, then subsided when Theodore laughed dismissively.

"He is to be your husband. Deuced sorry to have missed Robert's young pup. Haven't seen 'em in years. It's all arranged now that he's met you. That was his only condition to the marriage."

"He acted more like he was inspecting a mule than having a conversation with his betrothed! Father, why did you not tell me?"

Theodore swallowed his soup. It was thin and lacked seasoning. Silently he cursed Claud's parsimony, eager to be quit of her and his troublesome burden of a daughter. "Eh? Don't you like his looks? I hear all the women in Charles Town fair swoon over 'em."

"His looks are not at issue, Father. He is quite . . . handsome." She colored, realizing that she had almost said beautiful! "He was rude to me and seemed most displeased with the whole of it."

"Mr. Blackthorne would not have been displeased if you had looked the part of a lady," Claud remonstrated sourly.

"'Twas you, Aunt, who set me to beating rugs in the afternoon heat!"

"Only because you defied all my efforts to teach you God-fearing deportment!"

"Enough!" Theodore gave each of the bristling females a quelling look. "I'll not have bickering at table. It quite disturbs the digestion," he said, rubbing his ample abdomen. "Now, here is the way of it, Madelyne. You will return with me to your beloved Charles Town to purchase a suitable trousseau, then off you go to Savannah. Quintin Blackthorne is one of the wealthiest planters and traders in Georgia. You are fortunate indeed to make such a match."

But that cold, arrogant man doesn't want me, she pleaded silently, realizing that her father had taken the matter completely out of her hands. She looked at Claud's pinched face and pewter eyes. *At least I'll escape this hellish place,* she silently consoled herself. Yet a small niggling voice asked, *Have you escaped one hell only to plunge into another?* Eyes as cold and green as the Atlantic in December flashed into her mind, chilling her, scorning her.

May, 1780, London

"You are a disgrace to the Caruthers name! A young, unwed girl, running with that scandalous crowd. Lord Darth is the most infamous rakehell in London. Do you think someone of his ilk will ask for your hand?" Barbara's mother's eyes glowed like blue flames as she stared at her recalcitrant daughter, who remained totally unruffled, affecting a bored expression. Her face was the mirror image of her mother's twenty years earlier, a flawless, heart-shaped visage with patrician features, delicate yet oddly strong for all its beauty.

With complete indifference, Barbara smoothed the pompadour of her elaborate white wig and swished her pink satin skirts as she turned toward her mother, the Dowager Baroness of Rushcroft. "I wondered when it would all come down to this. Lord Darth, that fearful villain, paying attention to me—instead of you!"

Marianne took a swift step forward, then regained her composure. "Darth is twice your age. Not at all suitable."

"For me or for you? Everyone from London to Bath knows you were his mistress until he tired of you."

This time Marianne took that last step and slapped Barbara. "You will never again repeat that," she ground out in a low voice. "Never!" She whirled back, steadying the panniers of her peacock-blue gown before she reached for a pile of papers on the Queen Anne desk behind her. "How long do you think I'll continue to pay these?" She threw the markers at Barbara.

Like oversized snowflakes, they fluttered all around the girl, falling to the heavy Persian carpet. Barbara touched a note with the toe of her slippered foot. "I've just had a run of bad luck at whist the past few weeks, that's all. Twill turn in my favor again."

"You overspend your allowance every month. Your father gambled away a goodly portion of our wealth. I will not stand by and watch you dispatch the rest of it!"

"Is that the reason you so mourn the loss of Darth? Was he a generous patron, Mother? He'll never marry you either. At least I have the straight of that!"

"And no gentleman will ever marry you if you continue as you have. You're the daughter of a baron! You must wed advantageously. Considering your fondness for the high life, I would suggest you heed my warning." Marianne paused and studied Barbara consideringly. "The Earl of Wickersham called again yesterday morning."

Barbara stiffened, then made a moue of disgust. "Wickersham is a buffoon, fat, old—"

"And rich. He's in the market for a wife and is quite taken with you. I do believe he would even be indulgent enough to pay your gaming debts if you handled him properly." Marianne waited with one delicate brow arched.

"Never." Barbara shivered with loathing. "To win his indulgence, I'd have to submit to his foul breath, slobbering lips, and perversions! Or haven't you heard the whispers about town, Mother? His last wife killed herself because he forced her to join him in his sport with a young boy."

"Wickersham is an earl with land holdings from here to Ireland. You're just spreading unfounded rumors. A girl your age shouldn't even know of such filth, much less speak of it!"

"And our family needs his money, so it really doesn't signify what his morals are—or his looks. I've had other offers from far more pleasing men."

"But none as rich by half. Young fools whose fathers hold the purse strings."

"Understand this, Mother. I would *not* marry Wickersham if he was the last peer in the realm."

Lady Marianne's lips pursed and her eyes darkened with frustration. "Then you make your own bed, my pet. See who pays these." She gestured to the markers lying about the floor. I shall not stand behind your debts ever again. You are cut off from all further allowance as well."

"If Monty were here, you wouldn't dare treat me so!"

"But your brother is not here. He's off in that ghastly colonial wilderness fighting rabble. I am in charge of your expenses, not Montgomery."

"Then I shall simply have to pawn my jewelry. Darth will help me if I ask him," Barbara added, a dare in her voice. God, how she despised the procession of men who had traipsed in and out of her mother's bedroom ever since her earliest childhood memories, long before her father had died. Indeed, she had only taken up with Darth Kensington to infuriate Marianne. She liked him little better than Wickersham.

The two women stared at each other in a silent contest of wills. Marianne was still voluptuous and striking, but clearly past her prime. Her skin beneath the powders and creams was crepey and flaccid, her once magnificent blue eyes now marred by tiny wrinkles at the corners. Barbara had inherited her mother's perfect face and her father's height. Slim and supple, yet handsomely curved with strong young muscles and not a wrinkle or a sag anywhere on her body.

At that instant Marianne hated her. Never before had she considered her daughter to be more than an irritating nuisance, easily foisted off on nannies. Now she had become a rival—a woman who displayed the same mulish determination Montgomery had when he purchased his commission in spite of his father's threats and her pleas. Where did her children's willful strength come from? They must both be throwbacks to some distant ancestor, she decided.

Then as thoughts of Monty filtered through her mind, a new idea occurred to her. "Barbara," she purred, "you and your brother were always so close."

Barbara shrugged. "In the nursery. I've not seen him in six years. The army is his life now."

"Yes, he has done well, I suppose, a major serving General Prevost. Although he does find life in the southern colonies a bit more rustic than even Philadelphia, which I understand was pestilent."

"I never realized that you bothered to read his letters." Over the years, Monty's letters had grown fewer and fewer as his rank and duties escalated, especially since that dreadful war had begun.

"Oh yes, I've perused a few. Enough to know he's presently stationed in a tropical backwater of mosquitoes and roaches, surrounded by roving bands of rabble who terrorize the countryside." She paused. "If you find life under my roof so insufferable that you must resort to wild escapades, and you refuse the Earl of Wickersham's suit, then perhaps it would be better if you went to Montgomery. Your brother can deal with you. I wash my hands of you!"

"To Savannah!" Barbara fairly shrieked. "I won't go."

"You will—if I have to have the servants truss you up like a Christmas goose and haul you aboard ship."

Barbara looked at the venom gleaming in Marianne's eyes and realized that she meant every word she said.

Chapter Two

June, 1780, The Charles Town-Savannah Post Road

Madelyne stood in the rough, dusty road looking from the broken baggage cart to the nearly naked red savages approaching them. *I will not panic. I will remain calm for Jemmy's sake.* The young groom lay beside the collapsed cart. He had been pinned beneath a smashed wheel, which he had been trying to lift free and replace. Will Tarrant and the other men had quickly freed him. But now, from the corner of her eye, she saw Tarrant clutching his fowling piece apprehensively. "Don't be a fool. There are at least a score of them and but six of us." She added less certainly, "They are supposed to be friends of those loyal to the king."

All the Indians were indecently clad in scanty breechclouts and moccasins. The tallest of the group moved forward slowly, his right hand raised with the palm open. Madelyne studied his clear brown eyes, trying not to stare at the grotesque tattoos that lined his naked chest with dark blue ridges. Like his fellows, his earlobes were deformed and elongated, pierced with heavy copper ornaments. His head was partially shaven, leaving only a small fringe of hair around his forehead and one long strand adorned with feathers and beads which fell halfway down his back. His cheeks, too, were scarred with smaller versions of the hideous blue tattoos.

Gulliver growled low when he felt Madelyne's quiver of fear, but she patted the dog and soothed him. "He seems peaceful enough. Now let us pray he speaks English." The sound of her voice reassured the dog, who cocked his head and watched as the savage halted about ten feet in front of Madelyne.

"Good day, sir. We are in a bit of distress. Our cart wheel snapped and my groom was gravely injured when the cart fell on him. Can you help us?"

The savage listened intently, his face unreadable. Then he asked in guttural but understandable English, "You liberty men?"

"Most certainly not!" Madelyne drew herself up to her full five feet and one inch of height and stuck out her small chin pugnaciously. "We are loyal subjects of King George. I am Madelyne Marie Deveaux, betrothed to Mr. Blackthorne of Savannah."

At the mention of Blackthorne, the Indian's eyes suddenly lit. He struck his palm against his chest with a resounding thump and said, "I am Mad Turkey, brother to Blackthorne. What means betrothed?" He pronounced the word carefully.

Under his curious scrutiny, Madelyne knew she was blushing as she replied, "I am on my way to Savannah to marry Mr. Blackthorne—to become his wife." Good blessed heavens! Not only was Quintin Blackthorne rude and surly, but he consorted with wild Indians! To what kind of family was her father sending her?

"His woman?" He grunted, then quickly gave several curt commands to two of his followers who came forward. They ignored her four armed escorts and knelt beside poor Jemmy. After a cursory examination, another rapid exchange was made in their bewildering tongue. Then the one identified as Mad Turkey said, "The boy has many hurts. You need medicine man. You come, my camp."

Madelyne watched in growing consternation as several Indians began to fashion a crude stretcher from uncured deerhides, which they took from their pack animals.

"We go now," Mad Turkey said, pointing toward a twisting path leading into a dense stand of oak and hickory trees.

"Would it not be better to send for help and wait here with my bags? All my trousseau—my bride gifts—are in the wagon and my servant is injured too badly to travel." *They mean us no harm,* she told herself, smoothing the green twill skirts of her riding habit.

More orders were issued to the Indians. When they began to take the trunks and boxes from the cart and heft them up, Clyde and Avery looked at her questioningly and Will Tarrant seemed about ready to threaten the savages. Madelyne shook her head, whispering to Jasper Oldham, who stood closest to her, "If they wanted to loot our wagon, they had but to kill us straightaway. We'll go with them. We're close enough to Savannah. The leader will send for help. It won't take long, I'm certain."

"You may believe them stinkin' savages, but I don't," Will said sourly.

Madelyne ignored him and went to Jemmy's side, Gulliver loping after her. The lad was unconscious as they laid him on the makeshift carrier. As Madelyne and her escorts led their horses, following the Indians into the dark embrace of the trees, she prayed she was not making a monumental mistake—perhaps the last one in her life!

June, 1780, Savannah

The Blackthorne city house stood on St. James Square, just across from Governor Wright's official residence. As befitted the home of the most illustrious trader, planter, and stockman in the colony, the edifice was made of fired brick and stood three stories high. The candles in the chandelier winked from a front window. Tonight Robert Blackthorne and his son Quintin were entertaining senior officers of the British general staff in charge of the occupation.

"A pity Governor Wright could not be here. This is damned fine Madeira, Robert," Colonel Ashburton said as he swallowed the rich wine.

"I hope the governor isn't ill. Tis the season for ague," Quintin said.

"Nothing of the sort. He and General Prevost had to confer on plans for the sweep north," Major Oliver replied as a servant set a Wedgewood bowl before him. The delicate, spicy fragrance of turtle consomme filled the air. Taking a sniff, he said, "You do know how to set a splendid table, Robert."

The elder Blackthorne nodded his head, allowing a slight smile to ruffle his austere features. He wore no wig and his iron gray hair was unpowdered, a Georgia custom dictated by the heat, but the cut of his charcoal satin waistcoat and pearl linen coat was impeccable. A flawlessly arranged stock of black silk added to the mien of somber power that enveloped his person.

"Even among us colonials, Miles, there are a few who have cultivated the finer points of civilization." Robert's eyes swept the magnificent Chippendale table covered with an Irish linen tablecloth and set with fine china. Massive silver candlesticks held spermaceti candles, which bathed the whole room in golden light.

"I daresay we have every luxury in this house that one might find in the homes of England's finest gentry, and all we have to do is work for it." Quintin cast a look of challenge in Robert's direction.

"Quite so. Rather like we poor military men serving his majesty in this damned campaign—only our pay is always in arrears," Colonel Ashburton said cheerfully, taking another swallow of the excellent Madeira, unaware of the tension between father and son.

"Speaking of the campaign, I hear you're moving on Augusta soon," Quintin remarked as he sipped a spoonful of consomme.

"We'll be moving out within the week, royal militia along with several hundred of my regulars," Ashburton replied.

"I hope you drive those rebel scum into the river and drown every man jack of 'em," Robert said fervently.

"To the recapture of Augusta. Hear, hear," the colonel and the major echoed.

All four men raised their glasses in a toast.

"I say, Quintin, is your cousin still upriver with the Creek Indians?" the major asked. "They'll be useful allies when we sweep inland to drive those rebel pockets of resistance to ground."

"Devon may be anywhere. Boy's like the damned wind. Not like his elder brother, Andrew, who's solid as a rock," Robert replied.

Quintin scowled. "Devon has kept the Muskogee— or Creeks, as you call them, loyal to the British cause by delivering presents from his majesty to them, but as to using them in war . . ." He played with the crystal goblet of Madeira for a moment. "I think it most unwise."

Robert's face was like a storm cloud, but it was Colonel Ashburton who answered. "How so,

Quintin? They are fierce fighters."

"Yes, they are. Have you ever been in the back country and seen a massacre? Every subject born in this colony is familiar with what Indians can do when they go to war, I assure you."

"But the savages are under orders from British regular army, sir. I must protest," the colonel replied in affront.

Quintin scoffed. "Once loosed, no one controls a Muskogee war party. And they won't stop to ask whether a family is Whig or Tory before they scalp them."

"That scarcely speaks well for men like your half-caste cousin. He's always assured his majesty's government that his mother's people are loyal subjects," Oliver said.

"The poor devils only want to save their land. The army has promised to keep squatters out. That's one reason so many Georgians in the back country support the rebellion—land hunger. But I can guarantee you that if his majesty's government brings the Muskogee in on this war, it will drive a great many loyal subjects right into the arms of the Liberty Boys."

Colonel Ashburton considered Quintin's words, but his young companion snorted in derision. "Give us a few weeks in the back country and British steel will clean 'em out."

"Pray tell me more, Miles. When do you leave and who all is going on this sweep?" Quintin took a bite of juicy pink beef and washed it down with rich sweet wine. The dinner was progressing splendidly.

"I noticed you did not mention your impending marriage to our honored guests. Having second thoughts?" Robert sat in a wing chair in his library, his eyes narrowed on Quint.

"No." Quint untied the ribbon that had held his shoulder-length hair clubbed at his nape. Rubbing his neck, he looked down at Robert in cold amusement. "The chit will serve well enough. She's plain, healthy, and has a modicum of education, so she should birth me no morons."

"Plain, eh?"

"You know damn well I want no belle to charm all the men in Savannah and then let half of them lift her skirts." He took a drink of fine cognac, smuggled from France, then laughed. "God above, if that old Calvinist spinster who raised her is any measure, Madelyne should be appalled enough on our wedding night that she'll want no man to touch her."

"Just so you touch her—and plant an heir in her belly that you know is your own," Robert said.

Quint leveled dark green eyes on the man he called father and asked cynically, "Can any man ever trust his wife enough to be certain his children are his own?"

"I chose the girl myself. Known her father for forty years. Good blood. Raised in the country by maiden aunts. You're a damn sight more fortunate than I."

Quint tossed down the last of the cognac, which had gone sour on his palate. "No need to preach to me. I'll wed her and bed her, but I will seek my *pleasure* elsewhere."

"Serena, eh?" Robert looked faintly amused now. "As long as you never thought to wed her, I have no argument with that, other than to advise discretion. She is Andrew's cousin by marriage, after all, and a lady." Robert spoke the last word like an epithet.

Quint looked at Robert with frank incredulity. "God above, you truly take me for a fool if for one moment you thought I'd wed Serena! I'm going out for a ride."

As Quint turned on his heel and quit the library, Robert stared into the dying embers in the fireplace and murmured low, "You're not the fool, Quintin, I am."

Quint rode swiftly from the city in the still night heat. He patted the big black's neck and murmured, "Domino, I bet you wish this weather would break even more than I do." Horse and rider continued through the soft, sand-packed streets, Domino's hoofbeats muted and slow. Twice Quint was hailed by night sentries, once at Barnard Street and again as he left the city.

Every British soldier in Savannah recognized the son of the worthy Loyalist, Robert Blackthorne. No one questioned his riding to Polly Bloor's tavern for a bit of fun. He headed northwest, following the twisting curves of the river until he saw the dimly winking lights of the Golden Swan high on the western bluff.

He smiled, thinking of the first time a frightened lad of fifteen years had dared to set foot in the place, a purse clutched in one fist, asking for the services of a whore. Back then, Polly had been a toothsome wench if a man's tastes ran to big, fleshy blondes with wide smiles and ample breasts. She had been a good teacher for a green boy, Polly had, and he respected her honesty. She was a whore and made no pretense or excuse for it. Quint trusted Polly Bloor as he did no other woman.

Of course, he and Polly were engaged in a totally different kind of activity now. A grim smile slashed his face as he dismounted at the tavern door. Bloody hell, how he would love announcing to Robert Blackthorne what he was doing. It might send the old son of a bitch into an apoplexy.

A young stableboy who worked for Polly cheerfully took his horse. He flipped the lad a coin and entered the smoky interior of the tavern and coach house. Although the hour was late, business was still brisk. Two burly rivermen dressed in buckskins sat with huge tankards of ale before them, quaffing the warm, foamy brew and talking loudly. The scarred tables and chairs were made of sturdy oak and hickory, not the soft pine so prevalent in the area. Polly's customers were known to be hard on furniture from time to time.

He wended his way between tables, greeting coach drivers, rivermen, planters, half-caste traders, and even a smattering of gentlemen from the city who came to Polly's for a sporting time. During daylight hours, horse races were often held on the flat open ground stretching behind the coach house. A great deal of money passed hands in Polly's place. Quintin's eyes scanned the room, but he did not see the man he was to meet.

Polly Bloor came barreling through the doorway leading to the kitchen. "Quint, darlin', I been hopin' you'd get a thirst one of these nights," she said, thrusting her ample bosom against his chest and enveloping his lean waist in her fleshy arms. She was a tall, rawboned woman who did not have to strain to kiss him full on the lips, even though he was six feet in height.

"Yes, Polly, I had a thirst, but even more, I had a longing to see your beautiful smile," he said as they walked companionably to a table in a secluded alcove. She yelled to the barkeep to draw two stout drafts of her best ale, then sat with him until the drinks were served.

When the burly barkeep left, she winked at her guest and tossed off a stiff gulp of the ale. "Here's to old times, darlin'." Looking around to make certain they were not overheard, she added, "Solomon Torres is upstairs. First door on the right. Lucy's in the room across from him. I'll send her down to fetch you."

"Why all the extra precautions? We've always sat and shared a drink openly before."

Polly shrugged. "Solomon told me that he thinks he's bein' watched by some of Governor Wright's men. Most of the Jews in Savannah openly supported the rebel cause. Tis best if you aren't seen together."

"All right. Send Lucy down to entice me to her room," he said as he tipped his chair back against the rough log wall.

Lucy arrived, and shortly he was slipping into Solomon Torres's room undetected. The slim, sandy-haired man stood up at once and clasped Quint's hand in a firm shake. "I trust Polly explained our problem. We may need to change our rendezvous after this. You can't be linked to any suspicious characters, my friend." Torres's thin, angular face split in a wide grin, making him appear boyishly handsome.

"We'll work something out," Quintin said. "Our cause needs you, with your connections as a trader up and down the coast, as much as it needs me."

"What news have you got for me? I trust your father's bountiful table and wine cellar loosened the tongues of his guests?"

Quint smiled grimly. "If only he knew how well. Tis almost too easy, Solomon. They bray about how quickly they'll crush the Georgia patriots and then give out every detail about troop movements, ordinance, anything I ask. As we suspected, they plan a sweep north to try to recapture Augusta—leaving in three days. Ashburton is marching with a battalion and about forty royal militia." Quint proceeded to give a detailed account of men, weaponry, and marching order while Solomon wrote it all down in his own code.

"Good, although I fear we won't be able to muster enough men to hold Augusta now. At least the state officers can escape to a less accessible location. I leave before dawn with my trading wagon. Once we're well up the road, I'll ride ahead for Augusta and tell Stephen Heard what to expect."

"You're a good man, Solomon. Let's drink to a successful—er, holding action against his majesty's troops." Quint took the bottle he'd carried upstairs and poured two drinks, then handed one to Torres. "Rum is kosher, isn't it?"

Torres laughed and drank with relish. "If not, I'm a poor Jew indeed!" He paused and looked across the table, the flickering candlelight softening his angular face. "How did you come to the patriot cause? Your family is staunchly loyalist, longtime friends with James Wright."

"Governor Wright is a good man in an impossible job, as are many Englishmen on both sides of the Atlantic. Look at all our champions in Parliament, men like Edmund Burke, even the Earl of Chatham himself. Yet no one listened to their warnings, and now the die is cast. As for me"—Quint shrugged—"let's just say I had a natural predilection to defy my father, combined with the patriot influence of my mentor while I was at university in Philadelphia."

"Your mentor?"

"A most remarkable man. A writer of subtle wit, elected as fellow of the Royal Society for his brilliant scientific studies. He had no formal education beyond being apprenticed as a printer in boyhood, yet he's become our most brilliant statesman—Ben Franklin."

Torres's eyes widened. "Our ambassador to the French court, who negotiated the alliance with France and Spain?"

"Yes. A man of rare common sense. While everyone else was clamoring for war, Ben worked tirelessly in London for compromise, but when war was inevitable, he knew where his loyalty must lie. Tis not always an easy decision. Some, like my father, cling to German George with blind prejudice, but others genuinely believe we can keep our rights as Englishmen if we remain loyal and are patient. Once I hoped for that, too."

"But now it's gone past hope, and each man must choose sides." Torres sighed. "All my family has been in the patriot camp, but I know you and your cousin are on opposing sides."

"Yes, Devon is an ardent loyalist. I always knew he'd take his stand with the British. His mother is half Muskogee, and the Confederation has always leaned toward the Crown. British soldiers are their only protection from the encroachment of our settlers."

"Balderdash. The royal governor's wrung cessions of land from them repeatedly."

"But the royal governor has made them dependent on the trade goods we bring them. Remember, even a shaky ally is better than an avowed enemy. The Muskogee—"

Quint was interrupted by the sound of glass breaking, furniture cracking, and curses rending the air. A smile quirked his lips. "Something tells me that my cousin Devon has put in an appearance below."

The whole taproom was in chaos when Quint reached the head of the stairs. He scanned the melee of men punching and kicking, gouging and rolling on the planked floor, until he saw Devon's dark blond head in the thick of the brawl. His cousin was busily engaged in crashing a tankard of ale over the head of a huge, bull-necked fellow who obligingly collapsed onto the floor.

Just then a deafening report from Polly's blunderbuss quieted the uproar. Men froze with fists raised and turned to where the buxom owner of the Golden Swan stood atop a scarred oak table, with a second piece sweeping menacingly across the crowd. "All right, you rum-soaked coxcombs! Next man jack to break anythin' in my place gets a taste of scrap pot metal in his gizzard."

A few bellows of laughter erupted. Men just engaged in mayhem slapped their foes on the back, and everyone settled down to eating and drinking once again.

Quint, holding the rum glass in his hand, sauntered down the stairs, watching as Devon pinched a pretty young barmaid and then seized Polly from the table. Dev swung her, blunderbuss and all, to the floor as if she weighed no more than a feather. When he bent to kiss her, she scolded, "First you nearly wreck my place, now you'd charm me, you rogue."

"I had to defend the honor of Priscilla Watson from the slander Rafer Dooley was spouting. I'd defend you the same, Polly."

"You'd defend anything in skirts, then reach right up 'em—if she be pretty enough!" She allowed him to give her a fulsome kiss.

"I might have known it was you wenching again, Devon," Quint said.

"And well I may, as I'm still a free man bound to no woman, while you, cousin, are pledged." Devon's dancing brown eyes mocked Quint as a lazy smile slashed his face.

Quint did not return the smile. "I should've known you'd get word of my betrothal even in the back country."

"You're to be wed Sunday next, yet here you are consorting with Polly's lovely wenches. For shame, Quint."

"Tis no joking matter, Devon. You know my feelings about leg-shackling. I'd none of the chit if my need were only for a bed mate."

Devon threw back his head of shaggy gold hair and laughed, clapping one long arm about his cousin's shoulders. The two tall, slim men strolled across the noisy taproom, sidestepping broken pieces of furniture, heading toward a table by the rear door. "Be a love and bring us more of the fine libation

Quint is drinking, Polly my girl," Devon called over his shoulder.

As they took their seats on opposite sides of a narrow plank table, the dim light from a lantern made Devon's brown eyes and swarthy skin appear even darker, the only visible signs of his quarter Muskogee blood. The bold, sensual mouth, sculpted nose, and winged eyebrows were classically handsome and set off to perfection by his golden hair. He took a swallow of the rum Polly had set down in front of him and then said softly, "If you're so displeased with the chit as your black scowl bespeaks, you can leave her with the Muskogee."

Quint's eyes narrowed and he reached across the table, taking hold of Devon's shirt-sleeve. "What are you talking about? If this is one of your jests—"

"Not at all. I just received a message from Mad Turkey's temporary hunting camp. It would seem they're offering hospitality to Madelyne Deveaux, late of Charles Town and environs."

As Devon related the details of Madelyne's misadventure, Quint swore beneath his breath. "We've not even wed, and already she's causing me trouble. Why the hell did she travel through that boggy swampland with a baggage cart? Any sensible female would wait for a drogger and sail down the coast."

Devon shrugged. "Why not ask the lady yourself? That is, if you feel inclined to accompany me when I rescue her. If not, I could be prevailed upon—"

Now Quint's face split in a grin, but his eyes were like green ice as he interrupted. "I'd not trust you with the wife of a Salzberger pastor!"

Devon laughed heartily. "A pox on you, Quint. Our German settlers have hard-working, God-fearing women, but they do lack a certain—er, charm."

"Then you'll be disappointed in Madelyne too. The girl is plain and seemed dutiful. She won't tempt you, believe me."

"So, you did inspect your prize before agreeing to the marriage. Is she really paragon enough to make a confirmed misogynist like you end his bachelor days?"

Quint grunted and finished his rum. "You know I have to have an heir." At Devon's raised eyebrow and leer, his cousin added, "A *legal* heir. That does require being saddled with a wife, but I'm at least certain I've taken all precautions to have one who'll not play me false."

Devon shuddered. "Being not only the black sheep of the family but also a second son, I need have no qualms about marriage and heirs. Anyway, I still think my mother's people have the right of it—trace descent through the maternal line. That way there are never any doubts about inheritance."

"Still Muskogee law punishes adultery even more rigorously than does English law." Quint's green eyes locked with Devon's brown ones. "It would seem that men in all societies have reason to mistrust the wiles of women."

"Ah, but women offer us such compensations, I'm willing to overlook their defects." Again came the slash of white as Devon grinned. "I'm most anxious to meet your plain little puss. God, Quint, I do hope she has some bit of spirit from her Huguenot ancestors. She'll need it! You are an overbearing bastard, you know," he added with genuine affection.

"Quite right," Quint replied enigmatically.

Devon raised his glass after the pretty barmaid poured him a refill. "Here's to your bride, Quint. We'll ride to her rescue at first light."

Chapter Three

Quintin swatted a mosquito and felt himself sweat as they rode steadily along the rutted post road. "Now I remember why I decided against the trading end of the family business and settled for plantation life. Swelter to death in summer, freeze your ass off in winter—and ride through mud the year round."

Devon laughed. "You're getting soft, Quint. City life's corrupted you. I remember a time when you and I used to ride into the Muskogee villages and spend months hunting and feasting with them."

Quint's face softened. "It was a good life then, wasn't it? Paradise for a couple of growing boys."

Devon's eyes danced as he recalled their youth. "Yes, especially when we reached puberty."

"Speak for yourself. I bestowed my virginity on Polly Bloor. She was an uncommon fine-looking wench back then."

"And a willing teacher, I'd wager. I won't deny I've enjoyed a toss with her now and again, but the women of my mother's tribe are cleaner and no less enthusiastic."

Quintin looked at his cousin, his mood suddenly turning serious. "How is Aunt Charity? I know she's had a difficult time since Uncle Alastair died."

Devon's expression shifted to grimness, then brightened. "Yes, the Blackthorne family scarce welcomed a half-caste Muskogee woman as the second wife of the exalted Alastair Blackthorne, no matter that she was better educated than any of their women, including my beloved elder brother's mother. But that's all over now. My mother is happy living with her people. She runs a school for the children in the village. Says they have to learn to read and write English so the white men can't cheat them."

"No need to fear with men like you as royal agents, Dev."

"I do my best. The Crown is the Indians' only protection. If this war drags on . . . I fear what might happen if we lose it, Quint."

Quintin quirked one black eyebrow. "Surely you, the cockiest Tory in Georgia, don't for a minute believe we can lose?"

Devon sighed, then shrugged. "I don't know. Now that those damned Frenchies and their Spanish friends have entered to aid the rebellion . . . If only General Clinton hadn't rescinded the paroles of those rebels who'd laid down their arms. You can't give your word as an officer and a gentleman, then simply change your mind because the circumstances don't suit. That makes his majesty's cause seem as despicable as that of the rabble who lead this treason."

Quintin nodded gravely. "Revoking their paroles and calling up former rebels to fight for the king has driven thousands of them back to their old allegiance."

Discussing the war with Devon always made

Quint uncomfortable. With Robert, he loved the double game he played, but Devon was the only Blackthorne whose good opinion he valued. And one day he would lose it.

"Awfully pensive, cousin. Thinking perchance about your bride?" Devon whooped with delight. "Mayhap she isn't as plain and mousy as you first recalled."

Quintin grimaced. "Must you bring up such an unpleasant topic to compound an unpleasant day? The chit is plain enough, quiet as a wake, and already more trouble than she's worth."

After three days, Madelyne was finding life in the Creek camp quite pleasant, if a bit primitive. She had always loved an adventure and this was certainly an alien and exciting one. *It also keeps you away from your future husband for a while longer,* a taunting voice whispered as she sat dangling her legs in the cool waters of the stream. The harshly beautiful face of Quintin Blackthorne flashed in her mind with such clarity that it startled her. She had dreamed of him again last night while sleeping in the crude brush shelter the Creeks had erected for her.

They had been most fortunate that the trading party found them. The Creeks were on their way to another village, where the Crown's agent would trade them manufactured goods in exchange for their bundles of cured deerskins.

Her reverie was interrupted by the snap of a twig behind her. She turned and saw Will Tarrant approaching. The big man had an unpleasant way of sneaking up on people. He was carrying a suspiciously bulging haversack slung over one shoulder, as well as a shot pouch and musket.

"You look as if you're planning on leaving," she challenged.

He sneered. "You can set with them red-skinned

savages 'n hold Jemmy's hand, but I'm goin' to Savannah—fer help."

"You'll do no such thing," she said with rising anger. How dare this cowardly oaf speak to her so disrespectfully! "You're indentured to my father for three more years, Will, and until then you will do as he bids you." She climbed quickly to her feet and faced him.

"I done my duty, but I ain't livin' with no savages."

"You're just using this as an excuse, Will. Mad Turkey sent a runner to fetch his friends in the Blackthorne family and they'll be here soon."

"Pah! Them dirty redskins ain't got no rich white friends." He spat on the ground near the hem of her muslin skirt.

"You are the dirty one, Will Tarrant, not the Creeks who bathe in the stream every morning. Now go back to camp and do as Jasper tells you."

"Think again, Mistress Deveaux," he said with a sneer, reaching out for her with his big meaty hands. "Always figgered sooner or later you 'n me'd tangle."

Madelyne felt the breath crushed from her as he seized her in a tight embrace. Gagging from his fetid breath, she turned her head from his face and kicked at his shins, using the heel of her boot to grind down on his instep. He let out a yowl of pain and then struck her, knocking her to the ground. Once freed of his vicelike grip, she gathered her wind and screamed.

A Creek youth named Smooth Stone came flying from the heavy foliage and launched himself onto Tarrant's back. Madelyne struggled to her feet, searching frantically for a weapon to aid the boy, for Will was easily twice his size. As she grabbed a stout oak limb, she screamed for Gulliver, who had been sleeping at Jemmy's side when she left camp.

*   *   *

Major Montgomery Ashley Caruthers, leading a company of Kings Rangers on a special courier mission to General Cornwallis, heard the cry of a woman's voice, then men shouting and a shot being fired. "That was an Englishwoman's voice!"

The major wheeled his horse off the trail and plunged toward the burbling sound of the creek some hundred yards beyond a nearly impassable stand of trees and underbrush. There was no discernible path through the thicket stretching between them and the stream. "Scatter out, men. Arms at the ready!" The seasoned loyalists under his command unslung their Pennsylvania rifles and began to guide their mounts into the thick trees.

Lieutenant Nathaniel Goodly was the first to find his way through the woods. He saw a white woman of obvious quality kneeling beside a fallen white man dressed in crude frontiersman's clothes. A Creek Indian also knelt beside them.

Quickly dismounting, Goodly knelt to take aim at the savage, but the woman threw herself directly into his line of fire. Goodly cursed and lowered his Ferguson breechloader, then drew his bayonet and attached it to the barrel, preparing to charge the savage.

Madelyne screamed for the idiot soldier to stop, that the Creek was a friend, but it seemed he could not comprehend her. She did not hesitate, but seized the barrel of the rifle and clung to it like a leech lest its stupid owner kill Smooth Stone.

"Please, mistress. I know you're hysterical, but—"

Gulliver came bounding up as his mistress and the soldier struggled. He launched himself at Goodly, eliciting an oath of pain and surprise from the lieutenant. The dog had his jaws firmly clamped onto a large portion of his linen breeches and a sizeable chunk of his left buttock as well. Neither Madelyne nor Gulliver would relinquish their hold.

Madelyne shoved and Gulliver ripped in unison. The lieutenant went down, rolling on the ground with his bare rump most indelicately exposed, one plump white cheek bleeding profusely.

By now several more men dressed in the natty green uniforms of royal rangers had come crashing into the clearing around the creek. Madelyne seized the lieutenant's rifle and fired a shot in the air to get the attention of all her would-be rescuers, who were pouring from the trees like bats from a cave. "Don't shoot the Indian!" she shrieked at the top of her voice.

Major Caruthers, known in civilian life as the seventh Baron of Rushcroft, had never in his decade with the army encountered such a situation. The colonials, Whig or Tory, were a blasted perverse lot at the best of times, and this was certainly not the best of times. He knew enough not to act precipitously. Signaling for his men to hold their fire, he surveyed the scene.

One very young Creek stood stoically beside the fallen body of a coarse-looking white man. The woman had apparently attacked his lieutenant and set her dog on him as well. Now more Creek warriors were entering the clearing from the opposite side. Yes, he would most certainly not act precipitously.

He rode up to where Goodly lay thrashing on the ground and eyed the huge brown dog that now sat benignly with the seat of the lieutenant's breeches lying at his feet. Caruthers dismounted with extreme caution and muttered curtly to Goodly, "Bloody hell, man, cease that infernal yowling at once." He eyed the woman, who now lowered her rifle and smiled tentatively at him.

"I apologize for Gulliver's behavior. He only thought to defend me," she said, patting the great beast affectionately. "You see, the Creek boy saved me from that brute's attack." She gestured to the dead Tarrant.

Lud, the chit was a real stunner—not quite the thing back in London, of course, with all that dark hair and queer-colored amber eyes, but striking nonetheless. He returned her smile and bowed gallantly. "Major Montgomery Caruthers, at your service, mistress." He eyed the dead woodsman and the Indian youth uneasily.

Madelyne opened her mouth to explain the situation, but just then two more riders burst upon the scene. She let out a low groan as soon as she recognized the tall, dark man on the black stallion. *Damn Quintin Blackthorne!* Goodly, lying on the ground, let out another bleat of pain. There would be no helping her fiance's foul humor, but she could at least offer succor to the poor young soldier who had tried to be her rescuer. She knelt and said, "Please turn over and let me stanch the bleeding."

"Mistress, you must not. My men can take him to our surgeon," the major remonstrated.

"That's quite all right, Major. I've often assisted my aunt in caring for gravely ill and injured people." She pried the young man's hand from his bleeding posterior and examined the painful gashes Gulliver's teeth had made. She could hear the crunch of Quintin's boots on the gravelly ground as he strode toward her, but she refused to turn.

Quintin heard that voice and instantly recognized it. It *was* Madelyne Deveaux, but where had all that glorious mahogany hair come from? It spilled over her shoulders like mulled wine.

"But, mistress, this is no task for a lady!" Major Caruthers remonstrated, paying no heed to Quintin's approach.

"Ah, but this is no lady, Major," Quintin interjected. She raised her head and met his gaze. Quintin felt gut-kicked. Gone was the filthy urchin covered from head to foot in oversized gray clothing, eyes downcast and face smeared with soot. Clear amber gold eyes glared at him from beneath delicately arched brows. Her chin had a mutinous set, but the anger only enhanced a strikingly beautiful face.

"Major Caruthers, allow me to present my fiance, Quintin Blackthorne of Savannah." She returned her attention to the lieutenant, ignoring the glowering figure looming over her. "Mr. Blackthorne had little to recommend his manners in South Carolina," Madelyne went on. "Being at home in Georgia has done nothing to improve them, I see."

"Your manners have suffered enough since first we met to match us well, m' dear," Quintin said from between clenched teeth. He reached down and pried her bloody hands from the whining boy's backside.

Madelyne jerked free. "I can help him. Twas my dog that caused his hurt, all over a misunderstanding. The lieutenant was trying to be *kind* to me."

"A mistake I'm not likely to make," Quintin replied, turning to Caruthers. "Major, send for your surgeon. I'll see to my future bride."

Devon sat on his mount and watched the exchange between the trio with a wide grin on his face. Plain? Meek? His cousin must be losing his eyesight at an alarmingly early age, not to mention his hearing, if the sharpness of Madelyne Deveaux's tongue was any indication.

As Caruthers signaled two of his men to assist Goodly, Devon interrupted, "If I might be so bold, let me see what can be worked out with our hosts." He dismounted and conferred in the Muskogee dialect with Mad Turkey. "My friend here offers us all the hospitality of his camp, where the food is plentiful, as is medical care for the injured lieutenant. It's nearly dusk now, and none can ride safely tonight. There'll be no moon."

Caruthers appeared to consider as he studied Devon's buckskin clothes and obvious familiarity with the Creeks who now surrounded him. Doubtless one of those colonial half-caste bastards, he thought, realizing that it was a fortunate circumstance that these savages were friendly. "I appreciate the offer, Mr.—"

"Allow me to present my cousin, Devon Blackthorne," Quintin said with a grim quirk of amusement in his expression.

Madelyne watched the exchange, her own anger at Quintin's high-handed attitude toward her forgotten. Something was going on between the English officer and the two Blackthorne men. She observed Devon, looking for some family resemblance, finding none but their exceptional height. "The Creeks have taken splendid care of my injured coachman," she said. Smiling at Quintin's intriguing cousin, she continued, "Please forgive Quintin's lack of manners. I'm Madelyne Deveaux, Mr. Blackthorne."

"Yes, you certainly are, aren't you, lovely lady," he said with a wink at Quintin. He bowed and saluted her hand ardently while Quintin glowered at them. "What say, cousin? Shall we all partake of the Muskogee hospitality? Your fiancée gives them high praise and would abide a day longer." He pointedly ignored the British major.

Quintin nodded curtly. "We'll stay the night. The Creek Confederacy always welcomes his majesty's soldiers. If these gentlemen wish to partake of Muskogee hospitality, I'm certain they're welcome."

"Quite so." Caruthers saluted Mad Turkey, then issued crisp orders to his men. Lieutenant Goodly, assisted by two soldiers, followed at the rear of the motley crew who headed toward the Muskogee camp.

"More tea, Mistress Deveaux?" Lieutenant Goodly stood hovering at her side, kettle in his hand.

Madelyne looked up and favored him with a brilliant smile. Poor boy, he hadn't been able to sit since his unfortunate encounter with Gulliver. "Yes, another cup would be lovely, thank you."

Major Caruthers watched Madelyne with keen blue eyes as she sat surrounded by his officers and men, like a queen holding court in the midst of the wilderness camp of Creek Indians. "May I say, Mistress Deveaux, you look particularly fetching this morning. The green of your dress so favors your hair and eyes. You'd be all the rage in London."

Madelyne laughed as she carefully arranged her skirts, reaching down to give Gulliver a pat as Smooth Stone fed him bits of venison. "Ah, Major, you quite spoil me, as the boy here spoils my pet. I only unpacked one of my trunks and pulled out the first cool dress I could find. Twas bad enough wearing riding habits in this murderous heat while I was on horseback, but encamped this way . . . well, this is much more comfortable."

"I assure you it looks far more than merely comfortable," the major replied.

Madelyne studied him covertly as he and two of his junior officers made light conversation with her. The major was the epitome of an English gentleman, pale smiling face framed by light brown hair, with manners as impeccable as his uniform. She could imagine him easily in a Charles Town drawing room with his hair powdered, dressed in a satin waistcoat and velvet breeches. Yet her treacherous mind kept conjuring up visions of Quintin, whose hair was far too black to be powdered, whose face was harsh and unsmiling, whose skin was sun-darkened.

"A penny for your thoughts, mistress?"

Madelyne blushed and focused her attention once again on the gaggle of officers surrounding her. "I was only thinking of how fortunate we were to be rescued—not once but twice, by the Creeks and by his majesty's gallant soldiers."

"I still think you should return with us to Charles Town. It's not safe to traverse the back country post road in these troubled times. You could catch a drogger from there to Savannah and arrive in only a few days."

Madelyne shook her head. "No, no that's quite impossible. Father would be furious. Since he almost drowned at sea when a hurricane blew up along the coast, he never allows anyone in our family to sail."

Quintin had spent a perfectly miserable night because of Madelyne Deveaux. The sharp-tongued hoyden with all that glorious hair and those arresting eyes was far from the waif he'd met in South Carolina. But even yesterday's debacle could not prepare him for the sight of her dressed in a sheer muslin day gown, sitting surrounded by fawning British officers as if she were hosting a London salon. He snarled an oath and stalked angrily toward the cluster of men obscuring his view of his betrothed.

"Easy, my man, easy," Devon said, placing a restraining hand on Quint's rigid shoulder. They both watched the dandyish looking Major Caruthers kiss her hand.

Quint shook Dev's hand away and continued toward the assembly as Madelyne knelt and hugged the dog.

"Gulliver is quite a champion to the Creeks since he saved Smooth Stone's life," she said, rising with the assistance of Major Caruthers.

"They'll make a totem to him if you don't leave soon," a captain said.

Another officer added, "Perhaps it would be more interesting to see a totem with poor Goodly here on it, bare arsed and all—beggin' the lady's pardon."

Goodly blushed beet red and stammered as all the men burst into hearty laughter. Only Madelyne restrained herself with a mere twitch on her lips as she defended her misguided rescuer. "La, Captain, you and your fellows are too hard on the lieutenant by half. If you had been first to arrive, I'm certain any of you could have made the same mistake and suffered the loss of your breeches!"

"Well, it would seem, mistress, that you have found life with Indians and soldiers much to your liking. Your brush with danger has greatly improved your appearance."

Madelyne whirled at the sound of the clipped, cold voice. "I see your manners remain constant, even if my appearance does not," she replied over-sweetly, sketching a slight curtsy.

When she bowed before him, Quint quickly re-evaluated his opinion of her body. She was small but in no way deficient. The soft cloth hugged delicately full breasts and showed off a tiny waist before flaring into a froth of billowy petticoats draped with an overskirt of paler green.

After watching the exchange with detached amusement, Devon stepped up to Madelyne and bowed. "You look even more ravishing this morning, my dear cousin."

Quint's eyes were shards of green ice as he looked quellingly at Dev. "Pay Dev no further heed. He will be leaving us shortly, off to the Muskogee towns in the interior."

"I greatly fear my men and I must be off, too, dear lady. Are you certain we cannot prevail upon you to return to Charles Town with us?" Caruthers asked, ignoring Quintin and his half-caste cousin.

"Absolutely not." Quint answered for Madelyne. "We've been delayed enough, and it's only a day to Savannah. You had best look to your command, Major. I'll attend to my fiancée."

"But Jemmy is still too badly hurt to ride," Madelyne said tartly, angered by Quint's rudeness.

Quint turned to Dev. "I assume you can have your friends here see to his care until the fellow is well enough for travel?"

Devon nodded, turning to Madelyne. "I'll person-ally escort the injured boy to the nearest village—

it's far closer than Savannah, and he'll get the best of care there."

"In that case, I do thank you, Mr. Blackthorne." Madelyne favored Devon with a smile. "At least one member of the Blackthorne family is possessed of some courtesy," she murmured sweetly.

Quint seethed as Madelyne had her small retinue of servants load her trunks and bags onto horses lent them by the Muskogee. Having heard about the bondsman who attacked her and was killed by Smooth Stone, he felt obliged to offer the youth a handsome gift—his pocket watch, an item he knew always fascinated Indians.

Since it was only a day's hard ride, Quint decided to set out for Savannah at once. After formal thank-yous and farewells were made to Mad Turkey and the Muskogees, they also bade the British soldiers Godspeed, Madelyne with far more enthusiasm than Quint. Then only Devon remained, standing with legs braced apart, arms folded across his broad chest.

"Well, cousins." He smiled and winked at Madelyne. "I shall miss you. Be safe on your journey."

"Surely you'll be at our wedding," Madelyne said, liking the easy-mannered Devon instinctively.

His face lost its devilish glint of humor for a brief moment. "No, I fear not. I am not welcome in Uncle Robert's house. Quint can explain it to you in good time. Only be happy, Madelyne. You, too, Quint. And don't take life so seriously."

The cousins embraced each other, then separated. "Take care of yourself with the Muskogee. And, Devon, you're always welcome in my home—damn Robert Blackthorne and all his kind."

"I know, Quint. I'll turn up one day . . . like a bad penny." With that he bowed to Madelyne and turned back toward the Muskogee camp.

They rode out with Madelyne's great hulking brute of a dog trailing beside her horse. Jasper Oldham, a tough, wiry old Carolinian, and two other of the Deveaux servants managed the pack train of luggage wending its way behind them. As a courtesy and for added protection, Mad Turkey had also sent along six of his warriors.

"It was most gracious of you to give Smooth Stone the watch. He was very pleased," Madelyne said as they rode. Wanting to break the brooding silence between them, she was determined to be pleasant and draw the harsh stranger to talk with her.

"The boy obviously saved your life. Twas the least I could do." His profile was forbidding, and he said no more.

"Yes, he was very brave. Will Tarrant was a huge bully. I never liked him." She shivered, recalling his filthy, foul-smelling body.

"If he was so untrustworthy, what were you doing alone with him so far from camp?" His green eyes skewered her accusingly.

"I wasn't alone with him. He was trying to escape. He was my father's bondsman with three years yet to serve."

"And you, a small, unarmed female, felt compelled to attempt to stop him?" His voice was laced with scorn.

"It didn't quite happen that way," she replied defensively. "I merely happened to be at the creek when he came along. Gulliver had stayed with Jemmy, else the man would never have dared to threaten me."

Quintin looked down at the shaggy mountain of fur loping ahead of them, raised one eyebrow as if to question her further, then lapsed again into silence.

"Why are you so displeased with me?" When he looked at her with patent disbelief etched on his face, she hastened to add, "Oh, I don't mean about the episode with Will or Lieutenant Goodly's breeches or any of that. I . . . I just mean . . . me. When you came to Aunt Claud's summer house, you were very rude, as if you disliked me even before you met me. I know I looked a fright but—"

"Your looks pleased me far better then than now. As to my being rude, if you take it so, best get used to it. I will be honest, mistress. I did not seek to wed you. Twas arranged between your father and mine. I merely approved Robert Blackthorne's choice. Now I wonder if I made a mistake, but it's too late, isn't it, lady?"

"Perhaps you are not alone in feeling this match a most ill-conceived one," Madelyne replied stiffly, refusing to let herself give in to the tears stinging beneath her eyelids. Her throat thickened, but she forced down the lump of misery and held her head high. As they rode in silence, she cast furtive glances at his forbidding profile and wondered how she could allow this cold enigma to bed her on their wedding night.

Chapter Four

The remainder of their journey to Savannah was no better than its beginning. Late that afternoon, nearly past the supper hour, they arrived at the Purrysburg ferry, where they crossed the muddy and turbulent Savannah River. After growing up in South Carolina's swampy back country, Madelyne was well used to fording small, brackish streams and taking ferries across the larger ones, but when she reached the middle of the flat, wide river, she was certain her father's fear of water must have been hereditary. The small wooden ferry, scarce more than a log-lashed raft, bobbed and weaved across the churning waters, swollen from recent heavy rains. The horses skittered and the big black slaves pulled in stony silence, as if resigned to a watery grave.

Madelyne looked forlornly back at her men, waiting patiently on the South Carolina shore with the rest of the horses and her baggage. Sensing Quintin's eyes on her, she gripped the splintery log railing and looked ahead, swearing she would show no fear in front of the infuriating boor.

"We'll spend the night with some German friends in Ebenezer. It's only slightly over twenty miles into Savannah from there," was his only comment.

Madelyne determined to enter Savannah looking every inch the lady of quality. If her husband-to-be was not pleased with her, perhaps she could at least charm his father, who had arranged the match. From a few passing comments, Madelyne guessed that Quintin and Robert Blackthorne did not get on at all well. *At least that leaves some hope for the father.* Madelyne felt certain it would strain even the most loving parent to excuse behavior as surly as Quintin Blackthorne's.

The warm hospitality of the German settlers of Ebenezer was in marked contrast to Quintin's coldness. Madelyne chatted with the plump, friendly Frau Dussel, ate a simple but hearty repast, and slept in a clean, soft bed that night.

Early the next day, they were off to Savannah. As they rode, Madelyne speculated about what kind of a place the city might be.

Her father had made it clear that the Blackthorne family was fabulously wealthy. Considering that Georgia was the poorest and most backward of all the Colonies, she had been dubious. Weren't they all convicts and debtors brought over in the 1730's by misguided missionaries? She knew the utopia had floundered so badly that the trustees gave over their colony to royal authority in 1752. Still, nearly three decades later, stories of the meanness of life in Georgia persisted. To what kind of a man and a home had Theodore Deveaux sent his only child?

Madelyne sighed as they neared the city. Probably her father did not give a fig. All her life he had been but an infrequent visitor, a widower eager to return to his military duties. At last he would no longer have the burden of her care. She was Quintin Blackthorne's responsibility for the rest of her life.

Madelyne watched him covertly as they rode side by side. His mount was splendid and his clothing expertly tailored, from the fine woolen cocked hat on his head to the gleaming leather boots on his feet. He looked rich. He looked as beautiful as sin. She thought wistfully of all her girlhood dreams of a love match with a handsome, dashing man. Quintin Blackthorne certainly fit the description physically. Madelyne vowed to have patience with his sour disposition, even though the tolerant Isolde had always told her she lacked that virtue.

If she learned to deal with his peremptory ways, perhaps in time he might become reconciled to the arranged match. Yet Madelyne felt certain that no one, not even the formidable Robert Blackthorne, could force this man riding beside her to do anything he did not wish to do. He exuded a will of iron and the most disconcerting virility. Every time he touched her, no matter how impersonal the gesture, she felt electricity fly between them, much like the sort of thing Mr. Franklin had described in his experiments.

How can I be attracted to a man who so obviously disdains me? It was not as if Madelyne had lacked suitors when Isolde had introduced her for her one brief season in Charles Town. Of course, halfway through it, her beloved aunt fell ill and they retired to the country, where Isolde died. If not for that cruel quirk of fate, she would doubtless be happily wed by now to a man who wanted her.

Madelyne reminded herself that she had wanted none of those drooling, foolish young dandies for a husband. She decided she was just being perverse. Quintin was handsome and rich, certainly two points in his favor. If only he had a delightful, teasing sense of humor and ready smile, like his cousin Devon.

"Why cannot your cousin Devon attend our wedding?" The question just popped out.

"He is not welcome at Blackthorne Hill." Quintin's voice was tight, as if he guarded a secret.

"So he said, but that doesn't explain why. He's quite the gentleman and most agreeably charming."

"He is one quarter Muskogee. His mother was a half-caste who wed into our exalted family. Robert has never forgiven his brother Alastair. Neither has Devon's half brother, Andrew, although Andrew will inherit everything of importance."

"So that's why he's returning to the Indians. How unfair and sad," she said pensively.

Quintin felt a spark of admiration for her, but quickly squelched it. "Devon prefers to live with the Muskogee. He's an ardent supporter of the loyalist cause and feels he can accomplish more by acting as liaison between the Creek Confederacy and the British Army than he could sitting home counting money as Andrew does."

"And what of you? You aren't in service to his majesty, are you?" What insane urge made her say that?

"I'm in the Georgia Royal Militia. I fought at the siege of Savannah last fall when we withstood an entire French fleet, as well as three thousand rebels. Admiral d'Estaing was a fool," he said with bitterness in his voice.

"Yet we won and held Savannah. Why are you so disgusted by a man who obviously aided your cause with his incompetence?"

"I abhor senseless slaughter." He raised an eyebrow and studied her for a moment. "Something a female blinded by pretty uniforms and fancy military parades could scarcely be expected to understand."

Madelyne bristled but reminded herself of her vow. Patience, she would learn patience . . . if it killed her! They rode in silence through the thickening afternoon heat.

Suddenly Quintin announced, "We're close to

Blackthorne Hill. If we had more time we could stop to freshen up, but since we're already a week late . . ." He let his words fade and shrugged.

"My father made the travel arrangements, not I. And the cart's breaking a wheel was none of my doing either." She felt she must defend herself.

Quintin seemed indifferent. "Tis no matter now. Shortly we'll be at our city house, where my father eagerly awaits your arrival."

"I shall look forward to someone eagerly awaiting me. Twill be a novelty, I warrant."

He ignored the remark.

As they approached the northern perimeter of the city, Madelyne's heart sank. The buildings were scarcely more than rough-hewn plank-and-log shanties set in irregular patterns along the banks of the vast river plain, which was filled with wide, flat islands. The soil was sandy, and with every rise in what had earlier been a mercifully cooling breeze, the sand filled the air, fairly choking them and stinging their eyes.

As if guessing her thoughts, Quintin said, "Although it's far smaller than Charles Town, for a city scarce forty-five years old, Savannah boasts public buildings and squares of considerable grace and beauty. This is just the temporary overflow of new settlers who have built here."

"Is there a Presbyterian Church?"

Quintin laughed. "Yes. Georgia is teeming with Nonconformists. You saw Ebenezer, which is all German Lutherans. Baptists and your own dear Calvinists are well represented. We even have a sizeable and prosperous Jewish community. But since 1757 the Established Church is maintained by all." He turned and looked at her with those unnerving ice-green eyes, as if testing her reaction. "We'll be married at the family estate by an Anglican priest. That's one thing about which Robert Blackthorne will never compromise."

"He is a religious man then?" Somehow the Blackthorne family didn't seem especially pious, if one could judge from Quintin and his cousin Devon.

Quintin gave a nasty chuckle. "Old Robert is many things, but religious is scarce an adjective anyone would apply to him. No, he's Church of England because it's the proper, loyal way to be. You must conform, you see, else he'll break you."

"And has he broken you?" She smoothed a wind-blown curl back beneath the meager protection of her hood and waited for his reply.

"Hardly. Robert and I have reached . . . an understanding."

His face seemed to lose its harshness for a brief moment. Traces of pain, perhaps regret, softened it, then vanished. Madelyne felt an odd thrill of compassion and curiosity. "You call him by his given name so often. Do you truly dislike your own father that much?"

He turned in the saddle and faced her. "Let me put it as simply as possible. I feel toward Robert Blackthorne precisely the same emotion that he feels toward me. Unadulterated hate."

At that moment a crowd of ragged children came running up to their horses, begging coins and creating a terrible cacophony of squeals and shrieks. To Madelyne's amazement, Quintin talked with several of them, calling them by name as he tossed coppers, one by one, to each boy and girl.

"Their fathers work on the waterfront, for hire as boatmen upriver or loading and unloading ocean ships," he explained.

"A brief lapse into humanity that must be rationalized, Quintin?" She couldn't keep the arch tone from her voice or her expression. "Or is it that the Blackthornes as shipping traders exploit their fathers?"

He snorted in disgust. "You and my father should

get along famously if you challenge him at every turn," he said with heavy irony. "Perhaps he'll even call off the marriage."

"Then I shall apply myself with all diligence," she replied.

By the time they entered the inner city, Madelyne was forced to revise her opinion of Savannah. Quintin had not exaggerated when he said the buildings were grand. Even the frame houses were predominantly two stories high, and many of the others were of handsome fire-glazed brick. Almost all had real glazed windows. The streets were a bit on the narrow side, but the public squares, laid out at regular intervals throughout the city, gave a feeling of spaciousness. Lovely magnolia and myrtle trees shaded the walks.

When they rode into St. James Square, Quintin pointed out Governor Wright's imposing residence, as well as several other houses of influential men. Then he gestured straight ahead at one of the grandest houses Madelyne had ever seen.

"That is your city house?" Her voice almost squeaked.

Quintin smiled coolly, as if amused at her provincialism.

The structure was of brick, three stories high with six enormous windows across both the first and second stories. Handsome dormers were set into the roof for the third story. When they rode up to the entry, a young black servant waited to take their mounts to the stables. Quintin assisted Madelyne in dismounting, while Jasper and his men followed the boy to the rear of the house.

As always, when he touched her, she felt her pulse race and that odd breathless feeling washed over her. Madelyne found that she could not meet his mocking green eyes. *He knows how he affects me, damn him!*

"So there you are. About time. I've been waiting

all morning." The gruff comments came from a tall, spare figure with iron-gray hair. He stood inside the wide double doors held open by a liveried servant.

From his imperious tone of voice and arrogant stance, Madelyne knew he must be Robert Blackthorne.

She smoothed the folds of her gold brocade riding skirts and raised her head, carefully positioning her hood so a few gleaming mahogany curls were artfully displayed. Willing herself not to tremble in the face of the harsh-looking old man, she climbed the stone steps at Quintin's side and curtsied gracefully to her future father-in-law.

"Well, what have we here, hmm?" Robert took Madelyne's cool hand and saluted it gallantly. He quirked his eyebrows expressively at Quintin, almost as if sharing a private joke—one that was on Quintin. "You're quite a surprise, gel. Yes, quite a surprise. Never knew your mother. Looks must've come from her. Old Theo couldn't have given 'em to you."

"You are most kind, sir, although I know I must look a fright after a week crossing swamps and stopping in an Indian camp."

"Had quite an adventure, did you? She has real spunk, eh, Quintin? Real spunk and real beauty. A winning combination." Robert's blue eyes locked with Quintin's green ones in an exchange that could have dropped the steamy Georgia temperature by at least fifty degrees.

The old man's condescending amusement put Madelyne's nerves on edge in spite of his superficially kind words. Quintin held himself rigidly silent as he walked into the house with them. *His father is taunting him about me, but why, if I please him?*

Her ruminations about the charged hostility between father and son were put aside the moment she walked indoors. The entry hall was breathtaking. Gleaming oak floors were laid with elegant Turkish rugs in lovely shades of blue and gold. French silk wallpaper with soft pink roses covered the high walls that were finished with crown molding. An enormous chandelier of elaborately scrolled brass was filled with at least a hundred candles and hung with glistening crystal.

"Your home is lovely, Mr. Blackthorne," Madelyne said in awe. Even in Charles Town, far older and more established homes of this elegance were rare indeed.

Robert gave a mirthless laugh. "Yes, we do manage to surprise most first-time visitors to Georgia."

"If you think this anything to remark on, wait until you see Blackthorne Hill," Quintin said.

"Yes, the Hill. That's where you'll be married. This very Saturday, is it not, Quintin?" Robert's eyes dueled with Quintin's again.

"Yes, Father, this very Saturday indeed," was all Quintin would reply.

The bride thought they might as well be discussing an execution as a marriage.

Madelyne was too hot and overwrought to nap in the beautiful room she had been assigned. Knowing that she must meet Alastair's elder son, Andrew, and other relatives at dinner that evening only added to her restlessness.

She rang for a maid and ordered bathwater, then began pulling gowns from her trunks. "At least I shall meet the formidable Blackthorne family looking my best," she murmured, then recalled Quintin's peculiar words about her appearance—that her looks had far better pleased him when she was filthy and disheveled than when attractively dressed. "Well, I can scarce go about like a chimney sweep just to suit his fancy."

She seized a peach-colored gown of sheer watered silk from the pile on the bed and asked the maid to press it for her, then went off to soak and prepare

herself for the ordeal she knew was coming that
night.

Quintin watched Serena Fallowfield make her
grand entrance, sweeping off her light cloak and
letting it drop into the arms of a maid, knowing he
was watching her magnificent cleavage spill from
her purple brocade gown. The bit of lace tucked into
the deep vee between her breasts only heightened
the scandalous bodice, rather than making it more
modest. Her glossy raven hair was piled high in a
mass of ringlets and coils around a pompadour that
was a good eight inches high.

Her blue eyes narrowed as she floated across the
room to where Quintin stood. She presented one
porcelain-pale cheek for a kiss as she pressed her
breasts indecently against his chest. "Dear Quintin,
I am so relieved you've returned from those savages.
Have you rescued your bride?"

"Yes, but don't look too disappointed, Serena. You
might shock poor Andrew," Quintin said in a low
voice intended only for her ears.

Just as they made the exchange, Madelyne entered
the room. She froze in the doorway, watching the
voluptuous woman with gleaming black hair practically throw herself on Quintin. The two of them
laughed and sparred like old friends—or lovers.
Compared to her, Madelyne felt very young and
unsophisticated. *No wonder he doesn't want me.*

"Ah, there you are, m'dear. Come, boy, introduce
our guests to your fiancée." Robert walked across
the room, a glass of wine in one hand, and bowed
to her, then cast a challenging look at his son.

Quintin stood silently taking in the soft, rustling
concoction in peach silk. She looked as innocent and
lovely as the first day of spring. Abandoning Serena,
he strolled slowly toward Madelyne. He could feel
Serena's gaze riveted on his back like a dagger thrust.
Bitch. But at least she was a known quantity—and

he did not have to marry her. He stopped beside his
father and took Madelyne's slim hand as if accepting
Robert's challenge to a duel.

After coolly saluting her fingertips, he allowed his
eyes to sweep up to her face. Big golden eyes stared
reproachfully at him, filled with a mixture of shock
and hurt, which she quickly covered with sparkling
anger.

"My apologies for being tardy, but I see you were
well entertained in my absence," she said softly with
a waspish edge to her voice.

"Ah, yes, Serena. Allow me to present our—er,
cousin by marriage." A slow smile turned the corners of his lips as he led her across the room to
Serena. *The spoiled little chit is as jealous as Serena!*

Andrew stood watching the arrival of his cousin's
betrothed with narrowed eyes. Quintin had always
sworn he would wed a plain, retiring woman who
would stay on his plantation and devote herself
to domestic duties. This fiery little beauty seemed
anything but plain or domestic. And Serena, the
stupid cow, was furious, but it was her own fault
she had bungled things so badly. He glided toward
them while introductions were made between the
two hostile women.

"So this is your bride, Quintin. How sweet and
innocent she looks." Serena's pale eyes flashed with
a white fire. She looked up at him, as if sharing
some private joke.

"Qualities you left behind in the schoolroom,
Serena." Quintin's expression was one of grim
amusement.

She arched one slim black eyebrow and gave him
a playful swat with her fan. "How ungallant of you
to remind a poor widow of her losses."

Madelyne felt like an intruder. Then Robert presented his nephew, Andrew. He was a tall, rather thin
man with fine sandy hair and a long angular face
faintly marked with smallpox scars. When he bowed

and smiled at her, his pale brown eyes were warm and his smile was infectiously friendly, transforming what she had first thought a plain face into a most properly handsome one.

"My greatest pleasure, Mistress Deveaux. May I say you will be a proud addition to the Blackthorne family? Welcome to Savannah."

"Why thank you, Mr. Blackthorne." Madelyne returned his smile warmly.

"There are too many 'mister' Blackthornes present already. Would you be so kind as to call me Cousin Andrew?"

She dimpled. "Yes, of course, Cousin Andrew, if you will call me Cousin Madelyne." At last she had made one friend in this strange family.

The dinner was sumptuous, with courses of spicy turtle soup, abundant fresh vegetables, brook trout, roast suckling pig, and delicate pies filled with pigeon, venison, and duck. With every course, rich Madeiras and ports were imbibed liberally by the men. Serena partook more than was seemly for a lady, although it did not appear to dull her cutting wit in the least. Madelyne took care to sip very slowly from her goblet and allowed no refills.

Conversation moved somewhat awkwardly at first, since the hostility between the two women was apparent to all there. Robert and Quintin seemed amused, but Andrew graciously intervened to ease things for Madelyne.

"When will your father arrive, Cousin Madelyne? It was a shame he couldn't accompany you on your journey here."

"He has duties with the royal militia in Charles Town. We expect him within the week."

"Else the marriage might have to be postponed," Serena purred, then added, "I understand, dear, that you had quite an adventure with the savages and almost didn't make it to Savannah yourself."

Madelyne put down her goblet and smiled at the

beautiful woman. "Quintin and his cousin Devon came to my rescue, although I was never in any real danger. The Creeks are loyal allies of his majesty. They made me feel quite welcome."

"I couldn't abide a moment with those smelly creatures." Serena shuddered delicately and took another sip of wine.

"But they aren't smelly at all. They bathe every morning." Madelyne felt called upon to defend her hosts.

"Did you join them, pray tell?" Quintin asked.

"As a matter of fact, I was quite tempted. The weather has been so hot, and the stream was quite cool."

Robert laughed. "Well said, m'dear." As he drank a generous measure of Madeira, he stared at Quintin.

Andrew again intervened, changing the subject. "I say, what do you think of General Clinton leaving the Southern colonies' fate with this Cornwallis fellow? Is the rebellion that close to being crushed?"

"Hardly, with Liberty Boys and sharp-shooting rebel militia roaming the countryside from Virginia to the Florida border," Quintin replied.

"We'll show 'em. Need another lesson or two like Colonel Tarleton taught 'em at Waxhaus," Robert said. "Then they'll scatter like the cowardly rabble they are."

"We need no more of 'Tarleton's quarter,' Father. That kind of butchery of prisoners made his name hated throughout the South and drove many a neutral to the rebels' camp."

"As I understand it, there's been more than a little of that violence on the side of the rebels. Don't they call killing Loyalist prisoners a 'Georgia parole' down here?" Madelyne asked Quintin. "And what about 'Sumpter's Law'? Why, tis no more than plain stealing by that rebel leader to keep his ruffians fighting for him."

Quintin's face darkened. "Both sides have been guilty of barbaric deeds. Civil wars are always the ugliest kind. A very wise man once said there is no such thing as a good war or a bad peace."

"Sounds like a damned coward to me," Robert rumbled into his glass, upturning it. He signaled for the butler to refill it.

"Who is this paragon of wisdom?" Madelyne inquired.

Quintin's mouth softened for a fleeting moment as he answered, "One of those damned rebels, but no coward. Ben Franklin."

"Indeed, Cousin, you should watch such sentiments lest you be accused of leaning to the rebellion yourself," Andrew admonished.

"One need not agree with a man's politics to admire his common sense. Besides, Cousin, since I serve in the Royal Militia and fought during the siege of Savannah, I scarcely think my loyalty to his majesty is in question."

Andrew was not in the militia. Madelyne saw that the barb had hit home and felt it most unfair of Quintin. "A great many loyal men aid his majesty by raising crops and serving on government councils."

"I find discussing war and politics a crashing bore. Ladies prefer more refined conversation." Serena's cold blue eyes swept past Madelyne as if she were invisible, then fixed on Quintin.

He looked at Andrew. "What? No defense of your newfound friend, Cousin?"

"A lady such as Madelyne needs no defense by me or anyone else," Andrew said with a quelling look at Serena, who subsided into her goblet of port for the duration of the meal.

When the interminable evening was over, Madelyne retired to bed with a splitting headache, more confused about the peculiarities of the Blackthorne family than ever. *And soon I shall be a Blackthorne, too.*

The maid had dutifully turned back the soft linens on her narrow bed. As she brushed her hair, she stared from the oval glass in front of her at the reflection of the bed, wondering idly if Quintin's bed was wider. Would she be expected to sleep in it with him? Or would she be assigned her own room adjacent to his? Aunt Isolde had mentioned such an arrangement between her parents when her mother had been alive. With his obvious aversion to her, would Quintin ignore her much as her father had ignored her mother?

"If only I weren't such an ignorant ninny," she murmured as she walked to the bed and slipped between the sheets. There had been no woman but the cold, virginal Claud left to explain marital duties to her. Here she was, but days from her wedding, without the slightest idea of what to expect. She tossed in the oppressive night heat, praying for the temporary oblivion of sleep.

Chapter Five

Downstairs, Quintin paced in the library, also unable to sleep. The look of hurt in those wide golden eyes still haunted him. He swore and poured another generous glass of brandy. She was beautiful, damn her! And possessed of a fierce streak of independence— and jealousy. When she'd seen him with Serena, it had upset her. Why? Maidenly pride? Her Huguenot sense of propriety? In spite of the unfortunate way they'd first met and the uncomfortable journey from the Indian camp to the city, perhaps she was attracted to him. He stopped pacing and stared out the window into the small garden at the rear of the house. "Don't let yourself believe in fairy tales."

In his twenty-eight years, Quintin had learned that his looks dazzled women. They flocked to him, and he enjoyed the easy favors of tavern wenches and fineborn ladies alike. He'd always had one rule, though—never lie with a married woman. Through the years, many had made overtures, but he had always rebuffed them. What faithless creatures females were. If only a man did not need their sweet, soft flesh; if only he could enjoy it and not worry about getting legal heirs.

Fleetingly he envied Devon, who would inherit nothing and could enjoy the willing girls of the Muskogee and never have a care about entailing a vast estate to a male child of his loins. "But I must do my duty . . . with her, the willful, beautiful little termagant." Damn, why did she make him feel guilty? She was the one he'd caught holding court, surrounded by drooling young officers, all laughing because she'd set her dog to snatch a man bare-assed. And she didn't even blush as they laughed over it! What kind of a match was he making?

When he had first met her in South Carolina, Madelyne Deveaux had seemed to be just what he wanted. He had planned on doing his duty, bedding her until she bore him a son, even if he did not relish the task. But how did the transformation take place? It had been like a gut kick seeing her in that camp. During the ride to Savannah, when he had to assist her in mounting and dismounting from her horse, the callow little flirt fair scorched his hands.

He took another swallow of brandy and decided the only way to get some sleep was to drink himself into oblivion. Of course he would have the mother of all headaches when they rode to Blackthorne Hill in the morning. "It's either the brandy or Madelyne Deveaux." With a muttered curse, he poured another glassful and settled into the big easy chair in front of the window.

Madelyne clutched at the yards and yards of sheer white muslin floating about her as she made her way into Robert's library. Yesterday she had seen a volume of *Fanny Hill; Or, The Memoirs of a Woman of Pleasure* on the shelf right next to *Dryden's Poems*. Aunt Isolde's friends had whispered and tittered

about the scandalous book. On this hot, sleepless
night she decided it was well past time to complete at least one part of her education. Maybe the
adventures of a famous courtesan would shed some
light on what a man expected in a woman and what
exactly went on in the marriage bed at night.

She had heard the tallcase clock strike two and
knew not a soul could be stirring in the house, else
she would never have dared venture out dressed in
only her sleeping clothes and the sheer dressing
robe. *I'll just snatch the book and slip back upstairs.*

Madelyne opened the door and slipped inside the
darkened room. A full moon spilled creamy white
light across the carpet. Silently she crossed the
room to the bookshelves, raising her candle so
she could read the titles. There it was, between
the Dryden and Montesquieu's *Spirit of the Laws.*
A small smile twitched on her lips as she considered the incongruity of Mr. Cleland's scandalous
book wedged between such somber and respectable
works. Robert Blackthorne obviously was in need of
someone to order his library!

When she pulled the book from the shelf, several
larger and heavier volumes were disturbed, causing
a sharp *plop* as they fell on their sides. Quintin
awakened and sat bolt upright in the chair, sensing
another presence in the room. He shook his head to
clear it, taking a moment to get his bearings. Then
he noticed the wavering flicker of a candle from the
far corner. Some shadowy apparition swathed in
flowing white was moving along the wall of books,
headed toward the door.

He rose silently and crossed the carpet to head
off the vanishing ghost. The candlelight illuminated
her face. "Madelyne!"

She whirled and the candle flickered out. The
candlestick fell from nerveless fingers and clattered
across the oak floor. Clutching the book to her
breasts, she stood trapped with Quintin between

her and the only exit. His face was harsh in the moonlight, a study in black and white. He looked furious.

"What by all that's holy are you doing running about the house in your nightclothes?" His raspy voice broke the silence and echoed in the high ceilinged room.

"I . . . I couldn't sleep. The heat . . . I remembered your father's books and thought I'd take one to read." She raised her chin defiantly as he advanced on her. "Surely you don't object. You did ask for assurances that I was literate before approving me!"

He stopped two feet in front of her and crossed his arms over his broad chest. Even in the dim light, she could see that cynical smile begin to flash. "So I did. Let me see what you deem suitable reading to put you to sleep on a long, hot summer's night." He reached for the book. She backed up a step.

The brandy fumes were overpowering as he loomed over her. "You've been drinking, sir. To excess, I fear."

"Tis my brandy. I'll indulge if I choose. Tis also my book. Let me see it."

She hugged it tighter. Merciful heavens above, what would he think when he saw this scandalous book! She would not be cowed by his fierce scowl. "You're too foxed to even read the title. Tis merely an . . . edifying piece on housewifery."

Quintin's nostrils were filled with her subtle perfume. She smelled like honeysuckle, standing there drenched in moonlight with all that gleaming mahogany hair falling around her shoulders and spilling across her breasts. He shook his head to clear the effects of the brandy and almost lost his balance, then steadied himself by cupping his hands around her shoulders.

Madelyne panicked. He was so big, so forbidding, scowling at her, touching her. His long tapered fingers dug into her arms through the sheer white batiste, scorching her. His warm breath washed over her. He smelled of brandy and another unidentifiable essence, male and compelling. She pushed at him with the book, trying in vain to put space between them. He wrenched the volume from her hands, then seized one slim wrist. She lost her balance and tumbled against him, long hair and voluminous clothes wrapping about them both.

Quintin dropped the book and clasped her to him. His breath was labored and his whole body rigid with lust. He could feel her squirming against him as soft little mewling protests formed on her lips.

"Damn, don't you have anything on but this transparent stuff? Tis less than mosquito netting!"

"Let me go. You're drunk! I'll scream the house down," she gasped.

His grip was so strong that it squeezed the breath from her. "So, scream and bring my father and all the servants to see you half-naked, roaming alone through the corridors."

"You are despicable! First you insult me and make it plain you are loath to wed me; then you attack me. You are no gentleman, sir!"

"And you are . . . what are you, Madelyne?" He studied her small, heart-shaped face. The wide-set eyes glowed like amber and her hair—God, her hair—gleamed black as ink in the dim light. He tangled one hand in it and pulled her soft open mouth up closer to his. When she tried to turn away, he tightened his hold on her hair, immobilizing her head until she grew very still, staring up at him like a rabbit caught in a snare.

Madelyne watched those sculpted, elegant lips draw closer and closer to hers. *He's going to kiss me.* She tried to relax, but now the panic was being replaced by another, even more disquieting emotion. She became aware that his shirt was open and her fingers sank into the springy black hair of his chest. Every inch of him was lean and hard, splendidly made. *God help me, I want him to*—

Quintin kissed her, slowly at first, tasting the sweet heat of her mouth, feeling its pliancy as he worked his lips over it, slanting his mouth against hers, first one way, then another until he felt her respond. His tongue probed delicately at the seam of her lips until she opened for him; then he plunged inside. He was losing control, all inhibitions being thrown to the wind by liquor. The kiss grew deeper, more possessive, more savage.

Madelyne melted at the first brushing contact of their lips, thrilled at the firm way his mouth seemed to command hers, moving and tutoring her responses. When she opened and his tongue invaded, twining with hers, a hot jolt of raw pleasure bolted through her, right down to her toes. Her fingers involuntarily clutched at the hard muscles of his chest, but gradually his kiss seemed to go out of control. He ground his lower body against hers, holding one buttock in his hand, lifting her up to press into him as his caresses continued to roughen. Alarmed, she began to push ineffectually against the iron wall of his chest. His breathing was labored, and he began to shake uncontrollably as he pulled her down toward the carpet.

Just as he knelt, she gave one final, desperate shove and twisted free of his grip. Caught off balance, Quintin's hold loosened and she wrenched free, letting out a harsh sob of pain as his fingers tore loose some strands of hair where it had tangled around his hand.

"You bastard!" She backed away from him in terror, but Quintin remained frozen on one knee, looking up at her, his expression harsh, his eyes blazing.

"More than you know," he whispered.

Madelyne rubbed her stinging temple where the hair had been torn, then gathered up the folds of her robe and fled like a wraith from the man kneeling in the moon-drenched room.

The morning was hazy and overcast as she sat sweltering in the confined space of Robert's two-wheeled chair, a favorite conveyance on the rough back country roads of Georgia. The light-weight vehicles were built for speed but were sturdy enough to withstand mud, potholes, and deep ruts in the uneven trails that passed for royal highways.

Madelyne cast a cautious glance at Robert's profile as he held the reins in his strong dark hands. She could see little resemblance between father and son. Robert's face was craggy and blunt, while Quintin's was finely sculpted. He must resemble his mother.

Nothing had been said of the long-dead Lady Anne, an English noblewoman wed to Robert after his family had grown rich in trade. She desperately wanted to understand this troubled family, but feared to ask the fierce and unpredictable Robert anything of a personal nature. Still, it seemed unnatural that a woman of such illustrious lineage, as her father had described Anne Caruthers, would not be remembered by so much as even a single portrait in the huge city house filled with likenesses of all the Blackthornes.

Perhaps when they arrived at the plantation she would learn more of Quintin's mother. *I really want to learn more of him,* she admitted to herself. After his frightening and inexplicable behavior in the library, she had spent the rest of the night dreaming strange, disturbingly erotic dreams.

Just thinking of what he had almost done to her— no, truthfully she had to admit, *with* her—filled her with humiliation. But soon he would have the right to her body. What would happen then? He had been so angry with her last night, almost as if he blamed her for his bestial behavior. *But you did respond to his kiss,* a voice of conscience niggled.

On rising that morning, she had both dreaded and anticipated confronting him, simply to gauge his reaction to last night. Would he apologize? Or remain cold and aloof? Madelyne had her speech of reconciliation carefully rehearsed, determined to mend the breach between them and to understand the demons that seemed to drive Quintin Blackthorne. But damn his soul, he had not appeared at breakfast.

Robert had informed her that she was to ride with him to Blackthorne Hill. Quintin had some business in town and would be along later in the afternoon. She derived a small measure of satisfaction thinking of the headache he must be stricken with after consuming so much liquor.

On the ride to the plantation, Robert was morose and silent for the most part. Finally, after several false starts at conversation, she drew him into discussing his various business ventures. He was inordinately proud of the wealth he had accrued from buying and selling land and growing beef cattle and other livestock, especially fine horses. Blackthorne Hill also grew a substantial rice crop as well as being virtually a self-sustaining kingdom where all basic food staples were raised on the premises.

"Place has been in our family since m' father bought the first plots from Mr. Oglethorpe back in '35. Of course, the first house was of wood, a good bit smaller than the brick one. Sits on the river bluff. I can see my fields and my stock, survey it all from the front porch." Robert's voice was filled with intense pride.

"I understand the Blackthorne family is also commissioned as his majesty's agent in trading with the Creek Confederacy." She dared not ask about Devon directly but was curious about him and Andrew.

"We trade with about a half dozen of the Lower Creek towns. Deer hides for weapons, iron tools, cloth, rum and such like. It's profitable," he said in a detached tone as if it held little interest for him.

"Is it wise to sell rum to the Indians? I've seen it wreak enough havoc among the lower classes of white men."

Robert snorted in disgust. "Keeps 'em in line. The savages crave rum worse than whites, but they drink it in the back country. Only rebel squatters wandering into their lands are at risk from drunken Indians. Serves 'em right."

"Yes, I suppose that's true. Certainly Mad Turkey and his warriors were most hospitable to me. They were traders. Do they come to Blackthorne Hill with their hides?"

"Not that close. Those that bring goods to us deal at the warehouse on the river. Our men more often take shipments to them in the trading towns."

"Is that Devon's job? To live with the Creeks and regulate the exchanges?" His expression darkened, and he affixed her with slate-blue eyes so cold they reminded her of Quintin's equally icy green ones.

"You will be best advised not to discuss Devon Blackthorne with anyone, Madelyne. He is a half-caste and a rogue. The family is disgraced by what he is and how he conducts himself."

"Quintin seems on good terms with him," she dared to venture.

Robert's face was hard as he replied, "They are the same age and grew up together when my brother Alastair was still alive. I believe Quintin befriended Devon simply to defy me."

"On the contrary, I think they are genuinely fast friends."

Robert turned and faced her with his most daunting stare. "You are a bold and sassy chit, just as Quintin said. I fear Theo has misled me as to your biddable nature."

Madelyne bristled but struggled to control her anger. "That is scarce surprising. My father has seen me but a few days a year since my mother died when I was five."

A shout interrupted their confrontation. One of the servants riding ahead of them raised his hand and waved.

"Just around that bend will be your first view of Blackthorne Hill," Robert said by way of explanation.

Madelyne watched anxiously as the chair turned, following the narrow, rutted road into a clearing along the banks of the Savannah River. The river's course was sluggish and twisting here. Just where it made a sharp turn, a huge bluff rose majestically above the wide-open land along its banks. Pens filled with horses, cattle, and swine were laid out at the northern edge. A large dairy, a poultry house and a tanning shed all lent their pungent odors as they rode nearer. The loud ringing of a smithy's hammer on an anvil broke through the noises from the livestock. Situated right on the banks of the river stood a large wooden building set up on stilts to keep the flood water from inundating the first floor during rainy seasons.

"Is that the trading post?" Madelyne asked, fascinated by all the sights, sounds, and smells of the busy plantation.

"Yes. The trading pirogues can pull up to the front porch at high water to load and unload goods."

Several huge, unwieldy flat-bottomed boats burdened with cargo bobbed in the current next to the wharf that fronted the post. As Madelyne studied the craft, the sun suddenly broke through the sullen overcast, reflecting brightly on the muddy waters of the Savannah. She shielded her eyes and turned to gaze northward toward the bluff. At her gasp of astonishment, Robert actually smiled.

"Quite a sight, isn't it?"

"I've never seen its like in Charles Town." She was rewarded with the most sincerely pleased expression she had yet seen on Robert's usually harsh, scowling countenance.

As the chair climbed the winding bluff road, the extent of Blackthorne Hill's glory unfolded before Madelyne's amazed eyes. Plots of every imaginable sort of vegetable were neatly interspersed between apple, peach and pear orchards. Below on the swampy river plain hundreds of acres of rice fields lay under cultivation. Two big kitchen buildings were bustling with cooks preparing the evening meal for an army of servants and slaves as well as special delicacies for the family. An elegant coach house and a long, sturdily constructed stable stood near the road as it crested the hill. Formal gardens bordered by boxwood lent fragrance and vibrant color to the scene. But everything was merely a backdrop for the big house that sat in the center of it all, like a sentinel guarding all the workers and the wealth of Blackthorne Hill.

If Madelyne had thought the city house grand, this one defied description. It was easily twice the size, the massive brick walls symmetrically broken by huge windows, open to admit the steady breeze that blew across the heights. Towering live oaks shaded the shingled roof, cooling the interior.

Dozens of men and women, black and white, obviously all house servants, neatly lined up along the curving driveway leading to the front door. As they alighted from the carriage, Madelyne noticed one woman, plumpish and tall with coarse, mannish features and piercing black eyes, who stood apart from the rest.

She curtsied obsequiously to Robert, her gray buckram skirts rustling as she moved. Madelyne imagined her to be the kind who would starch even her undergarments. The plain white cap covering her salt-and-pepper hair was crisp and snowy in the wilting afternoon heat.

"Welcome home, Master Robert."

He nodded, then took Madelyne's hand and presented her to the staff, beginning with the head housekeeper. "This is Mistress Ogilve. She has run Blackthorne Hill most efficiently for thirty years."

The woman flushed a bit beneath his praise and simpered a smile at Robert, then turned hostile assessing eyes on Madelyne, the new mistress, as if warning her not to interfere in her domain.

Madelyne forced a bright smile and tried to look as cool and presentable as she could in the heat. Robert proceeded down the impossible-to-remember line of indentured servants, slaves, and free workers, presenting her as the future mistress of Blackthorne Hill. All she could think of was a cool drink and a long soak in a tub, but she kept the smile pasted on, trying desperately to put names with faces as each servant was introduced.

Whatever else the shortcomings of her marriage, she would be accorded wealth and prestige far beyond any she had ever imagined. The Blackthornes must be as prosperous as any family in the colonies. But Madelyne would have traded all of it if the man she was to wed truly wanted her.

When the ordeal was finally over, Robert left her to the care of Mistress Ogilve, who escorted her upstairs. "This'll be your room for now," the housekeeper said as she opened the heavy oak door and marched into a lovely small room near the end of the long second-story hallway.

Madelyne followed her into the tidy room, filled with Queen Anne furniture. The coverings on the canopied bed were solid dark rose, with the color repeated in the rose-and-blue carpet in the center of the room. Although tastefully decorated, the room seemed cold to Madelyne. Her pretty bedroom at Isolde's had been more simply furnished with a turned bedstead and delicately inlaid chest of drawers. The pale green-and-gold bed hangings and carpet had given it a warm and cheery feeling.

Even the walls of this room were covered with rich silk fabric in the same somber hues as the rug.

"After the marriage, Master Quintin may want you to move to the bedroom at the head of the hall." The housekeeper's eyes were crafty and assessing, as if waiting to see what Madelyne's reaction would be to the cryptic remark.

Refusing to rise to the bait, Madelyne asked instead, "Would you be so kind as to send a tub and bathwater up for me? And I'll need a maid to assist me in changing."

Tight-lipped, the housekeeper bobbed a curtsy. "Very good, Mistress Deveaux." She rustled out, leaving Madelyne to wait for a maid before she could even peel the linen traveling gown from her body. Her stays bit into her ribs, and her fine lawn undergarments felt as if they had melted against her skin.

Later, as she lazed in the tub, Madelyne reviewed her first impressions of Blackthorne Hill. She felt tremendously overburdened. For all the grandeur of the estate, there was a soullessness to it. The downstairs rooms were lavishly furnished with the older more baroque William and Mary furniture. The carpets, chandeliers, wallpaper—every furnishing and fixture in the house—was the best that Europe could yield. The decor was carefully planned as if by a woman's hand, each room elegantly outfitted to blend with the others and to please a man who wanted to flaunt his wealth while pretending to taste.

Had the dead Anne Caruthers selected the beautiful rose-and-blue patterns, the Sevres china, the Sheffield silver—all to please Robert Blackthorne? Then why was there nothing left of feminine warmth in the grand old house? Each room was meticulously clean and ordered, yet none of the small personal touches that said people lived and laughed and loved were present. The walls were hung with old family portraits, the most recent being one of Robert as a young officer at the opening of the late war against France in 1757. No portraits of Quintin as a child and none of the mysterious Anne seemed to exist. Why?

Hearing the clatter of hooves on the front driveway, Madelyne had an intuition that Quintin had just arrived. A fine prickle of goosebumps spread across her wet skin in spite of the sultry air. Quickly she rose from the tub and began to towel herself dry, feeling oddly vulnerable in her nakedness.

Quintin entered the cool interior of the house and went immediately to the large sideboard in the dining room where Delphine, the head cook, always kept a large ewer filled with tangy, cool ale. His head was splitting from the effects of last night's overindulgence, and the long hot ride had certainly not helped ease the pain. Pouring a tankard full of the foaming golden liquid, he downed it in several gulps, then wiped his mouth with the back of his hand and took a deep breath.

In keeping with his usual custom, which sorely irritated Robert's sensibilities, Quintin wore no coat when he rode, only a loose shirt of soft buckskin, with the lacing open down his bare chest. He looked as savage as Robert always accused Devon of being. Indeed, it was from Devon that he had learned to enjoy the unconventional but far more practical back country clothes.

Quintin took another swallow of ale, then looked down at the dusty leather pouch he had carried from the city. A slow smile played mirthlessly across his lips. He had been constrained to purchase the expected bridal gift for Madelyne, a gaudy and costly set of matched pearl jewelry, but this little token would give him far more pleasure than the pearls when he presented it to her. He opened the pouch and extracted it, then headed upstairs. After a bath and change of clothes, he'd seek her out and offer it to her, along with some sort of apology for his behavior.

He swore as he remembered the fiasco last night. He had lost control of himself and attacked the girl like a rutting stag! She had the damnedest effect on him, and he didn't like it. What insanity had brought her, half-naked, floating into his private domain at two in the morning? Grudgingly, he had owned up to the need for at least a few perfunctory words of regret for his actions, but she was scarcely blameless in the matter. He'd make that quite clear. His face felt hot as he recalled the stinging epithet she'd flung at him. How he'd grown to loathe that word. His earliest childhood memories seemed filled with it. *Bastard*.

Shaking off old nightmares, Quintin picked up his gift and headed up the large curving staircase, calling down to the houseboy below with instructions for his bath.

Madelyne stood rooted to the hall floor, watching the leather-clad savage bound up the stairs. Merciful heavens, was this her future husband? The man who had ridden up to Aunt Claud's dressed like a prince from a storybook? Now his hair hung loose about his shoulders, and he was wearing the buckskin shirt of a backwoodsman, unlaced at the throat, with an indecent amount of black hair curling through the open front. How well she remembered that crisp hair, those hard chest muscles, and the pounding of his heart beneath her hands as he'd held her!

Rubbing his chest, Quintin reached the top of the stairs and looked up. Madelyne stood but a few feet from him. He sketched a bow as he observed her appearance. "A fetching gown. You look cool and refreshed after the long ride. Yellow becomes you." So did the clinging soft muslin cloth. He forced himself to attend to the business at hand, ignoring the dewy freshness of her skin and the way her dark, lustrous hair gleamed in the afternoon light.

A few wispy tendrils escaped, still damp from her bath. "Allow me to apologize for last night. I was drunk."

Madelyne nodded woodenly, remembering her horrifying lapse into vulgarity, the awful word she'd hissed at him before she fled. "It would be best if we both forgot the encounter."

His expression revealed how likely he thought that eventuality. "Yes, it would. That might best be accomplished if you refrained from wandering through the house with scarcely a stitch to cover your charms."

Madelyne felt the blood rush to her face. She gave him a scathing inspection, from his wind-blown, unclubbed hair and unshaven face down to the leather shirt with its gaping lacing. He was actually rubbing those long tapered fingers across his chest! A frisson of heat snaked through her belly. Stiffening, she forced herself to reply to his taunt. "I would say the pot is calling the kettle black. I had no earthly reason to expect anyone to be about when I ventured out unsuitably clad. Yet you actually rode from Savannah dressed thus—and have the nerve to lecture me on deportment!"

"A man has prerogatives reserved to his sex, mistress. And you are under my roof now, so you had best heed my warning." His expression was harsh, then grew mocking as he extended one hand to her, holding out a book. "I believe you dropped this in your haste to escape my talons last night."

Madelyne forgot to breathe. Merciful heavens, it was *that* book! She had completely forgotten how she'd lost her prize! And he had retrieved it just to taunt her. "How kind of you to bring it all this way." She reached out, willing her hand not to flinch when his fingers brushed hers as she accepted the book.

"Most ladies of my acquaintance would be scandalized by the confessions of an infamous English courtesan. Surely this isn't the sort of fare your Aunt Claud would approve."

She clutched the book, refusing to back down. "That is precisely the reason I chose it."

"Has your education been so constrained you feel a need for this sort of titillation?" He quirked one black eyebrow at her, waiting for her response. "Perhaps it would be best if you didn't read it. I feel confident I can instruct you adequately on our wedding night."

"Perhaps I wish to broaden my education vicariously so I may make comparison *after* our wedding night." What had she said? Madelyne watched his expression close. He stepped toward her, then stopped short and clenched his fists at his side.

"Only be certain, Mistress Deveaux, that you confine your education to *vicarious* experience in this area. If not, I assure you, you'll have cause to regret it!"

Chapter Six

Madelyne awakened late the following morning. Her sleep had been troubled by feverish dreams in which Quintin towered over her in anger one moment, then held her in a fierce, devouring embrace the next. She had not the heart even to open *Fanny Hill*. By the time she dressed and made her way downstairs, no one was about but servants efficiently engaged in running the enormous household. Both Quintin and Robert had gone out on business for the day. Giving Mistress Ogilve a wide berth, Madelyne made her way through the house, trying to find some hint of warmth, something personal in the grand, cold rooms.

Looking out at the pleasure gardens on the hillside, she decided to cut some marigolds and daisies to bring at least a touch of something live and vibrant into the perfect austerity of Blackthorne Hill. On her way out, she called Gulliver from his assigned place beneath the back porch. She and the dog passed several pleasant hours gathering and arranging bouquets with the assistance of a slave girl named Hattie, whose irreverent sense of youthful fun reminded Madelyne of dear Essie, forced to stay behind with Aunt Claud.

"I'll just place this lovely Meissen vase in the small sitting room at the rear of the hall," she called gaily to Hattie. "That should be enough."

"More than enough, making a mess with falling petals and pollen dust," Mrs. Ogilve said, materializing from around a corner to plant her solid bulk firmly in the middle of the wide hall. "Master Robert has never wanted flowers in the house."

Madelyne held the heavy vase like a shield in front of her. A showdown with this rude, imperious woman was inevitable. "I bowed to your wishes and let my dog remain outdoors so he wouldn't shed on your carpets, but I see little harm in a few flower petals falling. There is an army of servants to clean up. If the master didn't want flowers in the house, it strikes me as odd that he allows such time and attention to be given to those enormous beds on the hillside."

"They were planted by order of the first master."

"Then it's high time we used their bounty," Madelyne replied, stepping forward and forcing the dour housekeeper to stand aside or be dusted with pollen.

"What a curious place," Madelyne murmured to herself as she entered the room and searched for just the right spot to set the flowers. The cosy little haven was bright, having two windows, one facing south and one facing west. Its furnishings were the cane sort popular in the West Indies. The colors were warm, vibrant yellows and lush light shades of green. She decided at once to make it her own sitting room since it appeared that no one in the house ever used it.

After placing the bouquet on a round cane table hung with a delicate yellow damask cloth, she looked about. Several chairs with high backs and plump stuffed cushions faced the magnificent view of the fields falling away behind the leafy branches of the majestic live oaks outside the western window. A settee stood against the inside wall, with a small, square table at each end. Madelyne made a thorough inspection, sitting in the chairs, then reclining on the settee, which she found to be most comfortable.

Suddenly a thought struck her. Could this room have belonged to Quintin's mysterious English mother? It fit with nothing in the rest of the house. Had Anne Caruthers ever spent time in the British Indies? Overcome by a premonition, Madelyne reached for a drawer at one side of the table and pulled it open. An old and very musty Bible lay alone in the small space. She took it out with trembling fingers and opened it. "Lady Anne Letitia Caruthers" was written on the flyleaf in a flowing, delicate script. There was no other entry. Madelyne replaced the Bible and was drawn irresistibly to the drawer of the other end table. It was stuck. She tugged until it opened.

Inside were several obviously personal items, some stationery, still faintly lavender-scented even though brittle and yellowed with age. A small bottle of ink had dried solid, and a quill lay neatly beside the ink. Then she saw it—just a faint glitter, wedged against the loose cane in the drawer's bottom. It was a miniature in a gold frame. Madelyne knelt on the floor so she could reach all the way back and pry the treasure free without scratching it.

"So, you were Anne," she whispered, studying the beautiful, sad face in the tiny portrait. She was exquisite, with luminous green eyes and dark golden hair. Now Madelyne understood from where Quintin had inherited his perfectly aquiline features. Anne had the same strong mouth and straight brow, elegant cheekbones and stubborn jaw. His was a stronger, masculine version of the same face, cast with his father's darker complexion and hair. She held the miniature to the light, absorbed in studying the hauntingly sad look in those green eyes when a tight, furious voice interrupted.

"What the hell are you doing snooping in here?" Quintin snatched the portrait from her fingers. Without even glancing at it, he threw it back into the drawer and shoved it closed.

Madelyne stood up on wobbly legs. "This was your mother's room, wasn't it? Why does no one ever speak of her?"

"You're right, Madelyne. No one ever speaks of her. She's long dead and best forgotten," he replied tightly.

After days of confrontation and bullying from this enigmatic man, Madelyne felt a bright crimson flood of anger wash over her. "Best dead and forgotten! Every room in this house is filled to bursting with portraits of ancestors from hundreds of years ago. The illustrious Blackthorne family evidently saw fit to haul them all the way across the Atlantic. Why isn't the Lady Anne worthy to be honored among them?"

Quintin seized her shoulders and almost shook her. Recalling his loss of control the night he nearly raped her in drunken lust, he released her as if scalded and backed away. "There is only one thing you need to know, and you'd best believe me when I tell you—never again speak her name aloud in this house! Never!"

Madelyne saw the stark pain underlying his fury before he could turn and stride from the room. She stood numb and shaken, all her earlier anger drained from her. "By all that is holy, what kind of a family are the Blackthornes?"

Tears stung her eyes as she quickly left the lovely little place she had hoped to make a haven. Madelyne felt in desperate need of a comforting embrace. She sought out Gulliver behind the house, where he had been banished. She threw her arms around him and sobbed while he licked her face and thumped his tail. Gradually, as she regained control of her emotions, Madelyne looked across the yard to where the stables stood. Perhaps a ride would be a good idea. She needed to work off some of her fright and frustration before she had to face Quintin at the dinner table.

She changed quickly and used the servants' stairs at the rear of the house to slip undetected out to the stables. Gulliver shadowed her as she instructed a groom to saddle her mare, Speckles.

"You'll be needin' a couple of boys to ride with you, Mistress Deveaux. The countryside's full of them rebel rascals, cutthroats 'n thieves, all of 'em. I'll—"

"No, no, that's quite all right. I have Gulliver here, and he's protection enough. I'll not go onto the main roads." She could see the worried look in the young Irishman's freckled face, but she felt in no mood to wait for grooms. She wanted to be free of every vestige of the Blackthorne family at least for this afternoon.

Madelyne retraced her ride down the bluff road and observed the activity at the trading post for a few moments. Then she headed along a narrow trail through the back country, knowing it was too dangerous to chance riding the busy post road alone. After about an hour, her stomach began to growl, reminding her that in all the turmoil of the day she had eaten nothing. The frugal Mrs. Ogilve would doubtless find a kindred spirit in Claud Deveaux, who allowed no food to be served between seven and noon.

"If only there's an inn somewhere along this road," Madelyne said to Gulliver. She had a few small coins in the purse at her waist, surely enough for a modest midday repast, although during these troubled times of war, the value of currency was in greater flux than ever.

The deserted back road held no hope of food, but if she cut across the fields toward the river bluffs, there was a lone inn she recalled passing on her ride here from Savannah. Madelyne knew it was dangerous to approach the post road alone, but this was Georgia, the only colony to retain its royal government. The rebel riffraff were scattered in the woodlands to the north. Feeling reckless and daring, she turned Speckles toward the post road.

After about half an hour, she scanned the bluffs ahead. A large frame structure stood silhouetted on the horizon. The wooden sign creaking in the breeze announced The Golden Swan, Mistress Polly Bloor, Proprietor. For all the grand-sounding name, the inn looked none too respectable, frequented by boisterous rivermen and sweaty planters. But surely if a woman owned the place, it must cater to respectable folk. She could see the insignia of the royal post carrier on one horse's saddle at the hitching post. Then a small, nattily dressed man with a meticulously groomed wig and velvet coat emerged from the inn. A handsome coach quickly pulled about, and he stepped in. Given the rarity of inns along the whole of the Charles Town–Savannah road, Madelyne knew it was here or nowhere. Her stomach growled. She approached the inn and dismounted, tying Speckles to one of the blocks, then venturing to the door.

The noise from inside sounded friendly, if a bit loud. *This is the Georgia back country, not a Charles Town coffee house,* she reminded herself as she stepped cautiously inside. If there was no private room for ladies, she would, of course, leave. Letting her eyes adjust to the dim light, she surveyed massive smoke-stained beams stretching across the low ceiling and sturdy oak chairs and tables scattered about in cluttered disarray. Men of all classes of society ate, drank, and engaged in vociferous conversation.

The fireplace at the far wall was immense, and from the large iron kettle bubbling inside its stone walls a delicious aroma wafted toward her. In spite of the warm, stuffy room and the boisterous hum of voices, Madelyne wanted to be served.

A large blond woman of middle years saw Madelyne standing hesitantly in the door and swished her ample hips through the tangle of furniture toward her.

Polly Bloor noted the young woman's expensive clothes and beautiful mahogany hair, then saw the dog guarding his mistress. The proprietress greeted the lady. "So, you're the girl Quint's going to marry." She gave Madelyne a thorough perusal. When the younger woman's level amber eyes met her hazel ones, Polly nodded approvingly. "You don't flinch. Need that if you're gonna stand up to the likes of Quintin Blackthorne—or that old goat Robert."

"How—how did you know who I am?"

Polly laughed, revealing several missing teeth. "Only thing travels faster 'n gossip on the post road is a hurricane blowin' up from the Indies! I'm Polly Bloor, owner of this place."

"I'm Madelyne Deveaux, Mistress Bloor, and I'm fearfully hungry. I know it's not proper for a lone female to dine in a public room—"

"That ain't anythin' to fret about. Ridin' alone with this gawd-awful war goin' on is risky, though." She studied Madelyne's set features and then looked at the large dog standing beside her, eyeing the men inside the taproom. "I've a nice cosy room in the back where you can have a bite, all respectable and proper. Here, just let me show you the way around to the side entrance."

In a few moments, Madelyne and Gulliver were ensconced in a small room just off the kitchen, where a servant was busily cutting sweet, honey-cured ham into paper-thin slices. The smell made her stomach growl, and the dog sat with ears cocked, his eyes glued to the juicy pink meat piling up on the wooden cutting block. Madelyne took a sip of lemonade and waited. So everyone in Georgia knew she had come to wed Quintin. Did they also know how unhappy her bridegroom was with the dismal prospect of her for a wife?

Polly bustled in with a plate heaped with sweet ham, sharp cheese, and crispy corn dodgers. Placing it in front of Madelyne, she added, "I got a pot of venison stew that's rich 'n tender. Want a bowl of it, too?"

Madelyne smiled ruefully as she slipped a slice of ham to Gulliver. "I fear I may not have enough coins to be such a glutton."

Polly let loose a great booming laugh and replied, "Eat your fill. Quint runs a regular bill here. I think he'll be able to afford all a little bitty thing like you can eat."

"If he chooses to pay for it," Madelyne blurted out, then felt color heat her face. What had she said? By tomorrow everyone in seven parishes would hear it!

A shrewd look came over Polly's round, kindly face. "So, Quint's not happy with old Robert's match. I figgered as much. It ain't you, dearie. It's just the idea of leg-shackling. Gets most wild young stallions like Quint real testy and chomping on the bit."

"Especially if his father chose the bride."

"Mind if I set down? We're in private, but you bein' a lady 'n all . . ."

"Please do join me." Madelyne waved the older woman into the scarred oak chair next to hers. She smiled at Polly, deciding she liked her. "You can't know how starved I am for the company of another woman, Polly."

"You were sent all the way from Carolina without any female kin. Then you met up with Serena Fallowfield in Savannah. That'd make any female right desperate."

Madelyne stifled a laugh, then grew wistful. "She isn't very pleasant—at least not to me, although

Quintin seems to enjoy her company a good deal."

"He's enjoyed more 'n her company. So's many another man what took her fancy. She's nothin' special to Quint," Polly hastened to add.

"At dinner in Savannah he seemed to feel differently."

"It ain't Serena you gotta worry about, dearie. Quint'd never marry a wild one like her. Couldn't trust her. Trustin' even a good woman don't come easy to Blackthorne men. Stand up to him and always tell him the truth. That's what you gotta do." She hesitated, watching Madelyne as she fed scraps of her meal to Gulliver.

Madelyne looked up, confused and uncertain about how much to discuss with this kindly woman. "You've known Quintin for a long time?"

"Since he was a lad. He's not had an easy time growin' up, but he's a good man."

"You mean the enmity between him and his father was always this bad?"

"Only thing they ever agreed on was to distrust the female sex."

"But why? This morning I found a hidden portrait of Quintin's mother. He practically threw it away and forbade me to ever speak her name. What kind of family are the Blackthornes? Andrew and Devon seem the soul of kindness, but Robert and Quintin . . . I don't understand them, yet I'll be bound to them for as long as we all shall live."

"Someday Quint will tell you about his mama. I got a feeling about that . . . in his own good time." She studied Madelyne, then said baldly, "You love him already."

"No! I don't. He's arrogant and rude, and he's made it perfectly clear that he despises me." Remembering his brutal yet nearly successful attack on her in the library in Savannah, Madelyne felt her face flame.

Polly patted her hand. "What Quint says and what Quint feels inside don't usually turn out to be the same. Just remember that and be patient. But mind, don't let him ride roughshod over you neither."

"My temper can be every bit as formidable as his."

"Good. He needs a female with spunk." Polly laughed, but Madelyne was not reassured.

They discussed the Blackthorne family and life at the Hill. Polly even shared a bit of gossip about Robert's brother Alastair and his black sheep son Devon, whom she obviously liked as well as she did Quintin.

Finally Madelyne realized the late hour. She had to ride for Blackthorne Hill. "If Quintin and Robert find I've ridden out alone, they'll be furious and I've already done enough to make them angry. I'd best be leaving. Thank you, Polly, for everything. I feel I've made a friend. I hope you do, too." Madelyne extended her slim hand.

Polly clutched it in her big red one and gently squeezed it. "That I do, Madelyne. If ever there's anythin' you need, you just come to Polly. I'll always be here."

As she rode back along the rutted road, Madelyne mulled over the day's perplexing events, glad to have found a confidant in Polly Bloor, yet disquieted by what the innkeeper had told her about Quintin. He and Serena had been lovers. He distrusted all women, yet obviously he enjoyed their bodies. Once again the disturbing passion that flared between them replayed itself in her mind. *You love him*, Polly had said. *Nonsense! I don't even like him*. But merciful heavens, something drew her to him. She could not begin to comprehend her own feelings.

So absorbed was Madelyne in her own thoughts that at first she didn't notice the dapple gray's limp, but when the mare stumbled, she dismounted and checked her right front hoof. "Oh, Gulliver, what will we do now? Speckles can't be ridden, and we're still an hour from the plantation." Quintin would be furious with her.

The sound of hoofbeats echoed on the afternoon breeze. Perhaps some gentleman from a neighboring plantation could offer her a ride. She waited expectantly, then felt a stab of dismay when a man dressed in greasy buckskins and wearing a coonskin hat rode into view, accompanied by another tall, thin rider dressed more like a gentleman in linen smallclothes and a handsome blue twill jacket. Gulliver began to growl. Madelyne stood her ground, hoping that they would be decent back-country settlers. Before she could address the one she surmised to be the leader, the other spoke.

"Well, what we got us here, Ephraim? Looks to be a real fine lady in trouble." The woodsman was thickset, with an ugly purple scar on his cheek.

"Mind your manners, Luke." The one in gentlemen's garb doffed his hat.

Madelyne's relief was short-lived when Ephraim eyed her coldly and inquired, "Are you a patriot, mistress, or do you follow German George?"

"Mr. Malvern, he be a member of the Georgia Legislature," the other ruffian said, scratching his fat belly.

"Well, mistress? On the road from Augusta, I heard some fascinating news. That rich royalist whoremaster, Quintin Blackthorne, has brought a comely bride to his river house." Ephraim's eyes were as cold as pewter and gleamed with hate.

"Heard she's got lots of dark red hair," the big fellow called Luke said, leering.

"My name is Madelyne Deveaux and I am a loyal subject of his majesty, as is my betrothed, Quintin Blackthorne. Surely you gentlemen don't carry your war to women?" She faced them with as much bravado as she could muster, but her knees were wavering like a newborn foal's.

Luke dismounted and stepped several paces toward her before Gulliver's growling gave him pause. "If'n you favor that dog, call him off," he said nastily.

"What are you going to do, kill me and my dog? Such brave patriots!" she said scornfully.

"Never think it, my dear lady," Ephraim sneered, his narrow face twisted with relish. "We just plan a bit of an object lesson—to humble prideful Tories like you and the denizens of Blackthorne Hill."

Why did I ever do anything so foolish as to ride out alone! Now I'm trapped. She backed up, seizing the riding crop from her saddle.

Luke reached for her with a snarled oath, but before he could lay hands on her, Gulliver leaped at his chest, knocking the big man to the ground. Luke struggled to free his knife from his belt, but as he and Gulliver rolled and thrashed on the sandy ground, the dog was decidedly winning. Cursing, Ephraim Malvern dismounted and drew a pistol from his coat. Madelyne's quirt quickly disarmed him and left a bloody weal across his wrist.

"For that, you Tory harlot, you'll pay dearly," he ground out as he reached for her whip hand while using his other arm to protect his face.

Madelyne quirted him again, but his longer arms and far greater strength swiftly enabled him to disarm her, ripping her bodice and chemise half off one arm in the process. "You're just like Blackthorne. I wish it was him I had here."

"You get your wish, Malvern. Now release Mistress Deveaux before I use my new Kentucky pistol on a most tempting target," Quint said, his voice like silk edged with steel.

Malvern turned quickly to face his enemy, shoving Madelyne away. By this time Gulliver was standing over the badly mauled Luke, looking toward her. When Luke yanked a knife from its sheath, Madelyne raised her hard-soled riding boot and kicked his wrist with every ounce of her strength, sending the weapon flying. The dog moved closer to his throat and snarled, his fangs dripping with saliva and a good sampling of his victim's blood.

Quint ignored them as he dismounted and strode over to face Ephraim. "So this is how a distinguished member of the patriot legislature behaves when no one is about to observe his actions."

"I am a gentleman and a patriot as well as a planter, sir. You may be a successful planter, but that is all I can say to recommend you," Malvern replied haughtily as he squared off against Blackthorne.

"You've always coveted our lands and our success, Malvern, but to attack a woman just because she is affianced to me is despicable even for you." Quint raised his hand and gave Malvern's face a resounding slap.

Ephraim smiled evilly, rubbing his jaw. "I had hoped to provoke you one way or another. At last your foolish little bride has accomplished the task for me. My second will call at Blackthorne Hill on the morrow to make arrangements. Being the one challenged I, of course, choose foils." He bowed curtly to Quint, then turned to Madelyne and did the same, his eyes nearly opaque as he took in her torn clothes and disheveled appearance. "My regrets, dear lady, but you have served your purpose. How fortunate I am to have encountered you. Come along, Luke," he called over his shoulder as he mounted his horse and rode away.

The bloody backwoodsman with torn buckskins scrambled to his feet with a muttered oath, backed away from the dog, and ran for his horse without even attempting to pick up the knife Madelyne had kicked into a clump of wild roses.

As the pair galloped off, Quintin turned to an ashen-faced Madelyne. "Are you satisfied? Malvern has wanted to challenge me for years."

"He obviously hates you. Why didn't he?"

She watched his furious expression turn to cynical humor. "Because if I were challenged, I'd have the choice of weapons and I'm a dead shot. He was trained to use foils by the best fencing master in New Orleans."

Madelyne saw red specks dance before her eyes and fought waves of blackness. "I didn't mean to endanger you, Quintin. Truly I didn't," she whispered, reaching out to touch his arm, as much to feel his warm, firm flesh as to steady herself.

He threw off her hand as if it were a viper and turned toward Domino, swinging effortlessly into the saddle. "Don't bury me yet, my unhappy little bride," he said as he reached down for Speckles's reins.

"She's lame. That's why I—"

"You were afoot at the mercy of Malvern and his trashy lickspittle because you did an insanely stupid thing. There is a war going on, in case it's slipped your notice! Women do not ride unescorted in these times. Ladies never do, but I'll not waste my breath on that issue," he added bitterly as he leaned down from his saddle and hauled her up in front of him.

Madelyne fell across the horse like a sack of seed grain, her belly bruised by contact with the saddle. As she writhed and kicked, Quint gave her rump a swat, cursed, and kneed Domino into a canter toward home.

Devon Blackthorne was in big trouble. He looked around at the drunken mob of Liberty Boys surrounding him, their faces red from drink, their voices raised in a bellowing roar of enthusiasm.

"I say we hang the savage-loving son of a bitch!" one voice cried out.

"No. Too quick. His damned Indians don't kill us that easy. I say we burn 'im," yelled another drunken voice.

"Tar 'n feathers, tar 'n feathers," went up the chant.

Devon cursed his stupidity for stopping in this back-country settlement for a cool draft of ale. He had been so certain that this far from the coast no one would recognize him as a Crown agent. But one of Elijah Clarke's men had chanced upon the same tavern. Now he was surrounded by a howling pack of mongrels. If they tarred him, he'd probably die of the burns or the attendant poisoning that so often accompanied them. At best he'd be crippled and hideously scarred.

Better to die fast and clean. He kicked over the big oak table in front of him, sending chairs, tankards, and ale flying in all directions as he drew a wicked-looking hunting knife from its sheath. Letting its silvery glitter arc back and forth as he tossed it from hand to hand, he dared the leader to step forward. "You'll have a hard time killing a Muskogee warrior, cowardly traitors! Come and die with me!"

A roar went up from the crowd, and several men shouted orders, contradicting each other, but no one would face Devon head-on. Finally, as he backed toward the corner of the big log cabin, two men came at him using chairs as shields. While he was engaged with them, another fellow slipped behind him with a heavy hickory club and smashed it into the side of his head. Devon went down to his knees, dropping his knife as he fell face forward onto the earthen floor.

They dragged him outside and headed toward the smithy's shop, where a good hot fire burned all year round.

"Strip off them moccasins 'n let's see how tender his feet get when we light a few coals 'neath 'em," the ringleader called out.

"Git the tar a boilin'," another commanded two youths, who scurried off toward another cabin across the street.

Devon regained consciousness slowly, his head throbbing mercilessly. He tried to reach up and touch his temple, then realized that his hands were bound at his sides. He struggled, trying to clear his vision.

A disembodied voice cut through the haze of pain. "He's awake. Now."

Devon bit back a scream as they put the coals to the soles of his feet. His body arched in agony. Then he slumped back into unconsciousness. When a bucket of warm, brackish water hit him in the face, he came around once again, only to smell the acrid stench of hot pitch. Rough hands ripped at his pants, baring his legs up to his thighs.

The burning, corrosive tar was poured gradually across one foot, then up his leg to his calf. He hurled curses at them, sweat beading his brow as he looked down in horror at what they were doing. When his left leg broke free of his tormentors' hold, he kicked at them, spraying the ugly black tar all about the circle of drunken faces. A meaty fist punched his face; then another struck his stomach until he subsided, gasping for breath. Then they began on his right leg.

Suddenly shots erupted and horses' hooves thudded dully against the hard dry clay. A clear command rang out. "You will cease this abomination and free that man at once!"

Devon lay bound on the hot, dusty earth while chaos broke loose around him. Men cursed and yelled as the sounds of gunfire blended with the solid thuds of fists striking flesh. It was over quickly. The mounted men in sweat-stained green uniforms quickly scattered the mob of Liberty Boys, who went flying into the surrounding woods, chased by soldiers wielding sabers and firing rifles.

Devon felt the ropes around his torso being cut loose. He turned to a stern-faced man with dark hair and shrewd blue eyes. "Whoever you are, you have my everlasting thanks," he rasped out as his rescuer assisted him in sitting up.

In a heavy Yorkshire accent, the man replied, "I am Thomas Brown, Lieutenant Colonel in the King's Rangers and Superintendent of Indians for the Eastern Department."

Devon cocked an eyebrow, then winced as one of his tar-covered legs rubbed against the other. "I've heard of you, sir. I'm Devon Blackthorne, late an agent licensed for his majesty's trade with the Lower Creek towns."

"You're Alastair's son by his Muskogee wife," Brown said with a nod of approval.

Devon grinned in spite of the agony pounding up and down his body. "I'd forgotten you lived for a year among my mother's people."

"Until those bloody damn rabble ran me out of my own land in Georgia. Did the same thing to me," he said grimly, gesturing to the tar.

"So now you lead rangers in raids against the rebels."

"And coordinate British military activities with those of our Indian allies," Brown replied, studying Devon with a question in his keenly assessing gaze.

"How would you like a brand new recruit, Colonel, sir?"

"I was hoping you'd ask that."

Chapter Seven

Quintin rode out before dawn. Fog blanketed the river and climbed to the bluff above it in thinning layers. As the hot late June sun rose, cutting through the cool gray miasma, he considered what the next few hours would bring. *Perhaps my death.* He wondered how that might affect Madelyne. Would she be happily rid of him and the alliance forced on her? Or was he preferable to a life with her estimable Huguenot aunt?

Certainly she'd played distraught and penitent when he rescued her from Malvern. He could still see those wide-set amber eyes filled with fear, the ashen pallor of her normally sun-touched complexion. She'd tried to reach out to him—just as any other manipulative female would, he thought in dismissal. Then why did he still remember the quiver of those soft lips? He shifted uncomfortably in the saddle, recalling how much he still wanted to touch her. *Soon you'll get your fill of her . . . if you live to claim your wedding night reward.*

Solomon Torres watched the sardonic smile grimly twist his friend's lips as they rode to the arranged place on the Savannah road. "I think you should call this whole insane thing off, Quint. Malvern's waited for years for this chance."

"And my bride helpfully supplied him with the golden opportunity." He shrugged fatalistically. "I can't cry off, Solomon. You know what that would do to my reputation. I'd be ruined, never accepted in society again. Think what that would do for my work. If I'm not received by the gentlemen of the city, I'm of no further use to our cause."

"You could always join the Continental Line. General Washington has need of some decent officers, the good Lord knows," Doctor Witherspoon said dryly.

Solomon looked at their companion, whose small, wizened face was made even more owlish by the wire spectacles perched insecurely on his nose. "Noble, you know Quint is far more valuable as an agent. Any fool can join the army."

"Yep," Noble Witherspoon replied sourly. "Charles Lee and Horatio Gates are living proof of that!"

With tolerant amusement, Quint observed the earnest young merchant and the cynical old physician, both lifelong friends. "Gentlemen, please. The issue of my skills versus the dubious accomplishments of Gates and Lee aren't at issue here. I'm bound to face Malvern."

"If only you could avoid the fencing foils." Solomon's expression was grim.

"I've been given a gentleman's prerequisite instruction with swords of various sorts, including the French foil, even if I lack the expert instruction of a New Orleans dueling master. Don't bury me yet, my friends. I've a trick or two planned."

Solomon looked at Witherspoon when the old man chuckled and said, "Ephraim was my patient several years ago before his republican politics forced him to flee Savannah. I didn't think it too serious a breach of my oath to mention to Quint that he has developed a very weakened right eye. Inherited, I'd say. His father had the same affliction."

"Combined with greed! Two generations of Malverns have wanted Blackthorne Hill. Ironic that Ephraim joined the revolution hoping to oust us from our lands only to risk losing his when the British recaptured Savannah and restored royal government," Quint said.

"We could turn him in to British authorities. After all, he is a member of the legislature," Solomon ventured, then subsided, seeing the stubborn set of Quintin's jaw. "I only hope the disease in that eye has made him stone blind!"

Ephraim Malvern was waiting at the designated place as the three riders approached. Quintin looked at the smug expression on his adversary's face. *Just keep that set of mind, Ephraim.* He dismounted beneath an enormous willow tree whose feathery branches provided some protection from the sticky heat. He slipped off his coat and waistcoat, leaving only his loose lawn shirt with its billowing sleeves.

Malvern did the same. Both tall men were unencumbered now, with complete freedom of movement, clad in supple buckskin pants and soft boots. Ephraim's second opened a long, polished-walnut case. Two beautiful foils gleamed evilly on the red velvet lining.

Red as blood, Quint thought. He chose one according to protocol and tested it with several thrusting and parrying movements. "This will serve, Malvern."

Witherspoon, as the physician of record approved by both men, made his last formal and useless plea that the duel not take place. Quickly, Quintin and Ephraim took their positions on the flat, open ground beneath the willow, a famous dueling landmark just far enough north of the British-held city to be safe for Malvern.

For the first moments after the ring of steel resounded across the marshy river bottom, it seemed that Ephraim would easily win. He wielded the delicate blade like a seamstress handled a fine needle, thrusting with sure strokes that marked Quint several times, then parrying every attempt of Quint's bold offense with negligent ease.

"I don't like it. Malvern's drawn first blood," Solomon whispered to Noble.

"Just nicks. Look how they're progressing from beneath the tree out into the sunlight," the old doctor replied, sotto voce.

Quint almost had Ephraim where he wanted him, if only he could stay alive long enough to complete the maneuver! His seemingly rash desperation amused Malvern, who enjoyed toying with him. *Just stay amused and condescending, you peacock . . . just for a few more minutes.*

When they moved from the sheltering shade of the tree into the hard, clay-packed clearing, Ephraim felt the sun's sudden glare. He noted with satisfaction that Quint, too, perspired heavily as they circled each other, thrusting and parrying and counterthrusting. Sweat beaded their faces and soaked the thin lawn of their shirts until the garments clung to their bodies.

Quint watched Malvern's face, noting the way he squinted in the bright light. *That eye's bothering him.* "Having trouble seeing, Ephraim?" he asked tauntingly. Although he never missed a move, Quint knew Ephraim wanted to turn and glare at Witherspoon.

"So, the good doctor has betrayed his professional ethics. I've learned to compensate, so it don't matter, Blackthorne." He renewed the attack, now with far more seriousness, attempting to drive Quintin once more beneath the willow. One particularly deadly thrust sliced a huge rip in the left side of Quint's shirt, but he parried successfully, retreating toward the shade, yet arcing slowly around to meet a low-hanging limb whose swaying branches reached within five feet of the ground.

Malvern was moving from his right side toward the branches as Quint carefully let him attack, allowing several dangerous openings and taking painful slices from Ephraim's punishing blade. When Malvern was within a foot of the leaves, suspended without movement in the heavy air, Quint lunged recklessly, as if desperate. Ephraim laughed as he saw his opening—Quint's exposed left side. With a growl of triumph he closed in and thrust for the heart.

As swiftly as Ephraim moved, Quint moved with him, pivoting away as the blade sliced the sheer lawn of his clinging shirt. Ephraim felt the rustling willow leaves brush him before he saw them. He turned his head in reflex, trying to avoid them while at the same time recovering from the ineffectual thrust he'd made at Quint. The two movements gave Blackthorne the split-second opportunity he needed.

All the air hissed from Malvern's lungs as he felt the sudden clean, hard sting. "Amazing, it hurts less than a mere cut on the wrist," he wheezed, dropping to his knees as Quintin withdrew his blade. It had penetrated between the ribs, cleanly into Ephraim's heart. He toppled forward and then rolled onto his back. By the time Dr. Witherspoon knelt beside him, Ephraim Malvern was dead.

Ephraim's second was a pompous cousin with hopes of inheriting the family estates now that the sole heir of Abner Malvern had been removed. He made a few token protests about the maneuver into the willow branches, but there was really nothing specific to reproach Quintin about, given the common knowledge of Ephraim's superior swordsmanship. It had been his intent to drive Quintin back into the shade. He had failed.

Solomon helped the dead man's cousin load the body onto his horse and then turned back to where Dr. Witherspoon was tending to several of Quint's freely bleeding injuries. Suddenly his eyes widened in startled surprise and he yelled out a warning, but it was too late. A small figure clad in ragged breeches and a gray shirt tumbled from the leafy boughs above their heads. The lad had lost purchase on a slender branch that snapped upwards with a rustling whoosh after being relieved of its burden.

Madelyne landed atop Quint's shoulders, toppling them both to the ground in a tangle of arms and legs. Her hair came free of the leather cap she wore and spilled like rich red satin around his face and shoulders. A pair of .30-caliber Queen Anne's turn-off pistols landed several feet from them. Quintin seized her by her shoulders and thrust her away from him, then grabbed one silver inlaid pistol and rolled to his feet, examining it.

She could still smell the mixture of male musk and blood from his sweat-slicked body as she lay sprawled in front of him, dazed and relieved. Yet she was frightened, too, for he was drenched in his own blood.

Quint glared down at her as Solomon and Noble stood rooted to the ground in shocked silence. "What in the hell are you doing here and how did you get here?"

There was such a deadly edge to his voice that she took a moment to unstick her tongue from the roof of her dry mouth. How awful she must look to him! His disgusted perusal of her body attested to the fact. "I overheard the discussion about the duel and followed the road to the river—early, before dawn. Gulliver and my horse are over behind that clump of cattails across the slew."

"And just exactly what did you intend with this?" He held the pistol in the palm of his hand.

She scrambled to her feet, feeling at a horrible disadvantage on the ground. "You're not the only one who's a dead shot, Mr. Blackthorne."

Solomon's low chuckle rumbled across the still hot air. "By the Almighty, Quint, she'd have shot the blighter to save your miserable hide!"

"I'm deeply touched, mistress, but I fight my own battles." His voice was as crisp and cold as a December frost.

"This duel was my fault." As she lowered her eyes from his icy green glare, she murmured, "I couldn't have your death on my conscience."

"You'd better let me clean and bind those slashes before you bleed to death and ruin your wedding. Then you can settle matters with your lady," Noble said, once more resuming his attention to Quintin's injuries.

"This hoyden is no lady. The wedding was ruined the day my father and hers proposed the damnable match."

If ever I see you in boy's clothes or in any other way improperly attired, I will tan that pretty little backside until you'll not sit a horse for a month. Madelyne stood in front of a large oval mirror in her room at Blackthorne Hill, recalling Quintin's coldly furious threat to her the afternoon of the duel. That had been a week ago. This was her wedding day. Ever since she was a young girl, Madelyne had dreamed of this day. Yet the pale face and haunted eyes staring back at her from the mirror did not reflect her dreams at all. *A marriage made in hell,* he'd called it. He despised her, and Madelyne could scarcely blame him after all that had happened.

She had reacted to his arrogant rudeness and irrational jealousy with a fierce temper and rash, cutting words. In that she'd been justified. But the misadventure with Malvern was sheer stupidity on her part, a reckless act that could have gotten Quintin killed. As if that weren't enough, she had not even been able to slip away from the dueling scene without being caught.

When her father arrived yesterday, over a week behind schedule, he had soundly berated her again for all her sins. Madelyne blinked back tears. No one had wanted her since Aunt Isolde died.

Madelyne ran her fingers lightly across the feather-light gold tissue of the overskirt, which was drawn up with silk tapes in the polonaise fashion over a darker gold brocade petticoat. The bodice of the gown was inset with a white silk stomacher elaborately embroidered with gold thread. A sheer gold tissue veil floated below her shoulders. It was fastened to a dainty turban perched among the elaborate curls atop her head. Soft slippers with high heels and gold buckles peeped from beneath her petticoats. The gown and its accouterments were exquisite enough to surpass any girlish fantasy.

But the weight of the Blackthorne family jewels lay like a millstone against her bare throat. She touched the elaborate gold chain set with a dozen glowing emeralds in gradations. The largest one nestled like an icy green teardrop in the vale between her breasts, where the low-cut neckline of the bodice revealed a wide expanse of creamy flesh.

Beautiful. Cold. Green. The stones mocked her as cynically as Quintin's eyes did. At the marriage, he would place his seal on her—the large, square-cut emerald ring that matched the necklace.

She fought the urge to tear off the heavy jewels, the lovely gown and headdress, to flee this crowded mansion filled with strangers. Yet reason won out; she could not escape. The door opened, and the maid entered and bobbed a curtsy. It was time to go downstairs and face them all.

People filled the hall around the curving stairway, and hundreds more stood crowded in the large front parlor where the Anglican priest waited. Gentlemen sweated silently in fine satin coats, gold watches glittering, suspended on ribbons from their satin waistcoats. Ladies gowned in billowing skirts and petticoats undergirded to Herculean proportions with hip pads, rumps, and buns, were bedecked with garnets and pearls. Even diamonds winked here and there. Many wore velvet face patches cunningly cut in the shapes of stars and quarter moons.

Although the heat had led most men to disdain wigs in Georgia, a few older men held to the custom, while others powdered their own queued and curled locks in various shades from snow white to dark tan. The women were a bit less practical with their long tresses fantastically coiffed with cotton pads beneath the hairdos, allowing them to rise a foot or more above their brows. Satin calashes and silk turbans were elegantly sprinkled among straw bonnets.

Overflowing the rear hall and out onto the grounds about the house were all the family servants, ebony faces mixed among the paler complexions of indentured bondsmen, all glowing beneath the hot afternoon sun. Everyone had turned out to celebrate the marriage of the heir to Blackthorne Hill.

Quintin waited at the foot of the stairs, his face expressionless as he looked up to where Madelyne would make her descent on Theodore Deveaux's arm.

When she turned the corner and paused at the top of the stairs, the bride could sense the ice-cold stare of her groom. Then her eyes met his and everything changed. The air, so still and thick, suddenly seemed charged with electricity, as if a storm had just blown inside the house.

She allowed herself to drink in the splendid maleness of him. He was dressed in a perfectly tailored black silk broadcloth coat, the cuffs lined with bottle green. His waistcoat was of matching dark green satin, and his long legs were snugly fitted with black satin breeches. Unlike many other men, he wore his raven hair simply clubbed back with a thin black silk ribbon, no curls, no powder. The white silk stock at his throat made his swarthy face seem even darker. The chiseled lips were straight, turned neither up nor down, but in his eyes she saw the fire—cold fire. Fierce anger burned in the green gaze that was riveted on her, anger . . . and something else.

God above, she is beautiful! Quint watched her float down the stairs encased in a golden glow, managing the elaborate gown as if it was no more than a simple shift. All that glorious mahogany hair was worked into silky curls spilling about her bare, creamy shoulders. Even before she came close, he could smell the enticing essence of honeysuckle, her special fragrance. Quint cursed his body, which defied his iron-willed determination to remain cool and detached through this endless day. He could feel the tightening of his loins, feel the heat steal from there and circulate all the way to his finger-tips. His heartbeat accelerated as she drew near. Then he stepped forward, taking her hand from old Theodore's, and walked with her through the press of people into the big parlor. A benevolently smiling priest waited with his *Book of Common Prayer*. He would wed them to each other for life.

Madelyne tried to still her trembling when Quintin took her cold hand in his warm one. She felt chilled in spite of the heat from the crowd. Somehow Quintin's steady grip gave her an odd sense of strength. As they knelt before the priest, she dared a glance at his profile. He was so splendidly hand-some, so strong. If only he did not despise her. If only he wanted the marriage . . . as much as she did.

This was her chance. Given some of the callow boys and fat, smelly old men who had courted her, Madelyne realized that she could have done far worse than this mysterious, vulnerable man who had some long-buried pain lurking beneath his facade of harsh words and tautly leashed desire. Surviving a childhood with Robert Blackthorne must have been a sad, bitter experience.

In spite of Quintin's mistrust of her, he did desire her. A spark flashed between them each time they touched. She had responded to it with anger and shock, but also, if she was honest, with pleasure. He was an enigma, a man with a mysterious background who mistrusted all women. She vowed, even as she uttered the solemn promises of the marriage ceremony, that she would teach her new husband to trust her . . . perhaps even to care for her one day.

When the priest gave his final benediction, Quint rose and assisted her with his warm, steady grip. She looked up into his eyes, but could read nothing. *He's schooled himself to hide his true feelings from everyone.* But brandy broke down even the strongest man's resolve. Perhaps he perceived her as his weakness and, mistrusting women as he did, resented her intrusion into his life. Madelyne dared a smile at her new husband as they walked through the parlor to the stately cadence of the recessional. He returned the smile, but somehow it did not extend to those icy green eyes.

"Gloating, madam?" he whispered with a flash of white teeth.

"Merely trying for a hint of appropriate amiability, considering the circumstances." She returned his whisper. All the while they both nodded and smiled at the press of well-wishers as they made their way from the crowded parlor to the front hall.

"We must show ourselves to all the servants gathered outdoors. Tis an old custom my grandfather began when he brought his first bride to Blackthorne Hill." Quintin led her out onto the long porch with its massive columns, where they waved to a sea of men, women, and children of all ages and colors.

"All these people work for the Blackthorne family?" she asked in amazement. She'd realized the plantation was large, but this was incredible.

"We have nearly six hundred black slaves in addition to over three hundred indentured servants. Then there are all the free men who work for our lumber mills and ship our trade goods and cash crops up and down the river."

"This is an empire. If you had searched in England, you could have married a noblewoman."

"My father did marry a noblewoman," he replied tautly.

A sharp retort froze on her lips. Until she had solved the mystery of Anne, she would blunder no further.

Quint assisted her down the low, wide steps into the crowd, and they accepted congratulations. Madelyne felt the sincerity and genuine joy radiating from the sea of beaming faces. She watched Quintin laugh with burly laborers, accepting handshakes, even fatherly pats on the back from wizened old men. He knelt and accepted hugs from giggling children, seeming to genuinely enjoy their affection. Would he be a good father? Here was a side of the cold, arrogant Quintin Blackthorne that she had never seen before. Several comely young women eyed her with thinly disguised jealousy and took advantage of the opportunity to kiss the master and "wish him happy," as Phoebe Barshan, the housekeeper's niece, said coyly.

Madelyne knelt in the grass and accepted a bouquet of fragrant magnolias from one shy little slave girl. The goodwill of these simple people touched her deeply. No one who worked for Claud Deveaux would have responded this way. *Perhaps I can make a home here . . . if only I can win Quintin.*

He watched Madelyne mix with his people, seemingly pleased to do what many a haughty Savannah lady would have found demeaning, and it touched him more deeply than he felt comfortable admitting.

Just then Solomon tapped him on the shoulder, drawing his attention from the celebration. "This message was delivered by our rider from Savannah," he said, handing Quintin a sealed letter. No one in the crowd took note as he slipped it inside his waistcoat.

Madelyne felt Quintin's hand curl beneath her elbow, lifting her from where she knelt, talking with several children. She turned expectantly to him.

"I've something urgent to attend to. If you wish, you can freshen up before the revelry begins."

After they returned indoors, Quintin excused himself and vanished toward the library. Madelyne quickly found herself surrounded by strangers. Their felicitations, although delivered in far more elegant language, did not seem as open and honest as those she had received outdoors. Her head ached, and she was swelteringly hot in the crowd of overdressed men and women awash in perspiration and perfume.

When Andrew Blackthorne took her hand and saluted it, she felt a warm sense of relief just looking into his earnest, smiling face.

"A bride so soon deserted by her bridegroom? I shall have to upbraid my cousin," he said with a wink.

"Quintin had business to attend to in the study. He promised to return in a few moments." She felt called upon to defend him.

"Soon the dancing starts. You and Quintin are to lead off the first reel. Tis a tradition in the family."

"This family is filled with all sorts of obscure and interesting customs, I find."

"I shall be more than happy to interpret them for you," Andrew replied, leading her toward the hall. "If you like, I'll escort you to a place where you can sit in quiet for a few moments."

"I would be most grateful."

Before they could make good their escape, Robert bore down upon them with several British officers in tow, including General Prevost, commander of the occupation forces in Savannah. With all due pomp, he introduced his new daughter-in-law to the doughty old Swiss mercenary, as famed now for his temper as for the amorous exploits of his youth. There was a stock joke that half the junior officers in the British army were Augustine Prevost's get. Tall, with a beaked nose and an imposing thatch of silver hair, the general saluted her hand with great relish.

Quint locked the doors of the library and drew the curtains, then opened the message, which had come all the way from France. He smiled at Franklin's cribbed, uneven penmanship and began to read a witty and detailed report on the latest news and gossip circulating in Paris, Vienna, Berlin— and most importantly, London.

Madelyne smiled until she felt her face frozen in place in spite of the heat. The more people questioned her about her absent bridegroom, the more she wanted to turn and flee the whole hot, crowded spectacle. When Andrew brought her a cup of refreshment, she took it gratefully and sipped. "What's in this? It's delicious but too potent for me, I fear."

"A special treat, quite in favor the last time I was in London," he said, drinking with relish. "Tis a special brandy, with orange peel soaked in it for flavor. Then tis watered down and strained. A most pleasant flavor, don't you agree?"

Watered or not, the drink went immediately to her head. She smiled at his kind face and took another sip. The musicians were playing, and it was obviously far past time for the bridal reel to begin. Where was Quintin?

Answering the unspoken question in her eyes as she scanned the room, Andrew said, "Let me send a houseboy to search for my absent cousin. I'll not see you neglected on this special day."

"Ah, there you are, m'dear," Robert said, working his way through the press toward her as Andrew excused himself. Her father was with Robert, looking harried and uncomfortable, the way he always seemed when forced to be around his only child.

Theodore harrumphed and cleared his throat, then said bluntly, "You're all settled now, and I must entrust you to the very good care of your husband and his father. I'm off for Charles Town as soon as I can get rid of these damnably hot satin and velvet fripperies. Cornwallis is in a pickle in North Carolina at Ramsour's Mill. Fool royal militia disobeyed orders." He ranted for several minutes, then gave her a swift peck on her cheek and was gone.

Andrew reappeared just as the orchestra struck up a reel. He turned to Robert and said, "With your permission, sir, I'd like to lead my new cousin out in the first reel, since we've been unable to locate Quintin. Everyone is grown impatient for the dancing to begin."

Robert scowled, then smiled cannily. "Why not? If that young whelp can't tend to his obligations, we'll not wait for him."

Andrew took her hand and they walked to the head of the wide open space in the parlor where the carpets had been rolled up to facilitate dancing. The oak floors gleamed with wax, stretching out a good fifty feet in length, room enough for a dozen couples to line up for the reel. With much clapping and toasts to the health of the king and the Blackthorne family, the dancing began.

Madelyne's hurt over her father's hasty departure and Quintin's apparent desertion faded as the dancing progressed. Andrew was solicitous and kind as well as a skillful dancer. After several strenuous reels, the music slowed to the gentle cadence of the minuet.

When they stopped for refreshment, two British officers and several young planters crowded around her, asking for the honor of dancing with the bride. If any marked the absence of her groom, they were discreet enough not to mention it. Madelyne forced the thought from her mind, smiled and danced, her head spinning from orange brandy. After several dances, Andrew again claimed her hand, laughingly sending young Lieutenant St. Clair away crestfallen.

Quint stood in the doorway watching Madelyne, once more surrounded by admiring men. The creamy, soft flesh revealed by her low-cut bodice was dewy with perspiration. Her eyes glowed and her cheeks were flushed. She leaned close to Andrew as they met in the center of the row and began to skip between the lines of dancers to the rhythm of the reel. She was laughing intimately at some jest of his as they parted at the opposite end of the floor.

When the reel ended, the pair bowed to each other and then headed to the huge cut-crystal punch bowl. Andrew's hand over the one she had placed on his arm seemed altogether too possessive to Quint. He stalked toward them, not at all certain what he was going to say, but quite sure that his bride would be taught a lesson in deportment.

Robert stood at the side of the room, next to General Prevost, watching his scowling son's progress through the crowd. "Looks like a storm's brewing again. She'll lead him a merry chase or I miss my guess," he said with relish.

Chapter Eight

"Admirers are apparently drawn to you like bears to honey," Quint said as he stepped smoothly beside Madelyne and Andrew and drew her possessively away from his cousin.

"Perhaps I'm simply irresistibly sweet," she said, smiling boldly up at his dark face.

"I'll find out the truth of that tonight . . . when I taste of you," he whispered low.

To Madelyne the words sounded more like a threat than an endearment. With a curt nod at Andrew, Quintin drew her away. She tried to pull free of his grip, but he merely tightened the pressure on her hand.

"You were most rude to Cousin Andrew. I wished to thank him for leading me out in the dancing—since you chose to absent yourself from the odious obligation." She knew she was huffing like a schoolgirl in a snit and hated the sound of hurt pride evident in her voice.

"Ah yes, dear Andrew, always the long-suffering

126

and gallant Blackthorne, the one who attends to proprieties." He paused and took her chin in his hand, forcing her to look up and meet his eyes. To onlookers it seemed a tender gesture. "But mark me, wife, you belong to me, not to my cousin."

"Then by all means, have a care for performing your duties," she snapped.

A slow smile spread across his mouth as he escorted her from the room. "As soon as our bridal feast is over I fully intend to perform my duties—to the fullest."

Madelyne's cheeks again flamed, but she bit back a retort and walked in silence to the dining room. *I'm no match for his skill with sly innuendo.* She thought about the night all too quickly approaching, and her flushed cheeks grew pale. If only she knew what he would do to her. *Fanny Hill* had been no appreciable help. In fact, it had rather frightened her.

They sat at the head of the great long table as a legion of servants served fish courses, followed by fowl baked in savory pastry, haunches of rich venison, and crisply roasted pork. Every imaginable fresh vegetable the gardens of Blackthorne Hill could yield was stewed and braised to accompany the meats. Puddings, floating islands, syllabubs and trifles laced with brandy and filled with sweet whipped cream and ripe fruits, were presented in a dazzling array.

Quint watched Madelyne shove a piece of roast pork about her plate until the servants took it away, virtually untouched, then said, "Unlike our Jewish guests, you're not forbidden to eat pork." She declined to comment.

"Delphine's desserts are unequaled," he taunted as he dug into a plate swimming in caramel cream. She merely stirred the layers of cream and fruit in her portion of trifle until it was a soggy mess, untasted.

"I seem to have lost my appetite," she said quietly.

"Bridal nerves?" he asked, not unkindly. His conscience was getting the better of him. The girl was sheltered and young in spite of her outlandish behavior. Surely she was a virgin and naturally fearful about tonight.

"Yes, I suppose I am nervous," she confessed, daring to meet his eyes. For once he was not scowling or mocking her.

"It will be all right, Madelyne." He darkened, recalling his earlier crude taunts, wishing he could call them back.

"I've had no one . . . no woman to talk with. . . ." Courage failed her, yet she felt the need to reach out to this kinder side of her mysterious husband.

"Yes. I can imagine your Aunt Claud would not have been of much help," he said, smiling.

Madelyne felt some of her nervousness leave her. Merciful Heaven above, if he smiled at her like that more often, she would melt! When he stood up and reached for her hand, she eagerly responded, glad to quit the crowded room filled with important people who had proposed endless healths to the bridal couple.

Quint ushered Madelyne from the dining room into the back hallway, where several older housemaids stood. He issued them instructions to escort his bride to his room by way of the back stairs and assist her in changing from her wedding finery. Then he turned from the knowing but kindly smiles of the maids and took Madelyne's hand. "Go with them and no one will see you've retired. I'd spare us both any further raillery this night. I'll allow you time enough to prepare before I join you upstairs." With that he saluted the back of her hand briefly and slipped through the heavy oak door which led to the crowded front hall.

*   *   *

Madelyne looked into the large oval mirror as she sat on a Chippendale stool, staring at her reflection while her new maid brushed her hair. She could see herself and Nell in the floor-length mirror—a slim, small woman huddled pale and still while her tall, angular companion fussed with her hair. Nell's face was reddened and creased with age, her once yellow hair faded to a dull gray, but her smile was genuine as she spoke.

"Here now, ain't this hair the loveliest color—so dark a red it looks ta be black till the candle's flame catches it. Then it fair glows like live coals." She bent from her waist with each stroke of the tortoise-shell brush, sliding it through Madelyne's hair.

As Nell chatted and worked, Madelyne remained silent, staring into the mirror, which reflected nearly all of Quint's big, masculine room. It was filled with heavy walnut furniture, and the wall panels were painted a deep green in a marbled pattern. An English hunting scene and several pictures of famous racehorses were the only concession to art, obviously carelessly chosen, as if Quint had not long occupied the room . . . or cared to spend little time in it. The dressing room off to her left was filled with coats, breeches, and boots, all arranged in orderly perfection by his valet. Next to a large easy chair, a pipe, tobacco, and a crystal decanter of brandy were the only indications that her husband did more than dress, bathe, and sleep in this cold, austere suite.

Unwillingly, her eyes were again drawn to the bed, which was wide and long, custom-made for a tall man. Thick, soft goose-feather ticking invited a weary body to sink into its depths and sleep, but Madelyne was far too agitated for that, even if such were allowed on a bridal night.

Seeing her mistress's covert glances toward the canopied bed, Nell gave a toothy grin and said reassuringly, "Ye'll be wantin' ta climb beneath the sheets. Here now, let me arrange the netting so the mosquitos don't bother that pretty soft skin."

"You're very kind, Nell," Madelyne said as she stepped onto the low stool by the bedside and climbed into the waiting bed while the maid lowered the mosquito netting around it, then rearranged the deep maroon bed curtains.

"It be warm tonight. Ye want me ta leave the curtains open for the evening breeze?"

Before Madelyne could reply, Quint's voice cut across the room from the doorway. "Leave them open, Nell."

She did as she was bidden, then bobbed a curtsy to the master and quit the room.

Madelyne looked so tiny, swallowed up in his big bed, pale as the snowy sheets she had pulled up to her neck. He crossed to his dressing room while removing his coat, which he tossed carelessly across a chair.

In spite of the warm night air, Madelyne felt a little shiver run down her spine. She could hear the rustling noises of clothing being removed. *I won't be a cowering ninny,* she scolded herself, straightening up. The silence lengthened until Quintin appeared in the doorway, dressed in a banyan of deep red-and-navy printed cotton. She could see the black hair on his chest curling out where the lounging robe hung open, carelessly belted at his narrow waist.

Freed of its neat queue at his nape, his hair made his face seem almost savage. Quintin, more than his cousin Devon, looked as if he possessed Indian blood. When his green eyes swept from her face downward, penetrating the sheer pale pink silk of her sleeping gown, Madelyne felt a frisson of heat stain her cheeks and move lower into her belly.

Quint stared at her delicate loveliness. He had wanted a plain, dutiful girl who would obey him and be a faithful wife and good mother to his children. There was not a meek, dutiful bone in Madelyne

Deveaux's body—no, Madelyne Blackthorne, he corrected himself.

For better or worse, he had wed her. At least he would enjoy the bedding. Just looking at her swathed in the voluminous silk layers made his body go rigid with excitement. He cursed himself for the past weeks of sexual abstinence. He was as randy as a stag in rut and he hadn't even touched her yet.

Madelyne watched him advance slowly, then sink one knee into the softness of the bed. His long legs needed no step stool to climb into it. For a moment, she feared he would remove the banyan; she was certain he wore nothing beneath it. But he did not, only leaned across to her while one hand reached out to her. He took a lock of her hair and twisted it slowly around his fist, then raised it to his lips.

"I'm glad you didn't cover your hair with one of those foolish mobcaps," he said hoarsely. "Tis glorious this way."

She warmed to the compliment but even more to the gentleness of his touch as he tugged ever so softly on the imprisoned hair, pulling her closer to him. Madelyne leaned forward. To keep her balance she had to stretch out her hand, and her palm pressed against the hard warmth of his chest. She could feel the beat of his heart and the crisp silky texture of the mat of hair beneath her fingers. When she splayed them and rubbed her palm experimentally where his robe gaped open, she felt his heartbeat accelerate.

Quint took a steadying breath, vowing to go slowly lest he frighten her, but the chit was not making his resolution an easy one. He tugged again on her hair, and she tumbled against his chest with a small muffled gasp. The tantalizing fragrance of honeysuckle enveloped him as he smoothed the masses of silky dark hair away from her face, then tilted her chin up and leaned forward to meet her lips with his own.

The kiss was brushing, light, experimental. She

felt like wax in the sun, melting, warm, and pliant. Would the delicate caress turn violent again as it had that frightening night in Savannah? Madelyne prayed not, for this was utterly wondrous, robbing her of breath. She gave in to the seduction, letting her lips mimic his, teasing, whispering across his beautiful mouth.

He moved to touch her eyes with his lips, then her temples, where a fluttering pulse beat swiftly. When his warm lips caressed her throat, she held fast to his shoulders and let her head drop back, eyes closed, breath quickening. She was drowning in hot, sweet pleasure.

Murmuring low, indistinct words of encouragement, he laid her back on the bed and ran his hand from her shoulder down the side of her breast to her slender waist, then back up to cup her breast and let his thumb circle and tease the nipple. It contracted into pebbly hardness, causing her to moan softly.

Quint wanted desperately to tear the seemingly endless folds of silk from her body and bare it. He fought the urge and instead let his hands explore softly through the nightgown. When she arched against his hand, he moved from one breast to the other to excite it in turn. She was innocently wanton, and her instinctive, unpracticed response inflamed him.

Once more his lips touched her throat, where her pulse was beating wildly. He moved up to her cheek, then centered his mouth over hers and kissed her, this time with more force, his tongue touching the seam of her lips until she parted them. Slowly he tasted her, restraining the urge to plunge inside and plunder as he had the first time. He could feel her nails digging into his shoulders, hear her ragged little cries of pleasure. His blood boiled, racing through his body, setting him afire.

Madelyne felt his kiss grow more demanding as his tongue teased hers, then withdrew only to plunge in once more. She felt an answering need to taste him and boldly let her tongue follow his lead. When he groaned and increased the ferocity of the kiss, she felt no fear, only hunger. One little hand came up and tangled in his shaggy, night-dark hair, pulling him closer, closer.

Quint slid his hand to the ribbon holding the neckline of her gown closed. He untied it, then pulled the gathered opening free, murmuring against her mouth, "I would see all of you."

Cool night air touched her bare breasts for an instant, but then the heat of his mouth covered one while his hand cupped the other. He teased the aching nipple with his lips and tongue, then suckled it until she cried out. When he repeated the exquisite assault on her other breast, Madelyne fairly swooned with the pleasure.

"Yes, yes," she whispered, arching toward his seeking mouth. She could feel his hands pulling the unfastened gown lower until it bunched about her hips. When he splayed one long-fingered hand across her belly, intense heat coiled low inside her, sending out dizzying waves of desire. She was shameless, unprotesting.

Quint slipped the voluminous folds of silk from her hips, slid the gown free of her legs, and tossed it to the floor. His eyes followed the trail of bared flesh from her pert, perfectly formed breasts to her tiny waist and flat little belly, then lower to where that cluster of dark russet curls beckoned him. He paused a moment in his perusal, then swept his gaze down her slim legs with their flaring calves and delicate ankles. As his hands followed where his eyes had already traveled, he breathed, "You are exquisite. Too damnably perfect . . ."

Madelyne could barely understand his murmured words, but she could sense the urgency in him, for she felt it hammer at all her senses. He had undressed her. Would he now bare his body for her

as well? Earlier she had feared it; now she wanted—
needed—to see him, to feel his hard body pressed
to hers, unencumbered by clothing. Her hands slid
inside his open robe and she explored, feeling a
heady sense of power when his heart slammed
against her palm. She moved lower. The belt
impeded her progress, but before she could untie
it, he ripped it free, then shed the loose banyan with
a swift, sensuous shrug. His eyes locked on her face,
studying her reaction to his nakedness.

She was so enraptured by the flood of new sensations sweeping over her that she could feel no trace
of modesty. His body was so different from hers,
so dark and hard, furred with ebony hair across his
chest, forearms, and legs. She let her hands caress
while her eyes drank in the beauty of his maleness, nowhere more evident than in the straining,
pulsing phallus that probed against her belly. But
her courage failed, and her hands did not trespass
where her eyes had.

"You've been exceeding bold, Mistress Blackthorne, until now," he said in a low growl as he
rolled atop her, supporting his weight on his elbows
as he let their hot, naked flesh meld together. His
mouth took hers again, this time not gently at all,
yet she opened for him, returning the passionate
kiss with a fire of her own. "I can wait no longer."

His knee moved between her thighs as he commanded hoarsely, "Spread your legs—yes, like that,
now wrap them around my hips—higher, higher."
He groaned as she complied with his instructions.
Then he reached between them and guided his staff
to the core of her.

Madelyne felt that hard male part of him touching
her where all the aching need seemed to center. A jolt
of raw pleasure shot through her when he guided his
phallus to rub against her nether lips, stroking and
teasing as he rasped unintelligible words against her
throat. She felt her body arching to meet him.

He slowly sank into her, then felt her stiffen when he pressed against the barrier of her maidenhead. Raising himself over her with a look of predatorial satisfaction on his face, he gritted his teeth and flung his head back, struggling to hold himself in check.

"Don't move, don't even breathe," he rasped out.

After a moment, he took a deep ragged breath, then lowered himself to kiss her once more, cradling her face in his hand and coaxing her to respond as she had earlier. As soon as he felt her begin to lose herself to the pleasure, he thrust once, penetrating her, filling her.

His mouth muffled her cry as he continued the seductive kiss, all the while holding himself still within the tight, wet sheath of her body.

A feeling of incredible fullness quickly erased the sharp twinge of pain from her memory. *So this is the joining that offers surcease for the ache in me.* Her hands ran up and down the ridged muscles of his back, then tangled in his hair, pulling him to her as he deepened the kiss. The burning sensation had quickly passed, and now all she could feel was an irresistible urge to move. Earlier he had commanded her to remain still, but now it seemed so natural to forget that, just as she forgot the pain.

Quint felt her move, wriggling her hips experimentally. With a muttered oath, he showed her the motion, sliding out, plunging back in, slowly at first, struggling to make it last. Breaking off the kiss, he raised his upper body once more and observed her as he increased the tempo of his thrusts. Her eyes flew open, then closed in ecstasy as she tossed her head from side to side, arching hungrily to meet him. Dark, lustrous hair pooled in shiny masses all about her head and shoulders, spilling like ruby ink across the snowy bed linens. She arched and writhed, holding tightly to him.

He studied the flush stealing across her breasts . . .

and was lost. Every nerve in his body vibrated as he thrust one last shuddering time and collapsed onto her beautiful little breasts. The aftershocks of his release still gripped him as he lay panting for breath, utterly satiated after waiting weeks for this moment. The thought was disquieting, but he forced it from his mind as he rolled off her.

Madelyne felt the surge of raw male power that culminated in a sudden swelling of his member deep inside her. When his body was racked with convulsive shaking and he collapsed, the delicious stroking done, she knew it was over. She clung to him, fighting a restless hunger that still burned inside her, although she intuited that his had been quenched. When he pulled out of her body and rolled to his side, she felt bereft and chilled in spite of the sweat that sheened their bodies in the warm night air.

A reckless desire for fulfillment led her to sit up and study his naked body in the moonlight filtering in from the large window across the room. Quintin lay with one arm flung across his eyes, totally replete, separate from her. Frustration and anger welled up inside her as she watched the slow, even rise and fall of his chest. The wretch, he was fast asleep!

Her eyes traveled down his long dark figure, noting small scars, ridges of muscles, cunning patterns of body hair. She tentatively reached out her hand, aching to touch, to feel his heat again; then she let it fall to her side. What use increasing her misery? Perhaps only men were supposed to enjoy the act, although that hadn't been what Mr. Cleland had written in his book, but then, he was a man too. She flopped back down, seizing the sheet and pulling it over them both. After restlessly tossing for a while, she fell into a fitful slumber.

Quint awoke several hours later. The moon was high in the night sky now, its silvery light filtering through the gauze netting around the bed. At once he felt Madelyne's presence. The room smelled of the heady musk of sex, combined with a faint essence of honeysuckle. He turned and watched her small body toss fitfully beneath the sheet. He could feel his body growing hard. *Damn, I only have to look at her!* That was his last coherent thought before he reached for the sheet and yanked it to the foot of the bed.

Feeling the sudden slide of the cover from her body, Madelyne awoke from her restless slumber to find her husband staring down at her with dark, brooding eyes. His mouth swooped down and found hers, forcing her to open to his fierce, persuasive kiss. Then he trailed wet licks and bites down her throat until his lips brushed her breasts, eliciting a moan from her. She arched up as he suckled and teased the rosy peaks, her whole body aching. Foolishly, she was again letting him fuel the fires inside her until she was driven mad!

Quint felt her feeble protest as she tried to twist free of his imprisoning grasp, but he only held her more securely, whispering, "I can help you, Madelyne . . . only let me. . . ." He parted her legs and thrust into her. She was wet and hungry, so sweetly, wantonly hungry. He began slowly, moving inside her satiny heat. She clung to him, her nails digging into his shoulders, her hips meeting his, thrust for thrust. He kept to a slow, steady rhythm, careful to retain iron control over his body, watching her as the tension in her built and built.

For Madelyne, the ecstasy was delirious, just as it had been the first time. If it ended again she could not bear it. She scored his back with her nails, glorying in the wickedly intense pleasure that kept growing, radiating from the very center of her being. Then she felt the first contractions, and she raised her hips from the bed. Her eyes riveted on his as she cried and writhed, her whole body throbbing in release. This time when he, too, cried out and shuddered with completion, she understood.

Tears slid from beneath her russet lashes. Quint traced the silvery trails down her cheeks with the pads of his fingers. He didn't know what to say, so he just kissed them, lightly, sweetly.

Her eyes opened slowly, dreamy and unfocused now as one small hand stroked the beard beginning to grow bristly on his jaw. "That was the most wonderful thing I've ever experienced," she whispered, snuggling into his arms as he rolled off of her.

Quint held her, watching with a perplexed look on his face as she fell almost instantly into a deep sleep. "So apt a pupil, my wife," he whispered on the still night air.

Dawn came hot and golden. Quint slid free from Madelyne's sleeping embrace and entered his dressing room to ring for a bath. Later, as he sat in the tub, he brooded over the preceding night. His wife was not only a beauty, she was a passionate little creature in the bargain, not at all the qualities he had wanted in the mother of his children. She had been as eager as the most experienced women he'd bedded, in spite of the virgin blood staining the sheets on which they slept. *Innocent yesterday, but for how long satisfied with one man?*

Quint was not vain; he knew he was a fine-looking man and an accomplished lover. But a woman could turn her pretty head as soon as a new man swaggered by and caught her fancy. God knew, he and Devon had traded enough women back and forth—doxies and fineborn ladies both. He could stand no such faithlessness in the woman carrying his name. There was nothing for it; Madelyne was his wife, for better or for worse. He vowed to guard her closely.

Madelyne awakened to the sounds of splashing coming from Quintin's dressing room. She sat up in the center of the big, rumpled bed and hugged her knees to her chest, remembering last night. How glorious it had been, beyond her wildest imaginings! In spite of the hostile and mistrustful way things had started between them, there was great promise in their marriage.

If she understood nothing else about Quintin Blackthorne's mysterious past, she did know he desired her—and she him. An excellent basis on which to build a marriage, she thought, recalling the words from the Prayer Book, "Therefore a man shall cleave unto his wife and they shall be one flesh." She smiled and hugged herself once more, then slid from the bed and slipped on her hastily discarded nightclothes.

Quint returned dressed in a white ruffled shirt, brown waistcoat, and buckskin pants. He stood in the doorway, arms crossed over his chest, regarding his wife, who was standing before his big dressing mirror, attempting to untangle her hair. At the sound of his polished boots clicking against the oak floorboards, she turned, her face wreathed in a shy smile and tinted by a blush.

"If you ring for Nell, she'll help you with your hair," he said, striving to sound detached when every instinct told him to stride across the room and take her in his arms.

She took a hesitant step forward, clutching the brush nervously in her hands. "I . . . I didn't wish to summon Nell until we had an opportunity to speak." He stood still, leaning with seeming indolence against the door frame.

"And what is it you wish to speak of, Madelyne?"

She felt the heat scorch her cheeks. He was doing nothing to make this easier for her! "Last night was . . . that is, after all our earlier—er, mishaps— well, now I feel we can have a good marriage, Quintin." She looked into those fathomless green eyes. Something in his guarded stance made her realize that he was holding himself back, trying to rebuild the wall that had broken down last night.

She crossed the distance between them and placed one hand on his chest. His heart accelerated. She smiled and said softly, "Last night was wonderful, Quintin. To say I enjoyed what we did seems far too weak a way to express it, but I did." She forced her eyes to meet his.

He answered her silent plea for a kiss, wanting only to give her a chaste salute, but once he tasted her and smelled her heady scent, he lost control and wrapped his arms about her, deepening the caress into a hungry ravagement of her mouth. She responded ardently, molding her slim curves against him and clinging to him. He finally broke free of the kiss but still held her in a bone-crushing grip.

His expression was harsh, his breathing labored as he said, "So you enjoyed my husbandly attention, did you? All too well, it seems." He shoved her away and turned on his heel, placing his arm on the door frame and leaning his head against his arm.

"I don't understand, Quintin. You pleased me, and I pleased you—I know I did," she added boldly, watching his shoulders stiffen. "What is wrong?"

He raised his head and turned to her. "Ladies aren't usually so forward about such matters, only harlots. A good wife's duty is to bear her husband's children, not wallow in carnal pleasures."

Madelyne felt as if he had just struck her squarely in her midsection. She struggled for breath, letting rage build up, shoving aside the terrible cutting pain and humiliation.

"You dare to call me a harlot for confessing that I enjoyed making love with my lawful husband? Yet you, you hypocrite, you've lain with every cheap serving wench from Savannah to Charles Town— and the likes of immoral women like Serena Fallowfield! Yes, I've heard of her reputation! She's worse than the lowliest prostitute on the Charles Town waterfront." She forced down the hateful surge of tears, quivering with fury and pain.

"I've found my own kind with Serena, it would seem. You lay my sins quite correctly before me. It takes a real bastard to seek his own level, Madelyne. And make no mistake about me—you named me rightly back in the library in Savannah. I am a bastard—a legal bastard. My fine lady mother, an English noblewoman, shared the morals of those Charles Town whores. She slept with her husband's own brother—and God knows how many others! I am not Robert Blackthorne's son, but I am his only heir, God help us both. I'll not be betrayed as he was and raise a son to know the shame I've locked inside me for over twenty years!"

Madelyne listened to his anguished outburst in numb silence. Only when he brushed past her and slammed the bedroom door did she come out of her shocked trance. Shivering, she crumpled onto the carpet. She clutched her knees and huddled in a ball, but this time it was not with joyous anticipation.

As he strode down the hall, Quintin Blackthorne, for the first time since he was a child, felt alive—and afraid.

Chapter Nine

"You have that smirking look about you, Andrew. What have you been doing?" Serena Fallowfield sat in the elegant front parlor of Andrew's city house, daintily sipping tea while she watched him with narrowed eyes. He pulled off his coat and tossed it to a servant, who handed him a glass of rum and hastily quit the room.

"Why, my dear, I've just returned from a visit with dear Cousin Madelyne. Poor child. Quintin is such a brute," he said theatrically. "When he isn't off with his racehorses, he's at the Savannah docks. Then when he does come home, he's wretchedly jealous of his neglected wife." He eyed her appraisingly. "Perhaps it's best you didn't succeed in luring him into marriage. If he mistrusts an innocent like Madelyne, imagine how he'd react to your escapades."

Serena set the delicate Staffordshire cup and saucer down on the tea table with a clatter. "I pursued Quintin to save our family fortunes—or have you forgotten the plight doting old Alastair left us in?"

"You pursued Quintin right where you wanted him—to bed. Once you let him sample your tarnished charms, he would never marry you. Tactical error, m'dear. I'm afraid his standards for a wife are rather unrealistically high." He sipped his rum and stretched out indolently on a maroon brocade sofa.

Serena stood up, smoothing the bodice of her low-cut, blue silk gown and preening before a round wall mirror. "The error wasn't mine but yours—for underestimating your uncle. Robert would've seen me dragged off by the savages before he'd have allowed me to marry his son. He arranged the match with that pitiful Huguenot child."

"And Quintin agreed to it, much as he appears to be repenting his bargain these past weeks." He waved his glass dismissively when she started to argue further. "We've failed to join our side of the family, deplorably cash poor, with Quintin's side, wherein all the wealth resides."

"If your father hadn't married that—that Indian," she ground out the word with loathing, "none of this would have happened. He went off with her and lived like one of them until he caught a fever and died instead of tending to business here in Savannah."

"My father was a fool to marry Charity. Bloody hell, do you think I haven't cursed his memory for saddling me with a half-caste brother? What money Alastair Blackthorne didn't give to his damned Indians, he'd already gambled away. This house, not to mention my plantation, are mortgaged to the hilt."

"He also mortgaged his sister's plantation. God, as if marrying Henry Fallowfield weren't punishment enough, to find out his inheritance was gone within a year of the wedding!"

"At least he had the good grace to die quickly enough after that," Andrew said, his light brown eyes looking condescendingly amused now. "Do sit down, Serena. Have a drink. Twill steady your nerves far better than tea."

"Henry may have died to suit our plans, but somehow I don't think Quintin is quite so careless—or so stupid. And now that he's married that rustic, he'll soon get a child on her, mark me. An heir for all old Robert's wealth. What will become of us then, Andrew?" She continued pacing.

"If something were to happen to Quintin before he breeds his little Huguenot, I'd be Robert's only remaining heir."

She scoffed. "Quintin is far too clever to fall into your traps, Andrew. He survived the siege in spite of your best efforts to have him shot from behind our lines. Without French and rebels storming the city, how will you plan another accident? Or will you kill him yourself?"

He appeared to consider, his eyes hard. "He may be my brother, you know. If the whispered story about Alastair and Anne is true . . . but then, who knows?" He shrugged. "No, I won't be so rash as to simply shoot him. I've hit on a better idea. Madelyne is lonely, isolated on that big plantation with only a bitter old man and a jealous young husband for company. I've been—er, cultivating her."

Serena laughed, a high pealing sound that she'd practiced since her nursery days. "You, charm a woman away from Quintin Blackthorne? Don't be absurd."

His pock-marked skin flushed darkly and he stood up, all his earlier indolent patience at an end. "Don't be insulting, Serena," he whispered, wrapping his big hand around the slender bones of her wrist with crushing force. "You've existed on my charity for some time now. At least pretend to like me a little. Anyway, I don't have to bed the chit—I only have to make poor jealous Quintin think I have. Then there'll be no grandsons for old Robert—only me!"

July, 1780, Off the South Georgia Coast

Lady Barbara Caruthers felt every wave of the storm as it lashed the ship, hurling her bruised body across the small, cramped cabin until she wedged herself against the support posts of the bed and clung to them for dear life. "God, I hate you, Mother! You've sent me to die in this hellish wilderness. First poor Katie perished, leaving me to the mercy of this ruffian crew; now I must endure this horrible storm!"

Until last week, the trip had been an uneventful lark, filled with smooth sailing over glistening, blue-green water. Then her maid and companion took a fever and died suddenly, as had nearly half the crew, including the captain. The first officer, who had taken over, was drunk more than sober and eager to press his unwanted advances on a lone, defenseless lady.

Suddenly the ship took a mighty pitch to one side, and a splintering crack reverberated from above decks. "I may drown, but I bloody well won't do it cowering below."

Barbara crawled from her berth and struggled toward the door to her cabin. By the time she had clawed her way up the stairs and onto the deck, the ship was listing at a sharp angle. Two masts had been shattered, their jagged broken bases jutting up defiantly toward the roiling iron-gray skies. Some of the sailors lay bleeding and broken, tangled in ropes and sails, while others screamed and cursed, struggling to lower a couple of pitiful lifeboats into the churning white waves.

"Lady Barbara, come with me," one skinny yeoman cried over the howling wind as he fought his way to her side. "We got a boat ready." He took her arm to assist her, but just then the whole ship gave a mighty lurch and began to slide under, bow first. The deck tilted crazily, and Barbara's grip on the yeoman was broken.

She rolled and skidded to the edge of the railing, which had already been smashed when the mizzenmast toppled across it. Desperately, she clawed for purchase on the broken pieces, but there was nothing left but splinters. The ship lurched again and she was swept over the side into the dark, churning water. She did not even have time to scream.

Rain sheeted down, blacking out the horizon. Powerful waves seemed to be dragging her under, then pulling her up again. She bobbed on the swells, being carried choking and crying wherever the caprice of the current took her. Suddenly the rain cleared for a moment just as she rose on one wave. Dear God, there was land all around her—flat and marshy, but land, nonetheless!

She was sucked down again into the blackness, as if the fates only wanted to tantalize her with sight of deliverance before claiming her for a watery grave. But again she broke the surface, bobbing now in the slightly calmer waters of the channel. She looked to be between two low-lying islands immediately off the shore.

Barbara held tightly to her billowing skirts and their underpinnings, which she now knew might save her life. Her underskirt was fitted with a cork-padded rump to puff out the voluminous petticoats and overskirt of her gown. Cork floated, although Barbara Caruthers did not, never having been taught the most unladylike sport of swimming.

The current was slower now, the storm's destructive frenzy beginning to pass. She was carried toward a land mass directly ahead. Finally, teeth chattering, body bruised and exhausted, she felt the sandy bottom beneath her feet. A sickly shaft of pale yellow light began to cut through the clouds. Barbara thought she saw a figure up ahead but could not be certain. Her vision blurred as she sank on her knees in the shallows and fell face forward on the sand. Everything went black.

She awakened to the sound of the surf roaring in the distance, and a man's voice cutting through it. He was holding her, trying to force some vile brew between her blue lips. She coughed and opened her eyes, blinking in amazement as she looked into a sun-darkened face framed by thick golden hair. He was so beautiful, she feared she was well and truly dead, mistakenly swept up by some Norse god into Valhalla. She looked at him warily, for his appearance was strange in spite of his striking countenance.

He was dressed in a green jacket with scarlet collar and cuffs, and buckskin pants. Even the peculiar-looking slippers on his feet were made of the soft leather. A wicked-looking knife was strapped to one hip and a pistol to the other. His head was bare, and he wore his hair queued back, tied with a simple leather thong. God above, was he one of those traitorous rebels?

Then he smiled, and his dancing brown eyes crinkled at the corners. "I feared you'd never come around. Here, drink this. It's a marvelous restorative."

She sniffed the pale golden liquid's bitter aroma and took a tiny sip, then grimaced. "Who are you?"

"Captain Devon Blackthorne, King's Rangers, at your service," he replied, then frowned, muttering, "although the timing for this service could have been better arranged."

Barbara breathed a sigh of relief. Her rude colonial was at least one of his majesty's officers! Then she felt his eyes on her. Her skin itched from caked-on salt water, and her gown—or what was left of a once lovely calamanco robe à la Francaise—was now nothing but a shapeless mass of dank, seaweed-encrusted filth, ripped beyond recognition. The fine hoops of her "hen basket" stuck out at jagged angles from beneath the shredded remnants of her petticoats. Barbara reached up to her hair, which had come loose from its pins and hung about her shoulders in ratty tangles.

Devon watched the half-drowned woman take inventory of her shapely body. Although she was bedraggled, he had already seen enough of trim ankles, full breasts, and long sleek legs to know she was a real beauty. And by the looks of her once-grand clothes, probably from a good family. "Might I enquire who you are and what you're doing washed up on a desolate Georgia beach?"

Suddenly she was aware that he was studying her with an amused smile twitching at the corners of his mouth. She struggled to stand up. He assisted her. "I am Lady Barbara Caruthers, en route to Savannah, where my brother, Lord Montgomery Caruthers, is awaiting me. He's a major under the command of General Prevost. How far is this ghastly place from the city?"

"A good day's ride."

"Excellent. We can reach Savannah by nightfall then." She looked past him at two horses of surprisingly fine quality and started to walk toward them.

"I'm afraid I can't escort you to Savannah just now."

Barbara turned and looked at him incredulously. "Surely you don't mean to leave me stranded in this desolate wilderness?"

Devon frowned, then shrugged and smiled helplessly. "No, I suppose that isn't quite the thing, is it? But you see, your ladyship, there's a war going on all around us, and I'm on assignment. I can't lose two days shepherding a shipwrecked noblewoman about the countryside. I'll just have to take you with me until I can find someone trustworthy to see you safely to your destination."

Barbara's eyes narrowed as she inspected the arrogant lout about whose "trustworthiness" she was beginning to have grave reservations. She would have tapped the toe of her slipper, if she hadn't lost it in the ocean. "Perhaps you don't understand. My brother is the Seventh Baron of Rushcroft. General Prevost will be most displeased if you don't respect my wishes—at once." What had begun on a note of oversweet patience ended on one of considerable imperiousness. He merely stood back with arms crossed over his broad chest and smirked at her.

"This won't be the first time old Auggie Prevost has been displeased with me, but fortunately I'm not under his command. I answer to Colonel Brown and Governor Tonyn in Florida, and they've sent me to catch a thief. Now, if you're able to sit a horse, I suggest we move along."

Barbara stamped her foot and was rewarded with the warm squish of mud between her toes. "Bloody provincial lout," she muttered, then called at his retreating back, "I'll not budge an inch until you agree to take me to Savannah."

"Rare as the word must be to your ears, no." He didn't even bother to turn around, just began to untie a bag on the saddle of his big bay stallion. He tossed her a small pouch which she caught rather than have it sail into her face.

"Now see here—"

"No, you see here, your ladyship. You're a long way from the haut ton. You chose to traipse into the middle of a war, and now you'll just have to pay the consequences. There's biscuits and dried meat in the pouch. You can eat as we ride. I've lost too much time already."

She hurled the pouch at his thick skull, but missed. It sailed over the horse and landed with a plop in the mud. "I'll see you court-martialed and shot for this, you—"

"Not hungry? Pity, for it'll be dark before we stop again to eat." He swung effortlessly onto the big bay and walked the stallion toward her.

She stood stubbornly with her fists clenched at her sides. "You've not even the courtesy to assist a lady in mounting," she spat, looking at the other horse, a handsome piebald.

Suddenly he reached down and scooped her, kicking and screaming, up in front of him. "Satisfied? I've just assisted you in mounting."

"I meant onto the piebald, you dolt," she said from between gritted teeth.

"You're not riding the piebald. He belongs to my companion."

Just then, as if summoned, a tall, copper-skinned savage wearing a scalp lock, an abundance of gaudy beaded jewelry, and little else materialized silently from the tall marsh grasses. His naked chest was scarred by blue tattooing, as were his cheeks. He wore an arsenal of weapons, a low-riding pair of buckskin pants, and those same odd, low-cut leather slippers.

"Who is that?" She struggled not to squeal as her eyes glued onto the frightening savage, who swung onto the piebald and looked to Devon for orders.

"If I told you his Muskogee name, you couldn't pronounce it. Translated it's equivalent is Pig Sticker. He's famous for killing wild boars with his spear. Oh, he's also my cousin," he added conversationally as he kicked his bay into a brisk trot.

July, 1780, Blackthorne Hill

"An' I tells ya, Aunt Agnes, she's got a fancy fer 'em, she does," Phoebe Barsham said in her thick London slum accent. The pretty dairymaid had a petulant turn to her full red lips as she spoke, darting her black eyes from side to side, making certain no one of consequence heard her speak so of the mistress.

Mistress Ogilve merely nodded as she sat working on her account ledger. Her whorish sister Tabatha's child had her mother's crass manner of speech and dreadful manners. Why had she ever suggested to Master Robert that he buy the worthless chit's papers? "I would agree that the young master's cousin Andrew has spent overmuch time visiting with the bride. Have you seen aught else?"

"Not exactly."

Mistress Ogilve harrumphed in disgust. "I thought as much."

"You don't like 'er any more 'n I do."

"Be that as it may, if you can give me no evidence beyond seeing Master Andrew squiring her about, there is no point in your petty jealousy. Oh, don't look at me so. I know about your cheap liaison with the young master—you and half the other foolish girls working on this estate. If you come to me with your belly swollen, I'll have Master Robert sell your papers in a trice!"

"Ain't no chance 'o that," Phoebe said sullenly. "Since he wed 'er, he ain't touched me—ner none o' the rest."

"Laudable restraint on his part, not yours," the chief housekeeper replied sourly. "But it's his wife's virtue, not the master's, that I would like to impugn. If you can do no better than this, off with you and back to the dairy. I have accounts to pay."

"'N cash ta pocket fer yourself, too," Phoebe said slyly.

One look from her aunt's cold black eyes was enough to send her scurrying from the small room.

After Phoebe had left, Agnes Ogilve considered the matter of Madelyne Blackthorne. The willful and highly educated chit could be trouble. Old Robert and young Quintin, although scrupulously careful about their business ventures, had never been concerned about how she ran the household as long as meals were on time, the servants obedient, and the place kept clean and orderly. But since Quintin had taken a wife who desperately wanted something to occupy her time, the housekeeper lived in fear that her account books would one day come under Madelyne's scrutiny.

She needed to find a way to discredit the wife, not the husband. All that stupid Phoebe was concerned with was Quintin's absence from her bed. She mulled on that and decided it might be a good sign. If the master got his wife with child, he might be satisfied and leave the running of the household alone.

"Still, if Phoebe's snooping can yield me anything at all, I'd best encourage the noxious brat," she mused aloud. There were few servants who had not taken to Madelyne. The only ones who disliked her were Quintin's cast-off paramours. Whereas every person who toiled in Blackthorne Hill hated the imperious chief housekeeper.

The subject of Mistress Ogilve's ruminations strolled through the formal gardens beside the big house, kneeling in the sandy soil from time to time to prune a rosebush or pull one of the few weeds that dared to crop up on the meticulously tended grounds. There was an array of servants to do this. In fact, there was an array of servants to do everything on the plantation.

Madelyne smiled ruefully. "Under Claud's roof, I complained bitterly about all my chores. Now I pine for tasks to do. I vow, I'd even beat rugs . . . if Mistress Ogilve would let me." She had to laugh at the picture of her in those long-discarded filthy rags beating a magnificent Turkish carpet while Quintin and the housekeeper looked on, aghast. Her reverie was broken when she heard Gulliver's sharp barking and a strange bellowing sound.

Standing up, she dusted off her skirts and walked from the gardens down toward the lane whence the racket was emanating. A plumpish young woman with long black hair was beating one of the fine Jersey milk cows with a pole.

"Ya bloody old sack o' bones! Damn ya. Get goin'. I'm late fer milkin' 'n it be yer fault." Phoebe gave the cow a sharp jab in the ribs, eliciting another loud mooing cry. Then she turned her attention to the dog. Gulliver jumped at her and barked furiously. She swung her weapon toward him with a snarled oath, but he was too quick for her. "Git, ya mangy cur! Tain't none o' yer affair." She menaced the large dog, who stood his ground, legs braced and fur bristling, growling low in his throat.

Madelyne saw the confrontation and shouted, "Gulliver, come here! You, girl, stop tormenting that poor cow." She picked up her skirts and ran down the road toward the pasture gate.

Phoebe turned and saw Quintin's wife, clad in a dusty brown sack dress of coarse calico, striding angrily toward her. She tightened her grip on the pole and stood mutinously glaring at the dog, who ceased his barking and trotted obediently to Madelyne.

"What is the meaning of this—Phoebe—that *is* your name, isn't it?"

"I'm Phoebe Barsham, Mistress Ogilve's niece," she said but deliberately did not curtsy.

"Why are you abusing this valuable animal?" Madelyne stepped in front of the bondswoman, hating her shorter stature which forced her to look up at Phoebe.

"Dumb beast won't move 'n it's well onta milkin' time."

"Well, terrifying her and causing her pain certainly won't solve anything." She turned to the cow, who stood silently now, head down but making no attempt to graze on the high grass at the roadside. Madelyne patted her and then looked at her feet. The right rear one was caught somehow and the animal twitched her tail and pulled on it to no avail. "She's caught—probably in an animal warren of some sort. Here, help me free her."

"Could be a snake hole. I ain't goin' near it," Phoebe said stubbornly.

Madelyne knelt and worked with the cow's right rear foot, which was wedged tightly. After a moment's feckless struggle, she looked up at the strapping girl and said angrily, "Get over here at once or I'll cane you with that pole!"

"You wouldn't dare. My aunt'd go to the master 'n he'd tell you ta mind yer sewin' and leave runnin' this here place to them what knows what they're about."

The truth of her useless position and Quintin's refusal to allow her any authority over the servants cut too deeply. Madelyne stood up and advanced on the larger woman with fire in her golden eyes. She yanked the pole from Phoebe's hands and hurled it into the tall grass, then reached for her shoulder, intent on dragging her to perform the task.

Phoebe slapped Madelyne's hand away with a crude oath and placed her fists defiantly on her hips, daring the little mistress to touch her again.

All the stress and humiliation of the past weeks seemed to well up inside Madelyne, like a dam bursting. She grabbed a fistful of black hair from beneath Phoebe's dingy cap and gave a sharp yank, causing the girl to lose her balance and pitch forward. "I am the mistress of Blackthorne Hill, and you are an indentured servant. You will obey me!"

"Bloody hell I will!" Phoebe seized the neckline of Madelyne's chemise and ripped it off her shoulder, then tried to kick with her heavy-soled shoes, but Madelyne's skirts offered some protection as she doubled her fist up and struck the bondswoman in her stomach. With black and dark red hair flying, feet flailing, and hands gouging, they fell to the dusty earth, rolling over and over as each struggled to subdue the other. Gulliver raced in a circle, barking furiously while the Jersey stood stoically by the roadside watching with round brown eyes.

"What in blazes is that racket?" Quintin muttered to Domino. He'd just spent a hellish day at the warehouse supervising the unloading of their fall trading goods for the Muskogee. He was hot, tired, and thoroughly out of sorts as he trotted the stallion up the road.

The scene before his eyes confounded him—two shrieking women, a barking dog, and an immobilized cow who let out a lowing cry of distress when the women rolled against her legs. The racket would shortly draw everyone from the plantation. Since one of the combatants was his wife, Quintin had to put a stop to it before that occurred. Madelyne had caused him enough disquietude already. He dismounted and strode furiously toward them, then reached down and plucked his gasping, disheveled wife from atop the housekeeper's harlot niece.

"Do you want everyone from Blackthorne Hill to Savannah to witness your disgrace, madam?" he hissed as Madelyne thrashed in his arms.

The moment she heard that cold, clipped voice, Madelyne froze in horror, all the rage suddenly drained from her. Once more, she and Phoebe had confirmed Quintin's belief in the wild, hoydenish way all women behaved—whether ladies or serving wenches. "I was trying to rescue the Jersey from her abuse. She was beating the poor creature quite mercilessly with a pole."

"I see no pole," he said with a scowl as he looked from the cow to Phoebe.

The dairymaid's sniveling turned into a smirk. "She attacked me, Master Quintin, whilst I was only doin' my job."

"That's a lie! I threw the pole in the grass and told her to help me free the Jersey. She refused."

Madelyne wrenched away from him and knelt beside the cow. "Here, see, she's caught."

Quintin swore and strode over, pushing Madelyne out of the way. He reached down with both hands and stroked the cow's leg as he examined it. "Pat her nose and keep her quiet while I work her leg free."

Madelyne did as he'd bidden her, all the while watching his hands—those lean, strong hands that had caressed her with such skill, now gently touching the Jersey with the same assurance. He deftly freed the hoof, checked it for injury, then stood up, brushing off his hands.

"She's fine, just wedged herself into a rabbit hole." He gave the Jersey a swat, and she trotted obediently down the road toward the dairy. "You'd best attend to your job, Phoebe," he said, dismissing the girl before she could protest. Then he turned to Madelyne. "I expect no better than churlish fighting from the likes of that one, but I'll not tolerate it from my wife. Look at you, half-naked, filthy, disheveled."

Madelyne's anger returned, roaring down on her like ocean waves. "She abused that poor animal, disobeyed me, and then attacked me! What was I supposed to do, let her strangle me? Perhaps that would suit you. Then you'd be rid of a wife you never wanted!"

She turned and began to run up the road, tears blinding her until she tripped. Gulliver followed her and then fell to licking her face as she knelt in the dust, utterly miserable.

Quint could see the rise and fall of her breasts where her chemise and bodice had been ripped loose. Her hair spilled across her shoulders in tangles. He wanted to scoop her up and carry her into the tall, sweet meadow grass where he could pull the rest of her clothes free and silence her tears and protests with a kiss, his hands caressing . . . Shaking free of the hold she had over him, Quint took Domino's reins and walked him over to where she and the dog were sitting.

He reached down and extended his hand. "You can't go running up to the front door in this condition, Madelyne. Come, I'll ride you around the back way," he said.

The odd note of gentleness in his voice broke into her misery like a ray of sunlight after a storm. This was as near an apology as she'd ever receive from this aloof, arrogant man. She reached up and took his hand, allowing him to help her stand. Then he mounted the stallion and scooped her into the saddle in front of him. Cradling her in his arms, he rode slowly across the pasture, circling toward the rear of the big house at the top of the bluff.

Neither of them saw Phoebe turn and watch them ride away. Her black eyes were filled with hate.

Chapter Ten

Madelyne sank back into the tub of warm, scented water and sighed. Her body ached from head to toe. She was scratched and bruised, but above all her pride was again in tatters. Quintin had let her off at the rear door and taken Domino down to the stables. "At least he didn't defend Phoebe, and he waited to berate me until after he'd dismissed her," she murmured to herself dejectedly.

As she soaked away the grime from her brawl with the serving girl, Madelyne thought about the past several months since Quintin Blackthorne had stormed into her life and turned it upside down. His shocking confession the morning after the wedding had explained many things about his behavior—and Robert's. She shivered in the warm water, thinking about the bitter, loveless childhood her husband must have had. Old Robert was not a forgiving man, not even to an innocent child.

Madelyne had renewed her vow to break down the barriers that separated her from her husband and to teach him to trust her, but her success seemed to reach no further than their bed. He made love to her each night with such feverish abandon that it brought a flush to her body even thinking of it. But his passion for her was itself a double-edged sword, for the more he desired her, the more he resented her for making him feel vulnerable.

He was so afraid to let down his guard and give his heart to a woman. Again she puzzled about the Lady Anne. Why had she betrayed her marriage vows and left an innocent child to suffer the consequence of her sins? How had Robert found out? How sad for Quint to have no memory of his mother, just a legacy of hatred for all of her sex.

Madelyne barely remembered her own mother, but what little she did was sacred, and she'd had a lifetime of love from Aunt Isolde as consolation. Quint had grown up with nothing. "If only he could love me as . . ." She sat up in the tub, splashing water all about the floor of the dressing room. The sentence seemed to complete itself in the still warm room " . . . as I love him."

Love him? How could she love a cold, arrogant whoremaster who had bedded every woman in the colony and despised them after—none more so than she! Yet all he had to do was look at her with those burning green eyes and she melted like wax in the hot Georgia sun. God help her.

She sank back into the tub, replaying the bitter pattern their life had become. Each night he came to her bed and claimed his right to her body. Her young, starved flesh always responded so wondrously to his touch. Yet Madelyne craved more—a warm smile, a tender kiss, to be held and cherished when their passion was spent, but Quint never offered those things. He simply rose and left her to sleep alone in her bedroom while he returned to his.

Hot tears slid down her cheeks and dropped into the rapidly cooling bathwater as she recalled the humiliating scene several weeks ago when she had finally worked up her courage to confront him.

Quint had just rolled away from her and slid from the bed, beautiful and arrogant in his nakedness. As he reached for a navy banyan and belted it about his lean hips, she had sat up in bed and clutched the sheets about her, gathering her nerve.

"Must you leave?" Her voice was husky, partially because of her satiety, but more because her throat was dry with fear.

He quirked an eyebrow and looked at her. "Our mutual needs have been assuaged, haven't they? Why should I stay?"

She felt her cheeks heat and lowered her lashes. "Because . . . that is, I had thought it the natural thing . . . for a husband and wife to talk, to have some exchange of civility or affection, not just . . ."

"Just bedsport?" He supplied the crude word easily. "Be grateful for your passionate nature, Madelyne. At least you enjoy the act. Many ladies, so I'm told, abhor it and its logical consequence—the breeding of heirs."

"And that's the only reason you wed me—to ensure a male heir for the Blackthorne property. No need for a shred of kindness between us as long as I perform my duty." Her voice rose with anger. "You leave the house for the day and confine me to it. You can't even abide the sight of me at the breakfast table! I can't live like a prisoner in a gilded cage, Quint!"

"Would you rather return to your aunt Claud's charming house? Considerably less gilding, but a cage, nonetheless."

"Not a cage of my choosing."

"Your father made you a good bargain, Madelyne. Here you have wealth, position, and a life of ease. I don't even require that you beat rugs to learn Christian piety—only that you give me a son."

"You make what we do so calculated, so heartlessly cold."

Quintin had laughed with withering scorn. "Ah no, my dear little wife, what we do is anything but cold."

Madelyne dashed the tears from her cheeks and forced herself to put the sordid confrontation from her mind. It had solved nothing, nor would rehashing it serve her. She was exhausted, physically and emotionally. Lying back in the tepid water, she let her mind go blank and drifted off to sleep.

Quintin gave Domino a thorough rubdown himself, trying to work off the baffling surge of anger that always followed his confrontations with his wife. She had looked so small and vulnerable kneeling in the dust of the road with tears streaking her dirt-stained face. Phoebe was vicious and jealous, traits which had quickly led him to abandon her bed. Doubtless Madelyne's story was true.

And yet you turned on her and hurt her again. He cursed, then gave the stallion an affectionate swat and headed to the house. He'd sluice off by the well and then go upstairs to change for dinner.

When he reached the top of the back stairs, Quintin paused to shake the excess droplets of water from his hair. He'd already unfastened his shirt and shrugged it off as he entered his room. The thick carpet muffled the sounds of his boots as he pulled them off and tossed them for Toby to pick up later. He kicked his trousers into the pile of clothes and headed for his dressing room, padding silently across the floor. The sight that greeted him when he opened the door caught his breath, then knocked it from his chest as if he'd been dealt a blow by a smithy's hammer.

Madelyne lay in the big brass tub in the center of the dressing room with her head laid back against the tub's rim. Long, silky, mahogany hair hung over the side, spilling onto the floor. Her chin was tilted up, her disturbing golden eyes closed, and her dark amber lashes fanned across her cheeks. She was sound asleep.

Quint walked closer and watched the rise and fall of those perfect little breasts. With each breath the warm, perfumed water lapped against their pink tips. Her legs were bent to fit in the round tub but he could still see the dark reddish curls at the juncture of her thighs, submerged in the water.

His body was hard, his breathing labored. Lust swept through him, just looking at her, smelling the musky honeysuckle essence of her. *I'm besotted by a slip of a girl*, he thought furiously. Yet he knew what he would do—must do. Seizing a soft linen towel from the chair against the wall, he strode to the tub.

Madelyne was awakened by Quintin's deft fingers stroking with silky insistence along her collarbone, then moving lower to break the water, teasing her breasts, which instantly sprang to tingling life. When she opened her mouth to emit a soft little gasp, half surprise, half protest, he silenced it with his lips.

Quintin lifted her wet, gleaming body from the tub, continuing the kiss as he carried her into his room, leaving a trail of water across carpet and polished oak floors.

"No, Quint. You can't do this. The servants—"

"You should have thought of that before you fell asleep in the tub in my dressing room," he whispered, continuing to feast on her wet, perfumed throat.

"Toby was out and Nell couldn't lift that heavy tub to drag it into my room—"

"Bother the tub," he said hoarsely, tossing her onto his bed.

"I'm soaking wet." She bounced up, leaving a wet stain on the brocade coverlet.

He took the towel from his shoulder and began to rub her dry, starting with her shoulders, then massaging lower to caress her breasts, belly, thighs.

When she moaned, he let a low growl of laughter escape, then buried his face in her damp hair, inhaling her fragrance.

She felt his warm breath against her skin. All thoughts of stained bed linens were forgotten. *I should hate him for using me thus....* But she didn't. Her arms wrapped around his shoulders, pulling him close. Already she ached for his possession, her hips arched and her nails dug into the muscles of his back. She could feel him tense as he roughly pulled the towel from between them and threw it to the floor. He parted her legs and thrust deeply into her.

With unconscious volition, her legs wrapped about his hips, pulling him closer and deeper as she matched his wild, abandoned pace. He muttered an unintelligible oath as his mouth again found hers and plundered it.

She was so tight, yet so wet, so perfectly made to sheathe him. With no other woman had it ever felt this way. Somehow he knew it never would with another again, but the disturbing thought quickly fled as he felt her reach her release and blindly followed her over the precipice, tumbling into hot, sweet surcease that robbed him of breath and speech and rational thought.

Slowly, as if returning to consciousness after a drugged sleep, Quint rolled to his side and raised his head to stare down at her. Taking a lock of sweet, damp hair in his fist, he held it up to the waning afternoon light, letting the burnished glory of it catch fire. His eyes were troubled when he turned them to meet hers.

"Why is it always like this between us? I can't stop taking you this way any more than I can stop saying hurtful things to you."

Beneath the puzzlement, Madelyne could sense wariness and pain—or was it merely regret? Never before had he seemed this vulnerable. Perhaps it was her chance. She reached up and stroked his cheek, tenderly brushing his shoulder-length raven hair back so it did not shadow his face. What could she read in those fathomless green eyes? *Listen to me, Quintin Blackthorne, my beloved. Listen to my body . . . my soul.* She placed her fingertips on his lips, then replaced them with her lips. She kissed him softly, like the fluttering of butterfly wings, lightly brushing his mouth with hers.

"We've made a rough beginning, perhaps, but we can still make things better between us. We're bound for life, husband, but it need not be so hurtful a union if only you will try to trust me . . . just a little bit."

The ghost of a smile played about his lips. "Trust does not come easily for a man like me, betrayed at birth."

"I know, Quint."

He looked uncomfortable as he admitted, "I've never told anyone, not even Devon, about my bastardy—no one until you."

"I knew that, too," she replied softly.

"Woman's intuition?" He actually smiled at her.

"'Tis a very private pain, Quint. You only released it in anger because you feared what was growing between us. You've fought it ever since that night in the library of the city house—and don't say it's merely lust."

His brow creased in a frown. "Then what would you call it, Madelyne? Love?"

I dare not reveal too much . . . too quickly. She caressed his brow, smoothing the wrinkles. "Perhaps not . . . exactly, but given time we might . . ."

A sharp rapping sounded on the bedroom door, and one of the houseboys called through the heavy oak. "Mastah Quintin, Mastah Robert wants you at the horse pens. One of yo hosses got hisself loose 'n can't nobody catch 'im."

"I'll be right out." Quintin disengaged himself from his embrace with Madelyne, then on impulse leaned over and kissed her on the top of her nose. "You have freckles," he whispered irrelevantly, then slid from the bed and gathered up his discarded clothes.

She watched the sinuous beauty of his hard body as he dressed. She could still taste the faint salty musk of his skin, feel the crisp black hair spread in such cunning patterns on his body. If only they had not been interrupted, what might he have said? How might he have responded to her questions?

Madelyne felt a heady warmth about her heart as she recalled his tenderness. This time he had not withdrawn in anger, cold and aloof when they finished making love. Perhaps this new openness was a sign that he was ready to meet her at least part of the way. She would make him love her. She would!

In the midst of buttoning his trousers, he looked over at her guileless expression as she stared at him. "I won't be long."

"I'm not going anywhere, Quint." *Not now that I've finally gotten as far as your room . . . your bed.*

After Quintin left, Madelyne stretched as lazily as a cat, then threw back the sheets and rose. She wandered into her room and closed the door lest Toby, Quintin's elderly black valet, return and find his master's wife undressed. She selected a gown for dinner and was about to ring for Nell to assist her with the lacings when the door to Quintin's room opened and closed. Surely he couldn't be back this soon. Madelyne walked through the connecting dressing closet and opened the door silently. Some sixth sense made her cautious. Peering through the slit of the opened door, she smothered a gasp.

Quintin's valet, Toby, had opened his master's desk and was extracting a volume that looked to be a ledger from inside the cabinet. But Toby, she knew, could neither read nor do sums. What was he about? The hair on her nape prickled as she watched him place an envelope inside the ledger, carefully close it, and replace everything undisturbed.

As soon as he left the room, Madelyne reentered it and walked to the desk. For a moment she hesitated, then pulled down the gate and slid the ledger out. Her hands trembled as she opened the heavy volume. The pages separated right where Toby had placed the message. *I shouldn't open it. It's for Quint—or is it? What's going on here that a servant knows about and I don't?*

Madelyne slid the folded pages from the ledger and began to read:

> British regulars from Gov. Tonyn sweeping up Florida coast. Alert E. Clarke. Good site for ambush at ford of Altamaha.

She paused as her eyes blurred over the seemingly incredible words that she must surely have misread. Against her will she read further, skipping down the page of tightly written notes and instructions:

> Cornwallis delays facing Gates until he can muster more ordinance. Expect British ships at Wilmington within week. Cargo manifest: 55 cannon, howitzers and mortars (amounts unknown), two ton shot, 2,300 pounds bullet lead, 30,000 gunflints. Once supplies reach Cornwallis's officers, the general will move into South Carolina with all dispatch. Americans must be warned . . .

The paper fluttered to the floor, dropped from her nerveless fingers. The evidence contained in the note was damning, and it was clearly the bold penmanship of Quintin Blackthorne. Madelyne struggled to breathe as scenes from past months flashed before her eyes. She could see Quint laughing and exchanging confidences with Govenor Wright, entertaining British officers, casually questioning and encouraging them when they discussed military matters, often urging them to drink more than her Calvinist sensibilities felt decorous.

My husband is a spy and a traitor to his king and country! How desperately she wished that she had never opened the bedroom door—or ever trusted naively in her foolish love for Quintin Blackthorne.

"And I was fool enough to wish for a wife who could read and cipher."

Madelyne whirled, her back against the sharp edge of the desk's drop leaf. She knew that every ounce of blood had drained from her face as she tried to swallow over the dry, hard lump in her throat. "It would seem there is more to your mysterious past than just your heredity. Tell me, is Robert also a traitor?"

He smiled, but it was not the beautiful smile that melted her bones. This one was ruthless and cold. "Robert Blackthorne is as blindly loyal to the king as you, but unlike the old man, you are tied to me in a rather unique manner—what was it the priest said? We are one flesh, Madelyne. You are my wife, and as such you owe me unconditional loyalty."

"And you are a spy and a traitor! How could you betray every principle of honor and aid these rebels? Sons of Liberty! Pah! Mobs of drunken malcontents too lazy to do an honest day's work."

"I quite agree with you about our local Liberty boys. They do the patriot cause far more harm than good, but they scarcely comprise American leadership."

"American leadership," she scoffed contemptuously.

He advanced a few steps toward her and asked, "Are you acquainted with Mr. Franklin or Governor Jefferson? Perhaps General Washington? No? Then don't be so quick to judge us all by the likes of a backwoods mob."

"How could you join the Georgia Royal Militia? You fought at the siege of Savannah." Her hand flew to her lips, and they thinned with anger. "Did you shoot your fellow Englishmen in the back while the French and the rebels charged from the front?"

His expression betrayed a fleeting glimpse of agony as he remembered those hellish weeks. "If you think me capable of such perfidy, there's little I can say to refute it. I sent that French fop d'Estaing word that Prevost was fortifying the city, but he delayed the attack. There was quite sufficient carnage on both sides without my shooting anyone— British or American. God, do you think I came to this allegiance easily?"

"Perhaps you only did it to spite Robert."

He appeared to consider that for a moment. "The temptation was great, but that wasn't the reason. I genuinely admire the British system of laws and government—so do all the men who signed the Declaration of Independence. Else we'd not have modeled our own new government on it. But we've remonstrated too long. The ocean's too wide and the king's ministers too intractable. Perhaps Edmund Burke summed up our feelings best when he said to Parliament that an Englishman is the unfittest person on earth to argue another Englishman into slavery."

"Slavery! That's nonsense. You're traitors, all of you." She stubbornly held her ground.

Quintin reached out and seized her fine-boned wrist with one hand, pulling her against him and holding her fast.

"You're hurting me!" She did not plead, only gritted out the words, then stood stiffly in his arms.

He took her face in his hand, forcing her to look up and meet his eyes. "Will you betray me, Madelyne? T'would rid you of a husband who's dealt you more than a few passing hurts. Robert would probably be glad to see the last of me, Lord knows." He paused, studying her confused expression. "Well, my fierce little loyalist, what's

it to be? I can scarce chain you to my bed."
He began to stroke her cheek with his fingertips, ever so gently. "You could watch them hang
me . . ."

Madelyne felt faint as visions of Quint's lifeless
body hanging from a gallows flashed before her
eyes. God above! She could never do that, never
lose him, no matter what he did. The bitter irony
of the situation did not escape her as she whispered
in a choked voice, "I could never wish you dead,
Quint, politics be damned!"

He continued holding her face and lowered his
mouth to claim hers in a fierce, possessive kiss, as
if sealing their bargain.

When they broke apart, both shaken, she said,
"So now you're forced to trust me at last—because you have no choice. Perhaps I have no
choice either," she added, reaching up to close
her smaller hand around his as it held her face.
She tiptoed up and let her lips brush his, gently
this time.

Quint's eyes were troubled as he released her. "I
have to take these dispatches to South Carolina."

"How long will you be gone, Quint? It's dangerous
on the roads. If the Creek learn you're a patriot . . ."
She shuddered.

He smiled grimly. "I'm still Devon Blackthorne's
cousin. Perhaps that might count for something.
Then, again, perhaps he'd turn me over to them."
His eyes were filled with pain now.

"You hate deceiving him, don't you?"

"Yes, above all, that. I dread the day he learns
the truth of my allegiance, as someday he must."
He released her and began to gather up the
papers, then turned to her and said, "The only
one on Blackthorne Hill who knows about my
work is Toby. You can trust him. Speak of this
with no one else. Will you swear your silence,
Madelyne?"

Please, trust me. I love you, God help me, I love you. Her thoughts were in chaos as he stared at her with those piercing green eyes, but all she answered was, "I swear, Quint."

Chapter Eleven

July, 1780, The Georgia Interior

Lady Barbara Caruthers had never been so miserable in her life. Soaked, bruised, and nearly drowned in the briny Atlantic, then abducted by an insolent half-caste and his frightening savage cousin. She supposed it was a miracle that she was alive. Her misery was intensified during the night, when she tried to slip one of Devon's pistols from his side. He rolled over and seized her wrist in a bone-crushing grasp as he pulled her to lie on his prone body.

Their faces were inches apart as he whispered low, "Don't ever try that again. I'm a very light sleeper, and Pig Sticker never sleeps." He glanced up to where the tall savage suddenly materialized from the shadows of a tree.

She looked at the Indian's impassive face, then down at his hand, resting lightly on the hilt of a wicked-looking hatchet. Her eyes quickly returned to Devon.

"Do you even know how to prime a pistol?"

"I've never touched one of the wretched things in my life. I only wanted to make you see common sense and take me to Savannah."

He laughed, enjoying her embarrassment as she lay sprawled atop him. "Best get some sleep, Lady Barbara. You'll need your strength tomorrow."

Then he had the audacity to toss her away from him and roll over, turning his back to her as if she were a doxy dismissed after he'd made use of her services!

Furiously, she'd crawled back into her blanket under Pig Sticker's baleful stare and tried to sleep. Morning came all too soon. Barbara rolled over and every muscle of her body screamed in protest. The ground, which had seemed so swampy and soft beneath the horses' hooves, felt entirely different when used as a bed. She clawed her way free of the mosquito netting and sat up, wincing with every movement.

A survey of her dismal surroundings did little to revive her spirits. The countryside was a flat, barren wilderness of scrub pines and tall weeds. She thought it so desolate that no creature could inhabit the hellish place, until Devon identified the track of a panther and mentioned she'd be wise not to stray far from their camp! They traveled at a breakneck pace all day, pausing only long enough for Pig Sticker to examine the marshy ground for signs of their prey.

By the time Devon Blackthorne called a halt for the night, it was full dark. Although she'd had to relieve herself since early afternoon, Barbara resolutely refused to ask her captors for the humiliating favor. Exhausted and starving, she straggled behind a copse of buckthorn trees to perform nature's functions, then huddled before a small campfire to devour a stone-hard biscuit and some stringy salted meat. She hadn't even bothered to ask what it was.

The second night, she made no attempt to wrest a pistol from Devon, but slept like the dead.

The following morning, Barbara awakened in even more misery, if such was possible. "Lud, I ache in places I didn't know I had!" She sat up gingerly and looked around for Devon, but saw only the savage. "Not that the white one was much better," she sniffed to herself. Of course if Pig Sticker was his cousin, he couldn't really be a white man, could he? She watched the Indian as he prepared a foul-smelling potion in a small tin cup. It seemed to be a ritual of some sort, for he stirred it reverently, held the cup aloft toward the rising sun, then drank it down in several swift gulps. Almost at once he doubled over and then walked toward a patch of tall grass where he calmly vomited it up.

Revolting! Barbara turned her head, battling her own rebellious stomach. Then she heard Devon's approach from behind a copse of pines. He exchanged a few words in their guttural dialect with the Indian, as the savage calmly peeled off his adornments and then his buckskin leggings. As naked as at the moment of his birth, Pig Sticker walked down the slight incline to the sluggish creek that meandered by their campsite. He dived in and began to vigorously scrub his body.

"Care to join us?" Devon said with a grin. He, too, was peeling off his clothes.

Barbara had thought herself a complete sophisticate two years after her come-out in London society, but this was making her face flame as if she were a schoolgirl. "Certainly not! You're as barbarous as that—that Pig Sticker person." Her eyes were locked on the flickering flames of the small fire. She would not look at him.

"You don't have to purge yourself with the Black Drink. I only do that myself on special occasions, but the Muskogee bathe every morning. A custom white civilization would do well to adopt."

"I take my ablutions in private, indoors," she said, her eyes never wavering.

"You'll be some time out in the heat before we see any indoor facilities, but suit yourself," he replied with a shrug. "When you begin to smell too bad, I'll make you walk—or dunk you myself."

She glared at him. "You wouldn't dare."

He grinned back at her. "Wait and see, your ladyship." With that he strolled into the water, giving her a splendid view of his backside.

She watched, fascinated in spite of her fury and chagrin. Although not as dark as the full-blooded Indian, he was bronzed from head to toe, including the lean, muscular cheeks of his buttocks. His lower legs were covered with pinkish-looking scars, as if the injury were recent. *What am I doing?* She quickly tore her eyes away lest he turn and give her another of those teasing winks.

Every movement was misery as she arose, crusted with itchy salt over every inch of her skin. At least her own discomfort kept her from stealing any further admiring glances at that golden-haired Indian! Her clothes, or what was left of them, hung in stiff tatters. "I feel like that bloody meat we ate last night," she said beneath her breath. What besides that horrendous black brew was there for breakfast?

She visited the bushes, then approached the campfire. What looked to be a large, dirty white rodent lay beside the fire, pierced with a single shot cleanly in the head. She shuddered. Surely *this* was not to be eaten? Devon and Pig Sticker returned from their morning ablutions and donned their clothes with no regard for modesty. She refused to watch, only listened as they continued to talk in that heathenish dialect. "Can you at least be courteous enough to speak English?"

Devon looked up, shaking droplets of water from his dark gold hair, an expression of annoyance on his face. "My cousin has bad news, I'm afraid," he said to her. "The man we're pursuing has obviously missed his rendezvous with a ship because of the storm. He's headed cross country with his loot—for New Orleans."

"New Orleans? Isn't that all the way into French territory? Surely you don't expect to drag an English subject there? We're at war with France and Spain."

He looked ruefully at the insignia of the King's Rangers on his buckskins. "That information is not news to me, your ladyship, I assure you, but you're the one who's blundered into the war. I'm only a humble soldier, under orders to catch a thief who absconded with a fortune in trade goods bound for the lower Muskogee towns. We should catch McGilvey in a few days. You've nothing to fear from the French."

"But more than a little to fear from you, I'll warrant," she muttered low. "Do you plan to starve me or are there more of those sumptuous biscuits? The tooth surgeons in London would get rich if I introduced them as a new colonial delicacy."

Devon laughed as he squatted by the fire. "I'm afraid we've run out of biscuits." He unsheathed a long, sharp knife from his belt and looked up at Pig Sticker, then over to Barbara. "I don't suppose you've ever cooked a possum . . . or anything else," he said glumly as he began to skin the dead animal. "We needed some fresh meat, and this was the first thing that ran across my sights."

"Surely you don't eat rats?" She choked, her earlier hunger forgotten.

"This isn't a rat. It's a possum. A little on the greasy side, but we don't have time to waste hunting."

She watched in horror as he methodically skinned and gutted the creature, then carved the carcass into several large hunks which he took to the stream and washed. Upon returning, he skewered them on small green sapling branches, which Pig Sticker had carefully peeled, then placed them over the flames to roast. As the fatty meat dripped into the fire, it gave off a sickly sweetish odor, rather like rancid mutton.

"If you'll forgive me, I think I'll forego your . . . possum roast," she said when Devon tore one of the chunks of meat apart and offered her a piece.

"You should've held on to those biscuits you threw at me the other day," he said with a grin, tearing into the fatty meat with strong white teeth.

When they finished the meal, Pig Sticker packed up the remaining meat. All Barbara consumed was some sour watered wine that Devon had in his canteen. Soon that, too, would be gone. Then he approached her with a small gourd from which he removed a stopper.

"Here, rub your face and all other exposed areas of your skin with this."

She smelled the stuff, a strange pungent oil of some sort. "What is it?"

"A special preparation my mother makes for fair-skinned women—to prevent sunburn."

"I'd not be risking sunburn if you'd take me to Savannah." She shoved the gourd back into his lean brown hands. How white hers seemed by comparison.

He looked at her as if she were a spoiled, half-witted child. "If you spend another day beneath this sun, you'll be blistered and feverish. People die of that in the southern colonies, your ladyship, and I've no time or inclination to nurse you back to porcelain-pink perfection." He advanced on her with the gourd. "Either you do it or I will."

"How dare you, you bloody loutish bastard!"

"My, my, the gently born are possessed of such refined vocabularies," Devon said, shaking his head. "Hold her, Pig Sticker, while I perform the task."

The big savage clamped his hand over her wrists and held them in one large hand. As she kicked, cursed and bit, he used his other hand to grab a fistful of silvery hair, yanking on it until tears of pain welled up in her eyes and she relented, immobilized by the stinging pull on her scalp.

Devon began with her face, smearing the oil over the delicate bones and silky white skin. "This would've been easier if you'd bathed the salt away first." When she spat an oath at him, he ignored it and continued stroking the oil down her slender throat with his fingertips.

He felt her pulse racing. In fury? Fear? Or something else? When he spread the oil across her collarbone and down near the swell of her generous breasts, he could see the tautening of her nipples through the thin fabric. *Yes, definitely something else*, he mused as he lifted her chin knowingly and her defiant blue eyes met his dark brown ones.

When she felt the shocking tingle of his callused fingers caressing her skin so intimately, Barbara wanted desperately to hate him, to despise his crude commoner's touch, but she could not. Many men had touched her, even kissed her and handled her, but their soft, pale hands never made her burn like this. It was as if she and Devon Blackthorne were alone. The brutish savage who held her was forgotten. She could not will the hot flush staining her cheeks to abate any more than she could prevent her breasts from tautening and the nipples from growing hard. *I can't find this half-caste desirable!* When he looked into her eyes, she held her head coolly aloof, returning his stare brazenly.

He knelt and lifted one long slim leg, rubbing the oil everywhere her petticoats had been torn away— even higher, up to her knees. "Astride the horse you'll bare more of your leg," he murmured, returning his attention to the sleek curve of her calf and shapely turn of ankle. Even filthy and bedraggled, she was magnificent.

When he'd completed the task, he stood up and

nodded to Pig Sticker, who released her. "I think we can go now," he said quietly.

Barbara said nothing, just waited until he mounted his big bay and pulled her up in front of him.

They rode all day, carefully tracking the crafty McGilvey. Several times Pig Sticker rode ahead, scouting to the left and right of them. Once they shifted course because he had made a discovery about the fugitive's trail.

"Who is this McGilvey fellow and what has he done?" she asked, trying desperately to take her mind off the heat, hunger, and thirst that plagued her— not to mention the half-caste's hard body, molded so closely to hers.

Devon grunted. "McGilvey's a crafty devil. Slipped into the compound outside St. Augustine and used a forged pass to take a half dozen pack mules loaded with muskets, powder, flints and steel, and a big cache of rum. Once he was licensed to trade with the Confederacy, but Governor Tonyn caught him stealing from the Indians and dismissed him. Then he pulled this trick—and at a crucial time, just when we need these presents for the lower towns to keep them from going over to the rebels' cause."

"How long have you been a ranger?"

"Not very long. I used to be a trader with the Muskogee myself," he replied.

"But I thought you lived with the sav—" She stopped in mid-sentence, feeling his body stiffen in the saddle behind her.

"Savages? Yes, to your eyes—and to most white settlers, the Muskogee seem savage. But I've seen things done by supposedly civilized men in this war that would equal or surpass the actions of the Muskogee. Men become animals in a civil war. They steal, rape, butcher, wantonly destroy homes, crops, lives—their neighbors' homes, crops, and lives."

Barbara shuddered. "I don't want to be here in this hellish conflict. When will it end?" She could feel him shrug in that smooth, careless way he had about him. He always moved like a big tawny cat, sleek and dangerous for all his flirtations and teasing ways.

"The way the rebels hang on in the back country, it may take a decade to subdue them." He did not voice his private fears that without more reinforcements from Lord Germain's government, the British cause might be lost in these colonies.

Just then the sounds of rushing water filled the silence as they rode. They came upon a thick stand of willows, whose weeping branches trailed into the rapidly moving current. "Heavy rains last week must have filled this stream." He cursed as he reined in and surveyed the roiling water.

Pig Sticker conferred with him, then pointed to a spot where the river curved sharply. Devon turned his bay in that direction and splashed into the rapidly deepening water.

"You aren't going to ford this without testing the depth? Surely there must be a bridge—"

His laughter cut her off. "A bridge?" His chest rumbled. "I doubt there are a dozen bridges in Georgia since the rebels burned what few lay between Savannah and Augusta. Here there never were any to burn."

She seized hold of the saddle with renewed strength. "I'll get soaking wet."

"Good. You smell like a bear pit after winter hibernation," he said pleasantly as the bay began to swim.

The rocking motion of the horse caused Barbara to slip. Devon's arm tightened around her waist, just below her breasts. His eyes traveled over her shoulder to view the tantalizing mounds of creamy flesh. The ripped gown accentuated more than it concealed of her lush curves. The sunburn oil he'd spread over her skin was beaded with tiny pearls of perspiration now, glistening in the heat.

Devon could feel his body respond and cursed to

himself. Why had he been saddled with an English noblewoman—and a beauty at that—while on such an important mission? So involved was he with the sweet curves of Barbara's flesh that he almost didn't hear Pig Sticker's shouted warning. A large piece of driftwood was headed directly toward them! He quickly turned the bay, but the horse stumbled and pitched to one side as it scrambled for footing on the uneven stream bottom. Devon struggled to hold on, but as the current washed over him, Barbara was wrenched away into the muddy, swirling water.

She screamed as she felt herself slipping, clawing at Devon's solid body. Her wet fingers could get no purchase. "I can't swim!"

Devon saw her blond hair bob beneath the water, then resurface several yards farther downstream. Throwing his pistols and knife onto the bank, he hurled free of his stirrups and dove into the water after her.

Barbara knew she was going to die. *So this is what it is like.* She went beneath the dark water again, sinking lower, lower. Then suddenly a strong arm wrapped around her waist and she was slammed into Devon's body. He kicked them to the surface and began to swim for the shallows. Holding her tightly, he finally succeeded in reaching waist-deep water, where he scooped her into his arms and walked slowly to the bank.

Barbara clung tightly to Devon, her head nestled against his throat as she let the steady pounding beat of his heart reassure her that she was indeed still alive. He laid her on the mossy ground beneath the spreading branches of a willow. When Pig Sticker called out for him, he yelled back in Muskogee, then knelt beside her and turned her over.

"Cough up the water. You probably swallowed half that river." He held her up by placing one arm beneath her breasts, then leaned her forward and pounded gently on her back until she choked up a gush of water. Then he let her recline on her back, gasping great gulps of air into her lungs.

Devon watched the rise and fall of her breasts as the wet linen clung to them. Her gown had been all but shredded during the shipwreck. Now she was down to only a linen chemise and part of one petticoat. Every ripe curve of her body was revealed to him.

"I planned a bath for you, but not this way," he murmured.

"I—" She coughed. "—never . . . bathe . . . outdoors."

He chuckled. "Well, you just did—and since you're already soaked, I suggest you remove these clothes and let me build a fire to dry them. You can't afford to lose any more." As he spoke he began to peel off his buckskin shirt.

Barbara watched the corded muscles play beneath the bronzed skin of his arms and chest, which was furred with coarse gold hair. Without realizing she had done it, she reached out and splayed her fingers in the mat of hair. His heartbeat accelerated.

He cocked one eyebrow quizzically. "Feeling grateful?"

She stiffened and pushed him away. "Grateful for what?"

"For saving your life!"

"Saving my life? If it weren't for you and your idiotic pursuit of some petty thief, I'd be safe in Savannah now!"

"You spoiled little bitch! I should've let you drown." He stood up, staring down at her, an insolent smile playing at his lips. "Well, it was almost worth it, just to get that stinking salt and sweat washed off you!" He inspected her body through the translucent wet linen. "You clean up very nicely, your ladyship."

Barbara cursed and bolted upright, then searched frantically around her for a weapon. Finding none, she clawed up a clump of mossy mud and hurled it at him. "Leave me alone!"

Sketching a mock bow, he backed off. "Whatever your ladyship wishes, but the fire and the food will be over there." He picked up his shirt and slung it over one shoulder, then sauntered from beneath the willow to where Pig Sticker waited with both horses.

Barbara huddled, glowering, beneath the tree, wet and miserable, for nearly an hour. Then she walked to the bank of the river and washed her hands. Devon had been right about her needing to dry her clothes, yet how could she? The sun was rapidly setting in the west, and she began to shiver as she sat finger-combing the damp, tangled mass of pale blond hair. Knowing nothing of how to dress her own hair, she simply let it hang in a long straight cascade which fell to her hips. If only Kate were here to tend to her as she always had. Poor Kate, dead of a fever—all because of Marianne Caruthers's vindictive jealousy. "I won't let her defeat me," she whispered with steel in her voice.

She stood up and did what she could to straighten her pitifully torn clothes. God above, she was half naked! It was a wonder that half-caste and his cousin hadn't raped her! *Perhaps Devon Blackthorne finds you so ugly he doesn't even want you.* She dismissed the oddly distressing thought and squared her shoulders, then walked defiantly toward the campfire.

Devon was kneeling on the ground, dumping several small rabbits from his game pouch. He scowled up at her, reading her mind from her haughty expression. Damn, what other woman alive could be left half naked, bruised, exhausted and twice nearly drowned, alone in the wilderness with two savage strangers, yet possess such stubborn spirit?

He smiled in spite of himself. "I see you've finally gotten over your pique. Now you can help us with supper. I snared these rabbits while Pig Sticker built the fire. He'll stand watch tonight and scout the area for signs of McGilvey. You can clean and cook the rabbits."

"Surely you're making a poor jest." She knew he was not.

"You watched me skin and gut the possum. These are a lot smaller and easier to dress." He tossed a small, sharp skinning knife onto the ground by her side. Then, reading the murderous look in her eyes, he added, "And don't think to sink that blade anywhere but into those rabbits, your ladyship." He patted the big, wicked-looking blade strapped at his thigh. "I'd hate to mar that lovely skin."

"I refuse to touch those . . . furry creatures," she said between clenched teeth.

"Then you don't eat," he replied levelly. "Not that I'd expect a spoiled stupid chit from London to be able to do a single useful thing."

Her stomach picked that most inopportune time to growl. He smiled and turned toward the western bend in the river, along which a thick stand of willows grew. "I'm going to investigate what Pig Sticker's found. We may be within a day of catching McGilvey, and he's not a man to take lightly. But then, neither am I, Lady Barbara." He walked off without a backward glance.

She resisted the urge to do just as he'd threatened her not to and plant the skinning knife squarely between those broad shoulders. She settled for piercing his back with her eyes, then looked down at the rabbits after he disappeared from view. Barbara kicked one small brown furball with her bare foot, sending it flying across the dusty ground. Stamping her foot in frustration, she muttered, "He thinks to come back after dark and find me huddled sobbing and cold at that fire, pleading for his help. Well, I'll show him!"

Her resolve was far easier spoken than accomplished. She almost cut off her finger on the first try at skinning one rabbit, but once she made the incision across its back, she grasped the skin on each side and gave a yank. It gave, and the meaty backbone was revealed. Forcing down her nausea, she continued to pull on the skin until she'd worked it free from the torso. She tried to remember how Devon had freed the legs, then began to pull and twist each half until she had extracted a reasonably intact carcass.

Throwing the bloody fur into the brush, she gritted her teeth for the worst. She must gut the creature next. By the time she'd cleaned out the body cavity, her roiling stomach had subsided. The trick, she concluded, was not to breathe through one's nose and smell the fetid stench of hot intestines. By the time she'd washed the rabbit in the river and spitted it over the fire, she felt a considerable sense of accomplishment—until she looked down at her blood-and-entrails-smeared body. And the other rabbit.

Slowly a smile spread across her face. She checked the perimeters of their camp. Neither Devon nor Pig Sticker was within sight or sound. If she were quick about it . . . She lowered the rabbit almost onto the coals to hasten its cooking time, then took the other one and threw it in the river along with the guts and fur.

By the time she'd washed the mess from her body and searched Devon's saddlebags for a clean shirt to wear, the rabbit was done enough to eat. She devoured more than half of it, tearing into the stringy meat as if it were the rarest delicacy ever set before her. Looking down at the meager remnants of meat and pile of bones, she burped, then broke into a peal of giggles, giddy with her success.

She tidied up the campsite, washed her greasy hands, then changed into Devon's shirt. It hung almost to her knees, and the cuffs fell below her fingertips, but she tied the tails of it about her waist, letting it blouse decently, then rolled up the sleeves.

Once fed, cleaned up, and dressed, she sat back and began to lose her sense of triumph. What would those two savages do to her when they returned hungry and found no food? Nervously she eyed the remaining leg and piece of breastbone next to the pile of scraps. "It serves them right," she said with a resolution she was far from feeling.

Needing something to occupy her mind, she returned to Devon's saddlebags and rummaged through them. Yes, just as she had recalled in her earlier haste, a book! A half-caste Indian, a backwoodsman, carried a volume of Jonathan Swift! Surely he could not read, could he?

What kind of an enigma was Devon Blackthorne, who had the book inscribed with his name, written in a bold scrawl across the title page. His speech, if not his etiquette, bespoke a man of education in spite of rude colonial dress. He was an officer in a colonial militia. Even though Barbara knew from Monty's letters how he regarded the loyalist militiamen, she grudgingly admitted that Devon possessed survival skills peculiarly fitted for success in the wilderness.

Putting aside her disturbing ruminations about Devon, she immersed herself in the outrageous satire of the scandalous Mr. Swift, who had long ago fallen from political favor. The adventures of Gulliver, however, were still entertaining.

Devon and Pig Sticker returned together, talking animatedly in Muskogee. They had found the trail of McGilvey's mule, not even two days ahead of them. Tomorrow would bring the reckoning. The smell of roasting rabbit remained faint on the air. Devon broke into a surprised smile. By God, she'd done it! He stepped into the light of the campfire and gazed down at Barbara's pale hair, spilling down her back like corn silk as she sat clutching a book.

He scanned the campfire area. "Where's the rest of the rabbits?"

"I ate my fill," she said, then returned to Swift.

"Two whole rabbits?"

She shrugged, mimicking his casual and infuriating gesture rather well.

Devon advanced toward her and yanked her to her feet. "You did not eat two whole rabbits."

She pulled free of his grasp. "You're hurting my arm."

"I'll do more than hurt your arm. I'll tan your backside with the flat of my hand if you don't tell me what—"

The deafening report of a Brown Bess musket echoed across the campsite, the ball narrowly brushing by Devon's shoulder. "McGilvey," he swore as he dove on top of Barbara, throwing them both to the ground. Then he shoved her from the circle of light around the campfire and kicked dust into it, snuffing it out.

At the first report of the gun, Pig Sticker had vanished into the willows from which they'd just emerged. Devon dragged Barbara into the tall grass, and they both dropped to their hands and knees. Devon's hand landed on the sharp rabbit bones and greasy leftovers she'd discarded earlier.

"So that's what you did with the rest," he whispered, then shoved her flat onto the ground and handed her the skinning knife, which he'd managed to grab before rolling away from the fire. "Move farther back into that heavy brush and hide yourself. Keep this knife and use it if you have to."

Before she could question him, Devon vanished through the grass. She could see nothing but dark shadows surrounding her. Out there among the whispering branches of the willows and jagged arms of the pines, the renegade McGilvey waited. She shivered, thinking of what a hunted thief like him would do if he caught her. But to do that he'd have to kill Devon. *Devon.* She could see him, lying bleeding, silent in death, that infuriating smile forever erased from his handsome face. *No, it couldn't happen!* She clutched the knife tightly and listened.

Devon worked his way in a circle and met Pig Sticker in the willow thicket. "He doubled back on us, damn his crafty soul," Devon whispered. "How many men do you think he's brought with him? We counted three riding with the mules."

"One would wait with the prize, the others come to kill us," the Muskogee said.

"That shot came from behind me."

Pig Sticker's lips curved grimly. "The one who fired it will not do so again." He showed Devon a Brown Bess musket. "Here is his weapon. I have spiked it."

Devon grinned and nodded. "We'll use knives in the darkness. I'm going to circle around the marsh grasses toward those trees to the east. You see if you can find where his mules are hidden. I imagine they're not all that far from here, probably due west by the riverbank."

"If I can set the mules to braying, that will flush our quarry quickly. He will not endanger his prize," Pig Sticker said, and was gone in an instant.

Devon moved stealthily through the darkness, listening. After a few moments he heard it. The soft squish of a man's large, moccasined foot stealing across the marshy ground. Devon drew closer until he sighted his prey, a big brutish man in buckskins with another Brown Bess clutched, primed and ready to fire, in his meaty fists.

What does the fool think he can hit in this darkness? He moved closer again, getting behind the renegade's back. Then he sprang up, but McGilvey's accomplice was as fast as a striking rattler and turned just as Devon jumped toward him. His gun was too cumbersome to use in such close quarters. When he tried to raise it, Devon kicked it away, then slashed wickedly across his foe's arm. Instantly, the renegade produced a knife of his own and the two adversaries circled each other in a dance of death. They thrust and parried, each scoring minor nicks on the other. Just as Devon feinted to the left and moved in to the right for the final blow, McGilvey's voice thundered out, distracting his concentration.

"I got yer woman, Blackthorne!"

McGilvey's man took advantage of the split second's distraction and sent his blade plunging into Devon's side, but Devon, too, was very fast. He managed to twist to the left just enough so the blow did not disembowel him, yet the tear in his side was agonizing. Not wasting an instant, Devon doubled over as if mortally wounded, but then brought home his blade in a killing zig-zag up the man's belly beneath his ribs.

"I'll kill 'er real slow, Blackthorne, then scalp all this yeller hair."

As the second renegade crumpled lifelessly to the ground, Devon turned and moved through the trees toward the sound of McGilvey's taunting voice. "I'm coming, you son of a bitch! Best you look to your own scalp."

Barbara struggled in the renegade's grasp, but he only laughed and shook her like a rag doll. She still had the skinning knife hidden in her skirt, but instinctively knew that if she tried to use it now, he would quickly overpower her. She had been a fool to leave the brush where Devon had told her to hide. *Wait, wait for Devon*, she repeated to herself as she heard his voice echo in the night. When he entered the clearing by the campfire, she gasped in horror. He was covered with blood!

Devon gritted his teeth against the pain and fought off waves of dizziness. He had bled a lot running to reach Barbara. "You've lost all your men, McGilvey. Now that Pig Sticker and I've dealt with them, I'll do for you."

The big, red-haired brute spat in the dust, revealing blackened teeth. One front tooth was missing. His yellow eyes narrowed with malice as he took in Blackthorne's injured side. With a grating laugh, he shoved Barbara roughly to the ground. "I can finish you real easy, half-breed. Then I'll have yer woman. Think on it while you die."

He lunged at Devon with his big knife gleaming in an arc of death. It narrowly missed the wounded man, whose reflexes were greatly slowed. The two men closed, and each seized the knife hand of the other, locking themselves in a wrestling contest that could end only one way. Devon felt his strength ebbing, his grip loosening on McGilvey's hand.

Barbara scrambled to her feet as they began their struggle. When McGilvey's back turned to her, she raised her knife and plunged it with all her strength into his back. He let out an oath of surprise and pain as he jerked around to face her. She quickly backed out of his reach.

"I'll kill you for this, real slow," McGilvey snarled, advancing toward her.

"McGilvey, you're a dead man," Devon cried out, desperate to distract the renegade. A Muskogee war cry rent the night air at that moment and McGilvey quickly forgot about Devon and Barbara. Clutching his left shoulder, where Barbara's blade was still embedded in his back, he shambled off into the darkness.

The last thing Devon heard before everything faded to black was Barbara's scream.

Chapter Twelve

"For the love of God, do something! He's bleeding to death," Barbara cried as Pig Sticker ran toward them. She had Devon's head cradled in her lap and was struggling ineffectually to stanch the blood flowing from his side.

The Muskogee glanced to where McGilvey had vanished into the trees, then knelt beside his fallen kinsman. Quickly he removed his knife from its sheath and reached for her tattered petticoats. "Cut for wrapping wound," he said in serviceable English.

Barbara at once obeyed him, pulling the tapes loose and then yanking one of her few remaining overskirts from her waist, being careful not to disturb Devon any more than necessary. In minutes, they had packed the ugly gash with cloth and wrapped it tightly to slow the bleeding.

"I return. Wait with my cousin."

As he quickly ran from the campsite, Barbara marveled that all along he had been able to speak

English and never said a word. Then she remembered some of her scathing insults and reddened in mortification. Good God, he could scalp her if the fancy took him!

When Pig Sticker returned, it was obvious that he harbored no ill will toward Barbara. In fact, although she did not realize it, he was most impressed that she had saved Devon's life by using the skinning knife at the critical time. He had secured the stolen trade goods they had been sent to retrieve and led the string of mules into camp, along with their horses. Barbara sat bathing Dev's face with cool water as Pig Sticker quickly and efficiently rigged a deer-hide sling between two mules. She helped him lift Devon onto the conveyance, and they set off toward a village which he assured her was only a day's ride away.

Traveling at night was very slow going, but the mules were surefooted and they had covered some ground by dawn. Before the sun rose, the Indian stopped and poured some of the vile libation he was accustomed to drink into a wooden cup. After performing the same disgusting ritual she'd witnessed the preceding day, he checked Devon and then remounted, ready to continue their journey.

Barbara was frantic with fear for Devon, and Pig Sticker was her only hope to help the wounded man. She had to understand this savage. "Why do you do that—drink that black brew that makes you sick?" He looked at her with fathomless black eyes, his face utterly devoid of expression. For a moment she feared he would not answer. Then he replied.

"Black drink makes me pure. Makes a warrior strong, not sick. Same way washing. White men do not wash in water. Weak, dirty."

Recalling Devon's comments to her about her filth-encrusted odor, she reddened with embarrassment. Changing the subject, she asked, "How long until we reach this village?"

"Soon," was the laconic reply.

He was equally noncommittal about Devon's condition. With increasing horror, Barbara watched the red stain soak through the bandage. The terrifying night replayed over and over in her mind as they crossed the flat, seemingly trackless land. She could still smell McGilvey's fetid breath, feel his big, bruising hands on her body, hear him cry out to Devon, "I got yer woman, Blackthorne." She looked down at Devon Blackthorne's still face, pale in spite of his swarthy skin. His woman? She could still feel the heady, scorching touch of his hands as he rubbed oil into her skin so intimately. What would happen to her if he died?

No, you can't die! I shan't allow it! He had come running to save her, leaving a trail of his own blood as he did so, taunting and attacking that huge brute McGilvey, even though he was in no condition to withstand any combat. What she would have given at that moment for one insolent leer or wink from his disturbing dark eyes!

The *Idalwa*, as Pig Sticker called the village, was a town of sizeable proportions, set out along the banks of a narrow but deep stream. The outskirts were filled with large mud-plaster buildings erected on wooden frames. Many were two stories high and had neat wood-shingled roofs. The arrangements seemed rather helter-skelter to Barbara as they rode through the twisting pathways between garden plots and buildings. Some structures were homes, some seemingly storage warehouses filled with deer hides and implements.

The people were overjoyed when they sighted the caravan of mules laden with trade goods, but became grave when they saw Devon. Barbara endured the curious stares of round-eyed children, all innocent of clothing in the summer heat. The women wore full calico skirts and brightly colored men's shirts, many of them bound at the waist with plaid sashes. The men were usually far less decently covered, many wearing only scandalous red breechclouts. Everyone was adorned with the disfiguring earrings that elongated their lobes, as well as beaded headbands, necklaces, bracelets, and belts.

Their open curiosity about the strange, bed-raggled-looking Englishwoman was neither hostile nor friendly. Barbara tried not to stare at the men's painted and tattooed bodies and simply looked straight ahead, her chin high and her back straight. *I'll show them what an Englishwoman is made of!*

The crowd parted to allow them to move toward the center of the village, where an immense round-domed building stood. To one side of it, what looked like a public square of some sort was surrounded by tiered and roofed seats on all four sides. A fire, tended by several young boys, burned in the center of the open area.

Pig Sticker reined in by the round structure and dismounted. A small delegation of elderly men, covered with tattoos and draped with ceremonial blankets, emerged from the entrance of the building and stood, waiting for Pig Sticker to approach. A rapid exchange took place in their language, with frequent gestures to Devon and to her. Barbara desperately wanted to know what Pig Sticker was saying about her. Then Devon moaned and began to twist his body in pain. At once she dismounted and went to him, placing her hand on his head.

"Quiet, Dev, quiet. You'll make the bleeding worse. We've brought you to a Creek village. They'll help you." *If only they can!*

After a few moments, one of the elderly men, whose face was as brown and wizened as a London mail pouch, walked to her and spoke in English.

"I am Kills the Bear of Wind Clan. Welcome to village. We take care of brother, Golden Eagle, who you call Devon Blackthorne. His mother of our clan. Is honor have him return here. We make strong medicine, heal him." He gestured, and two young men approached and unfastened the sling holding Devon, then began to carry him away.

"Where are you taking him?" She started to follow, but Kills the Bear placed a surprisingly strong hand on her arm.

"He be safe. Strong medicine. You rest now, eat. My woman take care for you." Again he had but to raise his hand and several young women, led by one older one, approached, chattering excitedly. Two of the younger women smiled shyly at her, but the third glared with sullen black eyes. The older woman, whom Kills the Bear introduced as his chief wife, Mocking Bird, nodded gravely and then led the way to a large, mud-plastered building.

Barbara swallowed the nervous lump in her throat and entered the rude dwelling as if it were the Tower of London. They climbed a sturdy ladder to the second floor, which was surprisingly spacious, orderly, and clean. Simple pallets of animal hides lay around the perimeter, and a variety of clay vessels and iron utensils were placed in one corner. Barbara took a seat as Mocking Bird directed her.

One of the friendly younger women diffidently touched Barbara's loose hair, obviously enthralled with its color. The Englishwoman smiled at the child, for surely the girl was barely past puberty.

"She thinks your hair is magic," the older one with venomous eyes said in perfect English. Her voice was as cold as her expression.

"Blond hair is common among my people, not magic," Barbara replied, wondering where the strikingly handsome female had learned to speak so well.

"Devon has golden hair. That is how he received his name, Golden Eagle. He belongs to me, skinny white woman. Do not think he will stay with you."

Barbara smiled coldly. "So that is how you learned English. Do not threaten me. I've learned to fight for my survival."

The hateful woman returned Barbara's hard-edged stare for a moment, then stood up gracefully and left the room. Mocking Bird ignored her departure and silently set a bowl of what looked like porridge in front of Barbara, along with a flat dish filled with griddle cakes coated in honey and some other clear, pungent substance. There were no utensils for handling the food. At first Barbara hesitated, but it was obvious that they expected the guest of honor to partake first.

She moved her hand toward the bowl and received a nod of approval from Mocking Bird. Cupping her fingers together, she scooped up a small amount of the sticky gruel and lifted it to her mouth. It tasted bland and starchy, but she was starving. After making a thorough mess of her hands and mouth, she eyed the cakes. Perhaps they had a bit more flavor? She tried one, breaking off a piece and sopping up the thick liquid from the platter. A most peculiar combination of suet and honey masked the taste of the crisp patty. She ate another.

As soon as Barbara had sampled all the foods laid out, including the later addition of some dried meat of unknown origin, the others all joined her. It seemed that her table manners were acceptable, for everyone ate with their hands and then licked their fingers by way of cleaning them.

"Now, you take bath. We bring clean clothes. Come." The chief wife of Kills the Bear also spoke English when she felt the need.

"Please, before anything else, I would like to see Devon. You've been most kind, but—"

"Golden Eagle be fine. You see soon. Come."

The old woman did not look like one to be crossed. Barbara decided to bide her time. Biting her tongue, she nodded.

Fully expecting Barbara to do her bidding, the woman began to descend the ladder. The two younger girls waited politely until their guest had followed, then did the same. They wended their way through the village to the river and followed it downstream to where a dense stand of willows dropped their leafy branches as a shield for modesty.

"Thank heaven I won't have to strip mother-naked in front of every man in the place," she muttered to herself as the girls laughingly pulled Devon's shirt and her much-abused skirts from her body. Just as she stood completely naked, surrounded by her companions, who were now busily shedding their own garments, the tall, hateful woman who claimed Devon reappeared.

Wrinkling her nose, she said, "You smell like all the English. I do not know why Devon kept you."

Mocking Bird said something in their language to the girl and she argued back briefly, then left in a huff, ostensibly on some errand.

Barbara allowed herself to be led to the water's edge, but when the two girls jumped in and began to paddle about like playful otters, she stopped short. "I cannot swim." She appealed to Mocking Bird.

"Not deep. You tall. Stand up." She commanded the girls to demonstrate. They quickly touched bottom. The water just off the bank was well over three feet deep, but safe enough—if she didn't lose her footing. Recalling her earlier brushes with watery death and how Devon had saved her life, she hurried on with the bath, praying that he was indeed safe and she'd be allowed to see him soon.

The girls used a spicy soap, obviously traded from the English. Although of inferior quality to what she was wont to use, it felt heavenly to have her hair and body sudsed and rinsed, then rubbed dry, even with coarse cotton cloth. As they worked, the girls repeatedly giggled and made remarks that seemed to be comparing the pallor of her skin to the duskiness of theirs, taking special notice of the pale gold curls at the apex of her thighs. She endured the innocent laughter with as much dignity as possible, until her nemesis returned and gave her body an insulting inspection.

"Your skin is as ugly as the underbelly of a fish!" She threw the bundle of clothes into Mocking Bird's arms and stalked off. Suddenly Barbara was aware that she had moved toward the bank, her hands fisted.

The old woman had the first hint of a smile playing about her lips as she watched the Englishwoman. "You, Panther Woman same size. These fit you."

So she was being given Panther Woman's clothes. No wonder the hateful creature had argued with Mocking Bird! Barbara allowed the girls to dress her. They weren't exactly ladies-in-waiting to Queen Charlotte, but they did an adequate job. The shirt was of deep blue cotton, a shade that flattered her eyes; the bright green printed skirt was crisp and cool, falling to just below her knees. They laced soft buckskin boots on her feet. She touched the silver chain belt they had placed snugly about her waist and wished for a mirror. *Lud, I've been deprived of civilization for too long if I feel glamorous in fishwife's clothes!* But she did.

The worst part was untangling her hair with a comb made of fish bones. Then the young women braided it in a long, fat plait down her back and even offered her some beaded copper jewelry.

"Now, may I please go to Devon?" she asked Mocking Bird.

The old woman grunted and walked toward the village. Barbara followed. When they entered a large building, it took a moment for her eyes to grow accustomed to the dim light, for the day was growing late and there were only a few high, narrow windows. Devon lay on a pallet at one side of the rectangular room. He had been stripped of all his clothing and lay with only a light piece of cotton cloth about his lower body. A tall, emaciated man with a craggy, cadaverous face leaned over him. Various pots and other implements sat scattered at his bedside.

She walked to the pallet and knelt beside Devon, her hand reaching out to stroke his brow. It was warm, but did not feel fevered. She looked up at the medicine man, whose homely countenance radiated kindness.

He smiled. "The Breath Master will not claim this one yet. He is a strong young eagle."

"Barbara?" Devon opened his eyes.

"How did you know—"

"I heard English and I felt your touch," he whispered, turning his head toward her. He winced as he raised his hand and grasped hers.

"Don't reopen the wound." She leaned over him, holding his hand fast but placing it on his chest. "Does it hurt terribly?"

He grinned. "I never had a knife slash that hurt wonderfully, but it's not deep. I just passed out from weakness—lost too much blood."

She looked at him with a puzzled expression on her face. "Then why do physicians bleed ill or injured people?"

Dev's chuckle broke off into a slight croak. "Because, your ladyship, they don't know any better!"

"White medicine men often do foolish things," the Muskogee healer added, not unkindly. "All this eagle needs now is to regain his strength. Then he will be fine."

Barbara studied his weathered face. He, too, was part white, although the blood obviously ran thinner than Dev's.

Answering her unspoken question, Devon said, "This is Tall Crane, my mother's brother, who has married a woman of the Bear Clan from this village."

"Like my sister Charity, I too grew up with our father and learned white ways. I am called Nathaniel McKinny among your people."

Barbara searched for some resemblance between the blunt features of Nathaniel and the chiseled handsomeness of Devon. Other than their warm brown eyes, she could see none, but she instinctively felt a liking for this soft-spoken man. "I am honored to make your acquaintance, Mr. McKinney."

"I have forsaken most white ways. Please call me Tall Crane, for I am Muskogee now."

He looked from her to Devon with sad, knowing eyes, then said to Barbara, "You are English born, of a noble family, are you not?"

"Yes. My brother is the Baron of Rushcroft. He's in Savannah. I was coming to visit him when my ship was wrecked."

"So Golden Eagle has told me." He sensed the attraction between the two young people from such diverse backgrounds. "Perhaps it would be best if I spoke with Kills the Bear. He would be pleased to send an escort with you and see you safely to Savannah."

"No." Devon's voice was surprisingly strong. "I'll be able to take her myself in a short while."

This was her chance for escape. She could be safely with Monty in a few days . . . but then she would never see Devon Blackthorne again. Only two days ago, that would have been her dearest wish. Now she was not at all so certain. She shook her head and said softly, "No, I shall stay and tend Devon. He's already pledged to take me to Savannah now that his mission has been accomplished."

"Better send that escort with the pack mules up to the Altamaha. The *micco* there is waiting for his muskets and rum."

Seeing the defiance in his nephew's eyes, Tall Crane sighed and nodded. "It shall be as you both wish." He rose with surprising grace for a man of such lanky proportions. "I will send women with food for you."

Barbara was uncertain of what the exchange had meant. "Does your uncle dislike me because I'm English?"

"No, not at all. He just knows what would happen if a half-breed like me were to overreach himself," he replied.

"I see," she said, her cheeks flushed as she realized that Devon was not the only one reaching for the unattainable.

"I should send you away right now. You saved my life. McGilvey would've made short work of me." His face was troubled, but still he did not relinquish her hand. The bile rose in his throat when he remembered the filthy brute's hands on *his* beautiful Lady Barbara. *I must stop this!*

She stroked his cheek and smiled. "And you saved my life—twice. As I reckon it, that still leaves a balance owed in my tally book. I'll stay, Devon Blackthorne."

Their eyes locked and they simply stared at each other in silence for a moment. Then a shadow fell across the door, and an angry hiss of breath broke the spell.

"I have brought food for you, Devon. Send her away so I may tend you." Panther Woman knelt, turning her back on Barbara, and set down a tray of stiffly woven cane. "I have sofky and fresh roast venison—even my mother's freshly baked ash cakes."

"You've been most hospitable, Panther Woman, but I shall see that Devon eats his meal," Barbara said in that silky, oh-so English voice that warned Devon of an impending volcanic eruption.

The handsome Muskogee woman turned with pure loathing in her eyes for the tall, regal yellow-hair. "You are the one who will go, else I will—"

"Don't you threaten me, you bloody bitch. I just put a skinning knife through a man's back, and he was twice your size. I'll make short work of you."

Devon fought the urge to laugh, knowing it would not only hurt like hell, but would also infuriate the two seething women. "Panther Woman, you do me great kindness by bringing this food, but I am honor-bound to keep this white woman under my protection, for she has saved my life. Please leave the food and I will eat."

"Devon—"

"Please." His voice was soft but firm.

The woman rose with a furious swish of skirts and glared down at Barbara, then quit the room.

Barbara turned frosty blue eyes on his guileless face. "You've been her lover, haven't you?"

He did chuckle now, then groaned. "And what if I have? Muskogee women are under no restraints to maintain their chastity before marriage. I did no dishonor to her."

"But doubtless a great honor to you, bedding every wench in the miserable colony!" *What am I doing! Acting like a jealous shrew!* She positively hated the slow smile that insinuated its way across his face. "Don't you dare smirk at me, Devon Blackthorne! It's ill repayment for saving your miserable life."

He creased his brow in a frown. "Speaking of ill repayments, I seem to recall the matter of two fat rabbits you were to roast for us—and ended up eating yourself."

"They weren't fat at all and I only ate one—or rather, part of one . . . all right, the best part of one. You'd been such an insufferable beast, I scarcely felt inclined to feed you."

"Are you inclined now?" His eyes had lost all traces of humor. Something else glowed in their rich brown depths.

She began to fuss with the food. Then she saw a wooden spoon on the tray and sputtered. "They made me eat with my fingers!"

He shrugged, then winced. "That's the usual and reasonable way, but those of us raised among the whites have grown to prefer using utensils."

When he struggled to sit up, she helped him, rolling up several heavy blankets behind his back to serve as a support. He watched her work, inhaling the fragrance of lavender soap and enjoying the way the simple cotton shirt and skirt flattered her voluptuous curves. "I like the dress, your ladyship," he said softly.

She almost dropped the spoon, then recovered. "Then you should see me all tricked out in a ballgown with my hair powdered and patches upon my face."

He took a lock of hair between his fingers and watched the light glisten as he rubbed it. "Never powder such glowing hair—it's like moonbeams and sunlight melded together."

"You'd best eat and regain your strength," she choked out, more disturbed by his eloquent compliment than by his scathing mockery.

"Yes, I will need my strength," he replied softly.

In the following days, Devon mended with amazing rapidity. Barbara spent most of each day tending him and warding off Panther Woman, who gave her furious looks and hissed insults at every opportunity.

Oddly enough, she found herself beginning to enjoy living in a Muskogee village. She had always been an adventurous child, curious and daring. The Indians were fascinating, not at all the stupid and filthy savages spoken of with shudders of distaste in London drawing rooms.

One morning Devon was amazed to find the imperious Lady Barbara with Mocking Bird and her daughters grinding corn in a big hollowed-out log. She had her magically beautiful hair braided, but small curly tendrils escaped about her face. As she worked in the warm morning sun, she brushed at the sweat-dampened curls and continued doggedly with her task.

He walked around the garden beside Tall Crane's house and approached her from behind. "I see you're helping the women prepare for the Green Corn Festival."

She nearly dropped the big wooden pestle she was so clumsily wielding. Rather sheepishly, she smiled at Devon. "Actually I only took on this task in a fit of pique when Panther Woman said I was useless and lazy. Everyone else is working so hard. . . ."

She looked around the scattered homes and garden plots. Women were grinding corn, harvesting their gardens, and cleaning their houses while men butchered and skinned freshly killed deer.

"The Muskogee year begins with the harvest of new corn. It's a special religious festival, a time of atonement for the Muskogee. People renew their lives and begin again. All crimes but murder are forgiven, and no one may harbor a grudge against his fellow," Devon explained.

"What a lovely idea. It would be so good to have all people everywhere end wars and hatreds and begin anew."

"Then you and your brother would return to England," he said softly.

"Perhaps. And what of you? Will you stay with the King's Rangers or return to live with your mother's people when the war ends?"

"I'm not especially good at following orders. I imagine that once my duty's discharged, I'll return to being a trader, moving between the settlements and the Muskogee towns."

"Does Panther Woman fit into your plans, Devon?" What made her ask that?

He smiled that sunny, boyish grin she had grown so fond of. "Panther Woman's plans are her own, not mine. We were lovers once, but I told her before that I'd never wed her."

"Won't you get in trouble with Tall Crane for taking such liberties with his daughter?" She strove for a lightness in her voice that she did not feel.

"No. She is not his daughter, else she'd be my cousin, and such a liaison is considered incest by the Muskogee. She was born to his wife before they wed, and no biological father claims her. Anyway, it's the maternal uncle or brother, not her father, who settles any matters of marriage."

"You say that so lightly, as if bastardy was no disgrace at all."

"If a woman has lovers before she's wed, having a child is no disgrace for her or the babe. Only after marriage are both husband and wife expected to be faithful. The punishments for adultery are very rigorous."

Barbara considered the irony of his words. "'Tis just the opposite among my kind. A woman must be as pure as new-fallen snow on her wedding night, but once deflowered, she can sleep about as much as she's inclined. So can her husband." A wistful look came over her face. "My parents couldn't abide each other. Mother was relieved when Father died, although she didn't wait for his death before taking a succession of lovers. What a world turned upside down."

Devon could sense the hurt behind her words. "You had a lonely childhood, didn't you?"

She raised the pestle and ground down with great force. "Oh, Monty and I had dozens of nannies and tutors. We were never alone."

"But you had no parents."

Her shoulders slumped and she turned to him, feeling suddenly an absurd need to reveal her innermost feelings. "Do you know why I was exiled to Savannah? I'd taken my mother's lover away from her." At the look of incredulity on his face, she added, "Not that I ever bedded Darth. The idea makes me want to consume a gallon of that black drink and purge myself."

"You led him on just to spite her," he said with dawning comprehension.

"That was only one of my sins. I ran up thousands at the gaming tables and traveled with altogether too fast a crowd for an unmarried female, even one of my class. I'm reckless and spoiled, Devon." She said it like a dare.

He touched her defiant chin and looked into her brilliant blue eyes. "Since we met, I've noticed your penchant for—shall we say, vengeful behavior from time to time." A light danced in his eyes, but the longer they stood there in the center of the bustling village, the more everything else receded, until he felt as if he and Barbara were the last people on earth.

A youth with a chunky ball and stick came dashing by them, nearly knocking Devon over in his haste to get to the playing field. He bowed apologetically, and Devon dismissed him with a fond smile and a pat on the back. The spell was broken.

"It's afternoon. Everyone will finish their chores for the day and go to the field to watch the game."

"I've heard the yelling and cheering."

He smiled. "And you're curious." He took the pestle from her and leaned it against the edge of the log. "Let's go watch the Muskogee's favorite pastime . . . well, their second favorite pastime," he added with a wink.

Barbara Caruthers actually found herself giggling as they set out across the village square toward a big open field with earthworks raised on three sides.

Two H-shaped posts stood at opposite ends of the field, and several dozen young men milled about between them, eager to begin.

When they climbed the steep, artificially created hillock, Devon paused for a moment to catch his breath. Barbara wrapped her arm about his waist and helped him the rest of the way.

"Are you certain you're not overdoing?" she asked dubiously.

"An English lady wielding a sofky pestle in the noon heat questions me? Best take care of yourself."

"I haven't had my side slashed open by a madman. Besides we Caruthers are a tough lot."

They watched the wild and fast game, cheering each time the Wind Clan's players knocked the small deerskin-covered ball through the posts. Each player was armed with two long sticks with small loops on one end. With one stick they carried and batted the ball; with the other they fended off their opponents.

Devon had loved to participate in the no-holds-barred game as a youth, but now he wondered if the fierce, bloody competition might shock Barbara's sensibilities. Then he recalled his father describing the English fondness for cockfights and bear-baiting. At least in chunky, it was the men who voluntarily played who were injured, not innocent animals. When she stood up with face flushed and began to yell wildly with the rest of the Wind Clan spectators, he was delighted. What a magnificent woman she was.

Watching Devon and Barbara as the days passed, Tall Crane became increasingly disturbed. Panther Woman had told him what was happening, but she was furiously jealous and spiteful. At first he'd dismissed her reports, thinking she was bitter because Devon chose not to wed her. Now he feared she was right. Devon Blackthorne was falling in love with an English noblewoman, a woman far beyond his reach. Only pain lay ahead for him if he pursued his present course. Should he have a talk with his nephew before the matter progressed any further?

Chapter Thirteen

They moved away from the crowd of laughing, chattering Muskogee who had watched the game, and wandered aimlessly toward the twisting course of the river. Soon they were far from the noise and confusion of the village.

"You're mending quite well," Barbara said.

Devon bent down and scooped up a handful of smooth stones, skipping them effortlessly across the surface of the slow-moving stream.

He flashed her a smile. "I had such a fine nurse, soon I'll be ready to play in the chunky games myself."

"I don't think I'd enjoy that—seeing you bruised and blackened. Those players are too rough."

"I've managed to stay intact until now, except for a few scars—and they didn't come from playing chunky," he added grimly.

"Did you spend much time in these villages when you were growing up?" His past was an intriguing mystery to her. Devon Blackthorne was educated, yet fully at home among the Indians.

"I grew up in two worlds." His dark eyes became haunted, his expression bleak. "My father's first wife was from a very proper Virginia family. Her father and his arranged the match, and soon Andrew was born."

"But they weren't happy." Barbara knew all too well about arranged marriages.

"They hated each other from all I can gather. She wanted to return to Williamsburg, and her mother said Georgia was a wilderness full of savages. She died in a few years, during a diphtheria epidemic."

"And then your father met your mother." It sounded exotic and romantic to her.

His expression was still bleak. "No, not right away. He was lonely and had quit his wife's bed as soon as their heir was guaranteed. I've only heard whispered gossip, rumors, that he was infatuated with his brother's wife, Lady Anne, I believe her name was. It was a very long time ago."

"Did it create a rift in your family? Was that what drove your father to live among the Indians?"

"He'd already been trading with the Muskogee. He and Uncle Robert had quite a profitable partnership in their youth. After my father's wife died, he and Robert must have come to blows over Robert's wife. They agreed he'd be better off living as far away from Blackthorne Hill as possible. He went to a large village, Coweta, where a half-caste woman whose father had educated her was teaching Muskogee children to read and write English."

"Your mother."

"Her name is Charity." A flash of warmth lit his eyes. "She healed his bitterness and eased his loneliness. They were married, and he brought her back to Savannah." His expression darkened again. "It was a mistake."

"The colonists don't approve of intermarriage with Indians," she said softly, understanding.

He scoffed. "That's putting it mildly. My half brother Andrew's mother came from a fine old Virginia family. They were aghast. So was Uncle Robert. Everyone treated my mother as if she were a leper. There were no social invitations. And then I was born. At first my parents were happy, but when they tried to hire tutors for me, no one would teach a dirty half-breed."

Barbara put her hand on his arm. "You must've had a sad childhood."

He shrugged in that familiar defiant way. "We visited my mother's people a lot when I was growing up. They accepted me, and there was always my cousin Quint. He and I sneaked away to meet on his father's estate often. Uncle Robert caned him for playing with me more than once.

"When it became obvious that I could pass for white with my blond hair, they sent me north to Philadelphia to complete my education. Quint was already there. We'd been close ever since we were children, far closer than Andrew and I could ever hope to be. Quint stayed in school to graduate, while I, I'm afraid, was not so diligent a pupil. After a couple of years, I came home."

"Did you miss Georgia?"

"Yes, but more than that, my father's health was failing and I knew how lonely it was for my mother, surrounded by whites who were polite only when they had to be.

"By the time I returned, my father had let his trading business go deeply into debt. Andrew tried to take over, but the two of them fought and matters only grew worse. Then father died, and Andrew inherited everything."

"Georgia has entail laws just as England does?" she asked.

"Yes. Mama and I always knew Andrew would get all my father's estates, but Papa had put aside some business investments to provide for Mama and held the Crown trading appointment for me."

"It isn't fair," Barbara said. "God, how I've hated the whole bloody system all my life." She laughed hollowly. "For all their babble about the rights of men, the colonials are just as class-ridden and hypocritical as the English nobility."

His expression softened. "Better watch out. You'll become a revolutionary. Then I'd have to shoot you, 'pon my honor as a King's Ranger."

They stopped now, alone in the silence except for the hum of insects and the rippling sound of the river. Their eyes locked and they stared, each powerless to break the spell.

Then Barbara said softly, "Isn't there something you'd much rather do than shoot me, Dev?" She'd meant it to be a teasing retort, but somehow it did not come out that way. *I want him to kiss me!*

You know there is! His hand touched her face, stroking it with a whisper-soft caress as his lips drew nearer hers. "This is madness, your ladyship," he said hoarsely, just before his mouth claimed hers.

Barbara had been kissed often since her "come-out"—by bumbling boys and lecherous older men. Mostly she'd found it amusing, occasionally repellent. Nothing prepared her for the jolt of breathless pleasure when Devon's lips brushed hers. Then he deepened the kiss, slanting his mouth over hers and drawing her tightly against his chest, encircling her waist with his arm. She felt one lock of straight gold hair brush her cheek. Her fingers touched it, then combed through the thick coarse hair, burrowing deep to his scalp as she pulled him down and the kiss grew fierce, passionate.

Devon let his tongue probe the seam of her lips. She quickly opened for him, welcoming him into the hot, sweet interior of her mouth. He could feel her breasts pressing against his chest, feel both their hearts thudding like a herd of galloping horses.

A twig cracked sharply, deliberately broken. It took a moment for the disrupting noise to register in Devon's passion-drugged mind. Unwillingly, he dragged his mouth free of Barbara's and looked up, holding her protectively in his arms. Tall Crane stood beside a large cypress tree, discreetly clearing his throat and looking with intent interest at a dragonfly lighting on a wildflower.

When Devon broke the kiss, Barbara felt bereft, her senses clamoring for more. Then she felt him stiffen and look past her. She turned in his arms and saw his uncle. When Devon gently set her away from him, she blushed like a green schoolgirl caught trysting with her first beau. The reproach she saw in Tall Crane's eyes brought a sudden flare of anger. Who was he—from a tribe where premarital promiscuity was allowed—to make her feel guilty?

"I would speak with my nephew in private, if you do not mind, my lady?" Tall Crane said, as politely as if they were in an English drawing room.

Her cheeks aflame, she dared to raise her eyes to meet Dev's. He seemed to hesitate for an instant, then let his hand fall to his side and nodded to her. "Please, return to the village. I'll be along shortly."

Barbara stiffened her spine and stepped regally past Tall Crane, retracing her path without a backward glance.

"She is angry with us," Tall Crane said.

Devon smiled ruefully. "She's angry with me for dismissing her like that." Although he was certain what his uncle was going to say, he had to ask, "What do you wish to speak of?"

"I have been observing you and the Lady Barbara for many days now, and my heart is troubled," the older man said gravely. "She is not only a white woman, but a titled English noblewoman. Her family will not allow you to wed her."

"I doubt Barbara would consent to wed me even if I were to ask her," Devon replied stiffly. "I know well enough the gulf between a half-breed and the white world."

"And yet you let this attraction grow . . . on both your parts. It can only end badly, Golden Eagle. You cannot live in her world, nor she in yours. Send her back to her own kind. I can have an escort of warriors ready at first light."

"No." Devon answered too quickly, then added, "I'll take her to her brother in Savannah in a few days. I'm responsible for her being here, and she saved my life. I'm almost fully recovered from the knife slash. I know my duty, Uncle, and I'll do it."

Over the next two days, Devon avoided Barbara as much as he could, leaving her with Mocking Bird and her daughters while he helped several of the men of his clan construct a two-story storage house. It was hot, strenuous labor, and Barbara feared he might reopen his wound, but he seemed to grow stronger each day.

She relived the magic of that kiss every sleeping and waking hour, wondering what might have happened if Tall Crane had not interrupted them. She knew Devon was avoiding her because of the old man's admonition. Why did he have to meddle in something that did not concern him? Soon it would be time for her to go to Savannah. Would she ever see Dev again?

Lady Barbara Caruthers was no stranger to cold reality. She had always known her future would be a marriage much like that of her parents. She and Monty had their duty, after all. *But why can't this be one small moment in time for me?* It was not fair. Life had never been fair to her or to Dev.

As she knelt in the garden plot pulling weeds, she watched Dev work, binding saplings for the frame of the building. She decided that just once, she would seize a bit of happiness for herself.

When the day's labor was done in mid-afternoon, most of the Indians ate their main meal and adjourned to the chunky field, but it was always Dev's habit to bathe when he'd finished working. She had observed him head to the river with soap and clean clothes the past several days. That afternoon, she followed him at a distance as he went far upriver, where no one would interrupt him. When she heard him splashing in the cool water, she quickly slipped behind the leafy bough of a willow and stripped off her own clothes.

The riverbed was secluded, shrouded with a canopy of tall willows. Cattails and other marsh grasses formed a thick curtain at the river's edge. She chose a spot just around the bend in the river and slid into the shallow water where she could perform her hasty toilette. The water felt heavenly after her strenuous labor in the garden. Indeed, she had grown as accustomed to daily bathing as a Muskogee maiden! After rinsing her long, pale hair, she flung the mane back and climbed from the water. Soaking wet in the midday warmth, she walked on noiseless feet across the mossy bank to where Dev was swimming.

Barbara watched him cut cleanly through the water, then reach the shallows and stand waist-deep in the current. The sun shone with blazing brilliance on his golden hair and deeply bronzed skin. Every droplet of water seemed to cling, glistening like silver on the swell of his muscles. Beads of water were trapped in the dark gold pelt of hair on his chest. She longed to bury her hands in the wet, springy mat.

He walked slowly from the water, as if preoccupied. This time she did not avert her eyes as his splendidly naked body drew close, but studied the beauty of his virility, enthralled. Her eyes traveled down the fascinating pattern of his body hair from his chest to where it narrowed in an arrowlike descent across his hard belly, then bloomed around his male parts. The slash across his waist was only a dull pinkish scar now.

Devon felt her eyes on him and sensed her presence just before he stepped out of the shallows. He stood frozen for a moment. "How long have you been here?" he asked in a strangled voice, unable to hide his body's immediate response to her. God above, she was wet from bathing. The thin strip of white cotton thrown carelessly about her lush curves concealed nothing!

Barbara did not answer him but walked silently to the water's edge, praying her courage would not desert her. She could see visible proof of his desire as he stood motionless, his hands clenched in fists at his sides. Taking a deep breath, she slid the cloth away and tossed it on the ground, then set one foot in the water.

"Don't," he pleaded hoarsely.

She ignored his command and drew closer, watching the look of tortured longing that blanched his swarthy face until it was almost pale. When she was within two feet of him, she paused, feeling the heat of their bodies calling one to the other. She watched for a moment, then said, "Please, Dev."

"This is wrong. You belong in England, in a fine mansion, surrounded by servants, not here in the wilderness." The words came out in a rush, raw and breathless. "You're a lady, you'll marry a man with a title, a rich Englishman—"

"Most probably so," she said with quiet sadness in her voice, "but first . . . first, Dev, I want what every Muskogee woman has the right to have. Is that so terrible? To want one time just for me?" *For love?*

With an oath, he reached out and crushed her in his arms, his mouth coming down on hers in a sweet, savage kiss. She melted into him, molding her wet, naked flesh to his while her hands glided over his shoulders and slid down his back, her palms flat, her fingernails biting into his muscles.

Devon trailed his mouth hungrily down her throat
and buried his face against her shoulder while one
hand found the curve of her breast. Then he moved
his head lower, capturing one pale pink nipple in his
mouth. He felt a thrill of desire race through him
when she keened out his name and arched against
his lips, offering herself to him. His mouth moved
to the other breast, repeating the soft suckling. He
cupped the milky globes in his hands, marveling at
their perfection—so lush, yet at the same time so
delicate.

Her eyes were glazed with passion as she felt his
hands on her breasts, cupping, teasing, his mouth
tasting her. Then he reached down and scooped her
into his arms and carried her to the bank, where he
knelt and laid her on the mossy earth. He leaned
over her with a question in his eyes.

She reached up and stroked his chest, urging
him to come to her. He held back, then whispered, "Once you said you'd taken your mother's
lover away from her, even though you didn't bed
him. Has any man—"

"No. Never." Her face flamed as she felt his troubled dark eyes study her. She forced herself to meet
his gaze. "I want you to be the first. . . ."

He knew this was madness, for he could not be
the last, the one to claim her in marriage, but when
those clear blue eyes implored him, he lowered his
body over hers and kissed her once more. He would
be the first.

As she enfolded him in her arms, all other thoughts
fled. Gently, reverently, he worshipped her flesh with
his hands and mouth, using the tip of his tongue to
flick at errant droplets of water that were caught
above her collarbone and in the vale between
her breasts. Her skin felt like wet silk against
his mouth. His body fought the restraint he was
placing on it. Never in his life had he been so

afire to take a woman, but Barbara was a virgin and deserved slow, gentle wooing.

She did not make his resolve easier, for in her innocent abandon she pulled him closer, taking her cue from the magical way he used his mouth. She tasted him, licking, biting, exploring . . . and growing hungrier, marveling at the contrast of her skin, so pale and soft, pressed intimately against his hard, bronzed flesh. When he took a fistful of her silvery hair and wrapped it around his neck, she felt a primitive surge of heat catch fire deep inside her belly.

As if understanding what was happening to her, Devon's hands traced a trail from her breast across the curve of her flat little belly, then lower. His mouth followed where his hands roamed. When his tongue circled and then probed her navel, she arched her hips and held his head in her hands. He moved lower, his hand gliding over one slender, rounded hip and thigh, then around to brush the soft curls between her legs.

Barbara was on fire, consumed by a nameless need. His fingers opened her nether lips carefully, patiently, as if he were unfolding the petals of a rose. She gasped and cried out his name.

He crooned low love words against her skin as he stroked her wet, satiny flesh, aching to plunge into her, desperately holding back. When she writhed against his hand, he knew he could wait no longer. He rose over her and took her hand in his, guiding it to touch him, wrapping it around his straining phallus.

The heat and hardness of it amazed her, and the velvety smoothness of it made her long to feel this ultimate caress. "Please, Dev, please," she whispered.

"Open for me. Aah, yes, that's the way," he gasped, his large hand wrapped about her small one as he guided himself into her, then pulled her hand away and held her tightly as he lay between her thighs, struggling to move slowly. She was small and tight, but wet and eager all the same. She arched against him. He gritted his teeth and slowed his steady invasion. "I don't want to hurt you, Barbara. Hold still."

The feeling of his hot flesh probing hers drove all reason from her. She bucked beneath him, and the thin wall holding him back was forever vanquished. Her nails dug into his back as she urged him deeper inside her. She could feel the incredible stretching pressure more than she could any pain. For all the foolish theatrics about it, losing a maidenhead was not a painful ordeal in any way. She tightened her legs about his hips and felt him move inside her. This was bliss!

Devon could feel the tearing of her maidenhead, but she did not hesitate or cry out, only urged him on—as if he could stop by then! Once fully inside her, he kissed her fiercely, possessively. *She is mine.*

But only for now, a voice mocked him.

He swept the disquieting thought aside and began to move. She moved with him, quickly catching the rhythm, as hungry as he. His tongue plunged into her mouth, mimicking the thrusting of his lower body. When she closed her lips around his tongue, he nearly went mad.

They rolled around on the soft, mossy ground until she lay atop him. He took her hips in his hands and raised them, then lowered them, never breaking their kiss. Barbara felt a heady sense of power when she lowered herself onto him and felt him strain up as she controlled the pace of their mating. And what a glorious mating it was, the pleasure building, delicious, compelling, the hunger consuming her. She longed for some unknown culmination; she longed for the ecstasy never to end.

Her hair spilled over her shoulders and covered them in a silken cocoon. Lost in their own world, they strove on, intent only on each other. She pressed her breasts against the hard warmth of his chest, letting his hair abrade her aching, sensitive nipples. He held her head with one hand as he ravaged her mouth, groaning and gasping for air.

Just when Barbara was certain she would die of the pleasure, that it could grow no more, a great swelling surge of intense ecstasy washed over her in successive waves. She rocked up and down, riding it out as her nails clawed at his shoulders. Then his body grew rigid and he shuddered. His staff swelled even larger inside her and he pulsed life into her in those same surging waves that she had felt.

Slowly, they grew still, their bodies sated, sweat-soaked and exhausted. Her fingertips traced patterns on his muscles, and her lips kissed the faint scars scattered across his upper body. "Thank you, Devon," she whispered, not knowing what else to say.

"Did I hurt you, Barbara?" he asked, although he was almost certain her discomfort had been fleeting.

Her hand gently soothed the scar on his side, and she chuckled. "Better if I asked you that question. For a man at death's door only a few short weeks ago, you've recovered marvelously, Mr. Blackthorne."

"I owe it all to your nursing skills, your ladyship," he said, kissing the tip of her nose. Then his expression sobered. *Your ladyship.* She was as far beyond his reach as the North Star, blazing with fiery beauty in the night sky.

"I'm not sorry, Devon," she answered in reply to his unspoken question. "Please, let us live one day at a time."

"For how long? You must go to your brother in Savannah, a place where I'm little welcome." He lifted her off him and sat up, taking her in his arms as they huddled together by the river's edge.

"There must be a way," she whispered fiercely. Having just had a taste of paradise, she did not want to speak of relinquishing it.

He stroked her cheek and then lifted that proud, stubborn chin. "What way? Could you live among the Muskogee? Scrape deer hides and cook over an open fire? No, your ladyship. You're destined for silks and servants. And I can't provide either."

She threw her arms around him with a sob of misery and he stroked her hair, rubbing her back to comfort her.

Panther Woman watched them return from the river. Her black eyes narrowed with hate as she looked from Devon to the pale-haired woman, who walked so arrogantly beside him. Although they did not even touch, she knew they had made love. There was a certain tension between a man and woman, an aura that glowed from their eyes as they exchanged covert glances. She saw the heightened color in the pale one's cheeks, the way Barbara's eyes followed Devon when he bade good day to her at Mocking Bird's house. Rage washed over her.

Always she had known that his white blood called to him, that he took white women when he traveled to their cities, but such were insignificant liaisons. He would never give his heart to a tavern wench. She knew this woman was different. She also knew Devon would never come to her bed again so long as the English one was alive.

"This evening I shall go down to the river and trap one of my pets," she murmured low and vanished inside the doorway of her house.

Tonight was the final and most important day of the eight days of feasting to welcome in the new year, the celebration called the *Boos-ke-tuh*, or Green Corn Festival. Devon escorted Barbara to the large town square, where four rectangular open shelters faced the center of the square. Since the seats were reserved by clan for the families of distinction, Devon, as a member of the prestigious Wind Clan, was allowed to bring Barbara to observe the ceremonial lighting of the new fires.

Already she had helped Mocking Bird's family clean their house and empty their hearth of the past year's ashes. All broken pottery, utensils, and tools were carefully gathered up and discarded. Special dances were held each night, and every morning the Black Drink was taken by all the men of the village.

Devon explained to her that sexual abstinence was considered an essential part of the religious ritual. "But I never was religious, either the English or Muskogee part of me," he said with a wink that made her blush.

He had felt obliged to join some of the communal male ceremonies at the opening of each day during the festival. He purged himself by using the Black Drink and by sitting in the sweat lodge with his uncle and cousins, then plunged into the cold river, although he did not join in the dancing.

Barbara noticed that there were few women seated in the assembly. Most of the females and a good minority of the males stood back beyond the perimeter of the square, watching at a distance. "They're men who haven't distinguished themselves in war or hunting, second wives, or just people of lesser clans. This is as class-conscious a society as any in Europe."

"Second wives?" she said with a raised eyebrow. So that explained the two older women who lived with Mocking Bird and did her bidding!

He smiled at her righteous indignation. "A Muskogee man can take a second wife—but only if his first wife consents."

"Why ever would she do such a thing?"

"To share the chores. It's considered a sign of wealth and prestige for a man to be able to provide for more than one wife. Many women think it an honor. Besides, if a woman becomes angry with her husband's treatment of her, she can divorce him and he has to leave her house, for all property remains with the woman's clan."

"How very interesting," she said, turning her attention back to the priests moving to the center of the square with four youths in their wake. Each carried a large log. The earth had been swept clean and sprinkled evenly with white sand. Now each boy carefully positioned his log on the sand, and the laborious process of building the fire began.

"Four is the sacred number, representing the sun, created by the Breath Master who makes the corn grow."

By the time all the rituals were performed, the fire blazed high in the night sky. It would burn without being extinguished until the next year's Green Corn Festival. Now the youths were sent to every clean, cold hearth in the village, bearing a live ember from this fire. Home hearths, too, would remain aglow for another year.

Barbara felt her eyelids growing heavy when they finally stood up and began to file out of the shelter. The night was warm and starry. They walked slowly back to the two-story building where Barbara, as a guest of the family, was sleeping. Devon stayed across the way in another large dwelling with his uncle and aunt.

"Sleep well," he said simply, aching to draw her into his arms and kiss her, but there were people everywhere, returning home after the festival.

Her eyes held his, troubled and sad yet tender. "I'll dream of this afternoon," she replied, then turned and vanished inside.

Her sleeping robes had been carefully rearranged, pulled up on the pallet, but the night air was much too warm for her to want furs swathing her already heated flesh. *I burn for him.*

As she unbraided her hair and combed it, Barbara sat pondering what she should do. Was Devon right? Could he never return to the white world with her? Although her time with the Indians had been an adventure, she could not imagine spending her life here. She thought of bringing Devon in his ranger's rifle shirt, buckskin pants, and moccasins to meet her brother. Monty would be aghast. Not only a colonial, but part Indian as well!

Tears blurred her vision as she realized the hopelessness of their love. At least for now, for a few more days or weeks or months, she would cling to her happiness, taking advantage of each precious moment with Devon Blackthorne. She yanked back the soft beaver pelts mounded up on her pallet and started to crawl onto the bed. A sharp hiss rent the stillness of the room.

Barbara jumped away from the dark pile of pelts. The room was unlit except for the bright moonlight pouring in from the windows. She seized the first weapon she could, a straw broom from the corner, and peered into the darkness.

The sinuous movement of a snake caught her eye as it slithered free of the pelts and glided across the pallet. Barbara clutched the broom in a death grip and screamed as loud as she could, over and over as the snake opened its white mouth and hissed again.

She had no idea how long it took before Devon bounded up the ladder, knife gleaming in his hand. He pushed her behind him and threw the blade in a silvery arc. The heavy knife sank into the snake's head, pinning it cleanly to the soft pallet. It writhed a moment, then was still.

"A cottonmouth," he said softly.

"They're poisonous, aren't they?"

"Yes, very. They're also known as water moccasins, and they don't live away from wet areas, certainly not in the dry second story of a house."

Her heart skipped a beat. "You mean someone put it here . . . to kill me?" *Panther Woman!*

Although he did not say it aloud, Barbara knew Devon was thinking just as she was. By this time Kills the Bear, Mocking Bird and most of their household had crowded around the ladder below. Devon's uncle, Tall Crane, climbed up and watched as his nephew freed the dead snake from his blade and tossed it out the window.

"I think the lady would be safer if you returned her to Savannah as quickly as possible," he said sadly. "I will speak with the brother of Panther Woman in the morning. He will see to her chastisement."

Thrill to the most sensual, adventure-filled Historical Romances on the market today...

FROM ▙ LEISURE BOOKS

As a home subscriber to the Leisure Romance Book Club, you'll enjoy the best in today's BRAND-NEW Historical Romance fiction. For over twenty years, Leisure Books has brought you the award-winning, high-quality authors you know and love to read. Each Leisure Historical Romance will sweep you away to a world of high adventure...and intimate romance. Discover for yourself all the passion and excitement millions of readers thrill to each and every month.

Save $5.⁰⁰ Each Time You Buy!

Six times a year, the Leisure Romance Book Club brings you four brand-new titles from Leisure Books, America's foremost publisher of Historical Romances. EACH PACKAGE WILL SAVE YOU $5.00 FROM THE BOOKSTORE PRICE! And you'll never miss a new title with our convenient home delivery service.

Here's how we do it. Each package will carry a FREE 10-DAY EXAMINATION privilege. At the end of that time, if you decide to keep your books, simply pay the low invoice price of $14.96, no shipping or handling charges added. HOME DELIVERY IS ALWAYS FREE. With today's top Historical Romance novels selling for $4.99 and higher, our price SAVES YOU $5.00 with each shipment.

AND YOUR FIRST FOUR-BOOK SHIPMENT IS TOTALLY FREE!
IT'S A BARGAIN YOU CAN'T BEAT! A Super $19.96 Value!

▙ *LEISURE BOOKS* A Division of Dorchester Publishing Co., Inc.

GET YOUR 4 FREE BOOKS NOW—A $19.96 Value!

Mail the Free Book Certificate Today!

Get Four Books Totally FREE— A $19.96 Value!

PLEASE RUSH
MY FOUR FREE
BOOKS TO ME
RIGHT AWAY!

Leisure Romance Book Club
65 Commerce Road
Stamford CT 06902-4563

AFFIX
STAMP
HERE

Chapter Fourteen

August, 1780, Blackthorne Hill

Dr. Witherspoon frowned and shook his head. "You've got to stay abed, Robert. Between this fever and your heart condition, you'll be dead in a fortnight if you don't."

"How can I stay abed," he drawled sarcastically, "while my son and heir is off gallivanting who knows where? On trading business, he says. Who's supposed to run this plantation? Most of our able-bodied men have either sneaked off to join those treasonous rebels or have been taken by the royal militia. There's no one to take charge of a bloody thing! Half my indentureds, even some of the slaves, have run away." Pale and trembling, Robert fell back against the pillows piled high behind his back.

The old physician turned to Madelyne, who waited quietly at the foot of the bed. "I have some medicine here that I want you to see that this old goat takes—pry his jaws open with the smithy's tongs if you must and pour it down his throat." Robert scowled blackly but Noble ignored him.

"What is it?" Madelyne asked, reaching for the small jar filled with what looked to be tree-bark chips.

"Rare stuff. Comes all the way from South America. I got it through a man I know in the West Indies. It's called cinchona and is supposed to arrest malarial fever. Damned expensive and hard to come by, or I'd have tried it before."

"Using me as your bloody guinea pig, eh, Noble?" Robert asked crossly.

The doctor turned his myopic gaze on Robert and said sternly, "You're to drink this. It might just break these fevers and chills. Worth a try. You've got a chance, at least—more than I can say for most of those poor devils dying like flies on battlefields across the South."

At the mention of the war, Madelyne paled, thinking of Quint, gone these past weeks without a word. Could he be ill or injured? *He's a traitor. You'd be well rid of him.* But the thought of life without him caused a squeezing pain around her heart. "How do I prepare this cin—cinchona?"

Witherspoon nodded to Robert as he latched his satchel and escorted Madelyne out into the hallway. He closed the heavy door and turned to her with a grave look on his face. "He's bad, Madelyne. The chills and fever have accelerated his heart, which has been weak for years already." He measured out some of the bark. "Steep about this much in a cup of water. He'll complain it's bitter, but make certain he drinks it all. Morning and night for the next three days or so. I'll be back to check on him by then."

As she took the medicine from him, Madelyne thought the old physician looked exhausted. "You've been working too hard, Dr. Witherspoon. Come have a cup of tea and some of Delphine's fresh cakes before you leave."

He took her hand and patted it. "You'd best not be talking to me about working too hard, young lady. You've been carrying a heavy load with Quint gone and Robert down ill."

"I'll be fine." The dark circles beneath her eyes belied her words.

Noble patted his small paunch and said, "I'm afraid Delphine's cooking isn't what the doctor ordered. I must decline your gracious offer and head up the post road toward Augusta. Seems Pickens and his men have had a little run-in with some royal militia. Both sides could use some patching up, I'd warrant."

"You be careful, Doctor," Madelyne admonished. Over the past months she had grown fond of the dour old physician with his acerbic wit. He always seemed able to walk a path between Robert and Quint, defending each to the other, yet retaining the friendship of both. She wondered what his politics were but never asked him, nor did the old man volunteer whether he was rebel or loyalist.

After Noble rode off, Madelyne walked around the side of the house and entered the kitchen where Delphine held absolute sovereignty. She gave the big black woman instructions about the cinchona, knowing Robert would be far less likely to argue with Delphine than with her. She returned to her chores, which this morning included supervising the making of soap. Madelyne eagerly took on the overseeing of the hot, laborious outdoor tasks that Mrs. Ogilve found beneath her.

Working from dawn to dusk, Madelyne fell into her lonely bed each night, too exhausted to dwell on her moral dilemma. She was married to a traitor, yet she could never betray him to the fate a traitor deserved.

Cousin Andrew visited frequently and was so solicitous and kind that she had almost blurted out her distress to him on several occasions, but she knew that would be disastrous. He'd be heartbroken that his own cousin had betrayed king and country. Then he, too, would be caught in the same tortured coil. No, he was too good and loyal a friend to lay such a burden upon.

She forced her grim thoughts aside. *I'll visit Polly when the soap is set. Maybe she can cheer me.*

In the past weeks of Quintin's absence, Madelyne had taken to making occasional visits to the Golden Swan. Polly was a wonderful confidant, buoying up her spirits when Robert's sarcastic coldness left her low. It was Polly who had urged her to face down Agnes Ogilve and assume control of the household. She had yet to wrest the bookkeeping ledgers and house slaves from beneath the old woman's iron fist, but she had taken command of all the rest of the domain.

Blackthorne Hill was run like a small fiefdom, with a dairy for making butter and cheese as well as more than fifty cows to be milked daily. Eggs had to be gathered from the poultry sheds, and the smokehouse larder had to be inspected, as did the pickling barrels in which beef and pork were cured.

Today a half-dozen huge iron kettles sat in the yard between the kitchen and the big house. The tallow and lye were bubbling slowly above carefully tended fires. Madelyne took a huge iron ladle from one of the slaves and stirred one kettle to judge how soon the soap could be set, a task she had watched both her aunts perform often since childhood.

Just then, the sound of drunken whooping and pounding hooves cut through the bucolic sounds of the plantation. Madelyne looked toward the road that led up from the river. A dozen men, roughly dressed and heavily armed, came thundering around the side of the big house, riding roughshod across her fine flower beds.

When she saw their leader, her furious anger was overlaid with fear. There was no mistaking the fat girth and scarred face of the late Ephraim Malvern's companion, Luke. He reined in his horse, dismounted, and swaggered toward her.

"Watch 'em, Miz Madelyne," Delphine said contemptuously from the kitchen door, "They's outliers. Steal from both sides. Ain't got no faith wif neither."

"Well, look what I done found now. And this time without any menfolk around to protect her." Luke's eyes scanned the yard furtively. "Where's yer dog?" He stroked his duck's-foot pistol.

Madelyne prayed Gulliver would stay in the woods with Jed and the boys, hunting deer. "I've protection enough from the likes of you, Luke. You'd best leave Blackthorne Hill while you're still able to sit a horse." She was proud of how steady her voice sounded.

Luke guffawed and spat from the side of his mouth, leaving a puddle of tobacco and saliva dripping from a peony bush. "Oh, I'll be able to sit a horse—after I ride you, you uppity Tory bitch." He stepped closer and reached for her.

Instinctively Madelyne's hands tightened around the iron ladle, and she flung boiling soap across his face. He staggered back, screaming and cursing, his fists balled in his eyes. Before the other men could dismount, Madelyne raced to the kettle nearest the horses, yelling to one of the big slaves, "Help me tip it, Ethan!" She wrapped her petticoats around her hands like potholders and heaved against the side of the iron kettle. Ethan put his shoulder to it and it overturned, pouring a river of slippery liquid soap across the grass.

The ground sloped slightly downhill toward the riders, whose terrified horses began to whinny and dance, then rear up as they struggled for purchase on the soap-slicked grass. The whole yard erupted in pandemonium, with guns going off wildly as horses fell, dumping their riders. Many of the beasts themselves were down, some rolling on their hapless owners.

Andrew Blackthorne and several of his men approached the big house from the opposite side. Hearing the commotion, he quickly dismounted, cursing as he readied his boxlock pistols. Signaling the men with him to follow, he charged down the hill. "Madelyne, I'm coming," he yelled as he raced toward her, gun raised. But before he could get to the scene of the debacle, Gulliver came racing from the trees and dived at his back, sending him sprawling facedown across the ground.

Andrew struggled to break his fall as he neared the soapy grass—to no avail. He slid like a greased pig into the chaos of flailing hooves and swearing men. Just as he narrowly missed colliding with a downed horse, one of his pistols discharged into the melee, creating even more havoc. As if his entry were not already ignominious enough, Madelyne's dog came at him barking and snarling.

Before the dog could do grievous injury, Madelyne's voice penetrated the cacophony and Gulliver quickly left Andrew and made his way to her side.

By this time, Luke and his boys were straggling from the yard, leading their terrified horses from the scene of destruction under the watchful eyes of Andrew's men, who stayed well clear of the mire. Most of the outliers had lost or discharged their firearms and all were covered with greasy soap, giving their rifle shirts and pants a peculiar shine in the morning sunlight.

As they limped away, Madelyne knelt solicitously by Andrew, who to his abject mortification was crying from the burning lye soap that had been rubbed into his eyes. He sat up cursing soundly as he contemplated the ruination of his fine clothes. If his soap-clogged pistol had been in working order, he doubtless would have discharged it squarely between Gulliver's eyes!

"Cousin Andrew, let me help you. I'm so grateful you and your men arrived when you did. Please forgive Gulliver. The sound of the shots must have frightened him. I can't imagine why he attacked *you!*" She placed his slippery arm around her shoulder, and together they struggled from the yard toward the house.

"Just so you're safe, Cousin. I'm glad I decided to ride out hunting this morning. When I heard the commotion, I rode here immediately. It's dangerous for you alone with Robert ill and Quintin gone."

"You're kind to worry, Cousin Andrew," she said as she helped him to a chair in the rear parlor and then issued crisp commands for bathwater to be readied for him. As she looked out the window at the ruins of the peony bushes and grass, fury infused her. *Damn you, Quintin Blackthorne! Where are you?*

Andrew was speaking. Madelyne turned apologetically. "I'm sorry, Cousin. I'm afraid I wasn't attending. What did you say?"

"I said, if you'd been armed properly you could have sent those men off before they entered the yard. Lots of ladies living in the back country have learned to handle weapons during these turbulent times. I would be happy to instruct you."

Madelyne's Aunt Isolde had already taught her the finer points of marksmanship, but poor Andrew looked so woebegone and earnest that she had not the heart to tell him that. She smiled brightly, always glad of his company. "I think that's a splendid idea, Andrew. Perhaps we could begin tomorrow?"

"I'll be here, dear lady, have no fear. You'll never want for protection while I draw breath."

Quintin rode toward Blackthorne Hill, letting Domino pick his way slowly through the undergrowth that encroached upon the seldom-used trail. He had a great deal to ponder. As if his personal life were not in enough chaos, the war was approaching disaster. British forces seemed to be triumphant across the Carolinas.

There was only one American commander left in the southern theater with brains and discipline enough to win, and Quint had just ridden away from that man—Colonel Francis Marion. When he'd reached General Horatio Gates's encampment, his information and advice were studiously ignored by the new American commander in the South. That was where he'd met the French Huguenot. Marion, too, had been ignored.

In spite of his dark mood, Quintin grinned ruefully. Francis did not exactly cut an imposing figure to command instant attention. He was thin and short, even scraggly, with stringy black hair and a great beak of a nose set in a small, intense face. But there was much more to the man on closer inspection. His mouth was resolute, and his black eyes burned with the light of keen intelligence. He was soft-spoken and cautious, but when he voiced an opinion it invariably made sense. He and Quintin had been drawn together immediately in their opposition to the arrogant and impetuous Gates, full of himself ever since his triumph at Saratoga nearly three years earlier.

When Marion asked to be allowed to return to guerilla fighting in the Carolina back country—skirmishing British supply lines and burning ferries and bridges—Gates quickly agreed, glad to be rid of the troublesome fellow. Quintin had joined Marion at his camp on the Santee River and participated in a number of raids.

Outraged, one British officer they captured had blurted out, "You do not sleep and fight like gentlemen, but waylay us like savages from behind trees!"

To Marion's way of thinking, that was the only sort of war that made sense. Quintin agreed and wished to remain and fight for the patriot cause, even though he had eaten little but sweet potatoes, slept on nothing but the damp, swampy earth and had scant opportunity for the amenities of a toilette in the past month.

A few days before he departed, dispatches arrived with grisly news. Gates had led his men against superior forces and was cut to pieces at Camden. One of the Revolution's most noble and skillful officers, Baron deKalb, was killed in the engagement. A scant two days later, that bloody butcher, Banastre Tarleton, led his battle-hardened dragoons against the Carolina partisan Sumter at Fishing Creek. Tarleton caught the ignorant popinjay Sumter bathing in the stream! Although the rebel narrowly escaped with his life, more than eight hundred Americans were captured or killed.

Marion had kept the news from his men, swearing Quintin to secrecy and pleading with him to return to Georgia and resume his intelligence work.

"A damned bloody spy, that's what I am. God, how I sicken of the deception." He rubbed his eyes, then felt the stubby bristle on his jaw. He would at least enjoy the luxury of a bath, a shave, and a decent meal. And then there was the matter of his wife. What would he do about Madelyne? It seemed nothing in his life was going as he wished.

He went over the excuse for his long absence again. Part of it was true. He had been caught between Cornwallis's and Gates's armies. The fact that he was a participant on the rebel side he would omit in recounting for Robert his business trip to Wilmington.

Convincing the old man would not be difficult. Robert was arrogantly certain that Quintin shared his disdain for the rebellion. That still left him with the problem of what to do with Madelyne. She was as much a loyal Tory as Robert or Devon. She knew his secret and could betray him. The irony of having to trust his life to the whims of a woman did not escape him.

When Blackthorne Hill came into view, Quintin felt the same emotional pull he always did after a long absence. *I may not be Robert's blood, but I share his obsession with the land.*

He kicked Domino into a canter and headed for the stables. As he rode around the back of the kitchen he noticed an enormous patch of dead grass. The area, once green and filled with flowering bushes, looked as if a herd of horses had been driven between the big house and the kitchen, or a battle had been fought there! He continued on to the stable with a sense of foreboding tightening his guts.

Abner Grimes, the head stableman, came out to greet him, a surprised smile on his pox-scarred face. "Thank the Almighty you've returned, Master Quintin!" When he bobbed his bald head, the sun shone on his pinkened pate.

Quintin dismounted, giving Abner Domino's reins, then followed the old man into the dim interior of the stables. "What the hell's going on here, Abner? The yard looks like a fire tore through here, yet everything else is in order."

"Well, sir, some Liberty Boys come callin'—outliers, really, they was. The mistress, she sent 'em flyin. Poured a vat of boiling soap on 'em, she did. 'Course, your cousin, Master Andrew, he 'n some of his men, they come along 'n helped her out. The mistress was that glad to see 'em, what with yer father bein' laid up with his fever again 'n you bein' gone. . . ." He rubbed down the big black as he talked.

Quint's face darkened. "So my cousin just happened to ride by and rescue her, did he?"

"Oh, not such an accident, I guess, what with him callin' so often. Sort of watchin' out for her in yer absence, sir. He's even been teachin' her to shoot a Jaeger rifle and a Queen Anne turn-off pistol. A woman needs protection in these troubled times."

The garrulous old man talked on, but by now Quint wasn't listening. *Protection, indeed!* "I'll be at the house. Domino's not the only one in need of some grooming." He stalked to the back door and strode down the hall in search of Madelyne, then nearly collided with the imperious old housekeeper.

"Thank heaven you're here! Master Robert is taken with that fever again and everything's in chaos, Master Quintin."

"So I've noticed," he replied tightly. "Exactly what did happen out there, Mistress Ogilve?" He gestured to the ruined yard he'd just traversed.

"Well, sir, it's not my place to criticize the mistress . . ." She hesitated, waiting for his urging.

"Just tell me what you know, woman!"

"She had one of the slaves turn a vat of soap over to frighten away some riffraff who'd come riding up. Of course, she needn't have done so, for Master Andrew was at hand with his men to protect us. Since you went away, he's been ever so solicitous— not that he wasn't before, of course."

"Of course."

"Well, after the whole debacle was over, the yard was in shambles. Needless waste, sir. I've tried to suggest, as much as it's proper for one in my position to do so, that the mistress leave the running of household matters in my hands. After all, your cousin and his men could have handled that man of Malvern's without her getting in the way."

His eyes narrowed. "Luke Vareen? A big brute with a scarred face?" *The bastard with Ephraim on the post road, the one her dog chewed up!*

Agnes Ogilve fought down a smirk of satisfaction as she nodded. "Twas that trashy one, yes, sir. Whatever he thought by accosting her here, I'll never understand," she added primly.

"Where is my wife now, Mistress Ogilve?"

She appeared to be flustered. "Well, she and Master Andrew went off shooting earlier today. I'm really not certain where . . . down near the slew, I think."

He spun on his heel and retraced his steps to the back door once again. As it slammed, the head housekeeper smiled smugly.

Madelyne swam across the pool of water at the far end of a small slew that fed into the Savannah River. It was well hidden, canopied by dense stands of bald cypress and willows, surrounded by reeds and water hyacinths. She had discovered it only a few days ago after she and Andrew finished a shooting lesson. Recalling how pleased and amazed he was with her progress, she smiled. Poor dear Andrew. If only Quint possessed his patience and kindness.

Quint. He had been gone for more than six weeks with only one cold, impersonal note saying he had been delayed in Wilmington. As if what they shared by night meant nothing to him—but then, she was afraid it did mean exactly nothing. He was using her to provide Blackthorne Hill with an heir. He did not love her. Why had she been so girlishly foolish as to let herself fall in love with him?

She closed her eyes and floated in the soothing water, willing her thoughts away from her husband. Recalling her small victories as mistress of the plantation over the past weeks, she smiled with satisfaction. Even Robert seemed to respond to her a bit better. She'd nursed him with patience and gentleness, although his behavior was enough to try a saint.

That hateful housekeeper was losing ground. With any luck she'd convince Robert to give her charge of the housekeeping staff and Mistress Ogilve's ledgers within a fortnight. There were certain discrepancies she wanted to—

"Enjoying your bath, my pet? I'm amazed my dear Cousin Andrew isn't about to frolic with you." Quintin stood with his shoulder against the trunk of a willow, his arms across his chest. He looked like an outlier himself, unshaven and dressed in filthy buckskins. Madelyne knew that look—he was furious.

She splashed water all around her as she faced him, sputtering and coughing. "So, you finally decided to return home. I thought the British had you in the Carolinas."

"Doubtless your devoutest wish, but no, obviously they did not." He began stripping off his clothes with rough jerky movements as he talked. "I've heard all about your escapades at the house."

"Distorted versions by that hateful Mistress Ogilve, I'll wager!"

"If you stayed indoors like a dutiful wife, you could have met me and forestalled her tale," he said as he finished peeling down his tight buckskin pants.

Madelyne felt her mouth go dry as she watched the play of light through the leafy branches of the tree make patterns on his lean, muscular body. He untied his hair and shook it loose about his shoulders, then started toward the water.

"What are you doing?" She couldn't keep a small squeak of alarm from her voice. He was so irrationally jealous. Surely he couldn't believe she and Andrew—

"I'm going to bathe, a luxury I've been denied these past weeks in the Carolina swamps." He looked around the hidden pool. "How did you discover this place? I thought no one had seen it since Dev and I were boys." He paused and scowled. "I forgot. Andrew used to come here, too—to spy on us and tattle so I'd get a caning for associating with my disgraceful half-breed cousin."

He dove into the water and surfaced beside Madelyne. She quickly moved away. "You've never liked Andrew, have you? Boys do petty things—things they should put behind them when they're grown."

He smiled but it was a cold parody of amusement. "Oh, we're all grown-up, all right. In fact, right now I'm thinking some very grown-up thoughts indeed, but first I'll wash the swamp stench from my body."

He dove beneath the water and came up several yards away, then began to swim across the pool to where she'd set her towel and some toilet articles beside Speckles. He left the water only long enough to grab her bar of soap, then plunged back in. When he broke the surface, he narrowed his eyes at her. "Speckles has no saddle."

"I like to ride bareback when I'm alone."

"You also like to swim naked . . . when you're alone," he added silkily. "Where did you acquire all these unorthodox tastes? Somehow I can't imagine your aunt Claud approving."

"She tried to break my spirit by taking away everything I loved—every simple pleasure Aunt Isolde taught me to enjoy. It was my mother's sister who raised me—to be free. Claud made me a prisoner."

"And you saw me as a means of escape?" He looked at her with obvious incredulity on his face.

"No, Quint, I saw only an angry man who didn't wish to wed me but agreed to it when he believed me to be someone I'm not. Tis you, not me, who repents our marriage." She turned in the water and swam away from him, fighting desperately not to cry.

Quint rinsed the soap from his hair and tossed the bar onto the shore with an oath, then swam after the water sprite whose floating masses of dark hair and milky breasts incited him to unreasoning lust. She was in the shallows when he caught her. He grabbed one slim ankle and pulled her back into the water with a loud splash.

"Perhaps I do repent our marriage, but tis done, Madelyne. You're my wife and I never share what's mine—not with Andrew, not with any man." He held her tightly against his body as she thrashed in the waist-deep water. Then, using one hand, he held her jaw tightly and forced her to look up and meet his eyes. "Did you let him touch you?"

Madelyne could see the anguish beneath the anger, and something inside her softened. He said he had put childhood memories behind him, but she could still see the scars of Robert Blackthorne's cruelty, set deeply in his pain-filled eyes.

"No one but you has ever touched me, Quint. Or ever will." She held his fathomless gaze, willing him to believe her.

Quintin studied her beautiful face, so earnest and imploring. Before he could think rationally, his body, so long denied, reacted. He bent down and took her mouth in a fierce, possessive kiss.

Joyously, Madelyne wrapped her arms around him and returned the kiss, letting her lips open and welcome his invading tongue. They stood locked in an embrace as the water lapped around them. Then Quint lifted her buttocks and whispered against her throat, "Wrap your legs around me."

She obeyed and he slid into her. She gasped at the hot, sudden pleasure as he began to thrust slowly while holding her in the warm water. The sensation was totally new this way and very erotic. Madelyne combed her fingers through his long, wet hair and kissed him again, moving her hips to the rhythm he set.

After a few moments Quint could not keep his body under restraint. He began thrusting faster, harder, out of control as he savaged her pliant body. And Madelyne clung to him, blind with passion, willing him to understand her love in the only way she could express it.

When his whole body went rigid and began to shake, she felt a sharp, piercing thrill. As he spilled his seed deeply within her, she joined him in the surge of swift, glorious release. He stood in the water, holding her as she clung tightly to him. Both of them were shivering and mute, unable to meet each other's eyes, afraid of what they might reveal.

Chapter Fifteen

September, 1780, Savannah

Phoebe Barsham opened the latch on the gate and stepped inside the high, enclosed courtyard at the rear of Andrew Blackthorne's city house. The smell of garbage assailed her nostrils, but she had smelled worse in London's East End. The glow of rats' eyes greeted her from the refuse heap by the fence. She didn't flinch, but tossed a stone at them and they scuttled off. She'd seen rats in London, too.

But now her lot in life was about to change. She knocked on the rear door and waited until an old harridan of a kitchen maid opened it.

"Go away. It's too late ta be peddlin' vegetables er the like."

"I ain't 'ere ta sell vegetables. I'm 'ere ta see Mr. Andrew Blackthorne." At the old crone's skeptical look, Phoebe shoved her aside and entered, drawing on her considerable height to intimidate the maid.

"Just tell 'im Phoebe's 'ere with some information 'e's been wantin'.''

She was shown into a small, dimly lit rear parlor. Andrew turned to her as soon as the door was closed and snarled, "Are you insane, coming here?"

"Well now, I was real careful. No one seen me."

"You stupid cow! You're just as incompetent as that bastard Vareen you sent to me. He botched the job. Madelyne scarcely needed rescuing from a pack of men who couldn't even stand upright!"

"T'weren't Luke's fault she threw boilin' soap in 'is face. 'E's blind in one eye now." She shivered in revulsion, remembering what Luke Vareen had looked like with his new disfigurements.

"Why have you come here? You were to send me word through the tavern by the waterfront."

"No time for that. I got some news you'll be wantin' . . . wantin' real bad."

His brown eyes grew darker as he narrowed them on her. "What news?"

"It'll cost ya. I wants me papers from the master. Wants ta shake the smell of cow shit 'n country from me shoes fer good."

"Tell me what you have and I'll consider it."

"You 'eard 'bout thet Jew feller bein' arrested last week? Solomon Torres. Now 'e's a real special friend of the young master."

The hairs on the back of Andrew's neck prickled in premonition. "Yes. He's accused of spying for the damned rebels. All those Jews are a pack of traitors." He waited, watching the greed in her eyes. She had come to Savannah with the Blackthorne household for the opening of the fall social season. Her aunt had seen to elevating her from the dairy to the parlor. In her new post as maid, what could Phoebe have overheard to send her rushing to him like this?

Reading his thoughts, the crafty chit said, "I ain't tellin' no more till you pays me." She stuck out her chin pugnaciously.

Andrew studied her a moment, then shrugged and walked over to an escritoire in the corner. Unlocking it, he opened a small box inlaid with mother of pearl and counted out a hefty portion of silver coins. "This should pay for your papers and allow you a good start in your new life."

Phoebe's eyes gleamed with avarice as she scooped the pile of silver into her pocket. "Tomorrow night, after Governor's Wright's ball, Quintin Blackthorne 'n some of 'is patriot friends er goin' ta row out to the prison boat 'n rescue Torres. I 'eard 'em plannin' it. Yer cousin, the fancy heir ta Blackthorne, is a rebel spy!"

A surge of elation swept over Andrew. He threw back his head and laughed. This was too good to be true, but a bitter street urchin like Phoebe was not clever enough to fabricate such an outlandish tale. It must be true. He could already imagine the horror on old Robert's face when he received word of Quintin's death—as a traitor! "Tell me all the details you overheard. Who's involved with my cousin? When and how do they plan this rescue attempt?"

Phoebe walked north on Abercorn Street toward Broughton, retracing her steps across the city from Andrew's house to the master's. But soon Robert Blackthorne would no longer be her master, and his son, who had rejected her in favor of that pale, skinny stick of a wife, would be dead. She would show all of them—especially her Aunt Agnes, who was always correcting her speech and sniffing at her morals. She would be free of them all. Slowing her step, Phoebe patted the coins in her pocket again.

It was a fatal mistake. A long thin arm caught her by her throat and yanked her back into a copse of cabbage palms. She kicked and fought, but her attacker was terribly strong.

A familiar voice whispered, "Surely you didn't

think I could allow you to live, knowing I betrayed
my cousin to inherit his fortune? Foolish, greedy
Phoebe."

She struggled harder as Andrew murmured a
sigh and cut her throat. Quickly he ripped open
her pocket and retrieved the coins he'd given her.
Then he rolled her deeper into the trees and vanished into the darkness.

Considering that the countryside was ravaged
by war, Governor Wright's gala appeared opulent
indeed. A slave orchestra played a sprightly tune
while a glittering assembly of satin- and lace-clad
ladies and gentlemen danced, talked and laughed.
Port and Madeira flowed freely, imported from
Portugal at great expense. The formal dinner would
be a sumptuous repast of dozens of courses, each
served with wine. The upstart rebels might terrorize
the countryside, but in the coastal cities of the South,
the Royal Navy protected ocean trade. Any luxury a
loyalist family could afford, they might purchase.

Serena scanned the crowd of powdered heads,
quickly catching sight of Quintin's black hair. He
always stood out—taller, darker, utterly splendid,
a lithe panther in a roomful of milling sheep. She
patted her own raven locks and began to make her
way toward him as he slipped through a set of open
doors leading into the gardens.

That pathetic little chit Madelyne had finally left
his side and was talking with Andrew. Poor fool.
She actually believed he was her friend! Let the
two of them discuss books and politics. Serena had
other plans. Her gown was the sensation of the ball,
cut low across her breasts, falling in a bouffant
train from her shoulders down her back. The brilliant crimson taffeta caught the candlelight, sending
off glittering sparks with every rustling move she
made.

"Are you tired of her yet? Or are you still trying

to get an heir on her, Quint darling?"

Quintin turned at the sound of Serena's purring voice and stifled an obscenity. "I'd prefer not to discuss my wife, if you don't mind, Serena."

"As you wish, Quint darling."

"I'd also prefer you to drop the endearment. It might be misunderstood if anyone overheard us."

She laughed and took his arm, leading him across the lawn toward the privacy of a tall box hedge. "How stuffy and proper you've become. Marriage must be taming you. Who'd ever have thought it."

Her remarks hit too close to the truth. Quintin felt a surge of anger. He quirked a brow at the coldly beautiful woman and said, "Being tame and proper are qualities marriage never instilled in you, nor ever could."

"Ah, Quint, if I'd but wed the right man. For you I'd be whatever you wished me to be." She put a note of earnest entreaty in her voice, then added sadly, "But you had to go and marry your little Huguenot. I miss you, Quint."

"You miss my attentions in bed, Serena, that's all. You don't really want marriage—at least not the sort I'd demand, with fidelity and children to inherit Blackthorne Hill."

She arched an eyebrow. "You're certain your little Huguenot wife is such a paragon of faithfulness, then? La, of course! She must be horrified at what you make her submit to in bed, but dutiful enough not to protest."

He laughed hollowly. "You just might be surprised, Serena."

She studied the harsh, angular beauty of his face in the moonlight. "You were right earlier. Let's not talk about her. Let's talk about us." She glided closer to him and wrapped her arms around his neck, drawing him toward her.

He began to unloose her clinging hands when she pleaded, "Just one kiss . . . it'll be good-bye, Quint.

I've lost you." She squeezed out a tear from beneath thick black lashes.

"You're a most unconvincing actress, Serena," Quint said with a mirthless chuckle, but he lowered his mouth and met hers. All the tension of the past days welled up in him as he savaged her lips. Was it defiance of the hold Madelyne had on him? Or simply frustration over Solomon's deadly plight? At that point he didn't care. A moment's uncomplicated passion freed his mind of all other thoughts.

Quintin did not hear Madelyne's soft gasp of pain when she rounded the hedge and saw him locked in a heated embrace with Serena. She stood frozen in astonished horror for an instant. Then fury swept over her. "You filthy hypocrite! Accusing me of your own sins! I hope you both rot in hell for this. You deserve each other!"

Quint broke free of Serena in time to see his wife turn and flee toward the side exit from the gardens. He untangled Serena's clinging hands and ran after Madelyne, who was surprisingly fleet of foot in the full regalia of a wide hen basket overlaid with layers of petticoats. Her peach-silk skirts vanished around the corner of the house, but he was gaining on her. Just as she reached the end of the passageway between the Governor's house and the garden wall, he caught up to her.

Madelyne felt his strong hands on her shoulders and tried to break free, but he easily turned her to face him. He held her immobilized with one arm around her waist while his other hand clamped over her wrist. "Let me go, you whoreson cur!"

"Lower your voice," he commanded. "I don't fancy having to duel half the idiotic men in the colony because I've offended your delicate sensibilities."

"My sensibilities are quite intact, thank you. Tis you who have none—not a shred of decency." The tears came now, burning and blurring her vision, dissolving the cleansing anger into pitiful, whimpering pain. "You humiliated me—castigated me for enjoying your touch, told me I was a harlot for ever speaking of such base physical cravings. Well, from now on, husband, you'll be better pleased with your wife. I despise your touch, and I'll never again respond to it!"

He held her, but she ceased struggling now, just looked up into his face with contempt that struck him like a blow. Quint felt a sudden sense of desolation. Perhaps one careless moment's indulgence had cost him something very precious.

"We need to talk, Madelyne, but not here, not tonight. I have to—"

"Toby told me what you're going to do tonight. God help me, I've even become party to treason for you."

"We'll be missed at the dinner if we don't return." He paused, then added, "Or do you want Serena to gloat? She's achieved her ends now."

"Frankly, Quint, I don't care a fig if Serena turns handsprings across Governor Wright's rose garden. Neither of you is worth the rope to hang you." She slipped from his hold and retraced her steps toward the house with him trailing after her. "Cousin Andrew has asked to escort me to table," she could not resist adding for spite.

The Tybee Island prison ships loomed like black mastiffs on the horizon, silhouetted in the waning rays of moonlight. The air was calm and still, awaiting dawn—and another day of hell for the hundreds of men who lay dying aboard them.

Quint crouched at the edge of the sound, looking toward the narrow neck of water where two flat islands met. "You're right, Noble. I can smell the stench from here. It's enough to turn a man's guts. How can civilized men treat prisoners this way?"

The old physician shook his head. "I've heard our government holds British prisoners farther north under similar conditions. War's never pretty, and this is the ugliest kind. When I was aboard to treat our men last week, six more had died of smallpox. Some of them tried to inoculate themselves by using fluid from the pustules of infected men. Sometimes that works, but under the conditions they're forced to live in . . ."

"Does Solomon have smallpox?"

"Not when I checked him, but he's weak, Quint, very weak. I told you about the rations."

Quintin cursed. "Forcing Jews to eat pork or starve. Those royalist militia guards know what men like Solomon would do, damn them to hell!"

Just then Tom Johnwalker came crawling through the low, marshy grasses to where they were concealed. He was a hulking backwoodsman, who moved with surprising agility for his size. His grizzled face split in a wide grin as he whispered, "All our men is ready, Quint, 'n German George's boys is all sleepin' real easy, thanks ta the rum ya sent 'em."

"An anonymous contribution to the cause, I assume?" Noble said, peering over his spectacles.

Quint snorted. "They didn't question where it came from, just swilled it down. Now let's go to work. Noble, you and Hosea's men are to wait here with the horses."

"If he's not in shape to ride, I'm taking him home with me," the doctor said stubbornly. He and Quint had not agreed earlier about the wisdom of that idea, but Noble was determined.

"Let's pray it doesn't come to that," Quint said grimly. He signaled to a small party of men who shoved two Indian canoes into the black water. As he climbed into the first canoe, he heard Johnwalker whisper.

"I'm coverin' you from the shore, Quint. Any sign of trouble 'n me 'n my boys'll be on 'em like stink on a skunk's tail."

"Just don't be too hasty, Tommy." Quintin and his

men glided into the water, silently, their oars muffled with thick woolen padding. The night was ink-
black now, the moon almost gone, the first rays of
dawn yet to come. This was a desperate gambit, one
he knew his superiors would disallow, but Solomon
Torres was rotting aboard that ship because he had
gone to the pier in Quintin's place, to receive a
message from Franklin.

The Muskogee canoes were far superior to clumsy
ship's boats—light, swift and easily maneuverable.
They glided up to the side of the hulk on which
Noble had ascertained Solomon was imprisoned. So
far, absolute silence reigned. Quintin tossed a loop
of rope about the rigging suspended over the bow of
the ship and secured it, then climbed up carefully.
Once he cleared the deck, he scanned the blackness
for any sign of the watch. A low snore from a crumpled figure lying on the deck greeted him. The fat
guard clutched an empty jug of rum on his chest.

Let it work. Quint signaled for the others to come
aboard, then followed the diagram of the ship Noble
had drawn him. He had committed it to memory
days ago. They moved down the companionway
into the back of the ship. Not a single guard
stirred. A prickle of unease raced up and down
Quint's spine. Then he heard the restless noise
of prisoners—moans, curses, coughs. The stench
was enough to pull at his guts by this time. He
struggled to breathe as he knelt at the grate to the
hold, then hefted it up. The creak seemed louder
than a screaming panther in the night stillness, but
no one came. Was everyone drunk?

Dressed as he was in his royal militia uniform, he
prayed none of the other prisoners would question
his taking Torres away in the middle of the night.
He signaled to one of his men to hold open the
grate, then climbed down the ladder into the bowels
of hell. Men lay everywhere, randomly sprawled
across the filthy, damp wooden floor of the hold.

The stench of excrement blended with the sickly sweet odor of disease. Some of the poor, ragged beggars slept, but most stared in the darkness with vacant eyes as his flickering candle passed them by. No one questioned him.

Finally Quint located Solomon in a far corner with two other men. He signaled to his friend not to give any sign of recognition. "Come with me, Torres. We've prisoners to bury at daybreak."

"Solomon is too weak for burial detail," one companion whispered, his own breathing labored.

"These are your fellow Jews who've died aboard the hospital ship. If you want them laid to rest by their own kind, better step lively," Quintin replied in a cold, clipped accent.

"If my cousins could come, too. Between the three of us, we could serve well enough," Solomon rasped.

Quintin shook his head. "No, they're as weak as newborn kittens. You, Torres. Just you." Once they were above deck, Quint stepped out in the open, ready to climb over the railing when the voice of Major Montgomery Caruthers called out.

"Quintin Blackthorne, you're under arrest for treason." The major stood by the stairs to the quarterdeck with a Wogdon dueling pistol in his hand. The twelve-inch barrel gleamed evilly in the torchlight. Half a dozen armed soldiers spread out around them.

"A trap. Was it my lovely lady wife, Major, who turned us in? No, don't answer. Quite unchivalrous if you did. I know the answer, anyway," Quint added coldly as he raised his hands. The two men with him did the same, while Solomon Torres stood in the shadows.

Suddenly a shot zipped narrowly past the major's head, knocking his hat across the deck. A volley erupted as Tom Johnwalker and three other men climbed over the railings. Caruthers aimed his pistol at Tom, but Quint dove at him, causing his shot to go wide and knocking him to the deck. As they rolled around, Quint seized Caruthers's wrist and tried to wrest his second pistol from him. Johnwalker knocked the militiamen aside as if swatting flies, using the rifle he had just fired as a cudgel. Two of the loyalists were down, shot by rebels, while the other four were engaged by Quintin's men. Even Solomon, weakened by near starvation, joined in the fight.

"Here, men, into the boats before them other lobsterbacks come to see who's shootin'," Jed Cooper yelled.

Quintin came up on top of Caruthers and slammed his fist into the major's jaw, then jumped free of the unconscious man and assisted Solomon, who was struggling to reach the railing. All the fugitives were over the side in a matter of moments.

"How did you know it was a trap?" Quintin asked Johnwalker as they climbed into a canoe.

The big man grinned. "Piece of real luck. Soon as you was inside the cabin, the moon cleared the clouds one last time, real dim-like. I seen that major's pretty red uniform movin' across the deck with a pack of militiamen behind him. Knew they wasn't there to help you free the prisoner."

Quintin turned to look back at the ship, readying his pistol to fire as their boat rowed furiously for shore, heedless of the noise now. Suddenly more shots rent the air, this time coming from another prison ship directly to the north of them. A musket ball caught Jed Cooper squarely in the chest. He was flung backward into the water, dead instantly.

The murderous fire cut into the men in the canoe, but fog and darkness soon shrouded them. The alarm was spread, and the fugitives could hear Major Caruthers barking orders while the ship's boats were hastily lowered into the water. The rebels made shore, where Noble Witherspoon and the balance of their men waited with the horses.

Hosea and Tommy helped Solomon from the canoe while the doctor looked on. "Are you able to ride, Solomon?" he asked dubiously.

"I can, but I think Quint's been hit," Solomon said to Noble.

Quintin shook his head. "Just a scratch I can get Polly to bind up. Caruthers and his men will be here in a few moments."

"My men 'n me are goin' back to Richmond County, Quint. Now that you've been recognized, you better come with us or they'll hang you, sure," Johnwalker said.

"No. I'll go north eventually, but not right now. You and your men ride hard and create enough distraction to throw the militia off my trail. I'll take Solomon to safety first."

"Is the Swan still a safe place to leave messages?" Hosea asked as Noble tried unsuccessfully to inspect the slash across Quintin's shoulder.

"Yes. Use Polly's place, but be damn cautious approaching it. She's our only agent left who can get into Savannah. I don't want her betrayed as I was."

"Who did this, Quint?" Noble asked.

"My wife," Quintin replied tightly as he swung up on Domino. He looked over to Solomon. "Shall we see what this royal militia uniform can buy us before word of my shift in allegiance reaches the countryside?" With that, he kicked the big black into a gallop.

All the men dispersed in the darkness as the shouts of Caruthers and his men echoed across the water.

Quintin and his Jewish companion rode southwest, away from the city, then veered to the north by way of a back trail he was certain the British in Savannah had never seen. It was full daybreak when they reached the bluffs on the river. Polly

Bloor's tavern awaited them. Solomon was struggling to keep his seat as Quintin scrutinized the area surrounding the inn.

"Let me go in first. I can out-distance any pursuers on Domino. If it's clear, I'll signal you." He paused, then added, "I'm sorry about your cousins, Solomon. I'd have taken them with us if I could have."

Torres gestured with his hand. "You had no choice. Malachi and Abraham have been there for months. They were so weak, they'd never have made it into the boats. I'm amazed I did."

"Soon I'll have you dining on a fine, fat chicken— of course it won't be kosher, but Polly's kitchen is clean."

"If it's food without maggots in it, I'll forego kosher and beg God's forgiveness later," Solomon replied.

Soon both men were in Polly's cozy private apartment with her fussing over them. As Solomon devoured a juicy chicken breast, she treated Quintin's injury with trembling hands.

"I don't believe Madelyne betrayed you, Quint."

"Believe it, Polly. She and Toby were the only ones who knew about our plans to rescue Solomon." His eyes narrowed as he recalled their furious argument in the garden and his cousin Andrew's fawning attention to her at dinner the preceding night. "She's a loyal little Tory," Quintin said bitterly. "I think she hoped to become a widow last night."

Polly shook her head but remained silent. She had seen that implacable look in Quintin Blackthorne's eyes before and knew there was no crossing him when he was this way. "Give me that shirt and coat, love. They're too blood-stained to save. I'll get rid of them 'n bring you clean clothes."

"I guess my days as a royal militiaman are over for good," Quint said, handing her the ruined clothes.

"What will you do now, Quint?" Solomon asked. "I've got family in Charles Town who will offer me shelter, even forge papers to get me past the British sentries. You could go with me and convert," he said, trying to lighten his friend's grim humor.

Quint laughed softly. "I've too great a fondness for shellfish and pork. No, I have other plans. When I was in South Carolina, I met a man called Francis Marion. A tactical genius who understands this war better than anyone we have in the South. I'll join him for the duration. In a way I'm glad the subterfuge is over for us, old friend."

"But at what cost, Quint?" Torres asked sadly.

Just then the door at the end of the hall creaked. Polly stood up and motioned for both men to be quiet. She started for the door to her private quarters, but before she could reach it, a knock sounded and it swung open.

"Polly, love, where are you? I've brought someone to meet—" Dev stopped in mid-sentence as his eyes moved from Polly Bloor to Quint and Solomon. "What the hell's going on here?" he asked as he looked at the red furrow across Quint's shoulder. "You've been shot."

Taking a deep breath, Quintin raised the pistol he had concealed beneath the table and leveled it at his cousin. "Come in, Dev, and bring the young lady with you."

Dev's eyes darkened in shocked bewilderment. He felt Barbara's hand on his arm and took it protectively in his, shielding her with his body. "I brought Lady Barbara to Polly for a change of clothing that will see her safely into the city. She can scarcely approach Major Caruthers's residence dressed in Panther Woman's cast-offs."

Quintin studied the sunburned blonde in the colorful calico skirts and shirt of a Muskogee maiden. In spite of her unconventional dress and simply braided hair, she was a real beauty, a nonpareil in London society, he was certain. "You're related to Major Montgomery Caruthers?" He could see the resemblance in their blue eyes and aristocratic features.

"The major is my brother," she replied. "I was shipwrecked en route to Savannah where I was to join him."

"I'm happy to assure you he's in splendid health," Quint replied dryly. "You see, it was the major who tried to shoot me last night—as I was helping Solomon here escape from one of the prison ships off Tybee."

Barbara gasped in amazement, but Devon just stared, mute for a moment.

"Yes, Devon. Your cousin has sprouted horns and a tail. I'm an American spy—or at least I was until my wife betrayed me to this lady's brother. The British are searching for me right now, doubtless offering a sizable reward, dead or alive."

Devon's face turned to granite as he realized that Quintin was in deadly earnest. "Why? In God's name, why? To spite Robert?" he asked with anger and disgust in his voice.

Quint sighed as Solomon carefully removed Devon's weapons from his person and ushered him and Barbara to the round oak table by the hearth. "No, Dev, much as my father and I hate each other, spiting him is no reason to risk my honor, my fortune, my neck," Quint said, moving his aching shoulder gingerly to keep it from stiffening further.

"Then why?"

"You said it yourself. This is a civil war. There are good men on both sides."

Devon snorted in disgust. "Patriots you call yourselves—yet you ally with Europe's most despicable despot and defy the lawful authority of an elected parliament."

"Many of whose members protested the way these colonies were being treated. We've grown apart from the mother country, Dev. Franklin spent years in

London pleading for reason. Neither he nor I chose rebellion lightly."

"But you did choose it. You chose to lie and deceive everyone who trusted you." Devon's eyes were almost black with anger now. The pain of betrayal stung bitterly.

"I'm sorry for it, Dev. A thousand times I wanted to confess to you . . . but I know you well. You'd have been forced to do your duty."

"And you couldn't have that."

"Not and do mine," Quintin said philosophically. He turned to Polly and pointed the gun at her. "Fetch some rope from that cabinet, Polly. I regret forcing you to hide us, but I do appreciate your hospitality. Now, be a love and tie up my furious cousin and the lady for me. I'll check the ropes after you do."

Polly responded with alacrity, and Quintin went through the motions of verifying that she had indeed tied the captives securely. After having her gather a large quantity of food for their journey, he tied her too.

"We'll be on our way now, Dev, Polly, Lady Barbara," Quintin said, trying to avoid Dev's accusing eyes. But just before he placed the gag in Devon's mouth, his cousin had the last word.

"The next time we meet, Quint, I'll be shooting."

Chapter Sixteen

As they rode toward Savannah from the Golden Swan, Barbara wanted Devon to say something to break the bleak silence, but he remained uncommunicative and brooding. *Oh, Dev, what's going to happen to us?* Would he just leave her with Monty and walk away without a backward glance? She knew she had asked for nothing more that first time when she had come to him, but during the weeks of their trek back to civilization, they had repeatedly made love. She had grown accustomed to sleeping next to him and waking up in his arms. And now after a scant few weeks, her time with Dev was over.

Unwilling to break her word and plead with him to stay, Barbara ended the silence between them by asking, "Are you still thinking about your cousin?"

The look on Dev's face reflected his sense of pain and betrayal for a fleeting moment. Then he said, "We grew up together. Quint is more my brother than Andrew. All this time he deceived me—ever since this accursed rebellion began. Damn him! The next time we meet, one of us will kill the other." His voice was as grim as the threatening gray skies overhead.

"I don't think he'll kill you, nor you him, no matter your politics. He left us bound so Mistress Bloor's servants quickly found us. And yet you did not pursue him."

Devon snorted in disgust. "We both grew up among the Muskogee. Quint's spent nearly as much time as I in the swamps and back country. No one can find him if he wants to hide."

That subject was obviously closed. As they rode on, Barbara mentally rehearsed the story they had arranged for Monty. Dev had coached her. Polly had outfitted her suitably in simple garments such as a fisherman's wife might wear. Gathering her courage, she offered, "Are you certain you don't want to come into the house with me and meet Monty? I know he'd be grateful that you saved my life. He needn't know about the rest." Her voice ended on a breathless note.

Devon turned to her with a scowl on his face. "We've been over this already, Barbara. As a quarter-breed Muskogee I'm not socially acceptable in the better circles of Savannah. And how would we explain your being alone with me for more than a month since the *Hyperion* wrecked? Your brother, being a gentleman, would be obliged to call me out. And, not being a gentleman, I'd be obliged to kill him," he added, his mood lightening for a brief moment. "No, tis best to say you were rescued by a simple fisherman and his family, who nursed you back to health and then brought you to Savannah."

"Where they were too noble to remain and ask for any reward." She parroted the ending to the story they'd concocted, hating every syllable of it. "Dev, I don't know if I can do this—deceive Monty."

"You can do it to save your reputation. People believe what they want to believe. Look at the way

Quint deceived me. I believed he was as loyal an Englishman as I am."

Barbara lapsed into silence. There was nothing to reply. The outlying shanties of Savannah were past them now, and elegant houses of brick had come into sight. Soon he would leave her to make her way to the assembly house on Reynolds Square. She had memorized the directions. *Dev, I love you.*

Her only answer was the wind blowing off the Atlantic.

When Barbara reached the assembly house, General Prevost himself was there for a meeting with Governor Wright. Both men, solicitous over her ordeal and delighted at her miraculous rescue and recovery, had sent her on her way to her brother with a young lieutenant as escort. She silently prayed she could retell her fanciful tale one more time.

When the lieutenant helped her dismount in front of an elegant, two-story brick house on Oglethorpe Square, he explained that it had belonged a rebel family forced to flee the city.

Barbara was trembling, fearful of convincing Monty with her story, but more than anything, she was bereft at losing Devon. He had ridden away without looking back. She turned her attention to the house, where a flash of red appeared at the door. Then Monty ran swiftly to greet her.

Sweeping her up in his arms, he said, "Barbara, is it truly you! Lud, I was certain you were dead when I received word of the *Hyperion's* wreck." He looked at the coarse, barleycorn skirt and linen bodice she wore, then inspected her sun-darkened face. "What's happened to you?"

She felt like asking him the same thing. One eye was blackened and his jaw swollen and discolored. Quickly, she recounted her story again as he led her into the house, where a visitor—tall and thin, with light brown hair and cold eyes—waited. He was expensively dressed, obviously a gentleman, and he had overheard almost all of her explanation to Monty. Barbara smiled uncertainly. Something about the stranger made her uncomfortable, as if he alone knew she had fabricated her tale of shipwreck and rescue.

"Barbara, may I present one of my closest friends, Andrew Blackthorne. Andrew, this is my sister Barbara, whom we all feared was dead." Monty was beaming with excitement, his pale face flushed with delight in spite of his bruises.

As Andrew took her hand and saluted it lightly, Barbara felt a peculiar thrill of revulsion course through her. *So this is Dev's half brother, who's ashamed of his Muskogee blood.* She saw no resemblance and decided that Andrew must take after his mother, since Dev had already told her that he was cut in Alastair Blackthorne's very image. She curtsied as Blackthorne spoke.

"I'm enchanted to meet such a beautiful mermaid rescued from the cruel clutches of the sea."

Forcing herself to smile at him, she asked, "How have you come to be such fast friends with my brother?"

"London, m'dear," Monty replied. "I was posted home back in '74. Andrew here had come over on business. The Blackthornes own one of the largest mercantile houses in the colonies."

"But of course, Lady Barbara, you were just a child in the schoolroom so many years ago. How old and stodgy any man past thirty must seem to a fresh and lovely woman such as you."

She inclined her head at the compliment but forbore to correct his description of himself. "You are too kind, sir."

Monty summoned an array of servants and set them to drawing bathwater, preparing food, and securing more suitable clothing for her, then turned back to his sister. "Of course you'll need to have a whole new wardrobe. We have some excellent dressmakers here in the city, I'm given to understand, and as I recall, there's nothing you love more than shopping. We'll have to get you outfitted before the Habershams' ball. Blast, I have to be at Fort Halifax all day tomorrow." He cast an embarrassed look at Andrew. "We've just had a spy escape and must plan to counter any damage he might do."

"I'd be honored if you'd allow me to escort you shopping tomorrow, my lady," Andrew volunteered.

His odd light eyes seemed brown one moment, then almost colorless, like a chameleon's. Barbara smiled woodenly. "I should be delighted, Mr. Blackthorne." *But you're the wrong Mr. Blackthorne. Dev! Will I ever see you again?*

Quintin stood outside the city house, looking up at his bedroom window from the darkness of the courtyard. It was midnight and every candle had been doused. The house was shrouded in silence. Did Madelyne sleep alone in his big wide bed?

"How inconsiderate of me not to die when her little trap was sprung," he muttered beneath his breath. He was a fool to have sneaked back into the city after seeing Solomon safely on his way to Charles Town. "I should be searching for Marion in the South Carolina swamps." But he had to see her one last time.

As a boy, Quintin had often climbed the oak behind the house to escape when Robert locked him in his room as a punishment. He climbed up its spreading branches and entered the rear hall by an open window. Although autumn beckoned, the nights were still balmy. Silently he made his way down the dark hall to his room and opened the door.

Moonlight bathed the room and spilled across the wide bed, filtering through the filmy gauze of the mosquito netting. Madelyne's slim body lay curled beneath a sheet, her dark hair spilling across the snowy pillows.

Quint closed the door and moved to the bed, pulling the netting aside. She slept as innocently as a newborn. A bitter smile curved his lips. How deceiving appearances could be. He knelt on the bed and placed one hand over her mouth as he secured her wrists in the other.

"Scream and I'll crush that slender white throat, wife," he whispered in her ear.

Madelyne came awake instantly, her eyes wide with shock as she stared up into Quintin's face. Again, she was struck by his cold beauty. *A fallen angel.*

"Surprised to see me alive? Or did Major Caruthers explain how I escaped? No? Perhaps dear cousin Andrew, his good friend, broke the sad news to you." He eased his hand from her mouth to her throat, daring her to try to cry out.

"As God is my witness, Quint, I did not betray you."

"Then who did?" he snarled. "No one but you and Toby knew I was going to free Solomon Torres."

"All the men who rode with you knew. It must have been—"

"My men are loyal—some of them are dead, thanks to you!"

"Quint, I'm your wife. I pledged my loyalty to you."

His low, husky laugh had a hard edge to it. "So did my mother to my father. Odd, I realized when I returned to the Hill yesterday, Robert Blackthorne and I are more alike than ever I imagined. Both of us bound to the land—and cursed with faithless wives. Did you know Anne haunts him still? He's obsessed with the woman he hates. But I'll not carry your memory with me that way. I'm going to exorcise you from my mind and body, for whatever time remains in my life." He yanked down the sheet and his eyes raked her slender figure, revealed clearly through the sheer lawn of her sleeping shift.

"No, Quint, not this way—"

"If you cry out, I swear you'll have cause to regret it," he said with silky menace in his voice.

Madelyne watched, frozen in silence as he pulled off his boots and stockings, then shed his dark shirt and tossed it on the floor. His buckskin pants quickly followed onto the pile. She was hurt and angry, but more than that, she was afraid—for Quint, for his life which hung by a thread, and for their marriage. Always on shifting sand, it would not survive if he believed she could plot to send him to his death.

Did simple revenge bring him back here to take her one last time in a hurtful parody of the passion to which he had introduced her? *He must feel more than hatred for me, to do this.* As he stood before her in splendid nakedness, his physical desire was clearly evident. She felt an answering response sing through her body. *Listen for what I do, Quint, for what it means, for how I truly feel.* She willed him to understand as she opened her arms to him.

Quint expected her to resist, hoped she would so he could inflict a measure of pain on her to match the agony that squeezed his chest every time he thought of her betrayal. Yet she welcomed him, damn her! Even in this final act of their travesty of a marriage, she was besting him. Roughly, he pulled her into his embrace and savaged her mouth with a rapacious kiss, plunging his tongue deeply inside, foreshadowing what was to come.

Madelyne could feel the raw hurt and anger inside him as he ravaged her with kisses. His lips traveled from her mouth down her cheek to her neck. She dug her nails into his shoulders and threw back her head, giving him full access to her throat and then her breasts. He ripped the sheer gown from her shoulders. She helped him by sliding it from her arms and shoving it below her hips.

Quintin wanted to take her quickly with no preliminary lovemaking, to touch her delicate body as cruelly as she'd touched his soul. But once he felt her insidious softness, smelled her honeysuckle fragrance, he was lost. All thoughts of betrayal and punishment evaporated like fog at sunrise on the river. He cupped one breast in his hand, and she thrust it eagerly against his palm. His mouth followed where his hands led, hot and seeking.

Moaning her pleasure as he suckled her nipples into hard, aching points, Madelyne ran her fingers through his hair, pulling his head to her wildly beating heart. *Feel what I feel, Quint. Love me!*

They tumbled to their sides and rolled across the wide bed, locked in an embrace neither would relinquish. When she reached down and took his hard, smooth staff in her hands, his hips bucked against her. He let out a muffled oath of pleasure and anguish melded together and pulled the frothy gown from her lower body.

As she guided him deep inside her and wrapped her legs around his hips, Madelyne thought she heard his murmur, "Damn you, damn you," but she was not certain. The same surge of ecstasy that gripped him also held her prisoner as they arched and thrust in a fierce dance of passion. Quickly their breathing grew labored, their bodies sheened with perspiration in the warm night air.

Quint rolled atop her and gazed at the delicate perfection of her breasts and belly. His hand caressed her nipples, then skimmed over her flat abdomen and touched her navel. When he looked at her, expecting to see triumph, he found instead that she, too, was caught in the web of ecstasy. Her hair spilled like ink across the white pillows, tangling as she tossed her head back and forth, writhing and grinding her body to the rhythm he set. Her eyes were closed in intense concentration, which he had learned meant she was on the edge of fulfillment. *I should pull away, leave her empty and aching.* But he could not. With a shudder that blinded him, he joined her.

Madelyne felt the wave cresting, but as the contractions began, he slammed into her, harder and faster, his member swelling and stretching her. He gasped loudly and was dimly aware that she had placed her hand over his mouth as he stiffened, his whole body convulsing while he poured his seed deeply inside her womb.

She clutched his hips tightly as she felt his release blend with her own. *Please, Quint, give me a child. Let us create, not destroy.*

He collapsed on her, panting and spent. When his awareness returned, he realized how tightly she held him and at once pulled away, unwilling to gaze into those fathomless amber eyes, glowing in the moonlight, seeing into his soul. He rolled from the bed and began to dress quickly.

Madelyne sat up in bed, dreading what would come next. Even expecting the worst, she flinched when he spoke.

"Whatever charm it is about you that makes men behave like stags in rut, you have my leave to exercise it. Perhaps my cousin Andrew already has sampled it. God knows he's sniffed about you long enough. Now that you've seen to putting a price on my head, I'll not trouble you for some time . . . perhaps never, the way this endless war drags on."

She swallowed bitter bile and clutched her discarded nightgown to her body like protective armor. "Where will you go?" was all she could think to say.

His glacial green eyes mocked her. "Considering how well you keep a confidence, dear wife, it would ill behoove me to tell you. Suffice it to say I'll join the American army in some capacity less despicable than spying. Not that Dev will forgive me any sooner than you or Robert."

Her eyes widened in shock. "Dev? He's returned and found out you're a rebel? I know how bitterly that must have hurt you both."

"The world is filled with hurt, Madelyne. It always has been. I've grown used to it, but I never relished inflicting it on my cousin."

"Only on me. You want to hurt me, don't you, Quint? For sins I've never committed."

"Beautiful liar," he whispered, then vanished into the darkness, closing the door solidly behind him as she sat hunched in the center of the big, lonely bed.

Barbara sat next to her brother, struggling to concentrate on the sermon being delivered by the rector of Christ Church. Useless. She let her eyes stray surreptitiously around the crowded church. By the standard of St. Paul's, it was a simple edifice, yet it had taken years to construct and had a splendid pipe organ. The gallery provided an excellent viewing area from which parishioners could watch the priest and various socially prominent members, who sat in their reserved pews down front.

The Blackthorne family owned the most prominent pew, directly facing the altar. From Monty's pew across to the left she could see old Robert Blackthorne, ravaged by illness, yet sitting ramrod straight as if defying anyone to impugn his honor because his son had turned traitor.

Andrew had told them at dinner last evening that the old man came from his plantation to the city just to make that fact irrefutably clear. The Blackthorne name had been besmirched with his son's treachery, but no one would accuse Robert Blackthorne of disloyalty or cowardice. Andrew sat at the opposite end of the pew with the chillingly beautiful Widow Fallowfield, whom Barbara had met at several social gatherings.

Serena did not interest Barbara. It was the small, slim woman sitting between Robert and Andrew who caught her attention—Quintin's wife, Madelyne. How must she feel, being socially ostracized and whispered about behind her back? Everyone wondered if she had known about her husband's crimes. Barbara studied her delicate profile and pale, haunted eyes. Madelyne had entered the church with dignity and a certain stubborn pride that Barbara had admired.

Barbara's speculations were interrupted when the rector closed his sermon and everyone knelt for prayers. When the worship concluded, she took Monty's arm and they waited their turn to file out of the church. That was when she heard a woman behind her murmur to her companion.

"She has gall, I'll give her that. Sitting up front as bold as if her husband wasn't riding with an enemy army."

"Theirs was an arranged marriage, you know. Everyone said that wild young Quintin would never marry. There was no love lost between him and his Charles Town bride."

"Maybe soon she'll be a widow. I think young Andrew would fancy that. He's buzzed about her ever since she came to Georgia to wed his cousin."

Monty frowned at the aspersions cast on his friend's good name and quickly ushered Barbara ahead in the line, leaving the two older women to gossip. Once they were outside on Johnson Square, Barbara looked about at all the conveyances, searching for Madelyne Blackthorne. She was being helped into an open carriage by Andrew as Serena looked on with a sour expression on her haughty face.

"I admire her courage," Barbara said to her brother.

"What's that?" Monty asked, drawing his attention from the flirtatious winks and titters of several young women who were obviously entranced by his scarlet uniform.

"Your friend Andrew's cousin—Madelyne. She faced down the whole parish as regally as Queen Charlotte. That took some courage after what her husband did."

"Blighter ought to be shot. Will be if I have anything to say about it. I wasn't too pleased to have him escape from me the first time. He won't get another chance. Andrew was devastated over his cousin's perfidy."

So was Dev. "She shouldn't be cut for Quintin Blackthorne's crimes."

"Quite so, yes. I met her before they were married. A lot of spunk and a real charmer. Even then Blackthorne treated her abominably."

"Then those gossips were telling the truth. It was a forced marriage."

Monty's eyes crinkled as he looked at his baby sister with amused tolerance. "All marriages between people of consequence are arranged, Barbara."

Barbara bit back a retort about their parents' disastrous arrangement and shifted the subject to Madelyne again. "I'd like to meet her. She seems . . . different from the rest of these simpering females I've been forced to endure."

He chuckled as he helped her into his chair. "I imagine we could arrange that, but it'll take some doing. You see, old Robert has held quite a dislike for our father's family. His dead wife, Anne, was father's elder sister. That blackguard Quintin is unfortunately our cousin. Aunt Anne and Robert were wed long before you were born. The family was scandalized, what with Blackthorne being a colonial upstart with only marginal wealth back then. Odd thing was, he grew rich but the marriage, which was supposedly a love match, went sour somehow. It was all hushed up at home. Andrew was rather vague about it as well when I broached the subject back in London."

"I suppose Andrew could act as an intermediary between us and Madelyne." Somehow the idea of Andrew Blackthorne paired with the quiet, sad Madelyne seemed monstrously wrong to Barbara, but she said nothing of her aversions to her brother's friend.

Monty considered as he slapped the reins and the horse took off briskly. "He is rather fond of the girl. I'll speak with him."

Madelyne sat in the front parlor, her hands holding the Caruthers' card. In the weeks since Quintin's defection, she had received precious few visitors or invitations. All of Savannah was slyly curious about the scandal. People eyed her suspiciously, looking for signs of her complicity in her husband's spying. At first she had refused to rise to the bait and went about the city marketing, shopping, and attending church as if nothing were amiss, but the long lonely strain was beginning to wear on her.

Now she had received a card from Major Caruthers and his sister, newly arrived from England. She had liked the witty and gallant young major. Perhaps he and Lady Barbara would not be like the rest.

As she sat considering what to reply, Robert entered the room. Still thin and pale, he had rallied remarkably from his last bout of fever. The shock of his son's betrayal had made him furious. Madelyne supposed she should have been grateful that he had come to the city to help her face down the scandal. She was not.

Smiling at his scowling face, she said, "We've just received an invitation to tea with Major Caruthers and his sister, Lady Barbara."

"So Andrew tells me. I forbid you to go, Madelyne."

"Why ever?" she asked, baffled and affronted at his high-handed manner.

"'Tis long buried in the past, but our families have not been on good terms—"

"But Andrew and the major are fast friends," she protested.

"That is Andrew's business," he replied coldly, considering the matter closed.

"I'm afraid you'll have to give me a more specific reason for refusing."

Robert turned from the window and skewered her with his cold blue eyes. The willful chit had altogether too much impertinence. Theo had neglected her proper training. Usually when he gave anyone that withering look, they immediately gave over, but not Madelyne. Her eyes met his saucily, waiting for an answer. He cursed Andrew for ever striking up an acquaintance with that damned Caruthers whelp.

"I'll not discuss such a personal matter with you. Do as you like, but I will not tolerate either Rushcroft or his sister beneath my roof. Is that clear?" Without waiting for an answer, he stormed out of the parlor.

Madelyne dressed with great care that afternoon, choosing a soft yellow gown of calimanco with darker russet petticoats. As Nell arranged her hair, the older woman was in a fine taking, still furious about the death of the downstairs maid, Phoebe.

"I tell you, that lazy baggage should've been left working at the dairy on the Hill."

"She was scarcely good at caring for the animals," Madelyne said, remembering Phoebe's cruelty with the Jersey.

"Better animals than people. She's left us short-handed belowstairs. 'N her no smarter 'n ta go shakin' her petticoats at that scum down on the wharfs. Got what she deserved, she did."

"No one, not even Phoebe Barsham, deserves to be murdered that way," Madelyne said with a shudder.

"Little Lottie Barnes was ta come work downstairs until that hateful Mistress Ogilve set up her niece. Now look where we are. That old harridan won't send Lottie."

"I shall speak with Mistress Ogilve, Nell."

Nell's big hands paused in their deft ministrations, and a troubled look came over her round plain face. "I don't want to cause you any more grief, Mistress. You been through enough sorrow already."

Madelyne smiled reassuringly. "I need something to take my mind from my husband, Nell. Perhaps a good set-to with Mistress Ogilve will be just the thing." *Something I've been meaning to do for a good long while.*

When Nell had finished helping with her toilette, Madelyne inspected herself one final time and decided the woolen bonnet with its saucy feathers was quite flattering to her face. "If only I had some color in my cheeks," she murmured to herself. The past weeks had been hellish for her, and she knew her appearance betrayed it.

Andrew watched her descend the stairs with resolution in every step. He smiled and saluted her hand with a chaste kiss when she reached the bottom of the steps. "You look enchanting, my dear."

"I look quite wan and pale, but I do hope Lady Barbara and the major won't mind. It was awfully kind of you to arrange this outing for me with your friends, Andrew."

"They'll think you quite as charming as I do. I'm always delighted to do anything to bring a smile to your lovely face."

"You're too kind, sir," she said, smiling as they departed from the city house.

On the ride across York Street, Madelyne considered asking Andrew about Robert's angry denouncement of the Caruthers family, but decided against it. They chatted of inconsequential things, never broaching the topic of Quintin's betrayal and flight to join the rebel army. Some things were simply too painful to discuss.

"I am so grateful to have your friendship, Cousin. Without it I would be quite lost."

"No, my dear, it is I who should be grateful." He coughed discreetly, then let the topic drop as the carriage pulled up in front of the Caruthers' house.

They were ushered inside by a stoic black servant, who led them to an elegantly appointed sitting room. The rebel sympathizers who had owned this house had supurb taste in furnishings. Madelyne's musings were interrupted by the entrance of a tall, striking woman with silver-gilt hair fashioned in an elaborately curled pompadour. Her gown was of pale lavender brocade, a difficult shade for most women, but splendidly carried off by the beautiful blonde.

Barbara smiled warmly at Madelyne and even managed to carry it over to Andrew. "I am ever so glad you could come to tea."

"And so am I—provided you've left your watchdog at home. I should hate to suffer Lieutenant Goodly's fate," Monty said with a twinkle of amusement as he stepped beside his sister.

Madelyne noted Andrew's flush of embarrassment at the mention of her pet. "Gulliver is sleeping on the rug in front of my bedroom hearth, Major. You're quite safe, I can assure you."

As they exchanged laughs, Andrew's face creased with annoyance, which he hid behind a benign smile. Monty quickly explained about his abortive rescue of Madelyne and her servants from the Creeks.

"I grew up with two hounds that I positively adored and was heartbroken when they finally died of old age," Barbara said. "I'd love to meet Gulliver. Is he terribly fierce?"

Madelyne returned Barbara's winsome smile and replied, "Only when he's defending me, but I know he'd take to you immediately." *Just as I have.* At last, Madelyne had made a female friend in Savannah.

December, 1780, Snow's Island, South Carolina

The place was low and marshy, making the icy frost crunch underfoot as ragged men moved with spare economy around smoldering campfires, sheltered from the gray winter skies by clusters of scrub pines and crude brush arbors hastily erected for protection. Some of the partisans cleaned muskets and rifles; others patched their worn boots and jackets as best they could with strips of greasy buckskin. They were bearded and filthy, their shaggy hair and unwashed bodies home to all manner of vermin.

The smell of roasting sweet potatoes, a staple of their diet, filled the air with sickly persistence. Quint looked around the quiet camp, observing the men he had fought beside for the past months as they prepared for yet another foray against Colonel Tarleton's dragoons that morning. If only they could have something more substantial to fill the gnawing hunger in their bellies than potatoes. They had little ammunition to spare for the luxury of hunting game here of late, and the rivers were mostly too frozen for successful fishing.

Standing up, Quint rubbed his grizzled chin whiskers and stretched the stiffness from a body now grown used to sleeping on the wet, icy earth. He looked across the camp to where a small figure sat huddled over a crude wooden table, his dark head bent in concentration as he sipped from a battered wooden canteen. Blackthorne strolled past the men, bidding good morning to some, silently receiving acknowledgment from others too battle-weary to speak.

When he reached the larger brush shelter that served as Francis Marion's quarters, he paused and cleared his throat, then said, "Good morning, Francis. How does it feel to be a general—after sleeping on the news of your long overdue promotion?"

Looking up from his maps and papers, Marion let a fleeting smile touch his lips. "A brigadier general, Captain," he corrected, then added, "and it's only a state militia appointment. I'm still a lieutenant colonel in the Continental Line. I'd gladly be a plain lieutenant again if we could only drive Tarleton from the Carolinas." He took another sip from his canteen, then continued reading the map. "I think our old friend Banastre the Butcher is here." He pointed to the map, indicating a swampy area on the shores of the Pee Dee River.

Quint sat across from his commander and looked at the map. "Could be. Cornwallis sent the right man after us. That bastard never sleeps and drives his men like an overseer."

Marion raised an eyebrow in amusement. "I've been accused of the same tactics." He offered Quintin his canteen. "Something for sustenance?"

Quint shuddered. "No, thank you, sir. You're made of sterner stuff than I, to drink vinegar water."

"Owing to my Huguenot ancestry, no doubt," Marion replied, then paused, seeing the brief flash of pain in Quintin's eyes. "Still thinking of your wife?"

Quint managed a smile. "Occasionally, since we've wintered here where it's quiet, but please don't think I equate all Huguenots with treachery just because of my little Tory wife."

Marion rubbed his jaw consideringly. "I knew her mother's family. The Ravenals were fine people. Marie and Isolde are both dead now. . . ." He looked over at his troubled young officer. "Your wife must have been alone before she married you. I also met Theo Deveaux and his sister Claud on a few occasions." He shuddered in distaste. "They couldn't have offered her much comfort."

Remembering the sour old woman and pompous royal militia officer, Quint replied, "I offered her a convenient means of escape. She found comfort for her loneliness elsewhere."

Marion knew when it was best to drop a subject with his brooding young officer. Quintin was one of his best men, cold and lethal under fire. Marion knew he had been a spy for several years before he had been betrayed to the British. Betrayed by his own wife. How many such tragedies must this war of sundered allegiance have spawned? He returned to consideration of the map.

"I've read Greene's dispatch," Quintin said as he looked across the camp. The scrubby land and moss-draped cypress trees looked menacing, especially in the icy cold of winter.

"What do you think of our new southern commander?" Marion asked.

Quint scratched his ribs through his greasy buckskin shirt. God, what he wouldn't give for a bath. "Old Nate Greene at least has better intelligence information than that idiot Gates was given."

A smile played across Marion's lips. "God did not see fit to gift Horatio Gates with overmuch intelligence, military or otherwise. Every pitched battle exacted too dear a price in casualties from him. Even when he won, his victories were pyrrhic. The British have more trained soldiers in the Southern theater and the Patriots, alas, have not enough. General Greene understands that what he can least afford right now is this sort of victory."

"He does appear cautious. God knows he can't stand to lose more men when he has so few. But I do wish he'd come to realize how important the back country partisans are to his strategy. He can't win without us."

"Never fear, Captain. He won't," Marion replied dryly.

Chapter Seventeen

December, 1780, Savannah

Madelyne sat ashen-faced in front of the fire, her skin sheened with a film of perspiration in spite of the damp day. Nell daubed at her mistress's forehead with a damp cloth, clucking as one of the kitchen maids carried the basin and its noisome contents from the dining room.

"There, there. T'will be all right. See if it won't. Just something a touch high in the breakfast you ate."

Madelyne scoffed as she took the cloth from Nell. "I had plain tea and two dry scones, scarce anything to spoil in that! I think we all know what ails me, don't we, Nell?"

"Are you happy about it . . . or no?" The maid's homely face was softened by the love and concern that shone from her dark eyes.

"I don't know, really. I—"

"So the rumors are true. You're breeding." Robert

276

interrupted her as he stalked into the dining room. He studied her with more interest than he had shown in months.

Madelyne dismissed Nell, but did not rise to greet her father-in-law. She remained seated at one end of the enormous dining room table, well away from the sideboard laden with fried meats, oatmeal and heavy cream, pastries and eggs. She watched as he walked stiffly to the table and took his seat at its head. A houseboy began to fill a plate for him, even though they both knew he was capable of holding down little more than she could. His strong, once handsome face was ravaged by the wasting illness, the skin hanging in sallow pockets beneath his eyes and jawline. He stared at her with fever-bright eyes.

The boy placed the heaping plate before him, poured tea, and quit the room at Robert's curt dismissal. "You didn't answer Nell. Are you pleased to be carrying the heir to Blackthorne Hill?" He waited like a hawk perched atop an oak, studying her as if she were a succulent rabbit caught in an open field.

"That's all you care about—your precious heir for all this." Her hand swept the opulent room with its crystal chandeliers, French silk wallpaper, and Turkish carpets. She clutched a Spode cup in her hand, wanting desperately to throw the delicate porcelain at the hateful man sitting so imperiously at the opposite end of the table.

His face darkened. "If Quintin Blackthorne had a shred of conscience or sense of duty, he'd be here, attending to business, not off fighting king and country as a treasonous rebel! But at least he's performed one duty properly in his whole miserable, misbegotten life." He paused then, his harsh blue eyes skewering her. "Or did he? I wonder if I might dare hope the Blackthorne luck with wives extends so far."

"What are you insinuating?"

His laugh was ugly and grating. "Why, only that this child might be Andrew's, not Quintin's."

She fought the urge to be sick again. "You sound just like Quint with your vile accusations. Tis an obscenity even to speak of such a thing. The child I carry is my husband's. None other."

He shrugged and took a bite of roast partridge. "A pity. I would far sooner it were Andrew's get."

"Because he's a staunch royalist—or because Quint's not your son?" She stared him down boldly, glad to have it out in the open between them.

"So, he's told you, has he?" Robert said, wiping his mouth with a linen napkin. His eyes turned so dark a blue they looked black, making his pale face glow like a death mask. "That bastard has never spoken of this to a living soul. I made it clear to him when he was seven years old what the consequences would be if he let slip the family disgrace. If you do, you'll have great cause to regret it as well."

"I've already been threatened by your son, Robert." She couldn't resist emphasizing the words *your son* just to spite him.

His face turned from pallor to the fiery ruddiness of apoplexy. "That traitor is no son of mine and never was. At last he's shown his true colors— he's trash, fighting with other trash in a stupid, lost cause. I'll see him shot before he sets foot on Blackthorne Hill again."

Madelyne felt his hatred lash her like a hurricane wind. "If you despise him so much, why haven't you disowned him and made Andrew your heir? Quint's certainly given you excuse enough now, although he was a model son before his allegiance was exposed."

His face seemed to collapse, just as his body, half-risen from the chair, crumpled back onto the cushioned seat. "To disown him would mean admitting publicly what *she* did to me. Never. Never . . ." He quickly composed himself and again glared down the table at her. "Just give me an heir for my empire.

I don't give a damn if it's that misbegotten bastard's
get or not—just an heir I can call a Blackthorne!"

After a sleepless night and a restless morning,
Madelyne dressed in one of her most elegant
gowns, a rust-colored brocade frock with the skirts
bunched in the polonaise style, revealing rustling
black brocade petticoats beneath. As she placed a
black silk calash on her head and tied the ribbons
beneath her chin, she felt it added an appropriately
somber note. The weather outdoors fit her mood.
Cold, steady drizzle had turned the streets into
such a quagmire that Madelyne resigned herself
to wearing cumbersome pattens to elevate her
silk slippers so they would not touch the muddy
ground or flooded curbs.

"Soon I'll not be able to navigate in these clumsy
things. What will I do then? Muck about like a
brood sow?" She knew, of course, the proper lady-
like answer, which was to stay indoors, confined
from public view until her child was delivered.

It was best to be out and about now while circumstances still permitted. Madelyne needed to talk
with a sympathetic friend. She had only one in all
Savannah, Lady Barbara Caruthers.

When she was ushered into the Caruthers' parlor,
Madelyne found Barbara seated at a small Chippendale table with a deck of playing cards spread
before her, a troubled expression on her face. The
look of pensive pique immediately changed to one
of delight when she saw her guest. Barbara tossed
down her cards, stood up, and brushed her aqua
silk skirts aside as she rushed across the large room
to welcome Madelyne.

"Madelyne, it's been ages. Are you feeling quite
the thing now? I do so hope whatever is ailing surly
old Robert isn't contagious."

Madelyne returned her friend's hug and laughed
in spite of herself. "I assure you, Barbara, what is

ailing me has been in no way contracted from my father-in-law. I am with child."

Barbara held Madelyne at arm's length and studied the blue smudges beneath her eyes. "Are you well now? When is the babe due?"

"I feel a bit queasy and tire easily, but otherwise . . ." She shrugged as she seated herself on the cabriole sofa beside Barbara. Her face warmed with a flush when she answered Barbara's second question. "The babe is due the end of June." As if to forestall her friend's mental calculations, she added hastily, "Quint visited me several days after he helped his rebel friend escape from the prison boat. We had one last night. Perhaps the last we'll ever have."

"Well, he certainly left behind a significant souvenir," Barbara replied tartly as she rang for the maid to bring refreshments. "Tis tea time, and you look to need some meat on those little bird bones, my dear."

Madelyne laughed in spite of herself. "We Deveauxs may be small, but we're squirrel-tough. I'll be fine, Barbara. Dr. Witherspoon assures me my appetite will return soon enough."

"Twaddle. What do men know! I want you to drink some hot tea, very sweet," she said as she sliced from the sugar loaf the maid had set before her. The tea tray was filled with all sorts of pastries, puddings, and cakes. "Eat!" She heaped a plate with sweets and waited like an indulgent mother until Madelyne took several bites.

They munched in companionable silence for a moment; then Barbara asked, "Do you want Quintin Blackthorne's baby, Madelyne?"

Madelyne's amber eyes stared down into her cup, as if looking for some sort of answer there. "Tis odd, but in spite of all his cruelties, the betrayal of our cause, everything—yes, I want his child quite desperately. It may be all I have left of him when this hellish war is done."

"You love the bounder, don't you? No, don't protest. I understand better than you might think, how tis people worlds apart can fall in love." A haunting sadness came over her face as she thought of Devon.

"Then you've been in love?" This was a subject the forthright and fun-loving Lady Barbara had never spoken of with Madelyne.

"La, dozens of times, but no one so suitable as to warrant a marriage contract," she replied, glossing over her deeply buried pain. Madelyne had enough to contend with now. She did not need another burden. "I imagine old Robert is fair turning handsprings," she added, wanting to change the subject.

Madelyne's face grew stony. "I may have fallen in love with a man who doesn't return my tender feelings, but I still resent being a brood mare for the glorious Blackthorne name. That's all Robert cares about. His grandson."

"Spite him. Have a granddaughter," Barbara said, wiping a dollop of whipped cream from the corner of her mouth with a napkin.

Madelyne smiled. "Yes, that would put him even more out of fettle. A difficult feat these days. He's been in a state of snarling anger ever since Quint left with a price on his head. Even Andrew hasn't been able to cheer him."

"Small wonder there," Barbara murmured beneath her breath.

Madelyne heard the comment and felt constrained to defend him. "I don't understand why you're in such a taking every time Andrew's name is mentioned. You've been positively rude to him when he calls. He is Monty's best friend, after all."

"Yes, Andrew Blackthorne is such a paragon. I'm surprised that old Robert didn't name him his heir when Quint deserted to the rebels. Monty has mentioned that more than once. You've often agonized over who might have betrayed your husband, Madelyne. Who had more to gain than dear Cousin Andrew?"

"Barbara! That's monstrous." Madelyne set down her teacup with a clatter.

"Is it?"

"Yes," Madelyne replied crossly. "And besides, how could he possibly have done it? He knew nothing of the plot to rescue Solomon Torres. He was nowhere near our city house for days before the trap was sprung."

Barbara chewed her lip in vexation. "We know for a certainty you didn't do it."

"I knew about the plot the night of Governor Wright's ball." Madelyne's level amber eyes met Barbara's blue ones steadily.

"You knew all along he was a rebel spy and said nothing? Lud, you are in love with the rotter."

"Quite hopeless, am I not? A traitor by proxy, if you will."

"You're just a woman in love, and love knows no politics."

"Robert lives and breathes politics. Oh, Barbara, he's eaten up with his hate. I share your wonder that he hasn't disinherited Quint."

Barbara shivered. "I can't imagine living with that old blackguard. How do you endure him?"

"At times it isn't easy, but news of the child has eased things a bit."

Just then the parlor door opened and Monty, resplendent in his scarlet uniform, entered. "Ah, the lovely Mistress Blackthorne. I wanted to pay my respects before I was off for the evening." He saluted Madelyne's hand with a flourish, then kissed his sister on the cheek. "Don't wait up, Puss. I'll be late. Quite a game at Major Southby's tonight."

"Do be a bit more careful about your gambling, Monty," Barbara said softly.

He chuckled indulgently. "Now look at the kettle calling the pot black. I seem to remember our dear mother writing me, something about you and a few gaming hells in London . . ."

The two siblings exchanged a measured look, then Montgomery Caruthers, Seventh Baron of Rushcroft, bowed formally to both ladies and quit the room.

"His debts quite put mine in the shade—and I had *dear mother's* purse to dip into. Here of late our family estates seem to have fallen on hard times."

"Has he been after you regarding Colonel Weymouth since last we talked?" Madelyne knew Barbara's brother was pushing her in the direction of the most eligible bachelor in Savannah.

"The Viscount of Leicester has his praises sung like matins every morning. Lud, I scarce need ever hear Morning Prayer in church again," Barbara replied with resignation. "I suppose, from the practical point of view, we would suit. He's rich, soon to sell out his commission and return to London, where a hundred girls of good family will doubtless fall all over themselves pursuing him. He actually finds me enthralling."

"And if you wed him, Monty's gambling debts would be taken care of?" Madelyne saw the answer in Barbara's proud, beautiful face. How her brother's weakness must pain her.

"I shan't do it, of course. I saw what our parents' arrangement came to—oh-so-suitable a match, it was. Made for every political, economic, and social reason. They hated each other."

Madelyne felt her heart break with the pain. She knew only too well that a forced marriage could cause hatred and sow heartbreak. She patted Barbara's clenched white fists. "You needn't marry Weymouth, Barbara."

Suddenly Barbara knew what Madelyne was saying and realized her own monstrous selfishness. "Please forgive me, my very dear friend. I go on about things so long dead in my past and cause you pain now. Let us vow to forget all this unhappiness for this afternoon and have a little game of whist."

Her eyes took on a gleam as she led Madelyne
to the card table across the room. "We'll play for
hairpins—and even in the unlikely event that you
have a rebel scruple troubling you, let me assure
you, these cards came direct from England with
not a pence of tax paid on them!"

They played for a while, laughing and talking of
frivolous things as Barbara scored a dozen points to
Madelyne's one, for Madelyne was a novice at the
game.

Finally Madelyne worked up her courage and
said, "I would dearly wish to get a message to
my husband, Barbara. I've tried what few contacts
I have among his rebel friends. No one trusts
me."

"You want him to know about the babe?" Barbara
asked sympathetically.

"Yes . . . but even more, I want word that he is
alive and well. Only that."

Barbara pondered as Madelyne finally won a
hand. "Monty entertains officers and officials here
regularly. I overhear a great deal. Let me see if I
can put together any information that might secure
you a message to Quintin Blackthorne, wherever he
is."

April, 1781, The Georgia Back Country

Devon Blackthorne was sick of war. Sick of the
stench and carnage. Sick of the senseless waste as
a people rent itself like a frenzied beast in such a
coil of anguish that it tore out its own entrails. He
kicked the cold ashes of the cabin and cursed.

McGilvey had been here. Lying in the burned-out
debris of what was once a neat and prosperous farm
were the mutilated bodies of a man, his wife, and
their three children. They had been murdered for
their livestock and a few bushels of dried corn. Of
course, McGilvey and his men had taken their obscene
pleasures with the woman and her two daughters

before the mercy of death claimed them.

He thought of how McGilvey had tried to do this to Barbara, and his blood ran cold. "And now the bastard is raiding right outside Savannah." He had to run the renegade aground before McGilvey found out Devon's yellow-haired woman was living in the city. God only knew what the brute would do to her if he got his hands on her again!

The marauder was known to frequent the Savannah waterfront. Perhaps this temporary reassignment to the city was not such a bad thing after all. In spite of the pain of encountering Barbara, Devon might well be able to save her life.

Of course, the way the war was turning now, mayhap she would soon return to England with her brother. Lord Germain's southern strategy was not going well. Loyalists eager to fight the rebels did not swell the ranks of the occupying British army. Many colonists stayed neutral, while others fought fiercely for their independence from British rule.

The forests, swamps, and rivers that crisscrossed the South were custom-made for partisans, who could raid overextended British supply lines and vanish back into the wilderness, burning bridges and ferries as they went. Men like Pickins and Clarke had become the scourge of Georgia, while Marion and his new comrade in arms, Lighthorse Harry Lee, chipped away one British foothold after another in the Carolinas. The little Huguenot's tactical genius combined brilliantly with Lee's daring cavalry sweeps. Even such a master of carnage as Banastre Tarleton, who had dubbed Marion "The Swamp Fox," was unable to catch him in his deadly lair.

"If we lose this bloody war, I still won't lose McGilvey. He'll pay for his crimes," Devon swore as he signaled to his men to remount and continue

on their way. Sooner or later, he would kill George
McGilvey.

The bell clanged noisily from the center of Ellis
Square, signaling the opening of the public market
for the day. Madelyne surveyed the bustling pros-
perity before her, amazed at how little touched the
place seemed in the midst of a war. Ships from
London still unloaded their cargoes downriver,
bringing every luxury to the city encircled by
marauding rebel bands. Those partisans somewhat
restricted the flow of raw materials and foodstuffs
into Savannah, yet there were plenty of farmers and
tradesmen who were far more interested in profits
than politics. They brought fresh vegetables and
livestock on the hoof as well as cured hides and
warm furs to be traded for every import item from
iron cook pots to pickled herrings.

Passing stalls piled high with rich fox and otter
pelts, bins of fresh turnips and peas, and haunches of
venison hanging in the cool morning air, Madelyne
strolled through the market, looking for Polly's
familiar rawboned figure in her bright red petticoats and crisp white apron. They had been meeting
at the market, as it was a convenient place where
Polly regularly purchased supplies for her tavern.
The first time, last November, when Madelyne had
accidentally bumped into the older woman, Polly
had been decidedly cool, but when Madelyne risked
Robert's wrath by riding to the Swan to assure her
friend that she was innocent of Quint's betrayal,
Polly had believed her.

Then through Barbara, Madelyne had learned of
Polly's connections with the rebels. She sought to
warn Polly that the British were watching her tavern,
only to learn that Polly Bloor already knew that and
was indeed an avowed patriot. Now that the back
country partisans were scoring so many victories,
Polly no longer hid her allegiance, baldly admitting

regret that she could no longer hide fugitive rebels. She added puckishly, however, that since it was becoming increasingly risky for British patrols to venture so far from Savannah, her services were far less essential in that regard.

Polly's feelings made sense to Madelyne—as much sense as anything in this brutal civil war. Both women had prayed for word that Quintin was alive and well. Until now, none had come. But yesterday Polly sent a cryptic message saying she had received information about him. Madelyne was to meet her at their usual place, the butcher stall of a Salzberger colonist, where Polly bought excellent smoked sausage for her tavern.

"There you are! And lookin' in the bloom of motherhood, too." Polly reached out and gave Madelyne a hearty hug, then inspected her well-rounded middle. "I see my herbal tea and pound cake have done their job."

"If you mean ended my stomach upsets and put a lot of weight on me, that's the truth," Madelyne replied ruefully. "I feel like a great wallowing sow," she whispered. A finely dressed British officer's wife with her retinue of servants passed by, looking disdainfully at a pregnant woman who dared appear in public.

"You look splendid 'n healthy. Keep to your exercise. Don't let no fool man tell you to take to your bed."

"Dr. Witherspoon is no fool, and he agrees with you. Now Polly, tell me what you've learned about my child's father." Madelyne held her breath for a moment as Polly fished in her apron pocket.

The older woman's face was grave, but her words immediately soothed Madelyne. "That young rascal's alive 'n well. Well's can be in them cursed swamps. He finally got a letter through to me. Seems like Solomon Torres is back in the mail business, real quiet nowadays," she said beneath her breath as

Madelyne clutched the letter.

Madelyne felt the tears sting her eyes. He had written Polly but not her. Not the wife he believed had betrayed him to a hangman's noose. She clutched the letter, half afraid to read it lest some disparagement of her be contained in its pages.

Sensing her fears, Polly patted her hand. "He don't say much personal, just tells me about how us patriots are whipping the sass from you loyalists. But since old Corny's took such losses at Guilford's Courthouse that he had to retreat clean back to Virginia, I reckon you know enough about that already."

Madelyne managed a wobbly smile. "Yes, for all I care any longer. All Barbara's brother and his friends can speak of is what General Cornwallis plans next."

Polly gave her a hug and a wink. "If you find out, you be sure 'n let me know! Now, be off with you 'n read about your man."

Madelyne hesitated for a moment, then said, "You mentioned Mr. Torres . . . Do you think he might carry a letter from me to Quint? I want him to know about the baby."

Polly rubbed her fleshy chin in consideration. "Don't know if he could get anything through. This ain't the first letter Quint wrote—just the first that got to me. But you write your letter 'n I'll see what I can do."

"Oh, Polly, do you think he'll ever believe in me again? *Will he ever love me?*"

"Once a man's holding his own flesh 'n blood—well, he usually comes around."

"If he even believes that this *is* his child," Madelyne said bitterly.

Polly seized Madelyne by the arm and began to lead her through the maze of stalls and milling throngs of people. "We need to set down and have us a talk. I know a place."

The place was a small chandler's shop just off Ellis Square. A Mr. Brewster was the owner, a long-time customer of Polly's establishment. He ushered them into a small sitting room, spartanly furnished with a six-legged wooden settee and two worn slat-backed chairs. The spicy tang of bayberries hung heavy in the air as he asked if they would like refreshment.

"That would be real kind of you, Ethan. I'd take it as an extra kindness if'n you could bring the young mother here an extra bit of sugar for her coffee."

When they were alone, Polly stirred her coffee and spoke quietly. "I never told no one this, dearie, but after all you been through, I guess you got the right. You know about Quint and old Robert . . ."

"That my husband isn't Robert's son. Yes, he told me—but he said he'd never told another living soul. He only blurted it out to me in a fit of fury on our wedding morning."

"He don't know he told me. He was drunk outta his head. Only sixteen years old 'n hurtin' real bad." Polly shook her head and paused to compose herself. "That old man is pure vicious, damned if he ain't. Quint talked—rambled really—all about growin' up alone in that big plantation house."

"With only Robert Blackthorne's bitterness surrounding him," Madelyne said.

"You can't imagine the half of it. I want you to understand why Quint can't trust you—can't trust any woman, least of all one who's got under his skin the way you have. Robert used to grieve really fierce for his English lady, but her playing him false with his brother made him near crazy. He wouldn't let Quint even speak her name aloud or ask anyone about his mum. He had all her things locked away, but he couldn't bring hisself to get rid of them."

"Why, Polly? Why did she do such a horrible thing?"

Polly wrung her work-reddened hands helplessly. "I don't know, dearie. I only know she left her child to bear the punishment for her sins—and punish him old Robert did. Caught the boy up in the attic where he kept her things when Quint was only seven years old. You know how children get curious, specially when they're forbidden to do something? Well, he beat the young master with a whip—one of them whips overseers use on field slaves."

Madelyne shivered in revulsion. "How could he be such a monster? Did Quint resemble her? Remind him of her?"

"No, near as I can tell, the Lady Anne looked like your friend Lady Barbara, her niece—all blonde and blue-eyed and fair skinned. Quint would've stood the beatings. Even then he was a tough 'un. No, it was what Robert said that really cut deepest. Called Quint's mother a bitch in heat 'n her son a filthy mongrel, not worthy of the Blackthorne name even if he was Alastair's get."

"He said that to a seven-year-old child!"

"Explained everything about barnyard facts of life so there'd be no mistakin' either. That's when Quint run away to his uncle Alastair. By that time Alastair 'n his Indian wife had left their plantation. He followed them into Creek territory. Quint never said what Alastair told him. Maybe he never got up the courage to ask if he was his pa. I dunno. He lived with them for near a year 'n then Robert's men found him and hog-tied him to get him back to Blackthorne Hill. Robert locked the boy up in one of them big rooms on the third floor—attic rooms where the mistress's things was stored. Fed him bread 'n water, waitin' fer the boy to beg his forgiveness ta get free."

"But Quint refused," Madelyne said, tears choking her throat as she saw a small, raven-haired boy, alone and frightened, starved and whipped, but never defeated.

"Yep. Finally when he was near dead, the old man give up 'n fetched a doctor. When the boy recovered his health, Robert told him he was his only heir. He'd inherit Blackthorne Hill 'n everything Robert had built, but if he ever spoke about his bastardy to anyone, he'd give it all to Alastair's older boy, Andrew."

"And Quint never did. I can imagine how he must've grown to hate his mother, blaming her for what Robert did to him. Then he let Robert's hate for all women pervade his own beliefs."

"Every chance the old man got as Quint was growing up, Robert tried to break him, to shame him, almost as if he wanted Quint to give up and admit he wasn't good enough to inherit the Hill."

"No wonder he's so jealous of Andrew. If he'd broken under Robert's cruelties, he would've suffered everything in vain and all his birthright would've gone to his cousin."

"But he never broke 'n he never got mean like old Robert neither. He's a good man, Madelyne. Scared and lonely, afraid to trust—especially to trust you. I watched it ever since he first brought you here. No woman ever got to him like you."

"Serena Fallowfield seemed to be giving an excellent imitation of rousing his passions when I caught them together at the Governor's ball," Madelyne said tightly.

Polly scoffed. "He knows her for what she is— and she's been stalking him, that's for sure. Maybe he used her to put a wall between you. Ever think of that?"

"Well, it worked. I flew into a hateful rage and accused him of all sorts of awful things that night. The next day he became a hunted outlaw, and he blames me."

"You read what he's got to say about livin' through a war 'n then you write 'n tell him he's gonna be a papa come spring. I'll find some way in hell to get word to the young fool or my name ain't Polly Bloor!"

*   *   *

Madelyne read the letter her husband had sent to Polly. It was long but hastily scrawled on odd scraps of paper and much blurred by dust and dampness during its arduous journey from the Carolina swamps. The desperate and dangerous conditions under which the men lived and fought frightened her, especially since she was certain he was downplaying their adversity to ease Polly's fears.

Quintin served under the infamous rebel partisan Francis Marion, the Swamp Fox, whom all Southern loyalists cursed for his ruthless and successful raiding tactics. He described the most recent victory Marion had achieved, at an obscure place called Ft. Watson, when a Major Hezekiah Maham built a high log tower from which daring rebels could fire into the British stockade. Quintin braved fire and gunpowder explosives to ascend the tower and use his marksman's skills until the fort surrendered.

"He could have died in a fiery inferno, or been blown to bits!" She paled, but read further. Other than a few scratches, he had come through all their skirmishes and frontal assaults unscathed. But for how long? When she read that some of the Georgia partisans occasionally slipped home now that the back country was no longer firmly under British control, she made a decision.

"Quint's baby should be born at Blackthorne Hill after all he's done to hold it. I'm going home to the plantation. Let the Liberty Boys do their worst. I'm the wife of one of their patriots."

Would Quintin return home to see his newborn child? She prayed that he would.

Chapter Eighteen

June, 1781, The Commons, Savannah

The sun, which had shone brilliantly when the gala outing began, had now vanished beneath a billowing gray cloud that promised a thunderstorm. But the weather did not deter the avid spectators any more than it did the participants. Georgians, like their English cousins, dearly loved a good horse race, and the dozen riders competing that afternoon promised to put on quite a contest.

The flat terrain of the Georgia coast lent itself admirably to racing, even if the sandy soil did slow the track a bit. Gentlemen dressed in fine satin waistcoats and brocade jackets sat with their ladies in the shade of magnolia and sweet bay trees. The women arranged their wide panniers artfully as they seated themselves on footstools brought by servants, who waved fans overhead in the still afternoon heat and served them cool lemonade and picnic delicacies.

The rougher element, always present at such races, did not mix with the gentry, but held their raucous gathering at the opposite end of the large oval racetrack, nearer to where the riders readied their mounts. Tradesmen in rough buckram pants and rivermen in buckskins mingled with an assortment of enlisted soldiers and their Indian allies.

"I say, Barbara, you've scarcely touched that sinfully rich cream cake," Colonel Weymouth said solicitously. "Are you feeling unwell in the heat?" His round blue eyes were a bit protuberant and his jaw slightly receding, giving him the appearance of a quizzical fish.

"I'm quite fine, thank you, Alex, just looking forward to the rain."

"Oh pooh! The rain will quite ruin the race, not to mention my gown," Serena Fallowfield said petulantly as she smoothed her pale hands over the deep rose satin of her elegant creation.

Barbara thought she looked ridiculously overdressed for a sultry summer afternoon, but said nothing, hoping the black-haired witch would catch Alex Weymouth's attention, which would please both women. Barbara certainly did not want it, and Serena had dragged Andrew, who detested racing, to the event simply to stalk the viscount.

"I think the rain will hold off long enough for the race. We have covered coaches to see you ladies safely home," Weymouth said, looking from Serena to Barbara.

"I say, Alex, isn't that the blood bay everyone's been talking about? Big brute. You suppose he can run?" Monty's eyes squinted as he studied the horses across the track, worried about the large bet he had placed on a dun horse owned by a lieutenant under his command.

Weymouth studied the big, dark-red stallion prancing nervously amid the crowd of ruffians and savages. Several mongrel dogs barked and chased each other. A fat man in a fine wool hat was taking a bet from a giant Muskogee Indian. "Demned savages do like to wager, don't they? The bay looks to be too high strung for a real competitor."

"Don't be too certain of that, your lordship. I happen to recognize the beast. It belongs to Andrew's half-brother, Devon. He rides like one of those accursed savages," Serena said sweetly, noting the angry color rise in Andrew's face. "I would never wager against a half-caste rider. Some say he's as good as his wild relatives."

At the mention of Devon's name, Barbara froze. What was he doing in Savannah? He'd left her and ridden off for Florida nearly a year ago. She scanned the crowd and immediately picked out his golden head among the men and animals milling around the track.

Wearing a royal ranger's green jacket with crimson collar and cuffs, he looked so handsome and splendid that her breath caught in her throat. As Andrew, Monty, and Alex argued about the merits of Dev's horse and horsemanship, Barbara felt everything around her blurring. She traveled back in time to the Muskogee village where they had been lovers.

Serena watched her infuriating rival, then followed her gaze to Devon Blackthorne. "La, gentlemen, I do believe an English lady has had her fancy taken by a roguish half-caste. Do warn her, Andrew, that in spite of his dazzling looks, he's nothing but a Creek savage disguised in white man's clothing."

"Will that horse win, Andrew?" Barbara ignored Serena's taunts.

Andrew felt sweat dampening his brow and wanted to kill Henry Fallowfield's widow. How he hated to be reminded of his father's disgraceful second marriage, as if the Blackthornes did not already have enough scandal to contend with because of Quintin.

He forced a smile for Lady Barbara and replied, "I know little of horses and care less. As to my *half*-brother's skills, I plead equal ignorance. I doubt he can compete with the several excellent British officers who are riding today."

"Yes, I see Armbruster. Now that dun of his—"

"I want to place a wager on Devon Blackthorne's bay." Barbara interrupted Monty, who turned to her incredulously.

Bloody hell! Monty knew his spoiled sister disliked his matchmaking with Weymouth, but this was too much to be endured. "Nonsense, m' dear. You'll only lose. Sorry I even mentioned it and piqued your interest."

"I'm afraid that in this colonial backwater, Lady Barbara, women of quality are not even allowed the fun of a harmless wager without jeopardizing their reputations," Serena said, noting with satisfaction that the Viscount of Leicester was growing rather agitated, but when he spoke, her mood quickly darkened.

"We Londoners are a rowdy lot. Please pardon our small vices, dear Mrs. Fallowfield." Then he turned to Barbara and winked rakishly. "I shall be happy to place your wager for you, Lady Barbara. Say ten pounds?"

"La, Colonel," Barbara rejoined, "I would have this be a worthy bet. Let it be fifty pounds?"

Monty paled. Already the butcher, the cobbler, and his tailor were dunning him. Soon he would have no credit left even if his horse swept the field. "Are you quite certain, little sister, that such a large wager is appropriate?"

Before Barbara could reply, Serena interrupted petulantly. "Well, I shall wager, too, then. Won't you bet against that hateful savage, Andrew? I'm certain some of the ruffians over there would take our markers." She watched as Andrew's complexion turned a near shade to crimson, while Monty looked positively green as he stood silently beside his sister.

Gritting his teeth, Andrew nodded to Serena, his eyes cold and dark with a fury that bespoke later retribution. "I shall place the wagers," he replied glacially.

Caught up in the spirit of the gaming, Weymouth, too, decided he would bet on the bay in spite of encouraging Monty to place a tidy sum on Lieutenant Armbruster's dun. "I must stand with the Lady Barbara against all the rest of you. I'll back the bay as well—stoutly, with fifty pounds—if a taker can be found in that camp of Indians and rivermen."

"What an adventure," Barbara said, encouraging the viscount. They set out, with Monty and Andrew following reluctantly behind. Serena waited alone, furious at her desertion, yet unwilling to go near the riffraff across the track.

Devon saw her the moment she and Weymouth stepped away from the crowd. Her glorious silver-gilt hair shone from beneath a rakish little hat and her face was as hauntingly beautiful as his nightly dreams envisioned it. She looked every inch the English lady, dressed in a delicate lime-green India-cotton gown, simple and cool for a warm day. He felt his chest squeeze with pain and forced himself to concentrate on taking bets. What madness had made him agree to race Firebrand? *I might have known she'd be here.* Perhaps that was why he had come, just to see her again after all the hellish lonely months.

Barbara and her retinue approached Nicholas Dundee, a keen-witted shipping merchant who was taking bets on the race. Grimly, with a bitter twist to his lips, Devon wondered if his brother would acknowledge him. He decided to see, just for the hell of it, and to hear Barbara's voice one more time.

Leading Firebrand by his reins, he strolled over and stood directly in front of Andrew. "Good day for a race. Even better if it rains before we begin. Are you betting for or against me, dear brother?"

Andrew turned to his half-brother, his eyes darkened with fury barely held in check. The damned savage was laughing at him! "Against you, of course, Devon."

"Never fear, my dear fellow, for you have the lovely lady here and myself wagering for you," Weymouth said with a flourish. He eyed Devon keenly, noting his startling handsomeness in the natty ranger green. The chap didn't look like a savage at all, except for his swarthy skin and dark eyes.

Devon gave the viscount a mock salute with his riding crop, then made the same gesture with a more rakish flourish for Barbara, who stood with her eyes glued on him. "In olden times, a lady gave her champion some token to carry into a contest. Might you favor me so, beautiful lady?" He gave her a measuring look, wondering what she would respond, and noting with satisfaction that Weymouth's condescending smile had evaporated.

Barbara fought to breathe, wanting against all reason to throw herself into Dev's arms and sob out how much she loved him. Instead, she assumed the flirtatious facade she had practiced since childhood and replied, "How could I not honor such a gallant request?" She took a small green feather from her hat and boldly fastened it in the scarlet lapel of his jacket.

"I'm honored, my lady," he said, all traces of humor erased from his face.

Just then Nicholas Dundee called for the contestants to mount up and move to their positions at the starting line. Devon forced himself to concentrate on the business at hand, sizing up his competition.

He had listened to the gossip among the soldiers since arriving in the city and knew that the man favored to win the race was a royal militia officer named Armbruster, a wiry New Jersey farmer. His dun was reportedly unbeaten. Devon studied the horse, noting the nervous rider who pulled harshly on the reins as he wheeled the dun into position.

Likely a fast starter, but did he have the stamina to stay the course, which consisted of two laps around the mile-long oval track? He glanced up at the threatening skies and prayed for rain. The track was sandy, as most of the coastal lowlands were, but he had ridden it, and one stretch was hard-packed clay, which would turn to churning mud with a good soaking.

As the starting gun sent the riders off in a storm of flying sand, Barbara thought frantically about how to get a message to Dev. She scoured the crowd and noted several boys who might be persuaded to relay a few words to him for a couple of coins. One stood not far from their coach. When the riders vanished around the curve of the track behind a low-lying copse of myrtle, she felt a fat raindrop plop on her nose.

Almost immediately, Serena let out a squeak and ran for her coach. On the same pretext, Barbara did likewise. Once certain the men were all occupied, she extracted several coppers from her pocket and held them up for the waif to see. Thin and grimy looking, he had a certain feral cleverness in his expression as he cautiously neared the grandly dressed lady.

Quickly Barbara relayed her message for Dev and paid him, then reached inside the coach for her shawl. Draping it about her shoulders, she returned to her vantage point. She was not going to miss the outcome of the race just because of a simple wetting!

By the time the riders had made the first lap, nearly half of them were clearly out of the race. Dev's big bay was still near the front. She cheered him on lustily.

Dev leaned low on Firebrand's neck, holding him back as he gauged the last half of the race. Several of the strong starters had lost out, but a gray and Armbruster's dun were holding strong. Rain began to pelt them in earnest now, and the crowd thinned as satin- and lace-clad ladies and gentlemen fled for the dry comfort of their covered conveyances. He saw Barbara near the edge of the track, yelling him on with ferocity, utterly oblivious of being soaking wet. Grinning, he passed her by in a flurry of flying sand and mud.

When they approached the last quarter of the track and Armbruster saw that he had not shaken the bay or the gray, he dug his spurs into the straining animal and quirted him frantically. All three horses approached the muddy area close together. By the second time around, it had become badly churned up and was treacherous. The gray's rider slowed his mount to allow for the uncertain footing, but Armbruster whipped his dun on, with Devon gaining quickly.

Just as they drew neck and neck, Armbruster tried to rein his horse closer to the inside circle of the track. It was a mistake. The animal stumbled on the slick chunks of muddy earth, sliding to his knees and sending the Jersey man tumbling over his head. Devon let Firebrand have his head now, knowing the Indian mount was used to muddy backroad trails.

By the time they had cleared the treacherous stretch, he was so far ahead of the gray that it was no contest. The winner sailed across the finish line to the cheers of his Muskogee friends as well as a good number of rivermen and farmers who had bet on him.

Surrounded by well-wishers, Devon searched for Barbara in the crowd. She stood at the edge of the press beside a very glum-looking Major Montgomery and a livid Andrew, while Weymouth strode over to collect on the bets he had placed. Hat abandoned, her hair hung in a dripping mass down her back, and her pale green petticoats were liberally sprayed with sand and mud. She looked glorious.

A small, grimy little hand tugged at the tails of his jacket as he received congratulations and was paid handsomely by numerous losing gamblers. Dev turned in irritation, expecting the urchin to beg for a share in his bounty, but when the boy whispered the message in his ear, he was amazed. He looked up and his startled eyes met Barbara's again. She nodded to him, then turned quickly and walked toward her carriage before he could shake his head in refusal.

As they rode toward Blackthorne Hill, Barbara wondered if Dev would follow her there. She had not dared to look at his face for more than a brief glance when the boy delivered her message. What would he do? If he did dare to come, what would she do?

"I say, Barbara, you are aware that my uncle Robert will be . . . difficult?" Andrew made a discreet cough as he waited for her to reply.

They rode side by side, accompanied by a dozen armed soldiers. Monty was taking no chance with the rebel partisans. Barbara looked over at Andrew's pale, intense face and was again struck with how little she liked the man, although he had done nothing untoward to her. She wondered how he would feel about seeing Dev at Blackthorne Hill, then answered his question with candor. "I realize that Robert Blackthorne hates the Caruthers family. But he's ill, often confined to bed with bouts of fever.

I doubt he'll be able to horsewhip me from the premises." *Or Dev.* "Anyway, Madelyne asked me to come, and she needs me now that her time is near."

Andrew flushed in annoyance. It was bad enough that Quintin's wife was breeding without this arrogant Englishwoman rubbing his nose in it. "I should think an unmarried lady such as yourself would be better off visiting after the blessed event."

She gave him an assessing look that revealed just a hint of her animosity. "But Madelyne needs me now." Her voice was flat as she kicked her horse into a canter and rode ahead. Monty had wanted them to use his chair, but the thought of being confined in such a small conveyance for hours with Andrew Blackthorne had made her skin crawl.

Madelyne could hear Delphine moving about the room, but her eyes were squeezed tightly closed as she focused on breathing.

"Jest relax now. Doan fight the pain. Only make it worse. Easy, easy." The big black woman's hands were as soothing as her voice. She had been repeating her encouragements and offering small bits of advice for hours.

The first cramping contraction had hit Madelyne while she was overseeing the candle dipping. Delphine had arrived immediately. To her surprise the cook, who was the senior midwife on the plantation, instructed her to continue her usual activities, walking around the yard. She assigned two girls from the kitchen to stay with her and hold her up when a contraction hit her, but for hours the pains had been irregularly spaced.

When they came around ten minutes apart, Delphine ushered her upstairs but kept her walking about the large bedroom. Madelyne couldn't help but stare at the big, lonely bed where she and Quint had made love so often. If only he were here for his child's birth!

When the cramps were less than five minutes apart, Delphine put her in bed and began to gently massage her rounded abdomen and press cool cloths to her sweaty face. She felt the last contraction ease and opened her eyes. "Delphine, do you think Barbara will come? It's been nearly a week since I sent the letter."

"She say she comin'. She be here. Doan worry 'bout nothin' else now but this here little one. Won't be long now."

Voices echoed from downstairs and then the sound of footfalls on the carpeted stairs. Shortly, the slight, rumpled figure of Noble Witherspoon appeared at the door.

"What you doin' here?" Delphine drew herself up to her full magisterial height of five feet ten inches.

By comparison, the five-foot-three-inch physician seemed puny, but he was undaunted. "I've been caring for Mrs. Blackthorne ever since she became pregnant. I'm here to deliver the baby." He opened his bag and began to sort through it.

"I been deliverin' *all* the babies born on Blackthorne Hill for forty years," Delphine replied, affronted.

"Well, Quintin Blackthorne is my friend. I've treated him and will do the same for his wife. You don't have leave to be such a tyrant just because Quint freed you, Delphine."

The big black woman made a snort of disgust and narrowed her eyes on the little doctor. "Jest cause he done freed me doan mean I free him—or his family!"

Madelyne began to laugh as the two antagonists squared off on opposite sides of her bed, but then another pain gripped her, far worse than any before it. "You two had better call a truce and attend to the business that brought us all together," she gasped. "I think the new master of Blackthorne Hill wants to be born!"

* * *

The slaves' grapevine moved with incredible speed. At Blackthorne Hill, the mistress had just brought Master Quintin's son into the world. Within a few hours word had spread to the Golden Swan.

Devon Blackthorne sat at a corner table, nursing a mug of ale and wrestling with his conscience when he heard Polly excitedly receive the news. Should he go to meet Barbara? No, of course not. It was a reckless, foolish thing to do. She was all but engaged to her fish-eyed colonel—who also happened to be a fabulously wealthy viscount, he reminded himself glumly. She was better off among her own kind. But he did owe it to Madelyne Blackthorne, living all alone with hateful old Robert, to look in on her and her newborn baby.

"You're fooling yourself, my man," he muttered as he shoved back his chair and rose.

"Where're you goin', you young devil? I got at least three of my girls upstairs pinin' somethin' awful to have you in their beds," Polly said as she gave Dev a hug. "You just arrived last night and didn't even ask for Moll. She's in a real taking, I don't mind tellin' you."

"Tell her I slept alone, Polly," he said. "Really, I was pining for you, but since you've reformed, well . . ." He gave her a wink and a kiss on the cheek.

Blushing like a schoolgirl, Polly chuckled. "Go on with you. Such honeyed words. You'll bring down a dozen black bears from the hills with such sweet talk."

"Well I'm heading for the Hill. Better to face a dozen bears than beard Uncle Robert in his own lair. Wish me luck, love."

Her ruddy, weathered face lost all traces of humor. "Dev, you know how Robert feels. Why—"

"I just heard the news about my cousin's heir. I've met Quint's wife. She's as good and kind as she is loyal. Quint doesn't deserve her. She's alone and could probably use a bit of cheering, don't you agree?"

Polly gave him a highly dubious look. "You, Andrew, and that fancy English ladyship all goin' to get on together?"

Dev shrugged, but his usual careless insouciance was missing. "I'm used to handling Andrew. I'll let you know about the Englishwoman," he added, patting her well-padded rump as he tossed a coin for the drink on the scarred table.

"Good luck, Dev. Yer gonna need it."

When Devon arrived at Blackthorne Hill, everyone was thrilled about the birth of the heir. The stableman who took his bay had been busily collecting on a bet with the smithy regarding the child's sex. He regarded Devon with round-eyed wonder.

"Ain't seen you, Mastah Devon, in many a long year, sinc't you be a tad. Growed up real good."

"Thank you, Obediah. I appreciate the welcome, knowing full well how my uncle feels about me."

"Good luck, Mastah Devon."

When Devon reached the big house, he stood on the front stoop for a moment, looking about the scattered buildings of Robert Blackthorne's kingdom. The creek he and Quint used to swim in was just over the hill, and the dairy where they stole cream was down the road. Bittersweet memories of a childhood long past and a friendship sundered by war flooded his senses. Even though Robert Blackthorne had forbidden their association, he and Quint had been like brothers, stealing off to play together in secret. He pushed away the melancholy thoughts and let the heavy brass door knocker fall.

Almost instantly it was answered by a small black girl, barely old enough to be serving as a maid. A raspy voice called out from behind her, "Place is becoming a damned wayfaring inn. Who—" Robert stopped abruptly at the foot of the wide circular staircase and stared in amazement at Devon. His face, pale and haggard, quickly darkened with apoplectic fury. "What, by all that's holy, are you doing in my home?"

"You've always been in a poor position to invoke anything holy, Uncle Robert," Devon replied as he walked slowly across the entry hall to where Robert stood.

"Get out, you mongrel savage!"

"I may be one quarter Muskogee, but at least I wear the king's colors—unlike your own treacherous son," Devon said with a smoothness he was far from feeling.

Robert's face went from ruddy to purplish. "I'll have you horsewhipped. I'll do it myself!" He took a step toward Devon with his fist raised, only to stagger and fall backward, clutching the newel post at the bottom of the stairs. His breath came in great labored gulps, and his face was beaded with perspiration.

Devon instructed the serving girl to run and fetch Delphine, but before she even reached the end of the hallway, Andrew had entered the room and took in the scene.

"I heard Uncle Robert shouting. Small wonder. What crack-brained whim possessed you to come here?" he asked as he knelt beside his brother, who had eased Robert to a reclining position on the carpeted steps.

"I've met Quint's wife and had a feeling she might enjoy a friendly face," Devon said, noting the way Andrew stiffened.

"I am her friend. She certainly doesn't need to visit with a half-caste scoundrel like you."

Andrew's voice sounded pompous and at the same time oddly wary to Devon's ears. Before Devon could reply, Barbara's voice interrupted him. He turned and drank in her radiant beauty.

"Carry him upstairs to his room," she instructed the two brothers, then turned to Toby. "Send for Dr. Witherspoon." When the elderly servant left, she watched Dev as he and Andrew lifted the unconscious Robert and ascended the stairs with him.

So you came after all.

"Why are you here? Don't give me that twaddle about seeing Madelyne, either," Andrew hissed as they laid Robert on the big walnut four-poster bed in his room.

"Madelyne did ask to see your brother, Andrew," Barbara said as she looked at Dev's hands, busy unfastening Robert's shoes. "And I wanted to talk with him as well. After all, he was responsible for my winning a great deal of money."

"Monty and I lost even more," Andrew replied stiffly, wanting desperately to get the troublesome female out of the room so he could talk to Devon alone.

"Your brother really is a reckless gambler if he let Andrew here influence his betting," Devon said to Barbara as he peeled down Robert's stockings.

"I know only too well how reckless Monty can be," she replied softly, her eyes locking with Dev's.

"Speaking of reckless, coming here was really a rash, inconsiderate thing to do. You knew how Uncle Robert would react," Andrew interjected.

"Here's Toby. Let him tend to Uncle Robert, Andrew," Barbara said as the valet entered the room and hovered worriedly at the foot of the bed. Delphine, with her medicine basket, followed immediately behind and began to shoo the useless white folks from Robert's sickbed.

Barbara linked her arm through Dev's and led him toward the door. "I fear I must take things in hand, Mr. Blackthorne, since your brother is being such an absolute beast. We were never formally introduced. I am Lady Barbara Caruthers."

"I remember you well, your ladyship," he replied, his voice laden with double meaning, "from the race-track. Devon Blackthorne, at your service." He lifted her hand from his arm and kissed it gallantly. The hairs on the back of his neck prickled in warning as he felt Andrew's cold pale eyes on the two of them. *This is madness.*

"You'll have to leave, of course," Andrew said peremptorily.

"He most certainly will not. Madelyne has just given Blackthorne Hill its new heir. She wished to see Mr. Blackthorne," Barbara said, giving Andrew one of her lightly scolding, frivolous-belle smiles as she whisked Devon down the hallway toward the stairs.

Andrew seethed with impotent rage, but held his peace. He knew which direction the wind blew. Ever since old Robert had fallen ill and Quintin had fled in disgrace, Madelyne had taken over running the plantation. Now that she'd also provided a male heir, no one would do anything on Blackthorne Hill without her approval. Even that prim-faced old housekeeper kept her distance. He would do nothing to displease his "dear cousin" until Quintin was dead and she safely wed to him.

As they walked downstairs, Andrew watched Barbara and Devon with interest. Was the chit so intent on foisting his half-caste brother on him just because she disliked him—or was there something between Devon and the arrogant English beauty? He dismissed the idea as absurd. There was no way they could even have met before the other day at the race. Still, Devon had always had a way of charming women into simpering idiocy. Again he cursed his father for his ill-considered second marriage and the fates for giving the offspring of that union his striking handsomeness whilst he, the pure-blooded heir, resembled his mother's undistinguished-looking family.

"While you escort Devon to see my dear cousin, I shall attend to some pressing matters belowstairs. Tell her I'll be up to see her and the boy before dinner." Lud, what a ghastly ordeal the meal would be, sharing table with his savage half-brother and the spiteful Barbara Caruthers!

"So, this is the new heir of Blackthorne Hill. A little on the small side, but I imagine he'll grow," Devon said as Madelyne lifted the mosquito netting from the baby's cradle. His eyes danced teasingly as he made his inspection.

"His name is James Quintin Blackthorne, after my grandfather and his father—and he is *not* small," Madelyne replied proudly as she lifted the dozing infant from the cradle. "Here, lift him and see for yourself." She extended the small wriggling bundle toward the young bachelor.

Devon threw up his hands in mock surrender. "I'll take your word for it, Madelyne. He looks right lusty."

Madelyne lightly caressed the cap of fine black hair on the babe's head. "He has his father's hair and soon will have the green eyes, too," she said softly.

"Have you been able to get word to Quint that he's a father?" Devon tried to keep the edge from his voice.

Madelyne shrugged helplessly. "I've as little liking for the Liberty Boys as they have for me, but I sent a message through indirect sources. I don't know how long it will take or if it will reach him." *Or if he even cares.*

"Nonsense, if even half of what we hear about those rebels is true, he'll receive every detail of young James's birth in a trice," Barbara said soothingly, knowing how heavily the matter weighed on Madelyne's mind. "I'm certain someone at the Golden Swan will get through to him."

"Polly's place?" Devon asked in amazement.

Barbara turned to Devon with a superior smile. "You've only just arrived in Savannah, Mr. Black- thorne. My brother has had Mistress Bloor on his list of suspected rebel sympathizers for some time now. You really should get on better with Monty, you know." She cocked her head at him coquet- tishly.

"Damn if a man knows who's friend and who's foe in this accursed war," Devon said in amaze- ment, recalling how he and Barbara had found Quint hidden at the Swan. Perhaps . . .

Madelyne's chin went up as she held her son. "I knew Quint was a rebel, Devon." She could no longer make herself use the word "traitor." "I couldn't betray him. Censure me for it if you will. I've already done so a thousand times, yet I would not see my husband die."

Devon sighed in frustration. "Neither would I, Madelyne, now that the shock of betrayal has worn off. But we're men on opposing sides in war."

"And nothing's to be gained by discussing this further," Barbara said, steering Devon toward the door as she spoke to Madelyne. "You feed the young master there, and I'll be up to help you decide what dress to wear to dinner tonight. With Devon as a guest and Robert confined to bed, we should have a perfectly delightful time of it."

"If we promise not to discuss politics," Devon said, smiling at Madelyne.

"My lips are sealed," she replied as the baby began to cry loudly.

"Mine, too, but obviously Master James's aren't." He gave both women a lopsided smile as he left the room.

Dinner that evening was Madelyne's first trip downstairs since James was born, and the ser- vants had gone to great lengths to make it fes- tive. Huge sprays of fresh summer flowers lent their fragrance to the succulent aroma wafting from Delphine's kitchens. Without Robert's somber presence and acidic comments, the meal should have been pleasant, but Andrew and Devon were almost as bad as their uncle.

As the men argued through dinner, Madelyne watched the subtle byplay between Devon and Barbara and, she noted, so did Andrew. Something was going on, but Madelyne could not decide exactly what. Barbara had always disliked Andrew. After observing the way he behaved toward Devon, she was inclined to see some merit in her friend's judgment. As always, Andrew was solicitous and gentle with her, but now that she had made other friends in his brother and Barbara, Madelyne was beginning to see her "dear cousin" in a new light, an unflattering one.

Perhaps he's just jealous of Dev's charm and handsomeness. Lord knows the rogue has entranced Barbara, and she's scarcely a green girl. But there was something more to the seemingly instantaneous attraction between her friend and the ranger captain. Dismissing the idea as fanciful, she intervened in the heated discussion between the two brothers over the conduct of the war.

"The man's a bumbling oaf, thinking to take on General Cornwallis headlong," Andrew said. "We sent him off with his tail between his legs after Guilford Courthouse."

"Nate Greene is no fool. He knew when to fight and how to retreat strategically. Guilford Courthouse was a pyrrhic victory of the first order," Devon said tersely.

"It would seem to me that since the battle ended in a draw, either side could claim it as a victory," Madelyne said carefully. "The fact is, both men quit the field and regrouped."

"But Cornwallis chose to regroup in Virginia while Georgia and the Carolinas lay exposed like fish in a dammed-up creek," Devon argued. "He's fighting a traditional war against non-traditional foes."

"He's fighting rabble," Andrew scoffed.

Madelyne colored in anger at Andrew's aspersion on her husband and his cause.

"Those rabble have the brains to realize what it takes to win a civil war," Devon replied. "They can't face down disciplined British regulars in conventional battle, but they're masters at disruption and skirmishing."

"But aren't such raids merely annoyances?" Barbara asked Devon.

"Scarcely. Men like Pickens and Clarke in Georgia have cost us a fortune in supplies and countless casualties through desertion and injury. Within the past weeks, they've taken Augusta and Georgetown. And that old fox in South Carolina has led Tarleton on a fool's chase for months. When Marion joined Greene, they almost took Ninety-six. Cost Lord Rawdon half his command."

"Francis Marion was a friend of my mother's family before the war," Madelyne said sadly. *And now my husband serves under him.*

"Let us drink to a swift cessation of this insane war," Barbara interjected, raising her glass in a toast.

"And to the triumph of his majesty's forces," Andrew added.

"Let us just see it done," Madelyne said.

"Surely, in spite of Quintin's allegiance, you don't mean that," Andrew remonstrated, taking Madelyne's hand solicitously.

"Ah, but she does, and so do I. Men make wars. Women who bring children into the world would only see it safe for them." Barbara smiled at Madelyne, whom she noticed had freed her hand from Andrew's grasp.

"Well spoken . . . for a woman," Devon said with a glint of humor as his glass chimed against Barbara's.

They could hardly tear their eyes from each other's faces.

"Yes, but women do not have a bent for political matters, I fear," Andrew said with a patronizing tone. "English-speaking children are scarce safe in a world where misguided rebels ally with Frenchmen."

"Who was it who said, 'the enemy of my enemy is my friend'?" Madelyne asked, distracting Andrew from the intimate exchange between Barbara and Devon.

She vowed to find out exactly what was going on between her friend and Devon Blackthorne.

Chapter Nineteen

Barbara waited until the house was completely silent. The tall clock downstairs chimed two. All the servants were asleep. Even Andrew, who was prone to staying up late and nipping at Robert's excellent brandy, had retired to sleep off his overindulgence. She belted the silk robe about her waist and slipped from her room into the dark hallway.

Madelyne had given Devon a room at the far northeast end of the house, accessible to the river breeze, overruling Mrs. Ogilve, who had spitefully assigned him a cramped dormer room on the third floor. As Barbara neared his door at the end of the hall, she felt her heart beating furiously. The night was warm, but not nearly hot enough to cause the dewy sheen of perspiration on her body.

I've summoned him and he's come. Now what do I do? Her pride demanded that he come to her room, seek *her* out and seduce *her* this time. But she knew he would not. As it was, his visit to Blackthorne

Hill must have been undertaken only after lengthy agonizing. A week had passed since they met at the racetrack. The very next day, she had arrived here to find Madelyne safely delivered of her son. And Devon had not come. Until now.

She did not knock but slowly turned the heavy brass doorknob. The door swung open on silent, well-oiled hinges. Moonlight poured in a window at the end of the hall, bathing her in silvery light as she stood in the doorway.

Devon sat reclining on a mound of pillows in the wide, soft bed. He wore only a pair of snug, soft buckskin pants, his upper body and feet bare in the warm night air. His eyes were riveted on her as she hesitated. "You've come this far . . . don't stop now," he drawled softly.

Devon fought the desire to run to her and embrace her, but the pain tore at him, watching her slim body silhouetted in sheer silk. Moonbeams danced on her pale hair as it fell around her shoulders. His indolent pose was a sham, but he would never let her know how desperately he wanted what he could never have.

Barbara stepped inside the room and closed the door. Dev still did not move, just watched her with burning dark eyes. "I'd almost given up hope that you'd heed my message."

"Perhaps I only came because I heard of young James's birth."

"Liar," she whispered, drawing slowly nearer, watching the increasingly rapid rise and fall of his chest. "You're not so indifferent to me as you would pretend." She reached out one hand and touched the golden mat of hair on his chest, running her fingers through it, then splaying her palm over his pounding heart.

He clasped her wrist and held it away from his chest. Her hand looked milky pale against his darkly bronzed fist. "Barbara—your ladyship—I cannot have you," he murmured softly, then pulled her toward him. She fell on top of him, her breasts pressed against his chest, her legs entwined with his.

Their lips were inches apart as she whispered, "You already do have me, Dev."

He ran his fingers through her hair. "Everything about you is refined, perfect."

"Everything about me is yours, Dev."

"But only for tonight, your ladyship."

"Then let us not waste tonight, Dev," she said, kissing him as he had taught her, brushing his lips, then rimming them with her tongue until he opened his mouth and savaged hers.

With a low growl, he rolled them both across the bed, until she was beneath him. As his hand reached between them and yanked the sash of her robe free, he said, "You came to me for this and I can't deny you, God help us both." The robe opened, revealing one smooth, milky breast. His dark hand cupped it, feeling the nipple grow hard as she arched into the caress. Her whole body seemed to open to him, invite him, envelop him.

He trailed hot, wet kisses from her mouth down the slim column of her neck and over her delicate collarbone until his seeking lips fastened on her breast, suckling, teasing, arousing. She writhed against him, her hands digging into his shoulders, urging him on as he laved the other breast and gave his attention to it. He was rough as he tore the sheer silk away from her hot, eager flesh. She helped him, pulling her arms free of the sleeves and kicking off her soft slippers.

Devon moved lower, his tongue twirling in the hollow of her navel until she whimpered. Then he let his questing lips move down her flat little belly to the golden curls at the apex of her thighs. When his mouth found her soft, wet heat, she gasped in shocked pleasure and seized fistfuls of his hair in her hands.

Barbara felt the wild, sweet caress of his tongue and lips, touching her so delicately, so deliciously. It was scandalous. It was sinful. It was bliss. She opened further for him, spreading her legs wide as he continued this magical new way of loving her.

The room seemed to be spinning around her as she thrashed in abandon. She was being drawn deeper and deeper into a dark whirlpool of passion, blind to everything else but the heat and the need burning at the core of her body, the need that only Dev could create and quench. Barbara felt the cresting of her climax as it built slowly, then suddenly burst upon her like cannon shot, fiery, fierce, overwhelming.

Dev felt her shuddering release as it surged, peaked, then gradually ebbed, leaving her panting and spent. He tasted the musky sweetness of her body, now replete, as he raised his head and studied her moon-sheened magnificence.

"You even taste noble, your ladyship." His eyes glowed as they swept hungrily up her body to meet hers.

Barbara watched him as he lay beside her. He was still clad in those tight buckskins, made even tighter by the hardness of his arousal. She reached down and cupped him, feeling his staff straining against the soft leather. Her mind turned over several tantalizing possibilities as she stroked him, watching the tension build in his beautiful lean body. Muscles and tendons stood out in his neck, shoulders, and arms as he arched his hips to the rhythm she set.

While she continued to fondle him with one hand, her other moved to the buttons of his fly. She reached for the top one and felt him hold his breath. Then she proceeded to unfasten them, slowly, one at a time. His breathing grew erratic and rough. When the last button was loosed, she tugged at the tight pants. He helped her slide them over his hips and his staff sprang free, erect and straining with need. She touched it reverently, lightly, letting her fingertips glide up and down the hard, velvety length of it.

"You witch," he gasped, kicking his pants free and shoving them from the bed with one foot.

"I only do as you have taught me," she whispered, appearing to consider how next to approach her wondrous new toy.

"You're enjoying this," he rasped out accusingly.

"You said it. I'm a witch. And you're under my spell."

He muttered an oath she could not decipher as she lowered her head over him and began to taste of his flesh. At first she went softly, slowly, not certain what to do or how to move. Then he instructed her with words and his hands, showing her how to take him in her mouth and pleasure him far more roughly than he had her when loving her this way.

Soon he was thrusting in a frenzied rhythm. Never before had she felt such a sense of power and at the same time such tenderness as when his whole body began to tremble, then grew rigid as he spilled his seed in great pulsing waves. He cried out her name as she took his offering, rich and sweet on her tongue.

"You, too, taste good," she whispered as she slid up into his embrace, her face nuzzling the crisp hair of his chest.

How long had it been? Dev counted the months, endless and empty since last he had held her. There had been no other. God help him, he must leave before first light and never see her again.

At least he'd taken care to see that there was no chance a child came of their loving. He could never destroy her reputation that way or leave a bastard of mixed blood to be raised and despised by some English lord. Thinking of the viscount who was courting her, he tightened his hold on her possessively. *Lie with me and let us sleep, my love, for only this one last night.*

But Barbara was not content to lie still. She raised her head and began to kiss his throat, then ran her tongue along the golden beard stubble on his jaw while her hands explored the hard muscles of his arms and back.

"Be still and sleep," he commanded.

"No, we must not waste the night, remember? Let's taste of one another and see . . ." She let her tongue flick across his lips, then opened her mouth and kissed him voraciously.

His curses were muffled in her mouth as he deepened the kiss, abandoning control.

"You see," she said feverishly as she trailed her lips across his cheeks and over his eyelids, "we blend together our tastes and scents anyway." Then she returned to his mouth and a fierce predatory kiss.

Dev gave up his resolve as she clamped her thighs together, imprisoning his turgid, aching staff. He rolled on top of her and buried himself deeply. She urged him on with words and hands, digging her nails into his hips, drawing him further inside her. When he began to thrust furiously, she slowed him to a languorous pace, whispering, "Let it last, beloved, let it last."

He struggled to control himself, then set an even rhythm, his hips rising and falling as her legs wrapped about him, holding him fast. She arched with every stroke, panting, whispering his name. Just as he felt them cresting, he stopped and held her still.

"I should withdraw from you before—"

She stopped him with an incoherent cry and bucked against him, driving them both over the abyss into the conscienceless oblivion of a shattering climax. When he tried to pull away, she tightened her long legs around his hips and held him fast until he collapsed on top of her, breathless and spent.

Barbara held him in her arms and watched him sleep for a while after that, studying every nuance of his splendid face—its finely arched eyebrows, strong straight nose, sculpted, sensuous lips. His skin was swarthy and dark in contrast to his tawny gold hair. Truly he brought the best of two worlds together, and he was her world, her life.

"I will not lose you, Devon Blackthorne." Her soft voice whispered on the night air as she kissed his closed eyes, then lay beside him and fell fast asleep.

Sunrise came early, for it was just past the summer solstice. Devon, used to riding with ranger patrols, awakened as the faint streaks of pale pink light crept over the river below them. He looked down at the sleeping woman as he gently disengaged himself from her. Then he dressed in silent haste, picked up his few belongings, and placed them in the saddlebags lying across a chair. He knelt and carefully pulled the wrinkled robe over her. *Be happy, your ladyship . . . for both of us.*

Barbara awakened when she felt the loss of his body heat. Disoriented, she sat up in the big, empty bed and felt the pillow beside her. It was still slightly warm. Instinctively she knew he had left her. And left Blackthorne Hill, never to return.

Madelyne heard James cry before Amy, the young black nursemaid, could reach the child. She motioned for the girl to return to her bed and picked up her son while Gulliver watched from his sentry post at the side of the crib. The sky was not yet light. "You're sleeping longer and longer between feedings," she said, praising him as he eagerly began to suckle at her breast.

When she had finished feeding him, Madelyne changed his napkin and put him back in his cradle. She debated about returning to her own bed for a few more hours, but her strength had returned quickly after the birth. Both Dr. Witherspoon and Delphine praised her pluck and each claimed credit from the other. Smiling, she dressed quickly in simple muslin skirts and a calico bodice with wide lacings down its front, now an essential style for her to be able to feed James.

The heat of June had not yet risen with the sun. Madelyne considered a walk among her flowers during the coolness of the early morn. She had just opened the door to her room when she saw a figure disappear down the back stairs. From the long, silver-gilt hair, she knew it must be Barbara, but what was her friend doing up at this hour—and dressed in only a filmy robe?

Heedless of her dishabille, Barbara raced barefooted down the stairs and into the back hall. The stables were south of the big house, most quickly reached by the rear door. She opened it and ran across the dew-drenched grass, to find Dev leading his bay horse from the stable door.

He stopped in his tracks, frozen as she ran up to him, dressed only in the sheer, badly rumpled silk robe he had virtually torn off her body the preceding night.

"Go back inside before you're seen, your ladyship," he said with quiet finality. He reached for the pommel of the saddle to swing up, but she grasped his arm, forcing him to turn and face her or throw off her hand.

"Don't leave me without saying good-bye." Her voice broke.

"All right then, good-bye. Does that make it any easier?" he asked raggedly.

"I don't want it to be easy." She stood with shoulders erect, head held regally as she met his anguished eyes.

"You're a titled Englishwoman, nearly affianced to a titled Englishman."

"Weymouth is Monty's choice, never mine."

"He's a viscount, rich as sin, and not a bad sort from what I hear in Savannah. You could do far worse than wed him." Every word cost him, and he knew she knew it.

"Yes, I imagine I could. I could wed you."

"Never. I can't offer for you, Barbara. I have nothing. You've seen how my own family feels about me. I'm not even welcome as a guest in Uncle Robert's house."

"Robert Blackthorne will soon die of his own spleen. Damn him."

"Even so, his life or death won't change anything for us," he said, taking her hand in his and kissing the soft white skin on the inside of her wrist. "You know what we've just done can't be repeated. It should never have happened."

Knowing what he had tried to do last night when she had come to him, she asked, "What if I am with child?"

His face grew stony. "I tried to warn you. We were lucky last year."

"But what if—"

"It won't be the first by-blow claimed by a peer of the realm. Don't try to blackmail me, your ladyship. It ill becomes you. Go to Weymouth."

"I don't want Weymouth!"

"Then find another your brother will approve. This only tears at us both, and to no end." He swung up on Firebrand, feeling her hands struggling for purchase on his jacket. She held the wide crimson cuff of its sleeve as the big bay danced, sensing the tension between the two humans.

"I love you, Devon Blackthorne."

"Good-bye, your ladyship."

Madelyne could not hear their words from the house where she stood frozen, but she understood their anguish as Devon rode away and Barbara slowly crumpled to the ground, holding back her tears until he was out of sight. Madelyne walked quietly from the back door and knelt beside her friend, enfolding her in her arms.

"It hurts so much. I know . . . I know," Madelyne whispered as Barbara began to weep.

Mrs. Ogilve was habitually an early riser, especially since the hateful new mistress had begun to supervise and question her about the running of the household. After a hearty breakfast, she set out to order the lazy upstairs maids to thoroughly clean and scrub the guest room Madelyne had insisted that half-caste savage be given. As soon as the kitchen staff told her he had departed at dawn, she decided to waste no time removing all traces of his presence at Blackthorne Hill. Once Master Robert was back on his feet, he would appreciate that, she was certain.

Officiously she strode down the long, wide hall to the last room on the northeast corner. She opened the door and sniffed in disgust. The savage had left the bed as rumpled as if he'd disported with a dozen serving wenches in it! Perhaps he had taken one of the slaves or indentureds. She would give the girl a good caning if she found out who it was. Such evidence would also serve to shame the mistress for allowing the likes of Devon Blackthorne into this house over Master Robert's protests. As she began to snoop, she thought of her wayward niece, Phoebe.

"Served the nasty chit right. Whoring in Savannah. She deserved to get her throat cut on the wharfs."

Just as the housekeeper was about to abandon her search for evidence, she stepped on something. Sniffing in disgust at the musky sheet, she placed her hand on the bed and knelt. Agnes was stunned in disbelief at her good fortune. She knew that the elegant blue-silk slippers under the bed belonged to Lady Barbara Caruthers.

"That Caruthers bitch. She can be handled just as her aunt was." She looked at the tangled bedclothes once more and imagined that bronzed savage entwined with the pale blond Englishwoman. "Disgusting," she sniffed, well pleased nonetheless. Clutching the slippers, she left the room, all thoughts of having it cleaned now dismissed from her mind.

She headed toward the master's room, then debated about wakening him so early. He was still quite ill, although he would be happy to know the Indian was gone from under his roof. Now the Caruthers woman soon would be as well.

Madelyne left Barbara resting fretfully. Her friend had told her all about her relationship with Devon Blackthorne, beginning with the shipwreck last year. No wonder she had taken such an instant dislike to Andrew, being in love with his brother, whom the whole Blackthorne family ostracized because of his Indian blood. She mulled over how she could bring the unlikely lovers back together as she headed toward the stairs.

Then she noticed Mrs. Ogilve standing outside Robert's door, clutching something in her hand. She turned from the stair rail and walked resolutely toward the older woman. When she saw Barbara's slippers in the housekeeper's hands, she guessed at once where she had found them. The smug look on the old crone's face only confirmed her suspicion.

"I'll take those," she said, quickly snatching the slippers from the housekeeper.

"You give them back!" Agnes hissed. "I found them—"

"I know where you found them and it signifies nothing. If you attempt to spread your spiteful gossip about my friend, whose brother in Savannah is a personal favorite of General Prevost"—she paused to give that idea emphasis—"I shall not only see you dismissed from Blackthorne Hill, but I'll be certain you never hold another position anywhere in the colony!"

Agnes Ogilve's eyes narrowed to two pewter slits. "You wouldn't dare. I'll tell Master Robert—"

"Master Robert is still asleep—an ill old man whose heart is so poor he can sustain no further shocks. You wouldn't want to be responsible for his death, now would you, Mistress Ogilve?"

"It's your bringing that savage under our roof that put the master in this state."

"Dr. Witherspoon would strongly disagree, since he's been treating my father-in-law's fever for months already. And, more to the point, until Robert is recovered, I am in charge of Blackthorne Hill. Do I make myself very clear, Mistress Ogilve?"

"Very," the housekeeper said between gritted teeth. Without another word, she turned and stormed down the hall to the stairs.

Madelyne felt her knees trembling now that the confrontation was over. Not that it had been her first face-off with Agnes Ogilve since returning to the Hill, but never had so much been at stake. If the housekeeper had succeeded in besmirching Barbara's reputation . . . Madelyne headed to the room Devon had slept in to make certain no other evidence had been left behind after the lovers' tumultuous parting.

July 1781, Biggins Church, South Carolina

Quintin stood in the small, sunlit room, staring at the letter. After reading its contents, he was relieved that his hand did not shake. Again he reread it.

Marion, sitting at a scarred oak table in Mistress Smather's kitchen, sipped from his glass of vinegar water and studied his captain. He knew the letter had come from Quintin's estranged wife. He hoped it meant the breach between them would be mended, for he knew Quintin was in love with the girl, even if the bitter young man did not realize it himself.

"What news, Quint? Is aught amiss at Blackthorne Hill? Your father's health—"

"Robert still hangs on to life tenaciously as a bulldog. No, it regards Madelyne. It seems she has borne a son, whom she named James Quintin Blackthorne."

His expression was difficult to read, certainly not the joy most men would reveal upon hearing such news. Guardedly, Marion asked, "And you are not pleased?"

Quint's eyes flashed with a spark of anguish that he quickly transformed into anger. "At least I'll wager it's well and truly a Blackthorne, as much time as my cousin Andrew has spent with her in my absence."

Marion's normally olive dark complexion drained of color. "I do not believe it. I know that girl's family. Quint, even though you parted in anger from her—"

"We parted nine months before young James was born. Rather a close count, wouldn't you say? Especially considering how she rid herself of me."

"There is but one solution. Of course you shall go to her."

"We've driven off Fraser and his Carolina Rangers, but I'm not sure it's a good idea—"

"Nonsense!" Marion interrupted. "Georgetown and Augusta are under American control. General Cornwallis is being kept quite occupied in Virginia. Your Mr. Franklin has even sent word that Admiral de Grasse will be on the Chesapeake within a month to unite with General Washington. I think you'll be better able to join in our final push for victory this fall if you settle matters with your wife now." With that, he began to scribble the pass Captain Blackthorne would need to move through American lines.

For all Marion's optimism, Quintin was little reassured as he rode south toward Blackthorne Hill. The British still controlled Williamsburg, Charles

Town, and Savannah, all key seaports. The rebel partisans had gnawed away at their inland forts and decimated their supply lines, but the cost to both sides had been dear. Loyalist partisans had raided the length and breadth of South Carolina and Georgia. Each side burned the crops and homes of the other. He observed blackened fields once green with corn and the charred skeletons of what had once been sturdy cabins and even large river plantation mansions.

"What a criminal waste," he muttered to Domino. When would it end? The fighting had begun in Massachusetts back in 1775. Seventeen eighty-one was more than half over, with no end in sight, unless French naval support for General Washington turned the tide. "Let us hope this de Grasse is a far more skilled fighter than that fool d'Estaing."

By the time he reached Blackthorne Hill on the fourth day of his journey, it was early evening, the dinner hour. He could imagine Robert sitting at the head of that long table with Madelyne at the opposite end, engaged in an ongoing battle of vitriolic words and brittle silences. Robert would, of course, attempt to bring down the British authorities on him and have him arrested, but he knew the people from the Hill. No one would betray him— except his wife.

Why had she written him about the child? He turned the matter over and over in his mind. As Marion had said, there was but one way to find out. He had taken the precaution of bringing half a dozen seasoned men with him. On his signal, they dispersed to prearranged sites around the plantation house to await any possible trouble.

For some inexplicable reason, he expected none. Madelyne wanted to see him—wanted him to see the child she hoped to pass off as his. Perhaps it was . . . but he very much doubted it. Recalling Marion's cautions to him about how to treat with his wife, he smiled grimly and rode through the walnut trees until he reached a tall field of corn. He dismounted. From here he could walk undetected to the smith's barn, from thence to the stables, then to the rear entrance of the house . . . and Madelyne.

Inside the house, Madelyne and Robert had indeed just finished their hostile meal. Since June, the old man had rallied enough to be up and about, but his health was still precarious. After an argument last week, he had railed at Noble Witherspoon and forbidden the physician to return to the Hill.

Madelyne simply bided her time, letting him make his caustic remarks and wander through the house like some ghostly wraith. As long as he did not abuse the servants, she let him vent his spleen on her at meals and ignored him. His favorite topic for weeks had been the new heir to Blackthorne Hill. He had taunted her repeatedly about the legitimacy of James until she silenced him by threatening to reveal his own lifetime pretense about Quintin's legitimacy. He had paled, studied her with those unnerving slate-blue eyes, and decided she was not bluffing. Thereafter, he abandoned the topic.

As she entered the nursery that night, Madelyne gazed fondly at her son. Quintin's son. Every day he grew more and more like his sire. "Soon his eyes will be green," she murmured as Amy handed her the babe. Gulliver was at his assigned place beside the crib.

As was her wont, she dismissed the girl for the evening and prepared to enjoy some time with James. She unlaced her bodice and placed him at one milk-engorged breast, then leaned back in a comfortable Chippendale armchair as he feasted noisily. Why would any woman be so foolish as to use a wet nurse when she could enjoy this pleasure herself?

Quintin stood in the shadow of the door, his eyes sweeping the room. Madelyne's big hound

awakened and watched him warily, but made no
sound, only cocked his head quizzically, waiting to
see what Quint would do.

He turned his attention from the dog to his wife
and her son. A deep, nameless ache gnawed at his
vitals. Had Anne loved him thus? Her bastard son?
Or had she consigned him to a wet nurse and forgotten him?

Of course he had no memories and no one ever
spoke of her, so he did not know. He watched as
Madelyne kissed the child's black curly head. Her
breasts were heavy with milk, pale compared to the
sun-darkened skin above the line of her bodice. As
he watched that tiny mouth pull on her rose nipple,
he felt an old familiar heat begin to flood his senses
and pool in his groin. He cursed her beauty as her
long mahogany hair fell like a curtain across one
shoulder, gleaming in the candlelight.

"Such a touching tableau, dear wife," he said
softly, and was rewarded with Madelyne's sharp
intake of breath as she looked up.

Chapter Twenty

Madelyne felt the color rise in her cheeks as his gaze moved from her face to her bared breasts. James had finished nursing and lay contentedly in her arms. She hurriedly covered herself, awkwardly lacing up her bodice with one hand, all the while studying his calculating expression. He did not seem pleased with his son.

Guardedly she said, "You received my letter. Does your heir meet with your approval?" The young mother stood and held the sleeping infant so his father could inspect him.

"He was born in mid-June. I left Georgia in mid-September. That rather casts my paternity in doubt, doesn't it?" He looked at the babe, whose infant face bore no resemblance to anyone as yet.

Madelyne felt the room go black before her eyes. This could not be—but, of course, with Quint's innate suspicions it could. It was. "You came to visit me that night before you fled—September twentieth, as I recall. Tis ample time, Quint," she replied softly. "Can't you lay aside politics and just love your son?" *If not me.*

"If he is my son," he said in a brittle voice.

"Would you hold him?" she offered, struggling to overcome the red rage welling up inside her. "Look at his hair, Quint—tis as black as your own."

"A baby's hair often changes color, as do its eyes." He turned away, refusing to hold the boy. Galling pain welled up inside him. To be subjected to the same cruel fate as old Robert—what irony in it!

"Will you beat and shame this innocent child as Robert did you?" She knelt and placed James in his cradle, then looked up at him, waiting.

Quintin stiffened. "Who could have told you about what passed between me and Robert?"

"It takes no great genius to imagine how a man of his temperament would react to being saddled with another man's child. But let me warn you, Quint. Whether or not you believe you are James's father, I am his mother and I will kill anyone who lays a hand on him—even you."

Her voice had a steely edge to it, a ring of authority that he had not heard before. He scowled. "I would never do to a living soul what Robert did to me. You can rest easy on that account."

"But you still persist in believing he is not your son."

He turned from her accusing eyes, unwilling to let her see the torment etched on his face. "I don't know, Madelyne. Perhaps as he grows older . . . now, I don't know what to believe."

"Certainly not your wife." Her voice was hollow with bitterness.

"My wife who spent every spare minute she could with my cousin Andrew."

"Your wife who found you in a heated embrace with Serena Fallowfield! Have you ever seen Andrew take such improprieties with me?"

His shoulders fell in weary defeat. "All the more

reason for your jealous spite, Madelyne. You see, neither of us can trust the other."

He looked so tired and haggard, his face unshaven, his rifle shirt and buckskin pants greasy and ragged. "You've ridden far. Let me summon Toby. He'll fetch you a bath and clean clothes." Without waiting for his assent, she walked briskly to the doorway and called down the stairs for Quintin's valet.

"You've assumed full authority in my absence. I find it difficult to believe that Robert has become so accommodating, or does the prospect of an heir for his domain please him so well? I warrant he'd be doubly pleased if it was not mine."

Madelyne felt a stab of pain as she recalled Robert's exact words on the subject when she had told him of the child. "Robert is ailing. Since last fall, Dr. Witherspoon has feared for his life. The cinchona bark keeps his fever at bay, but his heart is failing."

Quintin snorted humorlessly. "Small wonder, given its size."

Toby entered then, overjoyed to see his master safely returned home. The gray-haired man's wizened face crinkled in a wide smile of welcome as he thumped Quintin on the back with the familiarity of an old protector who had watched his charge grow into a man.

"I'll fetch two boys to haul water and I'll see to fresh clothes myself, Mastah Quintin. Won't Delphine be pleased! Bake her finest peach pie, yessir, she will." He looked at the baby, now fussing in the cradle. "Got you a fine boy there. Sturdy as a live oak and tough as a Georgia pine."

"Thank you, Toby," he said quietly. After the old man left the room, Quintin turned and watched as Madelyne took the baby to a small table, where she began to change his napkin.

Gulliver's keen eyes never left James. "I see the child has a fierce protector," Quint said as he watched her fuss with James.

Madelyne did not turn around, but continued her task. "Gulliver guards him every night."

Quint walked closer to her and looked over her shoulder, curious in spite of himself. She performed the task deftly, as if used to doing it. "Don't you have a nurse for him?"

"Amy. She's a dear, but whenever I can, I prefer to care for him myself."

"Even to nurse him when we must have a dozen wet nurses on the Hill?"

She looked up at him, her eyes blazing. "James will know love from at least one of his parents!" She turned back to the infant and carried him to his cradle.

Just then Quintin heard the sounds of warm water being poured into the big wooden tub in his dressing room. His body ached and he was filthy. He had endured days of dusty travel with only muddy creeks in which to sluice off. He headed toward the call of the clean, warm water, leaving behind the deeply disturbing presence of his wife and the child.

While Quintin soaked, Madelyne went downstairs to Delphine's kitchen, where the old cook was busily engaged in carving thick wedges of sweet smoked ham. A half loaf of crusty bread and a wedge of cheddar cheese were already sliced. A bowl of freshly picked strawberries sat on the table alongside a pitcher of cream.

"I'll be bakin' a peach pie. Have it for Mastah Quintin for breakfast. Lordy, so good to have him home, ain't it?" She beamed at Madelyne.

Returning the smile, although with less enthusiasm, Madelyne began to help dish up a feast for her husband. "This time you're right—he does look too thin and you can fatten him up. Oh, Delphine, the stories I've heard about the privations of the soldiers in the back country." She shuddered.

"Doan you be worryin' 'bout the mastah. I'll fatten

him right 'nough now we got him home."

Madelyne forbore to say that it was unlikely
Quintin could safely stay at the Hill even if he
wished to, which she very much doubted. She took
the tray, laden with food and a cool pitcher of ale,
and climbed the stairs with it, heading for his room.
She heard the sounds of splashing, then silence by
the time she opened the door.

Quintin lay with his head back against the rim
of the tub, dozing. He had shaved off his beard
and washed his hair. She studied his profile in the
soft evening light. Just looking at his wet, muscular
body made her breath catch. To break the spell, she
walked briskly from the dressing room door to a
small side table in his bedroom and deposited the
tray.

Quintin awakened instantly and looked up at her,
watching as she laid out the food. "Among all your
other new duties, I didn't expect you to act as a
kitchen servant."

"How gracious of you to exempt me," she said
tightly as she uncovered the food. She could hear
sounds of his washing, but refused to look at him.

"In the interest of preserving Mrs. Ogilve's carefully beeswaxed floor, would you hand me that
towel?" he asked, feigning a nonchalance he was
far from feeling. Quintin watched as she seized the
towel, walked briskly into the closet, and approached
the tub.

He was standing dripping wet in the center of a
braided rag rug. Her eyes traveled down his body
before she thrust the towel at him, but he could
see the battle she waged not to look further. A slow
smile spread across his face. It was not a nice one.

Madelyne realized she was staring at him in spite
of her resolve. She could feel her pulse thrumming
frantically and her knees turning to water. *I will not
show him this terrible weakness!* But she could tell
by the mocking, bitter smile on his face that she

already had. Then, as he took the towel and began to dry himself, she noticed him wince slightly when he rubbed an angry red scar, newly healing on his left arm.

Before she could stop herself, her hand reached out to touch it. "You've been shot."

"It's happened more than once. But I've been lucky. Nothing broken or gone poisonous."

"But it could. So could this," she replied, as her fingers lightly grazed another raw nick on his chest. She was rewarded when his breath caught. A small smile quivered on her lips as she said, "These need tending. I'll fetch my medicines. Are there any other places that I should see to?" The moment the words escaped her lips she turned crimson.

Quintin realized her gaffe and his own maddening response to her. He wrapped the towel around his hips and walked barefoot over to his bed, where he stretched out casually. "I'll await your inspection when you bring your medicines."

Odious, arrogant lout! Madelyne stormed through the adjacent door to her room and summoned Nell, who quickly fetched her small leather pouch filled with ointments, tinctures, and herbals. She steadied herself by leaning on the door frame and taking a deep breath before she reentered his room and approached the bed. Forcing herself to act as dispassionately as she did when treating sick or injured servants, Madelyne rubbed ointment on the reddish weal of scar tissue, then turned her attention to the cut on his chest. Actually it was more of a rip. "How did you get this? It looks so ragged."

"A New Jersey loyalist with a bayonet was rather intent on skewering me. His musket caught on a vine just in time to deflect his arm."

Madelyne shuddered. "You must've faced death a hundred times this past year." She applied a stinging vinegar to cleanse the wound, then worked in a daub of ointment.

"Tis practically healed," he said dismissively, shoving the bag of medicines from her side. He took her hand in his with a muttered oath and pulled her roughly into his arms. Before his lips could swoop down to claim hers, she wrapped her arms around his neck and held him tightly, as desperate to receive the harsh, punishing kiss as he was to give it. After a moment of savaging her mouth, he raised his head and said in a hoarse voice, "What black witchery is it between us, Madelyne, that neither of us can deny it?"

"Please, Quint, for tonight, let there be no war, no past, nothing but this." She ran her tongue along his jawline, then up to touch his ear. Her fingernails lightly raked his bare chest, paying particular attention to the hard male nipples.

He began working the laces of her bodice free. When they refused to yield quickly enough, he tore the thin cotton drawstrings from their eyelets and pulled the garment from her, leaving only her thin chemise. Her breasts, engorged from nursing, strained against the sheer lawn. His hands cupped them, thumbs rubbing the tips, which quickly hardened. She moaned and pushed them against his massaging palms. Quintin pulled the drawstring at her neck and roughly shoved the undergarment down her shoulders, pinning her arms to her sides.

Staring at her, he held her, panting, immobilized, for several seconds as their eyes met. Then he lowered his head and teased each breast with his tongue and lips, moving from one to the other, feeling her writhe beneath his caresses. He knelt, straddling her, and yanked the towel free from his hips. Madelyne's eyes at once fastened on his rigid staff. He was ready for her, and as his hands roughly pulled up her petticoats and grazed her thighs, she was ready for him.

Struggling, she tore her chemise, working her arms free so she could reach up to clasp his shoulders as he positioned himself between her legs. She pulled him down to her, feeling him slide inside the wet, welcoming heat of her body. Wrapping her legs securely about his hips, Madelyne gloried in the old familiar sensations as they claimed her. She thought she heard him murmur her name, but through the haze of passion she only knew for certain that she cried out his.

How sweet, how wondrous this joining, all pleasure and oblivion, no remembrance of the ways they had wounded each other, the harsh words they had exchanged. But after such long abstinence, they spent themselves all too soon. The swiftness and rough, searing ecstasy of the culmination left them both too exhausted to move. Madelyne held him fast and he did not try to withdraw from her. She ran her fingers through his tangled hair, still damp from his bath.

Quintin felt her caress, felt her soft, beautiful little body beckon him, and again he grew hard. The need was too powerful to resist in spite of his best resolve. Like a rutting stag, he took her yet again. All the long months without the comforts of a woman's body should have explained his hunger, but as he slowed the pace and savored the exquisite way they fit together, he knew it was more than mere abstinence.

He had never sated his lust with the slatternly, diseased camp followers whom the partisans met from time to time, but on a few rare occasions he had been sent to Georgetown and Williamsburg on secret assignments. The women there were clean, attractive, and more than obliging, but none of them fed this aching hunger like his wife did. This was homecoming, pain and glory all bound together. He was helpless to resist and it frightened him.

Madelyne felt the delicious heat building again, then finally, when she thought she'd go mad with the pleasure, her release came, slower, in a crescendo of rising, prolonged waves that left her so utterly breathless that she felt faint. Through the haze she felt Quintin's last swift, shuddering strokes as he joined her.

But this time, he rolled away from her, up and off the bed. Reaching for the clothes Toby had laid out, he began to dress.

She watched him in stunned silence for a moment, then realized the strumpet she must look with her skirts rucked above her hips, her stockings still on, her chemise hanging torn from her body. As she smoothed down her petticoats and pulled the remnants of her shift together, she asked, "Is this how it's always to be for us, Quint? Swift passion, then silence . . . regret?"

His eyes never met hers as he pulled on his boots. "Regret? Yes, Madelyne, I have regrets. But it's far too late for me to change anything." He shrugged wearily and headed for the door.

"You could change everything if you wanted to— if you'd let go of your past and believe what we just shared was—"

"What we just shared was animal lust," he snapped back, his eyes raking her disheveled appearance. "Damned if I know what it is about you—oh, the hell with it all!" He spun on his heel and left the room without a backward glance.

Madelyne sat on the bed, numb with pain. Then, hearing James cry, she stood up and made her way to the dressing room where she seized a robe from a peg on the wall. Quickly donning it, she rushed into the nursery to attend her son.

As he stalked angrily down the stairs, Quintin could still see the look of anguish on her face. "Let go of the past—as if it'll ever let go of me," he whispered to himself as he opened the library door, heading for the stock of liquor Robert always kept there. Although his stomach growled, he could not eat. He wanted a drink.

Robert Blackthorne had heard the servants' excited whispering when he retired to his room after dinner. The young master had returned home to see his son. He wondered if Quintin believed the boy was his. After spending the past year with Madelyne, Robert was reasonably certain it was. The foolish chit was obviously besotted with her husband. The thought left a bitter taste in his mouth. The damned traitor!

He could not sleep, and the tumbler of brandy at his bedside was empty. He reached for the bell pull, then stopped. He felt restless, in need of a walk. "Be damned if I'll hide in my room while he walks about the Hill a free man."

Robert put on his robe and opened the door. When the boy who was assigned to see to him in the night stood up obediently, he shooed the child away and slowly walked down the hall. By the time he had descended the stairs and reached the library door, his breathing was labored. God, how he despised being an invalid!

Quintin heard the door open and saw the dim flicker of a candle. He had been sitting in the darkness, sipping his brandy and brooding. When he recognized Robert, he stood up, raising his glass in a mock salute. "To the new heir of Blackthorne Hill."

"You traitorous mongrel! You have no right to be here. If I had the strength, I'd ride to Savannah and fetch the soldiers to see you hanged!"

"Good to see you again, too, Father," Quintin said with a shrug, turning his back to stare out the window.

Robert felt the red rage begin to build, just as it had every time Quintin had defied him since childhood. Now he was such a worthless used-up old man that the young bastard could simply mock him and turn his back. It was not to be endured. He walked to the hearth and seized a poker.

"You'll not dismiss me like some stable lackey! As if you haven't brought enough disgrace on the Blackthorne name by your very existence, now you betray your king and country like the bastard you are. I'll whip you the same as I did when you were a boy."

Robert came at Quintin with the poker raised, his whole body shaking with every step. It was all he could do to hold the heavy iron bar aloft as he staggered across the large room. Quintin could see the icy pallor of death on his skin, smell it in his sweat. He reached out one arm and knocked the poker from Robert's hand, sending it flying with a loud clatter.

"Your days of beating me are over, old man," he said with icy deliberation. "I may be a bastard, but I've done my duty for Blackthorne Hill, just as you did. Now that I've seen my heir, I'll leave you to rot in your own bile."

Madelyne heard the sound of angry voices coming from the library. Still holding James, she raced down the stairs to the open door, where she saw Robert collapsed against a tall-backed chair by the window. Quintin stalked toward her. Barring his way she said, "You can't leave him like this, Quint. You may never see him alive again."

"Damn you, get out of my way. I've had enough of you all."

Hearing her soft declaration over the roaring in his ears, Robert straightened his spine, clawing the back of the chair to do so. "It is my devoutest wish never to see him alive again. Let him go back to his outlaws and die with them."

He glared at Madelyne with glassy eyes and laughed, a dry rasping sound. "So beautiful and Madonna-like, just as Anne was. Is she as faithless? We are both of us cursed by an obsession with our wives." He saw Quintin's back go rigid, but the younger man did not turn to face the older. "You say you've done your duty for Blackthorne Hill just as I did. Does it mean you think young James here is a bastard also? What say you to that, madam?"

Madelyne clutched her son protectively and met his gaze unflinchingly. "I told you when I conceived that this was Quint's baby. You can both choose to believe whatever pleases you—and be damned to you!" She turned and walked to the hall stairs without a backward glance.

By the time she was at the top of the steps, she heard Quintin's horse galloping away. She summoned two young houseboys and sent them to fetch Master Robert to bed once he had drunk his fill. Only the look of unconditional love in little James's eyes, the warm feel of his body in her arms, kept her sane. "I shall live for you, little one. You'll not have a life fouled by their hate."

Madelyne spent the following months working each day until she was ready to drop with exhaustion. Blackthorne Hill was preparing for the coming winter. She tried to think of her absent husband and the acrimony of their parting as little as possible. Running a huge plantation helped. As the days of September grew shorter, her hours of toil grew longer.

Her days were filled with treating sick slaves and hearing reports from their overseers about the harvesting of cash crops and foods grown to sustain the hundreds of souls on the Hill. She ordered the slaughter of hogs and cattle, then inspected the smokehouses full of hams and great slabs of side meat and checked the barrels filled with salted beef.

By night she pored over household account books, deciding where purchases could be cut and various items made at the Hill. The battle for Mrs. Ogilve's ledgers had been a formidable one, but with Quintin gone and Robert so ill that even the hard-faced overseers answered now to the mistress, the housekeeper was forced to give over her books.

Sitting one night by the light of a branched candlestick, she rubbed her eyes tiredly and scanned a page of purchases—clothing and foodstuffs for the residents of the big house. Listed were a number of items she had never inventoried, such as twenty bolts of fine linen for sheets and dozens of boxes of expensive spices—ginger, nutmegs, and cloves. She made a note to discuss the matter with Nell and Delphine when she had time.

By the end of September, the plantation received word of further reversals for the loyalist cause in the war, and Madelyne forgot the irregularities of the account books. The great British fleet under Admiral Graves was fought to a standstill by the American's French ally, Admiral de Grasse, off the capes of Virginia. The last vestige of British naval power in the southern theater sailed back to New York, leaving General Cornwallis surrounded by the encroaching French and American forces of Rochambeau and Washington. Even the dashing, if overly brutal British dragoon, Banastre Tarleton, had sailed for home. Madelyne thought of the rebel militia taking over Blackthorne Hill and decided to resume practice with the .30-caliber Jaeger rifle that Andrew had given her.

As September gave way to October, British shipping of seemingly inexhaustible luxury items began to shrink because of French fleets in southern waters. With fine spermaceti candles no longer available, Madelyne ordered the dipping of bayberry candles, even for the dining room table. So far Dr. Witherspoon had been able to obtain cinchona bark, but Robert's fevers now waxed and waned in spite of it.

"I'm responsible for all these hundreds of people, and so ill equipped for the task," she murmured aloud as she trudged from the dairy up the hill to the big house. Again Madelyne cursed Quintin's rebel allegiance which had led him to fight so far from home. Yet if the Americans did win—something she'd considered unthinkable a scant year ago—at least his outlaw exploits might save his birthright.

In this time of privation, Madelyne's greatest joy was her son. That warm October afternoon, her flagging spirits were cheered when she saw Andrew's distinctive chestnut gelding being led by a stableboy for a rubdown.

Although the unavoidable rift between Andrew and Barbara had widened, Madelyne still treasured the friendship of both and relied on their frequent visits to keep her abreast of news in the city. Then she noticed Serena Fallowfield's dainty white mare outside the stable door, and her heart sank.

"I'm a mess, and she'll not hesitate to embarrass both Andrew and me by saying so."

By the time she reached the back door of the big house, she could hear Serena's voice carrying down the long hall from the front parlor. "I don't know how poor old Robert's kept this place running if all your reports about his failing health are true, Andrew. After all, Quintin has deserted his family for his traitor's cause."

"My husband may not be here to run the Hill, but I am. Good afternoon, Serena," she said, nodding briskly to the odious woman, then turning to smile warmly at Andrew. "It's been far too long since your last visit. I'll have Delphine fix us a lovely luncheon, and then you may regale me with the latest gossip from Savannah."

"Your friend Lady Caruthers is the talk of the town," Serena purred. "It seems she's spurned her brother's dear friend—quite a catch, too. A viscount no less. And Weymouth owns a fortune in Monty's gambling notes."

"Hush, Serena. What's between gentlemen regarding their gaming debts is best not mentioned by ladies." Andrew's voice was laced with annoyance. He smiled apologetically at Madelyne and said, "When I said I was coming to visit you, my cousin here insisted on coming along to see how Uncle Robert is doing."

Madelyne could feel Serena's eyes on her wrinkled, muddy petticoats and sweat-soaked bodice. Her hair hung in a single unruly plait without even the benefit of a cap. "Please forgive my appearance, but since I'm the only able-bodied Blackthorne on the plantation, I must see to the outdoor and indoor activities. Make yourselves comfortable in the parlor while I change."

Andrew took her hand gallantly, ignoring the odor of cow that clung to it. "Your work does you proud, m'dear. I only regret that Quintin isn't here to care for his family in this time of need."

"Has he even learned he has a son?" Serena asked oversweetly.

Madelyne felt her face heat as she nodded. "Yes. In fact, he paid a brief, unexpected visit in response to my letter, several months ago, just to see James."

"You never mentioned that to me," Andrew said with a wounded look.

"My, my, sending messages through rebel lines. Are you won to his cause, then?" Serena asked before Madelyne could answer his complaint.

"I'm scarcely a rebel. I only felt that Quint had the right to know about James. I didn't expect the visit, and I really don't wish to discuss it. Now if you will excuse me for a few moments," she said, turning from Serena to Andrew, for whom she smiled.

When they were alone, Serena tapped her finger against her cheek and whispered to Andrew, "Are you perchance thinking the same as I? If Quintin came home once in response to her letter . . ."

Andrew stroked his chin and turned the possibilities over in his mind. "If only we had the means to get a message to him."

"Perhaps if we're patient, it will work out. If that old devil is as sick as you say, Madelyne will soon be sending word that Quintin is the new master of Blackthorne Hill. That should bring him home again."

"To gloat, if nothing else. He and my uncle could never abide one another. Let me confer with my backwoods informant about the matter and we'll see what can be arranged."

"I'll volunteer to put hemlock in Robert's tea," Serena said with a cold chuckle.

Andrew only nodded, preoccupied with his plans.

Noble Witherspoon hated to be the bearer of bad news, especially to a beleaguered woman like Madelyne Blackthorne, who was left alone with a small baby, a large plantation, and a husband who unjustly accused her of treachery. Sighing as he climbed down from his chair, he handed the reins to a stableboy and turned to face the mistress of Blackthorne Hill. Her printed calico bodice and plain petticoats, without hen baskets or other padding, attested to her hard-working ways.

"Dr. Witherspoon, I'm so happy you're here. I'm afraid I need quite a bit of medical advice. Someone always seems to get hurt or ill when you're not available."

Noble studied her face, lovely and flushed, but beneath the smiling facade he sensed aching sadness and great weariness. "You're becoming quite adept at treating patients, Madelyne. Keep this up and I'll have to certify you to the Governor's board as a trained physician."

She laughed lightly at the absurd idea. "And what men in authority would ever allow a mere female to practice medicine?"

He shrugged as they began walking toward the house. "Bunch of damn fools."

"Have you brought my supplies?" she asked hopefully. "Robert's fever hasn't abated with the cooler weather as we'd hoped."

"I'm afraid I couldn't get the cinchona with all the disruption of the war. I was most fortunate to acquire some calomel, a tiny bit of laudanum, and some powdered foxglove."

"The foxglove helps Robert's heart, but he suffers most cruelly from the ague, pitching and crying out in his sleep at night. I'm afraid his mind is slipping away—at least when the fever grips him."

"No wonder you look so careworn and peaked. There are servants aplenty to sit up with that old curmudgeon. Let that prune-faced housekeeper he's always favored do it," Noble said sourly.

Madelyne's expression grew wary at the mention of Mistress Ogilve. "You've practiced medicine here for over thirty years, Noble. What do you know about that woman?"

"Why? I thought you'd settled the matter of who's running the Hill with Robert down and Quintin away. She giving you any more sass?"

"No. I've quite put her in her place, but . . . well, I hate to accuse her without real evidence."

"Accuse her of what?"

Madelyne sighed. "Embezzlement, I'm afraid. I haven't sifted through all the household accounts yet—there's so little time and so many things to be seen to with Robert ill."

Noble smiled. "Hah! Robert up and about would be a deal more trouble for you." He scratched his chin reflectively. "So, you have reason to believe she's been pinching from her household budget. I wouldn't doubt it. Robert and Quintin always left the running of the house to her, for all of their shrewdness in dealing with other enterprises."

"I'd like to dismiss her, but until I can take the time to go through the records more carefully . . ." She let her words fade as they entered the house and came within earshot of two kitchen maids. "I'll take you up to see Robert straightaway." Noble grimaced but followed her up the stairs.

After completing his examination, he left the sickroom and motioned for Madelyne to walk down the hall with him. "Without the cinchona to break the fever, I doubt he has long. You're right about his erratic mental state. One moment he's as lucid as Aristotle, the next he's off raving about Anne like a lovesick schoolboy."

Madelyne's eyes grew round with amazement. "No one has so much as spoken her name in this house since I came here. Quintin forbade me to ask about her. What do you know of the lady, Noble?"

He pushed his glasses up the bridge of his nose and seemed to reminisce for a few seconds. "There was some gossip around the time Quint was born. She and Robert didn't get on. No mystery there. Nobody but a cornered wharf rat's as mean as Robert Blackthorne when he sets his mind to it. She died in a cholera epidemic when Quint was only a babe. I was newly arrived here and didn't have the exalted Blackthornes in my practice then. Don't know much other than that."

"How extraordinary that after all these years, he's started to speak of her again." Madelyne was preoccupied as the old physician gave her instructions about treating her father-in-law. Then they visited the employees and slaves on the Hill who were ill or injured.

When Noble had completed his rounds, he delightedly accepted Delphine's offer of a basket lunch that he could eat while riding to his next appointment upriver. Lost in thought, Madelyne bade him farewell and returned to the big house. It was time to unravel some mysteries.

Chapter Twenty-one

Madelyne sat in her room surrounded by ledgers. Although Mistress Ogilve had not destroyed the records, she had placed them in the root cellar, piled in a corner on the damp floor where mildew and mice could get at them. Over the years, no one had ever asked to see them. Delphine had been able to tell Madelyne where they were stored.

One—dated January 5, 1751—had notes written in the margins in a neat feminine hand, questioning the number of bolts of calico cloth bought for slaves' clothing. Madelyne scanned further, flipping through the months, and found more such questions, very similar to those she had been asking herself since taking over the accounts of Blackthorne Hill.

An eerie sense of premonition washed over her as she realized that January of 1751 was less than a year after Anne Caruthers had wed Robert Blackthorne. Had Anne been trying to prove the same crime against Mistress Ogilve thirty years earlier?

Robert's cry interrupted her disturbing train of thought. It was well past midnight, and the house was silent but for the bitter old man in the bed down the hall, raving and crying for his dead wife, the wife he purported to hate.

Once Madelyne had realized how much Robert was revealing in his feverish rantings, she assigned only a few trusted older servants to tend him and exacted oaths from them never to reveal anything they heard in the sickroom. Quintin would never forgive her if she allowed gossip about his bastardy to spread. Of course, Quintin would never forgive her for many other things either, but this was one thing she could do for him.

With dread in every step, she walked down the hall to look in on Robert. Would he recognize her tonight or be off in the distant past, battling with ghosts? She entered the room and quietly dismissed Toby, urging the elderly man to get some rest. Then she sat by Robert's bedside and began to place another cool compress on his sweat-soaked brow.

His skin was yellow and hung in loose folds. In the dim light of the lone bedside candle, his eyes, once blue, now looked black as the pits of hell. She had never liked Robert Blackthorne. He had treated her, as well as Quintin, abominably, yet she wished this tormented death on no man.

"Anne! Anne, damn your lying heart. My own brother—how could you? I loved you! I loved you. . . ." His voice faded. When he resumed his raspy, disjointed speech, he was in a totally different mood. "So lovely, m'dear. The blue velvet quite matches your eyes. We'll buy out every merchant in Charles Town, see if I won't do it. Look at the cedar chest. Excellent protection against the mildew in Georgia's hot summers. You must have it for your pretties. . . ."

After a few moments, the opaqueness lifted from his eyes and he looked at her, a snarl twisting his face. "What're you doing? Come to gloat. Well, I'm not dead yet. You and your bastard can wait until I am."

Used to his verbal attacks, Madelyne wrung out a washcloth and placed it on his head in spite of his protest. "Small wonder your wife turned from you. You Blackthorne men have such a charming way with the ladies."

Robert tried to rise up. "How dare you speak of her!" He coughed and fell back on the bed.

"I only do so because you have. You rave about how much you loved her, how beautiful she was, how happy you were." She watched his expression grow wary, then furious.

"I was a fool to trust her. Any man's a fool to trust a woman."

"What about your brother? He betrayed you, too."

"He was bewitched by her, just as I was. Andrew's mother was prim, dull, homely. Alastair's was the arranged match, mine the love match." He scoffed bitterly, then turned his head to the wall. "Get out. Leave me to die in peace."

"You've never known peace in life, Robert. I doubt death will grant it either."

It was nearing dawn when he finally fell into a deep sleep, his dreams and nightmares over for a while. Nell came in and scolded Madelyne for staying up with him and shooed her from the room. Madelyne fed James, then collapsed on her bed for several hours, troubled and puzzled by her own dreams. Later that afternoon, she went to Anne's parlor, which she had converted into her retreat.

Madelyne felt drawn to the drawer where Anne's miniature lay hidden. How well she remembered Quintin's anger when he had found her with it. He'd cracked the delicate frame when he furiously threw it back into the drawer. She took it out and examined the lovely face of this enigma.

"I wonder when it was painted." Her eyes moved from the face to the bare ivory shoulders, framed by the low-cut bodice of a blue velvet gown. The one for which Robert had selected the fabric? "She must have had a whole wardrobe filled with gowns, riding clothes, pockets and gloves, slippers . . . perhaps other personal items."

For some inexplicable reason, Madelyne wanted to learn more about the Lady Anne, a woman so shallow as to leave her son to Robert's bitter wrath, yet a wife concerned enough about Blackthorne Hill to peruse housekeeping accounts and detect petty thievery. The two traits did not fit together.

Quintin had said Robert could not bear to destroy her clothes but ordered everything packed up and hidden away.

Half an hour later, Madelyne was climbing into the cobwebbed recesses of the attic. The floorboards were loose in places, and mice ran to hide from her intrusion into their domain. In spite of brilliant sun outdoors, the narrow dormer windows emitted only small shafts of light. She picked her way through a labyrinth of crates, boxes and barrels, over forty years of accumulation, now abandoned by the Blackthorne family. The enormity of searching through all the packing cases and trunks overwhelmed her as she wended her way from aisle to aisle.

Finally, just as she was about to despair, a faint essence of cedar, pungent and clean, filtered through all the musty staleness of mildew. Cedar—the chest Robert had bought Anne! Madelyne began to shove dusty blankets and rickety boxes aside until it became apparent that Anne's personal effects were indeed piled in this dormer.

One heavy trunk blocked her way to the smaller cedar chest. When she shoved it, the clasp snapped. Curious, she lifted the lid and peered inside, then carefully lifted what had once been a magnificent

ball gown of rose taffeta from the chest. Beneath
it were others, now moth-eaten and partially discolored. Yet in spite of the vicissitudes of nature,
they were splendid, made to fit a tall, elegant blonde
of slim, yet voluptuous proportions. At once she
thought of Barbara and realized how much her
friend must resemble the aunt she'd never met.
Madelyne wondered if all the Caruthers women
were fated to have tragic love affairs.

Sadly forcing aside Barbara and Devon's troubled
relationship, she replaced the gowns in the chest
and pushed it back, coughing on the plumes of dust
that rose in the stifling attic. She squeezed between
a barrel and the large trunk to reach the smaller
cedar chest. It was tightly locked.

Searching the cluttered attic, she found a heavy
brass key hanging from a lock on a leather trunk.
Using it, she pried and jiggled at the chest until
it suddenly popped open. Inside were bundles of
letters, all carefully wrapped in satin ribbons, a
number of miniatures, dance cards from London
soirees, and other obviously very personal memo-
rabilia. Could such items from the long-dead past
reveal the essence of the Lady Anne? They were
incredibly well preserved in the tight cedar confines
of the chest.

Feeling as if she were trespassing or invading
another woman's privacy, she lifted out a bundle
of letters and untied it. A quick perusal revealed
that they were exchanges between her and Robert
Blackthorne during their courtship. How young,
innocent, and full of high hopes they both must
have been. Once, at least, she did truly love him.
What could possibly have gone wrong?

Madelyne dug deeper through the letters and
trinkets, looking for she was not exactly certain
what, when her hands brushed the edge of a
leather volume. She carefully extracted it and
examined the smooth cordovan leather with gold

corner pieces and binding. It was Anne's diary! A quick perusal indicated that she had begun it on shipboard during her honeymoon.

Madelyne skimmed the entries, pausing here and there to read a passage that particularly struck a chord. How different Anne's marriage and welcome to Blackthorne Hill had been from her own. Yet in both cases, father and son had caused their wives great anguish. She understood about Quintin, but what had turned the man Anne called "my beloved Robbie" into a man who cursed her memory?

The entries during 1750 were mostly prosaic details about settling in at the Hill and opening their new city house. Then one entry caught her eye:

Mistress Ogilve is a well-favored woman of uncertain years with comely black hair, tidy and punctilious, yet I know she does not like me. She has been with Robbie's father for several years and has complete control of the household. I shall endeavor to win her over, but I fear she resents my intrusion.

Madelyne continued reading rapidly, searching for more entries regarding Mistress Ogilve, but then another passage caught her eye.

Alastair called again today while Robbie was out, although I have begged him not to do this. Again he declared his love for me in a most foolish and reckless manner. Poor, dear Alastair. My heart aches for him, but I love Robbie.

Madelyne backtracked, reading more entries. The honeymoon idyll of Robert and Anne had not lasted long before he became increasingly possessive and jealous. Winning such a prize as the Lady Anne Caruthers, toast of London, did not ensure that a colonial planter could keep her. Every social function seemed to end with a jealous quarrel. Anne bore it all, seeming to understand her husband's insecurities, although she did fear for his life when he fought several duels over her. But once his own brother was smitten with her—Madelyne could well imagine that tragedy was inevitable.

With a sense of foreboding, she continued reading, finding earlier entries detailing the growing ardor of Alastair Blackthorne for his brother's English wife. Alastair and his first wife had been bitterly mismatched. She was apparently not only thin and plain, but more importantly, possessed of a mean, humorless spirit. She despised her marital duties, informing her husband immediately after the birth of Andrew that she had provided an heir and would submit to his attentions no further.

After a succession of affairs and kept women, none of whom satisfied his loneliness, Alastair met Robert's breathtakingly beautiful new bride. At first Anne felt sorry about his unhappy marriage and tried to befriend him. For his part, Alastair fought the dishonor of falling in love with his brother's wife, but finally confessed to her that he was powerless to change his feelings, even though she did not return them.

His spitefully jealous wife, Vivian, was first to notice the tension between her husband and Anne. She went to Robert with the tale, convincing him that it was Anne who had bewitched Alastair. "A spoiled aristocrat but toying with us rude colonials," she had said after leading Robert to a secluded spot in the Kent family garden where Alastair was professing his devotion to a reluctant Anne.

Madelyne could feel the pain from each line Anne wrote as she described the bitter confrontation between the brothers. After that, Robert took to drinking, leaving Alastair to run their trading business at the Hill. But apparently Alastair could not continue living so close to the woman he loved.

Leaving his wife and small son behind, he traveled to the Muskogee towns as Crown agent. Upon receiving word of Vivian's death, he returned to ask Robert and Anne to care for Andrew until the boy was old enough to join him in the wilderness. But Vivian's family insisted on keeping Andrew as their ward. In spite of Anne's protests, Robert agreed, cruelly castigating her because she cared more for his brother's son than she did for her "duty" to produce her husband's heir.

On the rare occasions when he came to Savannah to visit little Andrew, Alastair tried to press his suit to Anne, urging her to abandon her increasingly unhappy marriage and come away with him. But then the whole situation changed dramatically late in 1752.

At last my prayers for Alastair are answered. He has found a woman who can return his love! She is half Muskogee, but has been educated by her white father. Robert is furious because of her Indian blood, but I feel only joy and a profound sense of relief in his happiness. Perhaps the news I have for my husband will hearten him. If only tis true. I think I am with child. I will wait a few more weeks to be certain. This babe must mend the breach between us caused by Vivian's vile accusations.

If only Anne had told Robert of her condition then instead of waiting. As Madelyne read further, the tragic end of the tale unfolded:

Alastair was so joyous that he had to share the news with me. Charity is with child. When I told him that I, too, was in that wonderful condition, he embraced me. Twas but a brotherly hug this time, but Robert did not see it as such.

He had been drinking and only heard my last few words to Alastair as he took me in his arms. "I, too, will have a child in April!" For once I thank God Robert was drunk, else he might have been able to kill his brother before Alastair could disarm him. As it was, Robert had to be knocked unconscious before he would desist. Alastair begged me to come stay with Charity at their plantation upriver until Robert came to his senses, but I refused. Whatever will come of this bitter misunderstanding, I must remain to face it.

And face it she did, bravely, foolishly. Recalling all the hostile suspicious confrontations between her and Quintin, Madelyne could well envision how cruelly Robert had treated Anne. He had coldly informed her that he would claim his brother's bastard rather than face the disgrace of admitting the child was not his. He had even told her that he would pray it be stillborn, except that then he would have to visit her treacherous bed once more to get an heir for Blackthorne Hill.

The entries after that agonizing outpouring grew more brief, less frequent, as Anne's confinement advanced. Robert watched with malicious glee as she suffered through a difficult pregnancy; he fell filthy drunk on the night Quintin was born.

The last entry in the diary was dated November 10, 1753. Anne's neat, delicate penmanship was now cribbed and spidery, written with an unsteady hand.

I am going to die. For myself I do not fear. Only for my beloved Quintin, whom I must leave behind. I have written to Alastair and Charity, beseeching them to care for Robert's son and raise him with their own Devon, but I fear Mistress Ogilve has not posted my letters. I am isolated in this big house, afraid for my innocent babe, and afraid for Robert, who suffers the pangs of the damned. Perhaps in time he and Quintin can heal each other. As for me, death beckons and it is welcome.

The light outside was fading now. Madelyne closed the diary and clutched it to her breast as great racking sobs welled up from deep inside her. Anne was just as much an innocent victim as was she. All Anne's prayers for Robert and his son to heal each other had been in vain. Instead, Quintin had grown up twisted by his father's hatred. "And now the cycle repeats itself." Madelyne did not know if she cried more for Anne and the sad little boy she was forced to leave behind, or for herself and the bitter man that boy had become.

"Mistress Madelyne? You up there? It be gettin' dark 'n the young mastah he cryin' fer his dinnah."

Using her petticoats to wipe the tears from her face, Madelyne stood up. "I'll be right there, Delphine. Is Master Robert's fever still down?"

"'Pears to be, but he be mighty weak. Say, you been cryin'? I declare, you been workin' too hard." The older woman observed Madelyne's chalky face and red-rimmed eyes, then put her arm around her young charge's shoulders. "Come. I fix yo dinnah while you see to dat pretty little one."

Madelyne felt too drained to protest as she climbed down from the attic and walked to the nursery, still clutching Anne's diary in her arms.

Robert sat propped up by pillows on his big bed, watching the candle on the table flicker low. After days of fever, his mind was clear once more, although that nagging pain in his chest was worse. He refused to drink the wine sitting at his bedside, knowing it was laced with medicine to make him sleep. He preferred the pain and a clear head, for however brief a span he might keep it. Noble said the pain came from his heart. He scoffed at the notion. "Anne destroyed my heart twenty-eight years ago. It don't exist," he had told the doctor.

And now, thanks to his feverish ravings, Anne's shameful betrayal was being bandied about by all the servants. He was certain of it. He cursed the weakness of his failing flesh. All too soon it would be over. Let Madelyne worry about Blackthorne Hill now. She would hold it for her son. At least on that matter, he felt at peace. The heir had been born before he died.

A light rapping broke his melancholy reverie. Madelyne stood in the doorway, holding something in her hands. He squinted in the dim light to see what it was, then noticed the peculiar set to her features. Something was odd here.

"You come with more of Noble's poison to force down my throat?"

"No. Although what I've brought will be poison—of a sort." She drew nearer and took the guttering candle from its holder, then used it to light a branched candlestick on the Chippendale side table across the room. When she set it on the candlestand beside his bed, he could see what she had brought with her.

His face blanched, then mottled with fury. "You've been snooping in her things! And now you have the gall—"

"And now I have the gall to offer you proof that your wife was innocent of all the crimes your bitter, twisted mind conjured up."

He sat bolt upright, raising his hand to slap the diary from her grasp. "Get out of here! Leave me in peace!"

"Peace? You've never known peace since you first suspected your wife and your brother were lovers.

If you wish to die a coward's death, in willful ignorance, so be it. But the truth is here. Quintin is your son."

"No! I saw them! I heard her tell him she was going to have his child."

"You heard her say, 'I, too, will have a child in April.' Alastair had just told her that Charity was going to have his baby. That was the reason he'd come to Blackthorne Hill. In your drunken fit of jealous fury, you misunderstood. After all these years, do you have the courage to face the truth? To face what you've done to your own son?"

She held out the diary. "The entries begin on your voyage from England and run almost to the day of her death."

Robert clutched the covers in balled fists, refusing to touch the leather volume. He had not seen it since he had shared a cabin with Anne on their shipboard honeymoon.

"Are you afraid, Robert?" she asked softly, still holding the diary out to him.

"I know her writing. If this is some chicanery of yours, some scheme—"

"It's no scheme. If you know her hand, then you'll know that what she wrote over those years was no lie, no scheme."

Robert felt his whole body begin to tremble as his eyes met Madelyne's. Her expression was implacable yet sad . . . so very sad. He took the book from her and opened it to one of the early entries from 1750. Reading Anne's declaration of love for her "Robbie," he felt the air sear his lungs. "You had no right!"

"I've earned the right by loving your son—all too well, just as she loved you."

Against his will, Robert was drawn into the past, his eyes following the flowing script of Anne's delicate handwriting as she recounted their early months at Blackthorne Hill. How happy he had been then! But all too soon, everything changed.

Madelyne sat quietly and watched as he read, turning the pages swiftly as he came to the series of events prior to Quintin's birth. For the first time in the years she had lived with Robert Blackthorne, she could see his naked, defenseless emotions revealed— the agony beneath the bitterness, the sorrow beneath the cruelty. His face froze when he came to Anne's recounting of the night he accused her of carrying Alastair's bastard.

"She didn't tell me about her condition until I'd seen her with my brother . . . and misread it all."

Madelyne heard the crack in his voice, but his eyes were dry, his face now a granite mask. "What effort it must cost you to maintain the facade, Robert. To hide your pain."

"Oh, Anne, my Annie. All the wasted years. If I hadn't been such a fool, she might have lived. I never really believed she died of the fever. She just couldn't endure me . . . and my hatred. She gave up. I destroyed the only person I ever really loved."

"You destroyed far more than your own life and that of your wife, Robert. What of Quintin? What of *your* son?" *My husband.*

He clutched the book tightly and stared unseeing at the far wall. "He never cried, you know. Always just like me—he hid his pain, no matter how much I abused him with words or blows. Once . . . once I locked him in the wine cellar for three days. He'd run away to those damned savages again. I thought it was Alastair's blood calling to him, but it wasn't, was it? He only wanted to escape from me. He's a survivor, hard and strong as they come . . . just like me. . . ."

"Then God help you both," Madelyne said quietly. She stood up and took the diary from his nerveless fingers. He made no move to stop her, did not even seem to know she was present anymore. Snuffing out all but one candle, she left the bitter old man alone to ruminate about the tragedies of the past. She must deal with those of the present.

As she walked down the dark hallway, Madelyne failed to see Mistress Ogilve's black-clad figure hiding in an alcove while she passed by.

Madelyne labored over the letter to Quintin, repeatedly throwing away draft after draft. How did one tell a man that the whole fabric of his identity had been rent asunder? He was not Anne's bastard—but worse yet, perhaps, he was the cruel and obsessive Robert's son. Finally, exhausted, she placed the letter aside and prepared for bed.

Although she knew Amy took excellent care of James and Gulliver guarded him, Madelyne felt compelled to look in on the babe one final time before retiring. Finding him fast asleep, she placed a kiss on his silky cheek and tiptoed from the nursery, too spent to sit and rock him as she usually did each night. Oddly, even the dog was sleeping so soundly he did not rouse when she entered the room.

Smiling tiredly, she closed the door and headed toward her bedroom, but froze in the doorway when she saw Mistress Ogilve standing in front of her escritoire. The housekeeper was busily gathering up the diary and all the papers lying around it.

Madelyne stepped into the room, furiously angry. "What are you doing here without my leave, riffling through my belongings?"

The big woman turned and faced Madelyne with a look of such malevolence on her face that it could have frozen the Savannah River in July. "I'm taking this diary and all your other papers that mention it. They'll make good fuel for a fire." Agnes set the diary on the mantel and picked up a poker from the hearth. She advanced on Madelyne slowly, menacingly.

"Get out." Madelyne struggled not to panic or let her voice break. "Have you lost your senses? If you try to harm me, Gulliver will tear your throat out."

The housekeeper smiled malevolently. "The dog ate a bowl of porridge laced with Robert's laudanum." She advanced on Madelyne again.

Madelyne gasped in horror. "You can't just kill me. Everyone would know—"

"No one will know anything, if you're dead. But you'd dismiss me if I allowed you to continue reading my account ledgers—or if that old fool Robert remembered to tell you twas me who sent him to the garden the night his brother came to meet his wife. A nice bit of timing, that." She smirked.

As she scanned the room for a weapon, Madelyne desperately stalled. "You wanted to discredit Anne— just as you've tried to undermine me. You're stealing from Blackthorne Hill."

"I've run Blackthorne Hill's household for over thirty years. I've given my life for this place and what thanks have I for it? A few miserly pounds' wages. I've only taken what I'm owed and I'll not lose my position. Never! If Master Quintin believes he's Robert's son, then he'll believe that James is his son. He'll believe in you and he'll let you turn me out destitute. I cannot permit that." She was within a few feet of Madelyne now, raising the poker.

Madelyne screamed, but the older woman just paused to laugh. "The only one you'll awaken is your son. I've also put Robert's laudanum in the upstairs servants' bedtime wine. No one will hear when you fall down the stairs and crush your skull on the newel post."

This time when she raised the poker and swung, Madelyne was ready. Dodging nimbly to the left, she pulled up her night shift and raced barefooted through the bedroom door. Mistress Ogilve was suprisingly quick, grabbing a handful of her hair. Instinctively Madelyne threw herself to the right as the poker arced past her head, striking the door with a sickening thud.

Wrenching herself free of the cruel hold, Madelyne scrambled from her knees and raced down the hall. *If only I can reach the front stairs, I can hide below and find someone she didn't drug to help me!*

In spite of her weight and the heavy clothes she wore, the housekeeper again caught up with Madelyne at the top of the stairs and seized her arm in an iron grip. Madelyne grabbed the banister railing and tried to pull herself free of her tormentor, but she was no match for the much larger woman.

The housekeeper drew back the poker, but before the killing blow could be delivered, the echo of a single shot rang out. Mistress Ogilve dropped the poker, which clattered down the wide, curving staircase. Her heavy body careened after it, landing at the bottom in a crumpled heap.

Madelyne pulled herself up, still clutching the railing in a white-knuckled death grip. Quickly averting her eyes from the wreckage of what had been the housekeeper, she looked down the hall. Robert Blackthorne stood with a pistol in his hand, a look of dazed disbelief on his face. Even in the dim light flickering from one wall sconce, Madelyne could see that he was chalk-white and trembling. She ran toward him, but before she reached him, he collapsed.

She knelt and cradled his head in her lap, rubbing his forehead and cheeks to revive him. He clutched his chest with one hand and made a choking sound. A death rattle. "Don't try to speak, Robert. I must fetch help from downstairs to get you back in bed."

His hold on her arm tightened as he gasped. "Too late . . . too late for that. Only tell Quintin . . . tell my son I've been a fool. He can learn something from that at least. . . ." His voice trailed off and his grip on her arm slackened.

Madelyne carefully laid his head on the cool hall floor and placed his hands on his chest, then rose and ran toward the sound of James's furious crying. Her

son and Robert had been the only ones to hear her
struggle with the deranged housekeeper. Gulliver lay
very still beside the crib, breathing erratically. She
picked up the baby and ran downstairs for help.

By morning's light, it seemed almost impossible
to believe the preceding night's events. Robert was
laid out for burial by Toby and Delphine. Madelyne
told no one the details of Mistress Ogilve's death.
She was quickly buried that morning in the servants' plot behind the family graveyard.

By noon, a very groggy Gulliver sat in Delphine's
kitchen, being fed warm milk. When he polished off
the bowl and bestowed a slurping kiss on Madelyne,
she hugged him and laughed joyously. "Oh, Gulliver,
if she'd killed you . . ."

"Praise be to da Almighty, dat debil woman is
gone fer good." Delphine said, rolling her eyes heav-
enward.

"And so is Robert," Madelyne said sadly. "He saved
my life, and for that I shall always be grateful. I must
send word to Andrew to arrange his funeral."

Few people would mourn Robert Blackthorne. He
had been a bitter and unyielding man ever since he
brought home a woman he adored but could never
learn to trust. Andrew notified friends and family in
the surrounding parishes who might wish to attend
the funeral, scheduled for the following day.

Devon was still posted with the rangers in the
city. Knowing Barbara would arrive at Blackthorne
Hill that evening, Madelyne decided to send word
to Dev as well. She knew Andrew would not do
so. If not for Barbara, there would be no reason
for Devon Blackthorne to pay his respects to his
Uncle Robert. But perhaps, if she could bring them
together again . . .

Chapter Twenty-two

As the priest said prayers, six burly slaves lowered the mortal remains of Robert Blackthorne into the damp Georgia earth. Chilly October rain sprinkled the assembly, a fittingly unpleasant omen for the close of the bitter old man's blighted life.

Andrew stood beside Madelyne, his hand solicitously at her elbow. All in all, a sterling turnout, he mused with bitter irony. Old Robert was finally gone, but Quintin was still alive and now, damn him, he had produced an heir for Blackthorne Hill. Andrew vowed that Quintin would not live to claim Blackthorne Hill or his lovely wife. Both the plantation and the widow would be his. He smiled to himself, thinking it was time to summon outside help.

As he calculated his future, his eyes swept the assembly, pausing for a moment on his brother, dressed in his ranger's uniform. Madelyne's friendship with Devon would end, as would her association with that spiteful English chit, Lady Barbara.

Monty had been useful, but his sister was a disquieting influence on Madelyne, one he meant to stop as soon as he had wed the heiress of Blackthorne Hill.

Barbara felt Andrew's dark gaze touch her and repressed a shiver in the cool October wind. She returned his stare and he looked away. *He knows I despise him.* Her eyes scanned the crowd, hungrily searching for Devon. Flanked by Monty and Weymouth, she could scarcely see a flash of his green uniform and golden head as he stood across from her, near the rear of the gathered mourners. Perhaps after everyone returned to the house for the meal, she could seek him out. But no, Devon would not stay. He would simply pay his respects to Madelyne after the interment and then ride off.

Ride off. A plan quickly formed in her mind, and she tugged on Monty's sleeve. "I've torn my skirt's hem," she whispered, gathering the elaborate folds of gray silk into a bunched mass so he could not detect her prevarication. "I'm going to slip off to the house and find a maid to sew it before anyone sees me looking so bedraggled. You and Alex can keep anyone from noting my absence. I'll join you at the house."

Before her bemused brother could frame a reply, she vanished into the crowd, which was just beginning to disperse after the final words had been spoken over Robert's grave. Barbara slipped from the family graveyard and hid behind a copse of tulip trees, then decided on the swiftest yet most concealed course to the road below the stables. She would have to run like the wind through a corn field and then come up behind the outbuildings.

Devon ignored the cool looks of disapproval from distant cousins and other shirt-tail relations in the Blackthorne family as he made his way to where Madelyne and Andrew stood receiving condolences.

He was relieved that Barbara was not close by. Just seeing her silvery beauty from a distance had sent waves of pain crashing over him.

Madelyne smiled warmly and took his hand in hers as he stepped up to her. "It was so good of you to come, Dev."

He returned her smile, saying, "I know you'll scarcely miss Robert's cheery presence, but his death does place an extra burden on you. If there's any way I can help you, just send word to me in the city."

"Madelyne has me to assist her with the Hill now that Robert is gone," Andrew said with a smile both brothers knew to be false. "I'm certain we'll get on famously, Devon."

"I do appreciate your offer, Dev. Won't you please come to the house for dinner and spend the night? You haven't seen James since he was a newborn."

"I'm quite certain my brother has military duties calling him," Andrew said smoothly.

"Just so, Madelyne. For once Andrew has the right of something. I must ride to catch up with my company. We're dispatched against rebel raiders to the south of here."

Madelyne felt a stab of disappointment as she searched the crowd for Barbara, who had mysteriously vanished. She bartered for time by asking trivial questions about his activities and the course of the war as they strolled slowly toward the house. But finally Devon withdrew, promising to call again after his mission was accomplished.

Barbara waited in the dark shadows, her breathing labored from running the last hundred yards or so without stopping. "I'm a weakling. Panther Woman would best me easily if we were to fight for Dev," she whispered to herself as she crouched behind the elderberry bushes that grew thickly along a bend in the road, neatly concealing it from any onlookers at the house. Of course, if anyone were in the dairy, they would see her waylaying Devon Blackthorne, but only serving wenches tended the cows. She would chance it.

Devon rode down the curving road, deep in thought. Then Firebrand shied, and the subject of his reverie materialized right in front of the prancing horse.

He reined in. "What the hell are you doing here? I could have run you over."

She had one hand on the bay's bridle and was breathless and disheveled. "Please, Dev—I ran down here to meet you. I knew you'd ride out when everyone went to the house."

"You've had a lot of exercise for nothing, your ladyship," he said tightly, turning the bay's head away from her grasp.

"You can't leave me. I fell and twisted my ankle. I can't walk back, Dev." She leaned against his leg, letting her weight fall against Firebrand as if she could not support herself.

With a muttered curse, he leaned down and lifted her up in front of him on the horse. At once she threw her arms around his waist and buried her face against his chest. "We have to talk, Dev."

"There's nothing to say, Barbara. Your antics are going to get one or the other of us killed." He turned Firebrand off the road, riding toward the rear entrance of the house.

"Dev, I want to go with you. Monty will force me to marry Weymouth and I—"

"Marry him. He can get you safely out of this hell. Don't you read the broadsides circulating in Savannah? Haven't you heard what's happened in Virginia? Cornwallis surrendered his whole bloody army to the rebels and their French allies! After three weeks of being besieged in Yorktown, he gave up. The last effective field army his majesty had in North America—over seven thousand men—disarmed. It's over, your ladyship."

"What will happen now, Dev? The British army in Savannah can't just sail away!"

"They can and they will. There's nothing for it but to evacuate the coastal cities under the protection of the Royal Navy. At least you and your brother can go home and resume your lives. I'm one of the less fortunate—Georgia is my birthplace and now I've lost even that."

She looked into his eyes, which no longer held their devilish glint. His expression was as grim as his words. Touching his jaw with her fingertips, she asked, "Where will you go?"

He shrugged, but the careless insouciance was gone from the gesture. "I'm not certain. First I plan to resume my search for McGilvey and his renegades and rid the countryside of them. When the rangers are disbanded, I'll probably go back to the Muskogee. Now that British rule is over, the American settlers will pour west like locusts into Indian lands."

"And you'll fight for your mother's people?" She felt a cold sense of dread. "You could be killed, Dev."

"I could be killed while I'm wearing this uniform, too. Maybe McGilvey will get me."

"No!" She held tightly to him.

He replied with forced lightness, "As you can see, your ladyship, my prospects—as an Englishman or a Muskogee—aren't all that bright. Go home. Forget me and begin a new life." In spite of his resolve, he grazed her tear-stained cheek with his fingertips and then kissed the salty droplets from her lashes.

Barbara tightened her arms around his waist and her mouth sought his hungrily. When she felt his lips respond and open to hers, she thought she had won and murmured between kisses, "Damn your prospects, I'll make a good Muskogee wife. Take me with you."

A good Muskogee wife. Her words hammered at him until reason and sanity returned. Firebrand had stopped behind the farthest outlying stable building. He forced himself to push her away and then deposited her, breathless and disheveled, on the muddy ground. "You wouldn't last a week on a forced march in the swamps, your ladyship. You'd best hurry and repair your gown and coiffure before anyone sees you. Good-bye Barbara." He turned the bay and kicked it into a gallop.

"Damn you, Devon Blackthorne! Damn the whole bloody rebel army! I won't leave Georgia," she called after his retreating figure, but he did not look back.

April, 1782, Golden Swan Inn

Madelyne held James's little body close to her, sheltering him from the spring rain whipping about her as she alighted from the coach. She signaled to Obediah and the rest of her escort to take the horses to Polly's barn, then entered the warm golden glow of the tavern's main room. Shaking the rain from his shaggy pelt, Gulliver trotted behind her. He kept a wary eye on anyone who approached Madelyne and the baby. At the Swan, only Polly could do so with his approval. The blazing fire in the fireplace was as welcome as Polly's broad smile and hearty hug.

"I been wantin' to see you 'n that little rascal," she said as she led them through the noisy crowd to her own private quarters in the rear of the Swan. "Tut, now, ain't he a love? Gettin' real good-sized, too."

"He's eating chopped meat as well as mashed-up vegetables now. And he has three more teeth." Madelyne unwrapped her prize and handed him to Polly for an inspection.

She tickled the baby and elicited burbles of laughter which revealed his new teeth. "Growin' so strong 'n so good natured. Got pink cheeks, luvie, don't you? Pretty soon you'll be havin' a birthday!" she cooed to James.

"Yes, soon he'll be a year old. And his father's not seen him since he was a newborn. I've heard talk in the city of a British evacuation. The war's over in all but name, Polly. What have you heard that you sent for me?"

Polly Bloor's chafed face reddened even more than usual as she met Madelyne's eyes. "Just let me get you some refreshment. Then we'll talk. And as for you, you rascal," she said, looking down at the wet dog, "I have a fine meaty hambone out in the kitchen." Gulliver followed her obediently, tail wagging.

Madelyne carried her son to a large, comfortable armchair and sat down with him. He regarded her with clear emerald eyes, following her every movement with avid interest. Polly returned in a few moments and set a lavish tray of food on the table, including a small bowl filled with finely minced venison and carrots for James.

As she spooned the mush into his round little mouth, she said, "Quint got your letter about old Robert's death. He didn't mourn much."

"I wrote him about the diary. His mother didn't betray his father. She was innocent. Didn't that mean anything to him?" Anger warred with pain. She had written so many letters in the past months, all ignored.

Polly chose her words carefully as she continued feeding the baby. "I reckon it means a lot to him, but the fact is, well . . . he ain't been able to write. Got hisself shot—now mind, it ain't bad," she soothed as Madelyne's face paled. "General Marion hisself wrote me for Quint, sayin' he'd be comin' home to the Hill soon's he can travel."

"How badly was he hurt? Don't sugar the medicine, Polly. Tell me whatever you learned." Madelyne held her breath, all the anger gone as stark terror for Quintin replaced it.

"Wound wasn't the bad part. Fever set in. They ain't got much in the way of doctors or medicine in the swamp. But he's comin' 'round. General says he should be able to ride within the month, but I don't want you countin' days and frettin' so yer milk dries up fer little James before he's got a full set of teeth."

Madelyne smiled in spite of her trepidations. "Don't you fret, Polly. I'll take care of Quint's son until he comes home—to claim his birthright."

Outside the tavern, a small man slouched in the stable, listening to the armed riders who had accompanied Madelyne Blackthorne talk about their mistress. He pulled his coonskin cap low over his greasy gray hair and spat a gob of tobacco on the dirt floor between the front feet of Mistress Blackthorne's fine carriage horse. No one paid any attention as they passed around a jug of rum, laughing and talking.

When one of the heavily armed riders mentioned the friendship between his rich-as-sin mistress and the common strumpet who ran the Golden Swan, the eavesdropper pricked up his ears. This was not what he had been sent to learn, but it might be very useful, very useful indeed.

"Mistress Blackthorne's been tryin' to reach the master for months to tell him about his father dyin'. Guess old Polly finally got her word through the American lines."

One of the stablemen laughed. "British been snoopin' around here for over a year. Never caught Polly spyin' yet. She's a shrewd one. Picked her the winning side, too."

"You think she finally got a message from Quintin Blackthorne for his wife? I'd sure admire havin' him home to run things. I don't much like taking orders from a snip of a female, even if she is pretty as hell."

The men continued to speculate about Polly's courier system and concluded that it was indeed likely that Quintin Blackthorne was on his way back to claim his inheritance now that the war was winding down and his father was cold in his grave.

Archie Baird spat another gob of tobacco and moved out of the shelter afforded by the stable into the mild spring rain. He had been hanging around the Swan trying to ferret out any word about George McGilvey. Devon Blackthorne was offering a fine reward for information about the renegade. But he also knew that Major Caruthers had an old score to settle with Quintin Blackthorne, from nearly two years ago when the rebel had trounced the fancy English lord and freed a prisoner from the prison ship he was in charge of guarding. The hell with McGilvey. There would be a fat purse from the Englishman when he learned Quintin Blackthorne was coming home. After he collected from Caruthers, maybe old Archie would pick up the raider's scent again and collect both rewards.

Whistling in the rain, he rode for the city.

Savannah

Major Montgomery Caruthers took a swallow from the tumbler in his hand and grimaced. "Damned filthy rum," he muttered, taking another swallow and wishing desperately that it was fine brandy such as Sir Alex drank. Alex would settle for nothing but the best.

At first, Monty had been flattered when Weymouth offered him friendship, even though it soon became obvious that the viscount was using him as an entrée to court Barbara. With the Caruthers estates being run through by their mother, it had become obvious to him that both he and his sister must marry well.

Monty congratulated himself on the fortunate accident that had brought Weymouth and Barbara together in Savannah. He did enjoy Alex's company, but wished the viscount had not encouraged his old compulsion for gambling. Alex held a fortune in his markers. With Barbara so unresponsive, Weymouth now asked that her brother exert his influence on the lady. If she could be persuaded to marry him, the viscount was hinting, rather broadly, that he would see his way clear to tearing up Monty's markers.

This was the solution to all their problems. He had only to convince his willful younger sister of the wisdom of paying more serious attention to Alex's suit. That might prove difficult, he realized as he waited for her to respond to his request that she join him for a pre-dinner libation here in the privacy of the library. She was late.

Barbara had spent two days at Blackthorne Hill and only returned to the city that afternoon. As she dressed in an elaborate pale-blue silk gown and had her maid coif her hair in a high pompadour, the realization had struck her—she would much rather be back at the Golden Swan with Madelyne and Polly, playing with little James. *I'd love nothing more than to have a baby of my own to love. Dev's baby.*

But such was never to be. He had made that abundantly clear from the start. After a cursory inspection of her toilette, she headed for the library with a falsely bright smile on her face.

Opening the door, she greeted her brother. "Good evening, Monty. Frightfully sorry I'm late, but the roads are so difficult between here and Blackthorne Hill. I vow I was fair soaked from the rain."

He frowned, wondering how to initiate the delicate matter he had to discuss. Handing her a glass of sherry, he bussed her cheek perfunctorily and said, "You spend too much time with that Blackthorne woman."

"Quint and Madelyne are our cousins—as well as Andrew's. I thought you and he were as thick as thieves," she replied crossly. "Surely you can't blame Madelyne for Quintin's actions."

He waved his hand in a dismissive gesture and smiled. "No, of course not, it's just that I fear for your safety on the roads. You know how rebel partisans lurk everywhere these days. Alex expressed concern for your safety just yesterday." He observed her as she nervously played with her sherry glass.

"Weymouth is a dear sort, but entirely too fussy for my taste. Anyway, I had an adequate escort."

"Nonsense. We've few enough men to spare. I'm afraid you'll have to curtail any further excursions into the country."

"Then I shall go without an escort. The way things are headed, just telling Elijah Clarke's rebels that I'm a cousin of Quintin Blackthorne would allow me safe passage," she replied waspishly.

"Dammit, Barbara, there's a bloody war going on out there!"

"So I've repeatedly been told." A haunted look came into her eyes as she recalled Dev's words to the same effect.

"Don't be angry with me, Puss," he said, crossing the room and raising his crystal tumbler to toast with her wineglass. "We've something to celebrate. Some wonderful news."

"Is General Clinton sending his army from his stronghold in New York?" she asked dryly.

"No politics. This is of a personal nature." He could see a warning look come into her eyes, but persevered. "Weymouth has offered for you, Barbara. The catch of the season. You've landed him."

"Well, I'll just throw him back then. I've told you and Alex that I'm not interested in his suit."

"He's a bloody viscount! What are you waiting for, the Prince of Wales? Really, Barbara, you have a head on your shoulders. You know the straits our family is in—"

"I know the straits our famous Caruthers profligacy has placed us in, yes. I was guilty of it myself back in London. That's why mother shipped me off, if you recall. Now she's run through everything at home and you've amassed more debts here. Well, I'm sorry, Monty, but I won't marry a man who repels me. I don't care if I have to take in sewing!"

"How quaint a notion. Did your little Huguenot friend put it in your head? I knew I should have kept you from spending so much time rusticating in the country with her, pining away for a life of bucolic tranquility."

"It's not bucolic tranquility I want, Monty. It's love," she blurted out, then blushed to the roots of her hair in mortification.

"Love?" he scoffed. "Now I know I must forbid you to associate with that traitor's wife."

"My feelings have nothing to do with Madelyne's influence."

"What, pray, brought on this ridiculous impulse?"

"A man." She paused, knowing that she had his full attention now. Well, why not? Barbara saw her future stretching bleakly before her and felt goaded to tell the truth. She wished she had from the time Devon had left her at Reynolds Square with her carefully rehearsed tale.

"Everything I told you about my rescue after the shipwreck was a lie, Monty. There was no kindly fisherman and his wife."

"Some colonial found you?" His throat was dry. He crossed to the desk where the rum bottle sat and poured himself another drink.

"Devon Blackthorne found me."

"That ranger? Andrew's half brother . . ." He paled.

"Yes, Monty, that's right. Andrew's Muskogee brother, tainted with savage blood. He saved my life and took me to one of their villages. I lived among them all that time I was missing."

"And I suppose you and Blackthorne were lovers?" he asked coldly, certain by the look on her face that it was true.

"Yes, Monty, we were lovers. I still love him. I always will, even though he's repeatedly refused to take me with him." She gave a sad, ironic little laugh. "Odd really, but Dev used much the same arguments you have—urged me to marry Weymouth and flee the colonies before the final debacle. But I'll never go back to London." Her voice was whisper-soft, but steely with determination.

"Yes, you will! I'll have you bound hand and foot and carried aboard ship if I must."

She laughed mirthlessly. "Almost the identical threat mother used to send me here. I'll not stand for it, Monty. You, mother, society—even the overvalued Caruthers name—be damned. I'll not be coerced or manipulated any further." She set down her glass and made a mock curtsy. "If you'll excuse me. I've quite lost my appetite for dinner."

Monty stared into the glass of rum he had repeatedly refilled after Barbara's shocking revelations. His own sister, the little silver-haired imp he had been so fond of since she was in the nursery—lying with a filthy savage. Bad enough that Devon Blackthorne was the ne'er-do-well younger brother of a colonial merchant, but he was an Indian as well!

A rapping on the library door brought him out of his self-pitying reverie. "Tell cook I'll not be taking dinner, Hawkes," he said, thinking the butler had come to summon him to eat. He, too, had lost his appetite.

"Begging your pardon, my lord, but there's a frontiersman here to see you—says his name's Archie Baird." Hawkes's voice dripped disdain for the filthy, rough-mannered visitor who dared presume to darken the hallway of the Baron of Rushcroft.

"Baird," Monty repeated. Then his liquor-impeded brain recalled the fellow. What the devil did he want? "Send him in, Hawkes."

June, 1782, Blackthorne Hill

Quintin did not take the same precautions as he had the year before when he returned to the plantation. The danger of a British patrol capturing him was almost negligible these days. They were in the midst of preparing to evacuate Savannah. He doubted very much that any straggling loyalists or British regulars would be patroling this far north of the city. The countryside belonged to the Americans now. Soon the cities would, too.

He flexed his aching shoulder and wished once again that the interminable conflict were officially over. His last communication from Franklin indicated that the peace process was creeping along at a snail's pace.

"But for me, the war's over now," he murmured to Domino as he surveyed the prosperous plantation house and all its surrounding fields and outbuildings. The sullen noonday heat made him feel faint as he dismounted too quickly. He took his canteen, walked over to a cluster of rocks shaded by a hickory tree, and sat down to drink. The army doctor had warned him about overexertion and cautioned more rest before undertaking such a long journey, but Quintin was heartily sick of lying abed and desperately anxious to return home.

Understanding his feelings, Marion had signed his release and bidden him Godspeed. Parting from the little Huguenot had been one of the most difficult moments of Quintin Blackthorne's life. The taciturn older man had become not only an honored commander and dear friend, but more nearly a father to Quintin than Robert Blackthorne had ever been.

It was still difficult—no, impossible—to think of Robert Blackthorne as his father after a lifetime of being told he was a bastard. Now Robert was dead, penitent for his sins far too late for Anne or for his son. On the long and slow ride home, Quintin had thought a great deal about what Madelyne's letter said. Was Anne really an innocent victim? If so, was he guilty of the same jealous and ill-founded treatment of Madelyne? *I must read that diary for myself.*

Madelyne. She had been in his thoughts continuously over the past year. He dreamed of her, even raved about her in his feverish delirium. James was a year old now. Would the boy resemble him?

He stood up and capped the canteen. No more postponing the confrontation. He remounted Domino and rode directly toward the big brick house on the crest of the bluff.

Madelyne was in the smokehouse selecting a ham for that evening's dinner when she heard the cry go up from the big house. Quintin, returned at last! And here she was, sweaty and dressed in dirty old clothes. Even the lacing on her bodice had been torn loose by James's strong little fingers.

"There's no help for it," she murmured philosophically as she tried to smooth her hair beneath her mobcap. Springy mahogany curls fought her trembling fingers until she gave up and tossed the limp headgear aside and shook her hair free so that it flowed about her shoulders. With her heart pounding in her chest, she walked swiftly up the path to where Quintin was surrounded by a crowd of joyous servants.

Sensing her presence, he turned and looked down the road to where she stood, a small solitary figure in shabby clothes. She hesitated for a moment, then resumed walking toward him with a wary expression on her face.

Her eyes swept over him, noting the pallor of his beard-stubbled face, the thinness of his tall body, the way he favored his left shoulder. His brow was beaded with perspiration and he looked ready to drop.

"Oh, Quint, you could have died in those swamps!" Her step quickened into a run as the crowd of servants parted to let her pass.

Quintin stood still, staring at her with an unreadable expression in his green eyes, letting her come to him. At the last moment, before she reached him, Madelyne stopped short of throwing herself against him. Somehow he felt that had been her first instinct. Instead she stood with her hands out, palms open, waiting for him to make the next move.

"Welcome home, Quint." Her voice was ragged and breathless. Would he do nothing but look at her as if she were a beggar wench?

Quintin took her hands in his and felt his own pulse leap with the contact. The world faded away as he stared into her fathomless amber eyes. "Tis good to be home, Madelyne."

Holding hands, they walked toward the front door without saying another word. The servants chattered curiously about the reunion between their master and the wife who was accused of betraying him.

Chapter Twenty-three

As they neared the front door, Toby swung it wide and stood with tears in his eyes. "I'm so happy you're home safe, Mastah Quintin."

"Thank you, Toby. I'm happy to see you haven't changed—just as proper as ever." He reached out and embraced the old man, who returned the hug heartily.

"You look fair starvin', Mastah Quintin. I gonna fatten you up!" Delphine waddled into the front hall to inspect him with sharp black eyes. She held him at arm's length, then enveloped him against her pillowy girth. "Lawd above, you skinny as a newborn colt! You 'n Miz Madelyne go talk private while I start cookin'." She turned and retraced her steps down the hall.

"I'll see to a nice cool bath, if you like, suh," Toby said.

"That would be splendid, Toby. I could count the baths I've had in the last year and a half."

"Would you like to rest in the study while things

are prepared, Quint?" Madelyne asked after the two
of them were alone. Nervously smoothing her dusty
skirts, she added, "I need a bath, too." Then her face
pinkened in embarrassment at the unintentional
connotation.

Quintin smiled wolfishly. "I'd offer to share mine,
but I fear I'm too dirty. Then again . . ." His voice
trailed off suggestively.

She blushed as her hand came involuntarily to
her breast. "I must feed James. He's almost weaned,
but this is the one time of day . . ." Her eyes met his,
challenging him. "Would you like to see your son,
Quint? He's grown to look quite like you."

Would you recognize your own son? Robert didn't.
Quint had never known a father's love. Could he give
his son what he had never experienced? Suddenly
he was afraid. "Perhaps it would be best if I cleaned
myself up first," he said awkwardly. His voice rang
hollow in his ears. *Coward.* "I'll go upstairs and bathe
and shave while you feed him."

"How long will you stay, Quint? Is the war over?"

"For me it is. Marion gave me a full discharge
because of my wound and the fever. Just these past
weeks have I been able to ride. I've been of little use
to him for months, but then, there's been precious
little for us to do. The peace process is under way,
Madelyne, even if loyalists and patriots still skirmish in the back country."

"You've won. Everything, Quint. If you choose to
take it," she added softly, then turned and walked
away.

He debated following her to see their child. James.
His son? Just as he was Robert's son. He felt hot
and dizzy, still accursedly weak after his days in
the saddle. Or was it just being here, facing his
wife and the painful past she had so dramatically
resurrected?

He climbed the stairs and entered his big bedroom. Two houseboys had just filled the tub in

the dressing room. He stripped unceremoniously, so accustomed to dressing and undressing himself that he knew Toby would be appalled. Dismissing the boys with thanks, he sank into the cool, fresh water with a sigh of relief.

Toby entered the room and deposited a stack of fresh linen towels beside the tub, then gathered up his discarded clothes, clucking about how they should be burned.

"Do with them what you will, Toby. Just bring me anything clean and I shall be everlastingly grateful."

Madelyne fed James and laid him down for his afternoon nap. "Soon, little one, soon he'll know," she crooned, stroking his soft black hair as he fell into a deep sleep.

Hastily she stripped off her dirty clothes and scrubbed her body from the large basin of water Nell had fetched. Then she donned a fresh cotton day gown of deep yellow and tied back her hair with a matching ribbon.

Looking nervously at the door to the dressing closet joining their bedrooms, Madelyne decided not to interrupt his bath. Instead, she went through the hall and entered his bedroom, where Toby was setting out a veritable feast of sweet smoked ham, sharp cheese, crisp corn dodgers, and fresh raspberries with clotted cream.

He opened a bottle of chilled white wine and poured it into two crystal glasses, then turned to Madelyne, smiling. "I'll be downstairs, if you need anything else," he said.

Appreciating his understanding, Madelyne smiled warmly. "Thank you." When Quint entered the room a moment later, she raised one glass and offered it to him. "Delphine has outdone herself," she said, motioning him to join her at the Pembroke table near the window.

"As long as it isn't sweet potatoes and fish, I'll love it," he replied lightly, raising his glass to hers, then drinking down a hearty slug.

Madelyne took a sip, then placed her glass on the table and walked over to his desk. She withdrew the old leather diary and placed it on the table. "Would you like to read it now?" she asked gently.

"No. I'll need time . . ." *More time than I ever realized*, he thought miserably.

Clearing her throat for courage, she said, "I know this is very painful for you, Quint, but after he read it, your father was hurt far more irreparably than you—his life was over and he'd misspent all of it. He begged your forgiveness."

"So you wrote. . . . I don't know if I *can* forgive. Or forget," he said, staring at the worn leather volume pensively.

"Do you want to repeat your father's mistakes? You have to face the past so you can leave it behind and get on with the future."

He pulled out a chair for her and then seated himself at the small table. The intimacy of the arrangement struck him oddly. "I still desire you, you know. No matter what I believed—right or wrong—about you, I couldn't free myself from the hold you have on me."

The words seemed torn from him as he spoke in a low, swift monotone. Madelyne placed her hand over his and felt the fire that always leaped between them. "Then perhaps there is hope for our marriage yet. We have all the time in the world now, Quint. Let's not waste it." She raised her glass and proposed a toast. "To new beginnings."

Studying her with those unnerving green eyes, he silently chimed his glass against hers and drank, then turned his attention to the food, although just looking at the diary had erased his appetite.

They ate in tense silence for several moments, each imbibing of the wine more freely than was their wont.

Quint broke the silence first. "Delphine is as

splendid a cook as I remembered."

"I know how you hated the charred sweet potatoes and dreamed of her corn dodgers smothered in honey," she said, then flushed as he stared at her.

"How did you—"

"Polly let me read your letters to her," she replied, struggling to keep the accusatory tone from her voice.

He put down his fork and sighed, running his fingers through his long hair, then cradled his head in his palms. "I was certain of so many things then, Madelyne. Now I don't—"

A loud crash and a hoarse scream interrupted his sentence. Both of them stood up rapidly, but Quint was first to reach the door and fling it open, only to be met by a Brown Bess musket pointed at his midsection. A fish-eyed young corporal held the weapon levelly, backing Quint into his bedroom as Major Montgomery Caruthers ambled in, accompanied by half-a-dozen more soldiers, all armed to the teeth.

"So, at last we meet again, Blackthorne," Caruthers said smoothly, brushing a speck of lint from his immaculate scarlet uniform. "Luck has finally smiled on me. Imagine my delight when I heard that the infamous American spy had returned to his home."

"Monty, you can't arrest Quint! The war's over. You're leaving—"

"Tut, m'dear. You and Barbara will be much better off without the Blackthorne men in your lives," he soothed, patting her shoulder comfortingly.

Quint looked from the hard-eyed corporal to the smug major. He could see no means of escape as the soldiers ringed him. Then he turned to Madelyne, who had Caruthers's hand on her shoulder. "I wanted to believe you on . . . God help me, I did believe you," he said in a hoarse, harsh voice. His icy green eyes stopped her as she tried to reach out to him.

The major motioned for the soldiers to seize

Quint's arms and bind them roughly behind his back. "Now, I've recovered my escaped prisoner. Never fear, Madelyne, he'll not get away again to trouble you further."

"Please, Monty—he's my husband. Don't do this," she cried as the soldiers dragged Quintin from the room.

Quint did not even look back at her as she stood alone with fists clenched impotently at her sides.

As they tied Quint on Domino, Caruthers said casually, "Quite a splendid piece of horseflesh. Once we get to Savannah, it will be his majesty's property, of course. Perhaps I shall purchase him." Jauntily he mounted his chestnut and tossed a purse to Archie Baird.

The grimy backwoodsman, who had been watching the house for weeks, eagerly accepted his payment, then rode quickly away from the hate-filled looks of the servants who realized what he had done.

Quintin watched Archie ride away and wondered if Madelyne had hired him to lie in wait. If so, he must have been watching the Hill since she sent the letter about the diary and Robert's death. Quint willed himself not to think of the fool's paradise he had almost believed existed.

Savannah

"Well, what did she say?" Alex Weymouth asked, rubbing his sweaty palms nervously on his tight breeches.

"My sister consents to be your wife, Alex. I think this calls for a bit of a celebration, don't you?" Monty Caruthers replied.

"Most certainly!" Weymouth rang for a servant and ordered a bottle of his best Madeira to be opened. He motioned the major to take a seat in the lavishly appointed parlor of the elegant townhouse appropriated for his use during the occupation. "Can't say I'll be sorry to bid farewell to this sandy, mosquito-infested little sinkhole." He stared out the bay window at the street below him. "At least the rebels who owned this place stocked a decent wine cellar." The viscount took a sip, then turned and regarded the major over the rim of his goblet. "May I call on the morrow? Barbara and I should discuss the wedding."

Monty swallowed a gulp of the Madeira as he replayed last night's bitter confrontation with his sister. "Marrying the viscount is for your own good," he had remonstrated.

"My welfare has nothing to do with this. I'll wed the viscount to gain Quintin Blackthorne's freedom. In return, Weymouth will pay off your gaming debts. Tis a bargain made in hell, Monty. The only good to come of it will be Madelyne's reunion with her husband." Barbara had spoken with such bitter loathing that he had quit the room at once.

Returning to the present, Caruthers picked up the threads of conversation with Weymouth. "Er, yes, I imagine you may call in the afternoon, but first there is the matter of arranging that damned spy's release. Bloody awkward business, that, but you know how women take notions. My sister thinks herself Madelyne Blackthorne's dearest friend. All the better when we'll no longer have to associate with these colonials."

"I do wish we were leaving with the colonies still firmly under his majesty's control, however," the colonel replied.

Raising his glass, Colonel Alex Weymouth, Eighth Viscount of Leicester, proposed a toast. "To the Lady Barbara and to his majesty!"

"Hear, hear. To your health, as well," the major added, drinking deeply as he thought, *You're going to need it, wed to that she-cat against her will!*

After spending a fruitless morning at General Alured Clarke's headquarters in Savannah, Madelyne was exhausted and frightened nearly witless.

In spite of the inevitable end of the war, they were holding Quintin for trial. The captain she had spoken with was the soul of kindness as he explained to her that if her husband had merely been an American soldier, they would not have held him, circumstances being what they were. But Quintin Blackthorne was known to have been a spy, and the higher military and royal authorities felt that was quite another matter.

She had begged to see the new military commander, but he refused, and she was politely but firmly ushered into the street where her horse and chair waited. Desperately, she thought of anyone in authority upon whom she could prevail, but she was an outsider, with no influence now that Robert was dead.

"Andrew, of course!" He was not only a close friend of Major Caruthers, but also of that viscount, Colonel Weymouth, who was said to have General Clarke's ear in all matters. Andrew and Quintin may have had bitter differences over the war, but they were bound by blood after all. She climbed quickly into the carriage and instructed Obediah to drive her to her cousin's city house.

Andrew watched her alight from the carriage and studied her pale, haunted expression with satisfaction. She had obviously dressed to impress the authorities in an elegant caraco jacket of russet silk over voluminous green silk petticoats, but her efforts had been wasted. She must have learned how hopeless it was to petition for her husband's release. Even if Andrew's odious partner had not been able to locate Quint and kill him, this would serve just as well—perhaps better. Once Quintin Blackthorne was shot by a firing squad, Madelyne would come flying into his arms for comfort.

When she was ushered into the parlor, he took her hands and kissed them, drawing her to sit on the Serpentine sofa. "In spite of the warm day, you feel positively chilled, dear Madelyne."

She smoothed her silk skirts nervously. "I'm most distraught, Andrew. Yesterday a British patrol under Major Caruthers's command arrested Quint within hours of his homecoming. They mean to execute him."

"I know, my dear. I dined with Monty only last evening," he replied neutrally.

Madelyne placed her hand on his jacket sleeve and squeezed his arm. "I understand you and Quint have had bitter differences, and I regret the disgrace he's caused you, but he is your cousin, blood of your blood. Surely you can talk to the major—to Colonel Weymouth—someone must intercede with General Clarke to free him."

"I regret very much, my dearest Madelyne, that such is quite impossible. Quintin Blackthorne is a spy. There's no changing that fact, is there? Think, Madelyne, think of your honor, your Deveaux name, your loyalty. You've never belonged with a scoundrel and a deceiver like Quintin. No one blames you for his crimes—I have gone to a great deal of trouble to see to that." He enveloped her cold hands in his and squeezed them, then brought them to his lips, brushing them with a wet kiss. "In fact, dearest, I shall offer you consolation once he's removed from your life for good."

She stiffened in premonition, studying the ardor glowing in his pale brown eyes. "What do you mean, Andrew?" She withdrew her hands from his.

He smiled placatingly and patted her hand. "I know tis too soon for it to be seemly to speak, but I have always held a great *tendresse* for you, my dear. I couldn't abide how cruel Quintin was in his dealings with you. He never loved you, Madelyne. I do. And after a decent period of mourning, I know everyone of account in Savannah will expect us to wed. After all, you'll need someone to run Blackthorne Hill."

Madelyne sat round-eyed, stupefied with shock

as he gushed on. Then, recovering herself, she said coldly, "You seem to forget, *Cousin* Andrew, that I've been running the plantation alone and unaided for well over a year while Robert was ill and Quint off fighting with the Americans." She stood up, desiring to get away from Andrew before she said something she would later regret.

He, too, rose and stood stiffly, towering over her, his pock-marked face flushed with anger. "Don't act the fool, Madelyne. You've always been exceedingly bright for a female. You need the protection of marriage to me to shield you from the scandal of Quintin's death."

He reached for her, but she jerked away. "No! Quint isn't dead yet, but you're talking about him as if you wish he were."

"And why ever should I not? He and Devon have always been the lucky ones—wild, irresponsible, favored with pretty faces to charm weak, foolish women."

"Well, that lets me know your opinion of me and the rest of my sex. I shall go to Barbara. Perhaps she can persuade Monty with some of her weak, foolish wiles to spare my husband!"

He snorted in disgust. "Lud, you are naive. The Lady Barbara has seen common sense even if you refuse to. She's to wed Viscount Weymouth in a fortnight—just before they sail for England."

"No! She can't. She doesn't love him." Images of Barbara crumpled on the ground, sobbing as Devon rode off flashed through her mind.

"Love between a viscount and a baron's daughter has little to do with the arrangement. Marriage for the better classes is always a matter of property and social position. You'd do well to remember that, Madelyne," he chided, struggling to bring his anger under control.

She looked up at him with tear-blurred eyes. "Property and social position be damned, Andrew.

I love Quint and will not let him die!" She turned from him and fled, slamming the door behind her.

Andrew watched her ride off from his vantage point at the window, stroking his chin in consideration. "You'll come around once he's dead, stupid little chit." He imagined her soft, perfectly formed little body lying naked on the big bed in Blackthorne Hill's master suite, her lush mahogany hair spread like silk across the pillows. "Soon, Madelyne, soon," he murmured with a sly smile.

When Madelyne reached the Caruthers' house she was told the Lady Barbara was not receiving that day, having just returned from an outing with a migraine.

"I simply must speak with her," Madelyne informed the goggle-eyed butler as she imperiously shoved him aside and ascended the stairs while he gaped in amazement. Ladies, even colonial women of quality, simply did not behave this way!

Madelyne found Barbara lying on her bed, dressed in a soft cotton robe, with a wet towel pressed across her eyes. When she sat up in response to Madelyne's entrance, she removed the cloth.

"You've been crying." The telltale red rims of Barbara's puffy eyes spoke as eloquently as the look of bleak despair in their depths. "You don't want to wed the colonel."

"Considering that I finalized the nuptial plans with Alex an hour ago, that seems rather irrelevant now. My wishes aren't the issue, Madelyne. Let it rest."

"Let it rest? You love Devon Blackthorne."

"Devon won't ever marry me," Barbara replied softly. "And anyway, there are other matters to consider, such as Monty's gaming debts."

"You told me not a fortnight ago that you'd let the authorities cart Monty off to debtors' prison before you sold yourself to save him." Madelyne watched Barbara nervously twist the damp cloth in her hands. She did not meet Madelyne's eyes.

"The viscount is a very powerful man, Madelyne—and quite kind, really. Dev . . ." She paused as her throat thickened. "Dev told me I could do far worse than to marry Alex."

Suddenly Madelyne understood. "Colonel Weymouth is influential and he desires you, and Monty's desperate to settle his gaming debts. They've struck a deal, but it isn't just for your brother's debts is it, Barbara? You'd never throw your life away just for that. Monty and the colonel are going to free Quint—in exchange for you, aren't they?"

Barbara managed a wobbly smile. "You always were too clever by half. Small wonder you drove the arrogant Quintin Blackthorne to distraction."

"You can't do it. I won't have it, Barbara. Quint would never ask such a sacrifice. We'll find another way. How are they going to arrange it—bribe the guards?"

Barbara shrugged. "Something of the sort. Alex is paying for it, and Monty is handling the details."

"Oh, Barbara, what a true friend you are!" Madelyne hugged the taller woman.

"You love Quintin, and in time, once he's free, he'll believe you're innocent. Be happy, Madelyne, for my sake."

"Not at the price of your soul. You love Dev."

"But I can't have him. You already have Quint."

Madelyne turned away. "Quint is my husband, yes, but he may never return my love, Barbara. I'll find a way to get you free of this tangle. See if I don't!"

Blackthorne Hill, at the Riverfront

The warehouse was dark and musty as Madelyne made her way through its labyrinth of crates, barrels, and boxes with Gulliver padding silently behind her. The pungent odor of cured hides mingled with the spicy fragrance of tea, now a rare and hoarded commodity. The sheer size of the place had always awed her, even viewed from a distance when she had ridden up the hill to the plantation house. Now, for the first time, she ventured inside. It was night and no one was about. Her lone candle flickered feebly in the darkness as she stepped cautiously from one creaking floorboard to the next.

Madelyne and her canine protector had slipped past the sleeping guard. Since Andrew had refused to help free Quint, she knew he would refuse to allow her access to the warehouse. He would certainly not approve of her diverting funds to bribe a royal official for Quint's freedom. She lifted the latch on the office door at the rear of the warehouse and entered the interior, which smelled of ink and mildewed paper. It was cluttered with piles of dusty ledgers and loose papers.

She sighed and set her candle on a high desk after clearing a place for it. Then she located another one and lit it to provide more light as Gulliver watched with curious eyes. This was going to be a long night, she thought as she climbed onto a high oak stool in front of the desk and began to sort through the papers.

Monty's debts, in addition to the bribe for Quint's jailers, amounted to much more than all her household budget. She would have to sell off or trade some of the valuable items from the warehouse. Perhaps the listings of luxury imports on some of the cargo manifests might give her a clue as to what would be best to barter.

She had no more than begun to read when Gulliver's low growl alerted her to danger. Then the sound of loud cursing echoed through the long warehouse. She quickly doused her candles and ducked behind the desk.

"Them damblasted Frenchies'll be waitin' fer these pelts 'n the British rum and muskets. It's a damn long ride across the hill country. Git the men in here, and I'll tell them where to start loadin'," a raspy voice commanded.

"Why is it we always have to risk our scalps crossin' Creek country while Blackthorne sits all nice 'n safe, waitin' ta collect the biggest share of the profits?" another high-pitched voice whined.

The first man cursed some more, then added, "Cause he's the boss . . . at least until the war's over 'n them fancy redcoats leave."

"Aw shit, McGilvey, we oughta just clean out this whole warehouse right now 'n sell everythin' in New Orleans. I got me a woman there . . ."

His words faded as he and the man called McGilvey turned another direction in the vast warehouse. Madelyne stood frozen in the darkness. They were stealing British trade goods intended for the Creek and selling them to England's enemy, the French! And Devon was responsible for their treachery! How could she have so misjudged a man? Barbara loved him. Surely it could not be true, but if not Devon, then . . . Suddenly Madelyne remembered Quint saying that Andrew's wastrel ways had led him near penury.

Could it be? She must learn which Blackthorne brother was the thief and traitor. When her eyes had grown accustomed to the dark, she made her way out of the office, creeping stealthily toward the muted voices. Gulliver now held his peace, but his hackles bristled as he moved silently at her side. Half-a-dozen men were carrying rum barrels, boxes of muskets, and bundles of deerhides from the warehouse under the orders of a big, rangy man with stringy hair and cold yellow eyes. He looked like one of the outliers who preyed on both sides during the war. She crouched behind a pile of boxes marked china—a commodity they would most certainly not find profit in transporting overland.

"Be on the trail a month before we see any French silver fer this stuff," one scrawny man with odd, puffy eyes wheezed, hefting a cask.

"Part I hate worst is havin' ta split th' loot with Blackthorne," the whiny-voiced man replied.

Puffy Eyes spat a gob of tobacco juice on the floor and chuckled. "That skinny, pock-marked bastard don't get all his share and you know it. McGilvey always sees to it we short him."

Skinny, pock-marked! Stunned, Madelyne had her answer. It was Andrew—Andrew who had always been so kind to her, Andrew who wanted Quint dead so he could woo her and take over all the wealth of old Robert's estates.

Trembling, Madelyne crawled away from the scene of pilferage and climbed out the window in the office. The dog jumped agilely to the muddy ground below, but the drop was too great for her to risk it. She scrambled down one of the splintering log supports that held the warehouse above floodtide waters. As she made her way back up the hill to the plantation, she considered what to do.

"No wonder Andrew was always so solicitous about taking care of Quint's business for me. It provided the perfect opportunity to steal me blind!" She racked her brains for a way out of the coil. "Who can I trust to help Quint escape?" she rhetorically asked the dog.

The Outskirts of Savannah

Devon stared incredulously at the small, bedraggled woman who stood in the center of the austere log cabin he temporarily occupied. He was still groggy after being awakened by Madelyne's insistent pounding. After several days on patrol searching fruitlessly for McGilvey, he had just returned to the city. "You can't be serious!"

"Dev, I would scarcely have ridden through the night to awaken you with such a tale if it weren't true! Andrew wants Quint dead so he can inherit. God only knows what he planned to do to James once he had Robert's estates under his control. Barbara was right about him, and I was such a blind fool."

Dev stiffened as the pain lashed at him again. "Barbara's taken care of herself very sensibly."

"No! Barbara's marrying Weymouth to save Quint. The colonel was to forgive all Monty's gaming debts and bribe the watch to free Quint. That's why I went to the warehouse in the first place—to search for some means of raising funds to get Quint free without her having to pay such a terrible price. She loves *you*, Dev."

He raised one golden eyebrow skeptically, then shrugged in resignation. "And you love Quint."

"Can you not forgive him his deception? He believes in his cause just as passionately as you do in yours. It's men like Andrew and that awful McGilvey he employs who have no honor."

Dev caught his breath. "McGilvey! He was the man in the warehouse? Describe him to me."

"Tall and heavyset, wearing greasy buckskins, stringy filthy hair—I think it was red—cold yellow eyes—"

"Enough. That's him. My pious brother and that pillaging butcher. Bloody hell, what's this world come to?" Dev ran his fingers through his tousled hair and shook his head, dazed.

"The war has done terrible things to us all, but you and Quint have fought for principle—even if on opposite sides."

The old familiar grin that Madelyne had not seen on Devon Blackthorne's face in many long months flashed once again. He threw up his hands in mock surrender. "All right. I'll gather some of my Muskogee brothers for a rescue mission. We have access to military headquarters. The British regulars are used to me and my Muskogee scouts by now."

Madelyne threw her arms around Dev's neck and hugged him. "Oh, Dev, thank you! You're the only one I could turn to. Perhaps this will mend the rift between you and my husband? After all, if you're willing to save his life . . ."

He smiled sadly at her and shrugged. "Perhaps. In the meanwhile, I want you to return to Blackthorne Hill. Stay well clear of Andrew. I'll deal with him after I see to Quint."

"She was a real shapely wench, she was. Wouldn't mind tumblin' her if'n only I could find her agin." McGilvey took a swallow of rum and belched, then wiped a big paw across his beard-stubbled chin and leaned back on his chair.

Andrew winced in distaste and looked nervously around the crowded riverfront alehouse where he had summoned his minion for a report before the expedition to the French departed. "I don't like it, seeing a woman snooping around the warehouse while you were transferring goods."

"Bloody hell, she was just some indentured from th' plantation, probably comin' back from meetin' her man down at the riverside. Little bit of a thing, but she had this big brute of a hound with her. I wouldn't like to tangle with him. Sure would've liked to tumble th' wench, though. She had lots of pretty dark hair—looked reddish when th' moonlight struck it."

Andrew almost dropped his mug of ale. "A small woman with reddish hair and a big shaggy dog?" God above, could it be? He cursed and stood up, tossing a coin on the table. "Be off with your wares and don't try to cheat me this time, McGilvey. I'll see to the matter of the wench."

Chapter Twenty-four

"Tall Crane has been gone too long," Pig Sticker said in the Muskogee dialect. He was leaning against the wall of a barracks, across the street from the weapons storage depot of the military headquarters.

Dev replied in the same dialect, "He's well known and trusted by the British officers. It was best that he check on the position of the guards." He scanned the chaotic scene about him with keen eyes while lounging with seeming indolence beside his savage-looking Indian companion. "They're getting ready to pull out within a few weeks or I miss my guess."

"Do they wait for orders from the big chief to the north?"

Dev grunted. "More likely the bigger chief from across the waters. Britain is conceding these colonies, leaving her loyal subjects to emigrate or remain and face at best a very uncertain future here."

"What will you do? Surely you would not live in the cold country with the redcoats." Pig Sticker

398

studied the pensive, bitter expression in Golden
Eagle's eyes.

"No. I'll return to my mother's people."

"Panther Woman will rejoice." The Muskogee
waited for Dev's reaction.

With a shuttered look, Dev replied coldly, "Panther Woman would do well to look elsewhere for a
husband."

Before Pig Sticker could frame a reply, Tall Crane
strolled past them and engaged a half dozen of Dev's
Muskogee scouts in conversation, using a mixture
of English and their own language. Very casually,
Dev and Pig Sticker drifted over to join the group.

Speaking in English for the benefit of a few British
soldiers who happened by, the Indians discussed
their upcoming search for the renegade McGilvey.
When no one was nearby, they used Muskogee to
set up a plan for freeing Quintin.

"The wooden house where he is held is filled with
soldiers—too many for us to overcome. But there is
another way for us to free the prisoner," Tall Crane
said.

"I do not like going against our allies and aiding
an enemy," one of the younger men said, looking at
Devon with undisguised anger.

"Look around at your allies. They prepare to desert
us and give over this land to the settlers. We would
do well to have one such as Quintin Blackthorne as
our friend," Tall Crane interjected.

Devon stepped forward and faced the malcontent.
"You have been a good warrior, Walks the River,"
he said in English. "If you do not wish to follow me
on this mission, I will understand."

Walks the River looked at Tall Crane and the
others, then back to Devon. "I will follow you."

"Good." He studied each face, then looked to Tall
Crane. "What is your plan?"

"Soon it will be dinnertime and the men will
return here to eat. The barracks are not far

from a large stockpile of powder in the armory . . ."

Quintin sat in the musty, windowless little room, furnished only with a bare cot, a battered old wooden cabinet with a cracked pitcher full of rancid water on it, and a noisome slop jar in the far corner. The evening heat was as oppressive as a mud-soaked wool blanket, cocooning him in sticky misery.

He stared at the cracked chink in the wall but did not see it. He saw only Madelyne's tear-streaked face, heard her imploring voice begging Montgomery Caruthers not to arrest him, then begging his captors to let her see him. He had overheard her dispute with his jailors through the locked pine door. She had been here twice that first day, then again the second. Today she had not come. Had she given up?

At daybreak tomorrow he would face a firing squad. The military trial had been brief, thorough and very legal in spite of the British army's preparations for evacuation. Major Caruthers was a man who apparently held a grudge—and had influence in the highest military circles of Savannah. Quintin had been a member of the Royal Militia, caught in the traitorous act of freeing a rebel prisoner. He was a spy. His execution would be perfectly legal.

But the legalities of his impending death bothered Quint far less than the reason he had been apprehended. Had Madelyne sent word to Caruthers? Then why did she repeatedly return here begging to see him? And why did he hope against hope that her protestations of innocence were true?

"I'm a fool," he muttered to himself as he stood and began to pace in the small, stuffy room.

He was interrupted by the guard with his evening meal, no doubt another bowl of that unidentifiable grayish meat, with sour wine to wash it down. Just as the armed sergeant unlatched the door to admit an enlisted man with a tray, a roaring blast of noise filled the air.

"Gor, what was that! Them rebels blowin' up the whole bloody city?" the soldier asked as the tray clattered to the floor, splashing food and splintering crockery across the room.

The sergeant cursed and prodded his underling with the butt of his musket. "Clean up that mess, you imbecile!"

Pig Sticker moved behind the sergeant with silent swiftness and struck a blow to his head with a warclub. Before the hapless private could rise from his knees, he too was rendered unconscious in the same manner and fell ungracefully into a puddle of congealing grease.

Quint looked at Pig Sticker and smiled uncertainly, then saw the gold of Dev's hair in the dim light. "Dev! You're the last man alive I'd expect to rescue me—or have you come to beat the firing squad to their job?"

"No time to talk. Blowing the armory powder kegs will only keep the soldiers busy for a short while." They made their way from the room into another larger one, where two more soldiers lay sprawled. "I hope when they wake up they won't be able to identify any of us," Dev said as the Muskogee warriors filed out of the small building and vanished into the twilight. Then he grimaced. "Of course, in a short while it won't matter. They'll all be gone."

He looked at the chaos outside as smoke billowed in black plumes from the wooden building at the end of the sandy road. Soldiers and civilians raced to see what had happened. Dev motioned for Quint to follow him. "Horses tied behind the building," he said as they slipped outdoors and circled the squat edifice.

"Domino! How the devil—"

Dev swung onto Firebrand and said with a smile, "I owed Monty Caruthers some payment. You're not the only one he's harmed. I figured stealing his new prize was as fair a way as any to even the score. Let's ride and hope the sentries at the bridge are occupied with the explosion."

As Devon had wished, the whole area was in complete disarray. They passed the last sentry checkpoint without being stopped, but just as both men began to relax, a challenge rang out.

"Captain Blackthorne, what are you doing with that prisoner?" A short, thickset man with a face like a bulldog's stepped into their path with his Pennsylvania rifle raised. He wore the uniform of the Royal Militia, the same as Dev.

"This man is no prisoner, Captain Kirker," Dev replied, measuring the distance between them.

Kirker spat. "The devil you say, you lyin' half-caste. It's your cousin, the one to be shot for a spy. I'd know that arrogant face anywhere." He drew a bead on Devon.

"A pity for you, old chap," Quint said as he leaped from Domino and landed on the captain, knocking the rifle from his hands before it could discharge. The two men rolled in the sand for a couple of turns; then Quint came up on top and landed a solid blow to Kirker's jaw. The captain went limp as Quint leaped to his feet, then looked questioningly at Dev. "He can identify you."

Dev shrugged. "As I said, in a few weeks the British will be gone. And so will I, but I owe you my life. Kirker always hated me because of my Muskogee blood. He'd have shot me before you."

Quint smiled broadly. "Then we're even. That firing squad would have made short work of me come daybreak."

"No, as a matter of fact, one way or the other you'd have been freed. The women in our lives have seen to that."

As they rode from the city, Dev explained about

Barbara's bargain with her brother and Weymouth to secure Quint's freedom. "If I hadn't agreed to break you out, she'd have married the viscount and you'd have been let go by his men while the guards looked the other way."

"Madelyne came to you, asking you to betray king and country for me—and you did it?"

"First she went to my brother." At Quint's snort of disgust, Dev nodded, then went on to detail what Madelyne had learned about Andrew and his involvement with McGilvey. "So you see, she couldn't get help from Andrew and she couldn't let Barbara wed a man she didn't love. That left only me."

Quint's face split in a lopsided grin. "Does your being here mean you've forgiven me?"

Dev returned the smile, but his eyes were haunted. "Yes, I've forgiven you. The things I've seen in this war . . . it's senseless and barbaric, yet you rebels believe in your cause just as honestly as we loyalists believe in ours. I only wish it could've been settled without all these years of blood and death."

"I've often thought the same. I've ridden with Marion the past two years. Skirmishing in the back country, you see a lot of things—brutal ugly things done by both sides. Marion controlled his men but, I've heard stories about Clarke and Sumpter . . ."

Dev sighed. "They're no worse than Brown or Tarleton, God knows. I'm only glad it's over, even if we did lose."

"You plan to live with the Muskogee, but you don't have to, Dev. Andrew will pay for what he's done and once he does, his land and property will go to you. After all, I can vouch for the reformed man you've become."

Both men reined in their horses on the bluff above the city. It was dark now and time for them to part. Devon appeared to consider Quintin's words. His mouth was a grim slash as he said, "Andrew's not been brought to justice yet."

"He will be. I'll see to it."

"No. He's my brother, Quint. I'll see to him. This has been brewing ever since we were children."

"You can't go back to the city now. That Captain Kirker will have a hue and cry raised against you," Quint protested.

Dev's expression lightened. "Neither can you. I'll think of some way to deal with him. I'm to meet with Tall Crane and his men in an hour. Go home to your wife, Quint. She's risked her life to save you. She loves you."

"I've been pondering that. . . . Mayhap it was Andrew all along, playing us both for fools. I've treated her abominably, Dev. She ought to hate me."

"Instead she's given you a splendid son and all the devotion a man could ask. Go to her now."

Quint rubbed his beard-stubbled chin. "I guess the reckoning between us is long overdue. Lie low with the Muskogee for now, Dev. We can both deal with Andrew after the British evacuate. He'll have nowhere to hide then."

Dev shrugged. "Maybe I'll have Pig Sticker and my other Muskogee cousins do some checking on this connection between Andrew and McGilvey." He paused, then extended his hand to Quintin. "Good luck at the Hill."

Quint clasped his hand and replied, "Take care, Dev, until I hear from you—and thank you."

As they rode their separate ways, their eyes were glazed with tears. The war was over, at least for two men.

Blackthorne Hill

"You must be mad if you believe you'll succeed in this," Madelyne said to Andrew as she knelt protectively over James's cradle where the child fussed.

Of all nights for me to have allowed Gulliver to go hunting with Obediah!

"Just pick the child up and come with me." He waved the boxlock pistol in his hand toward the small bed.

"You'll waken Nell. How did you get into the nursery without the servants questioning you?"

Andrew's thin face was wreathed in smiles. "Why, I'm your beloved cousin Andrew. When I said you had sent for me, no one dreamed of questioning me. I sent them all back to bed. Tis late, but not too late for us to take a stroll with little James here down to the orchard. Tis a warm night with a full moon. And, grieving, soon-to-be widow that you are, who'd think it strange that you want my moral support at such a time?"

Her eyes narrowed. "All right, I'll come, but there's no reason to bring James."

"Bring him." All traces of his smile were erased.

"Why did I never see beyond your mask before?" Madelyne asked, more of herself than of him. His pale brown eyes were as cold as a viper's, and his face bore the stamp of vicious cruelty. What was he capable of? "You mean to harm my son," she said, standing up and placing herself between him and the cradle.

Andrew swore in disgust. "You spoiled little chit. You could have wed me once Quintin was executed. How long I've waited and planned for that."

"You were the one who betrayed him as an American spy, but how—"

"That pea-brained Phoebe was quite a talented eavesdropper for all she was such a stupid cow."

"You killed her." Madelyne shuddered with the realization. *He's going to kill me and James, too!*

"I could scarcely have her about saying I'd turned in my own cousin. That would have quite ruined my chances with you."

"You never had a chance with me. I thought of

you only as a friend, more fool I."

"And you adored that arrogant swine, Quintin, worshipped the ground he walked on no matter how badly he treated you. He and Dev—always the pretty faces to charm women—you're fools, all of you, and you'll pay. I'd planned to create a tragic accident in the orchard, but you leave me no choice. I'll end it here."

He raised the pistol's broad butt and swept it toward her head to knock her senseless, but Madelyne threw herself at him, using the disparity in their heights to her advantage, knocking him off balance. She cried out as Andrew's strong, bony fingers clawed at her throat.

Quint had heard the low murmur of voices as he climbed the stairs and followed them toward their source, the nursery. Standing outside the door, he overheard the exchange between Madelyne and his cousin. The enormity of his folly and Andrew's perfidy held him rooted to the hall floor until Madelyne screamed. When he kicked in the door, Andrew was kneeling over Madelyne, choking her.

"You bloody cur," Quint growled as he launched himself at his cousin, tearing Andrew's grip from Madelyne's neck.

She rolled free, coughing and gasping for air, then crawled to James's cradle and laid her body across it. Horror-filled, she saw the two men struggle, even as her eyes frantically scanned the room for the pistol Andrew had dropped when he began choking her. It had been kicked across the floor by the two men who now rained punches at each other in a savage fight for survival.

Andrew was unaccustomed to the rough life of a soldier, but desperation lent his tall, rangy body incredible strength. Still, Quint's war-toughened reflexes dodged or absorbed every punch, while he pummeled Andrew mercilessly. Knowing that his only hope was in using the pistol, Andrew maneuvered toward it, then dropped to his knees as if reeling from a blow while he bent over and reached for the weapon.

"Quint, watch him! His pistol's on the floor," Madelyne screamed.

The two men closed and then a shot reverberated through the small room. Slowly, Quint rose and the pistol clattered to the floor. During the struggle, the gun had twisted so that it discharged into Andrew's abdomen, ripping upward to his heart. A look of incredulous disbelief spread across Andrew's features as he felt his life's blood gush over his waistcoat, covering his body. He toppled forward onto the floor, dead.

Madelyne ran to Quint's side, frantically running her hands over him to see if he had been hurt. He gently took her small hands in his and kissed them each in turn.

"You're all right. He didn't shoot you! Oh, Quint, thank God, thank God." She buried her face against his chest as he held her tightly.

"I heard your scream from outside the door. I heard a great deal else, as well. Thank God you sent Dev to free me, or Andrew would have murdered you and our son in cold blood."

"Dev and his Muskogee work very efficiently," she hiccupped, still holding on to him fiercely.

"He told me everything about Andrew and that renegade, and about how you risked your life trying to raise funds to save me. I've been a fool, Madelyne. I—"

James's loud, fear-filled bellow erupted when his softer whimpering cries yielded no response. Madelyne smiled and reached up to caress Quint's face. "Come, see your son," she said softly, leading him by the hand across the room. She knelt and plucked the little boy from his bed and lifted him in her arms, offering him to his father.

Quint looked at the thick cap of inky hair

and round, deep-green eyes of James Quintin Blackthorne, his son. When he took the boy in his arms, he felt his chest tighten. "I doubted you," he said hoarsely. "I was always afraid to trust you. That's why I refused to see James when I came home. If my father couldn't recognize his own son, could I?"

Madelyne read the naked anguish in his face and saw again the small boy, brutalized and castigated by Robert Blackthorne.

Before she could reply, Toby appeared, brandishing one of Robert's old swords. Delphine with a rolling pin and Nell with a pressing iron stood behind him. All three were dressed in nightclothes, round-eyed with amazement as they took in the scene.

"Toby, be so kind as to see that my cousin's body is taken to the root cellar for the duration of the night. We'll see about a burial tomorrow," Quintin instructed as he held James in one arm and draped the other protectively about his wife.

"Lawd above, never did like dat man," Delphine said. "Mastah Quintin, you look fair onto starved. I's goin' ta start cookin' right now!"

As she waddled back downstairs, everyone burst into laughter.

The Georgia Back Country

Devon sat with Quint's letter in his hand, staring into the campfire. The site was well into a swampy area where neither British nor American patrols ventured. His brother was dead. Dev felt no grief, only relief that Madelyne and little James had not been harmed by Andrew's insane greed. He was happy for his cousin and his family, but distressed by the rest of Quintin's message.

His cousin wanted him to come forward after the British evacuated and claim Andrew's share of the Blackthorne inheritance. He was no longer a

Crown agent, but with hard work he could become a prosperous merchant trading with the Muskogee. *But without Barbara, I don't want that life.*

Devon's troubled reverie was interrupted when two warriors approached him. They had obviously come from a lengthy reconnaissance in the back country.

"The one you seek has been seen with six men, far to the west of here. They travel with guns and whiskey from the English Father, meant for us but destined for sale to the French."

"How many days? Show me," he commanded.

The warrior who had remained silent knelt and began to draw a map in the dust using the point of his knife. "They cross the Altamaha so, head west, so."

"Right for New Orleans. How quickly can you ready horses and men enough to journey after them? I would kill George McGilvey and you may have his stolen prize."

"We will have all in readiness by nightfall, Golden Eagle."

Dev folded Quint's letter and tucked it inside his buckskin rifle shirt. He no longer wore his green ranger's uniform. The war was over and he had chosen to remain in Georgia, for better or worse. But before he faced any future, he had to settle things with McGilvey. He owed the loyalists and the rebels that much for all the agony and destruction the marauder had wrought. Devon Blackthorne owed it to himself, too.

Blackthorne Hill

Late-morning sunlight poured in the window, covering Madelyne and turning her skin to gold and her hair to rich, red mahogany. Quint set a pot of fragrant chicory coffee and two cups on the bedside table, then leaned over his sleeping wife and gently touched the bruises on her throat and shoulders. She awakened and smiled up at him with sleepy amber eyes.

Neither had gotten much rest the preceding night. James was cosseted and put back to sleep after his room was cleaned up. When a British patrol had come to search the house for the fugitive, Quint had hidden Andrew's body and himself in a secret chamber in the cellar while Madelyne convinced the enraged Monty Caruthers that the last place to which her husband would ever return was Blackthorne Hill. After searching unsuccessfully, he had departed in high dudgeon.

Once Obediah returned with Gulliver, the dog was loosed to patrol for any more British soldiers. Delphine had prepared a feast to celebrate the master's deliverance, which everyone took part in. Quint and Madelyne had collapsed in exhaustion at first light, content merely to sleep wrapped in the security of each other's arms.

"What time is it?" Madelyne asked, rubbing sleep from her eyes and sitting up as Quint poured her a cup of steaming coffee.

"High noon and past time you were up preparing for our picnic. I thought we might go to the pond." He paused and studied her over the rim of his cup. "It does hold certain memories."

Recalling their impassioned lovemaking there, she felt the heat scorching her cheeks. "Yes, Quint, it does." Her lashes fluttered down, and she sipped her coffee. He took her chin in one hand and raised her head. "I've made you feel ashamed of your warm, wonderful instincts. I'm sorry, my love, so very sorry for that. I've been such a fool." He took her cup and set it on the bedside table, then enfolded her hands in his. "I always thought I wanted a plain, meek woman to bear my children, one so prim and cold she'd hate her marital duties and never enter into a dalliance with another man."

"As you were told your mother did," she said softly.

His face revealed his anguish as he squeezed her hands. "She was innocent . . . all these years I hated her, cursed her name for crimes she never committed. And I mistrusted all women, especially beautiful ones," he added, brushing her lips softly with his. "I read the diary this morning, Madelyne. Even if I did not already love you, I would love you for finding it and unlocking her tragic secret."

Madelyne smiled radiantly. She cupped his face between her hands and returned his gentle kiss, murmuring, "That is the first declaration of love you've ever made to me, Quintin Blackthorne."

"Believe me, it won't be the last."

James's cries interrupted the interlude. "Let me fetch our son, then we can discuss that picnic," he said as he rose from the bed.

In a moment he returned with James in his arms, but before he reached their bed, he knelt down with the boy and stood him on his sturdy little legs. "Now, let's do again what we did earlier this morning," he coaxed.

To Madelyne's delight, their son walked a somewhat erratic but unbroken path from his father's arms to the bed, where he stood, pulling on the covers and beaming up at her as she squealed her praise and lifted him into her arms. "Oh, you little rascal, all these months of one or two steps and then, boom! You show off for your father!"

"I taught him how to do it," Quint said smugly.

Madelyne's expression told him what she thought of that opinion. "Come join us in our morning romp." She took James by his hands and began to bounce him up and down on the bed. He shrieked with delight as both his parents joined in the game.

After seeing to James's feeding, while Quintin watched with another sort of hunger in his eyes, Madelyne tucked the exhausted little boy in his bed. Placing his arms about his wife's waist, Quint whispered in her ear, "Now that you've assuaged my son, you must attend to his father."

She raised one eyebrow. "Must I indeed?"

"Saucy wench!" He nuzzled her ear and turned her into his embrace. She went willingly.

The afternoon was hot, but the water was cool and inviting down at the pond, shaded as it was by bald cypress trees. They laid Delphine's feast of honey-fried chicken and sweet spiced peaches out on a blanket. While Quint poured two glasses of cool ale, Madelyne cut up a loaf of crusty bread and spread it with butter, then heaped two plates with all the largess of the imperious old cook's kitchens.

"Delphine's cooked almost continuously since you returned home last night, so you'd best eat every morsel," she chided.

"I did my duty in the middle of the night—to keep from 'fair wastin' away'. Now it's your turn."

They ate in silence for a few moments, sipping the pungent ale and licking bits of grease from their fingers as they finished the chicken. Then Madelyne felt Quint's eyes on her and looked into his hungry gaze.

"I think you need a bath to clean off all that chicken grease. Allow me to assist you."

He reached out and took her hands in his, teasing her palms with his tongue, then sucking on her fingers. With spare efficiency, he unlaced her bodice and pulled it off, then untied the tapes of her lightweight muslin petticoats. She helped him by pulling them down and kicking them aside. He pulled off her slippers and peeled down one sheer cotton stocking, letting his tongue trace a teasing pattern over the curves of her calf.

"Mmm, no chicken grease there. Let's check the other leg." She giggled as he followed through with his leisurely seduction. Then he reached for her chemise and untied the neckline. When he pulled it free, he again saw the darkening bruises Andrew had left on her perfect little body. His mood immediately shifted. "How close I came to losing you, Madelyne. While that greedy madman stalked you, all I did was accuse you of his crimes."

She rose to her knees and enfolded him in her arms, raining kisses on his face and neck. "I, too, was a fool, Quint. Barbara always told me not to trust him, but I fell under his spell like a bird charmed by a snake. The more you spoke against Andrew, the more I defended him."

"You always were a stubborn, willful woman, but I'd have no other."

"Not meek, submissive, and dutiful?" She sat back with her sleek little buttocks resting on her heels, preening like a cat under his heated gaze.

"Meek—never. But submissive and willing to do your wifely duty—with enthusiasm—now that's quite another matter."

He groaned when she reached out and began to unfasten his shirt, sliding it from his shoulders. When she turned her perfectly curved derriere to him and tugged at his boots, he whispered raggedly, "Why did I ever imagine I wanted a plain, frigid woman? Beautiful, passionate ones are much to be preferred."

Madelyne completed her task of removing his boots, then turned to unbuckle his belt. He took the opportunity to cup a breast in each hand, hefting their weight, then teasing the sensitive nipples with his thumbs. "You've been feeding my son for over a year. . . ." He flicked his tongue across one and she let out a small, incoherent cry.

"James is almost weaned," she gasped.

"Then by all means, allow me to examine the way he has been feasting," he whispered harshly, lowering his head to circle one rosy-pink nipple with his tongue, then suckle on her breasts, moving from one to the other. She arched against his voracious mouth, and her fingers dug into his shoulders as she clung to him. "My son is very lucky," he said as he nibbled wet kisses up across her collarbone and throat, then met her mouth.

Their lips brushed and caressed, their tongues dueled and tasted as they fell to the ground and rolled back and forth on the soft, springy moss. When her soft mouth left his, it moved down to his chest, where she buried her face in the thick black hair. When she licked and nibbled at his hard male nipples, he groaned. "Woman, what are you doing?"

"Checking you for chicken grease," she replied as she sat up and began tugging at his pants. She wriggled lower and unbuttoned his fly, then began to pull down the tight pants, pausing to stroke his swollen phallus when it sprang free of its confinement.

He raised one eyebrow wickedly. "Well, aren't you going to check there for chicken grease?"

Taking the dare, she tasted of him with several long, darting licks, then took his pulsing staff in her mouth until his hips arched and he gasped.

"Madelyne—oh, my darling Madelyne, yes, yes."

When he could withstand the exquisite torture no more without spilling his seed, he pulled her up and kicked off his pants, then lifted her in his arms and walked into the sparkling water of the pool. "I need to cool off."

"Spoilsport," she said as he lowered her into the pool. Then, as their slicked bodies glided against each other, she wrapped her arms and legs around him, but he did not plunge into her. Instead, he rolled back into the water, letting her recline on his chest as he propelled them across the pond.

"Let's go slowly and savor this," he whispered.

"Like the first time," she murmured in his ear. "That was so beautiful for me, Quint."

"Until I ruined everything the next morning.

This time I promise I'll make everything perfect, Madelyne."

"Everything is perfect now, Quint," she said as she nuzzled his ear and rubbed her body against his in a most enticing manner.

He speeded up their swim around the pool. She chuckled and continued her seduction until he reached the shallows and swept her into his arms. Walking out of the water, he knelt and laid her on the blanket. His hands traced the trails of glistening droplets, lovingly curving around her breasts, belly, and hips.

"You are so perfectly formed, so exquisitely beautiful . . . I love you."

"And I love you," she echoed, pulling him down to share a deep, sealing kiss.

Quint tore his mouth from hers at last, moving his lips in suckling, brushing caresses down her body as if laving her dry after her bath in the pool. He paused at her breasts and feasted, then moved to her navel and twirled his tongue in it until she writhed and ran her nails up and down his back. When he spread her thighs and moved his head lower, he could feel her stiffen in anticipation, but as soon as his mouth found the velvety wet heat at the core of her body, she arched in uncontrollable passion.

"Slowly, gently, my love," he murmured against her flesh, then continued the delicate torturous ministrations that had her head rolling from side to side as she moaned with pleasure.

I'm drowning, drowning in a whirlpool of such unbelievable . . . All thought fled as she reached the achingly sweet, subtle peak and hung suspended there, held in thrall by his deft caresses.

When Quint felt her body begin to spin out of control and heard her cry out his name in the throes of release, he raised his head and moved up to cover her body with his, thrusting into the sheath of fiery glory that contracted and enveloped him.

Gritting his teeth, he held back from joining her climax, then continued to stroke deeply inside her, long, slow, slick plunges that left them both breathless. As he felt her again ascending to another, even higher plane of release, he let go of all control and gave in to her urging, moving harder and faster until they were both sweat-sheened and panting.

Madelyne felt the ultimate swelling of his staff as he teetered on the brink of release and went tumbling into the vortex of blind ecstasy once more, this time, taking him with her. He raised himself with his arms on each side of her body and watched her face, then rasped out hoarsely, "Look at me, Madelyne."

She opened her eyes and locked them with his as he spilled his seed deeply within her body, then slowly sank atop her, where he lay, breathing harshly while she ran her hands up and down the muscles of his back and shoulders.

When he took her in his arms and rolled over to place her on top of his body, she nuzzled his chest. "Now we both need to bathe again." She paused and licked a droplet of perspiration from the small hollow of his Adam's apple, then chuckled. "We could eat more of Delphine's chicken first. I always did like salty things."

He roared with laughter, then pulled her closer for a long, thorough kiss. "Don't ever change, Madelyne. Be you, for me."

"Bareback riding? Swimming naked? Working in the dairy?" She challenged him.

"Plant rice or barter with the Muskogee for pelts— I don't care. Only forgive me for my cruelties and never stop loving me."

"We were both victims, Quint, but the past is past. Now there's only the future. The war's over and we can build our life in peace."

A small smile played about his lips. "The Americans have won. Does that mean you'll change your politics?"

"When it comes to loving you, Quintin Blackthorne, I have no politics."

Chapter Twenty-five

July, Western Georgia

Dev paused by the edge of the stream to let Firebrand drink. He dismounted, knelt down, and ducked his head in the cooling water. Several of the Muskogee with him, dressed sparely in breechclouts, plunged in and splashed about.

"He crossed here less than a day ago," Pig Sticker said to Dev. Rising and shaking the water from his hair, he followed his cousin to a narrow curve in the course of the twisting little creek. "See the hoofprints."

"Shod horses and pack mules. No doubt it's McGilvey." He knelt and examined the soft earth where the crossing had been made. "We'll catch up to him tomorrow?"

Pig Sticker nodded. "The whiskey and guns are heavy. We travel light. Before the sun reaches the top of the sky, we will see these men."

That night, Dev lay on his bedroll, listening to the

hum of insects and the soothing ripple of the creek. The guttural conversation and occasional bursts of laughter from his companions did not disturb his reverie. He could see Barbara's face etched in the night sky. Her beauty burned brighter than all the stars of the heavens. Again the pain of losing her sank into him like razor-sharp talons. But, as he reminded himself, he had never *had* her to lose. She was always destined for Weymouth or someone like him.

Yet she seemed so desperately unhappy at the prospect of wedding the viscount and had agreed to the betrothal only under the duress of saving her brother's honor and Quintin's life. "Well, I can do nothing about Monty's gaming debts, but I have saved Quint's life," he murmured to himself, sitting up restlessly to skip a pebble across the stream.

He wondered if Monty had convinced her to go through with the marriage in spite of Quint's escape. Madelyne had been convinced she would not. *It makes no difference. She will be gone when you return. Accept it.* Yet the thought of some soft, pallid English nobleman touching his beautiful Barbara filled him with bitter loathing.

Yer yellow-haired woman, McGilvey had called her. And he had been right. She would always be his woman, even though an ocean separated them.

"Your thoughts are deep," Tall Crane said quietly as he squatted on his haunches beside Devon. His nephew grunted a monosyllabic agreement. "You think of her. The English noblewoman." Knowing the answer to his rhetorical question, Tall Crane continued, "I see how you hurt and it troubles me."

Dev grinned. "Not half so much as it troubles me. But it'll pass. She's going home."

"The British soldiers are going home. . . . I have been thinking."

"Back when I was a boy in your village, Uncle, that used to mean I was in trouble."

Tall Crane chuckled. "Perhaps you will yet think you are in trouble. Your brother is dead. You will be your father's heir."

Dev raised his hand. "Quint has already mentioned that fact, but Andrew was out to kill my cousin to inherit his estates. He'd already run through everything Father left him."

"The trading company will still be yours. If you worked hard at it, I think you could prosper well enough to take an English wife."

"She's gone—or she will be as soon as her brother and his men receive orders to evacuate Savannah. She may even be married. There was talk of a betrothal between her and a colonel, a viscount. I don't know what will happen to her, but it won't include me, whatever it is. I'd rather not talk about it, Tall Crane."

"I understand, Golden Eagle." The Muskogee clasped Devon's shoulder, then rose and walked off, leaving the troubled younger man alone, staring at the night sky.

Early the following morning, Pig Sticker tracked the marauders with their pack train of stolen trade goods to a campsite near a sluggish stream. Five men were breaking camp in a haphazard fashion, obviously the worse for a night spent overindulging in the contents of one of the rum casks. A big brute sporting a livid red scar on his chin seemed to be in command, cursing and ordering the others to hurry with the reloading of the mules.

"They have no sentries posted," Pig Sticker said contemptuously to Devon as they crouched in the marsh grasses, observing the scene across the stream.

"I don't see McGilvey. Only five of his men. It seems unlikely he'd take the dawn watch."

"The Big Fire Hair is not with them. I have moved around the whole of their encampment," Pig Sticker replied with finality.

Devon cursed. Was McGilvey always to slip from his grasp? He gave the signal for the Muskogee to disperse, ringing the camp in a semicircle while the thieves struggled with tying heavy casks onto recalcitrant mules.

"Try not to shoot the rum barrels and waste good liquor," Dev whispered to Pig Sticker. He stood up and yelled for the marauders to surrender.

As he expected, they dove for their muskets and reached for their knives, but the fight was an uneven contest. Dev and his seven battle-hardened Muskogee warriors made short work of five rum-soaked marauders. "Take at least one alive," he yelled as he deflected the blade of a small, squirrel-faced man who snarled as he pulled free and tried again to carve up his prey.

As they circled, knives gleaming evilly in the bright morning light, Dev asked, "Where's your boss? I want McGilvey."

Squirrel Face cursed, and the red veins in his temples stood out as he lunged for Blackthorne. Dev spun wide and grabbed a fistful of greasy hair at the same time that his knife slashed his foe's arm. The smaller man's knife dropped from his hand as he screeched in pain and fell to his knees clutching his bleeding arm.

Dev looked around the camp and found the skirmish was over. Three of the raiders were dead and another wounded. The Muskogee waited for further orders as Pig Sticker held a knife at the throat of the wounded man.

Noting the emotionless way the big brute held steady beneath Pig Sticker's considerable menace, Dev decided to try his luck with Squirrel Face, who was rocking back and forth, cursing and sobbing as he cradled his arm.

"Rags! I need rags to wrap my goddamn arm. I'll bleed to death." He let loose another string of oaths.

Dev took a proffered strip of linen from Tall Crane and held it before the little outlaw. "If you want me to bind that arm, start talking. Where's McGilvey?"

Squirrel Face's eyes moved from side to side, taking in the fierce savages with gleaming bronze skin and beaded scalplocks. "Yer gonna let 'em kill me anyways."

Dev ran his finger caressingly across the length of his knife, then said, "There's dying . . . and then there's dying."

Squirrel Face blanched, then choked out, "He left us two days ago. A man he knowed come ridin' in, half killed a horse gettin' to the boss. He had a message from someone in Savannah. George, he left Macklin there in charge." He pointed to one of the dead men.

"Who sent for McGilvey? What was the message?"

The little raider grimaced in pain, then whined. "I only heard part of it. Something about that toff whose warehouse we take the goods from. Him bein' dead."

"Andrew Blackthorne? What about him?"

"Whoever sent for McGilvey wanted him to come back to Savannah because of it. Like I said, I couldn't make out all they said. I only know he rode out of camp two days back, headed for the city."

Dev motioned for Tall Crane to assist him as he bound up the raider's slashed forearm, then had him and his wounded companion tied to their horses. "Pig Sticker, you take the muskets and powder to your village. Tall Crane, I want you and two of your men to take the rum and these fellows to whatever passes for the rebel authorities in Augusta. They've burned and raided the Americans even more than the loyalists. I expect the new government might want to hang them," he said cheerfully.

"Why not just kill them now and keep the rum?" Pig Sticker asked reasonably.

"We will need to curry favor with our American

neighbors and their new leaders. This is a small beginning," Tall Crane explained.

Dev nodded in agreement.

"Do you think you will capture this McGilvey before he reaches the city?" Pig Sticker asked.

Devon shrugged. "He knows the land well enough, but I expect a Muskogee can travel faster than a white man. Since I know his destination, I'll not slow down to track him. A man like McGilvey won't be hard to ferret out in the city. I wonder who the devil summoned him that he left this prize and backtracked all the way to Savannah?"

"You will doubtless learn that and many other things when you reach the city," Tall Crane replied enigmatically.

July 11, Savannah

The waterfront was a scene of pandemonium as all manner of small sailing craft, pirogues, and flatboats took on cargo and passengers. A smattering of women dressed in fine silks ordered servants to have a care with their trunks and boxes while nursemaids fussed with crying, frightened children. Hard-looking rivermen dressed in greasy buckskins spat and swore as they poled their overloaded craft down the river toward Tybee Island, maneuvering past other craft and occasionally colliding with them in the melee.

Smartly dressed officers in scarlet barked commands at enlisted men and civilians alike as muskets, cannons, and ship's victuals were loaded for the journey downriver. Columns of soldiers marched with a brisk efficiency, oddly at variance with the chaos surrounding them. The British army was evacuating Savannah.

Inside the Blackthorne city house on St. James Square, Lady Barbara Caruthers and Major Montgomery Caruthers faced each other at the foot of the massive spiral staircase in the front entry.

"You look quite resplendent, Monty. I'm certain there will be lots of rich young heiresses waiting in London, fair swooning for the chance to marry a war hero. You'll land on your feet."

"I simply cannot sail off and leave you here all alone with this colonial riffraff." Monty's voice was imploring, almost desperate.

"I'm scarcely alone. Quint Blackthorne is our cousin. He and Madelyne have offered me their protection and this beautiful house to live in until I settle my life. I'll not have to take to the streets to support myself."

"You're waiting for that half-breed, aren't you?" he asked bitterly.

Barbara ran her hand nervously back and forth along the polished walnut newel post. "Yes, Monty, I'm waiting, but even if he doesn't return, or if he does and refuses to marry me, I still choose to live here."

"Why in the name of God? Weymouth—"

"Weymouth, not God, has everything to do with why I'll never go home. If you and mother didn't force me to marry him, it would only be someone else like him. I'll not go back to that kind of life."

"Don't be a lackwit. Would you rather live among savages?" he asked contemptuously.

"If I have to. I'd prefer the Muskogee to the London *ton*. The Indians are kinder—and more honest."

"You've taken leave of your senses." He took two steps toward her, but before he could seize hold of her, Barbara produced a turn-off pistol from the folds of her muslin skirts.

"It's primed and ready to fire, Monty. Madelyne taught me how to use it."

"You are mad! You can't shoot your only brother!" He looked at her set jaw and glacial blue eyes.

"I'd much regret it, and being a cripple would prove an impediment to finding a rich wife. Good-bye, Monty. I'm sorry it has to be this way." Although the gun did not waver, she was relieved to see two of the Blackthorne family servants enter the hall. One politely opened the front door while the other stood patiently, awaiting her orders.

"You'll soon enough come to regret this rash act, Barbara. Damn Devon Blackthorne for rescuing his cousin! You'd have wed Alex if not for that."

"And been unhappy for the rest of my life. It would seem the Blackthornes care more for me than you do."

"Balderdash! I only pray I can repair the damage to your reputation in London by the time you come to your senses and return." With that he spun on his heel and stalked out the door.

Barbara let the pistol fall to her side and leaned against the newel post as tears filled her eyes. "Goodbye, Monty," she called after him.

The following morning dawned sultry and hot. Dull gold light poured in the window of Barbara's bedroom, and dust motes danced on the heavy air. Pulling aside the mosquito netting, she slid from the bed, feeling restless, cut adrift. She had asked Madelyne for this time alone, foolishly hoping Dev might return from his dangerous hunt for McGilvey and come for her. If he would not have her, she would need time to think of how she might spend the rest of her life without him.

Rather than ringing for a maid, Barbara stretched and yawned, then walked over to the enamel pitcher and bowl on the Chippendale dressing table by the window. After splashing her face with cool water, she sponged off her sticky skin as best she could and dressed in a simple riding skirt and shirt. She studied the heavy linen riding jacket and then sighed in resignation as she slipped it on.

"I'm enough of a social liability to Madelyne and Quint just being English, without adding the disgrace of riding in public improperly attired."

She finished dressing and left the house without

any of the servants seeing her, although she could hear the cook preparing the morning meal as she passed the kitchen on her way to the stable. Soon she was riding with her hair flying free, cooled by the rise of a slight breeze. She could smell rain in the air.

Barbara rode without purpose or direction, only feeling the need for exercise. Bilbo, a young groom, stoically followed just behind her, having been roused from sound sleep to accompany the mistress. Dev had been gone for over two weeks now and she feared for him, but Madelyne had reassured her, saying he had Pig Sticker, Tall Crane, and half a dozen other trusted Muskogee scouts with him on his dangerous mission.

It still seemed incredible that the fastidious Andrew Blackthorne had been in league with that vile raider. No wonder her immediate instinct had been to dislike and mistrust him and that witch Serena Fallowfield.

As she rode through the sandy streets, she noticed absently that Serena's house was at the next square. "I wonder what she'll do now that she no longer has Andrew to bedevil," Barbara murmured to herself as she nodded good morning to a pair of well-dressed matrons riding in a carriage. Outside of a few busily scurrying tradespeople, the streets were still quiet.

Just as she was about to pass the corner on which the Fallowfield city house was located, Barbara noticed a big, roughly dressed man unlatching the side gate and slipping furtively inside.

"How odd." Something about the fellow sent a prickle of apprehension racing along her spine. Frontiersmen dressed in greasy buckskins were a common enough sight in Savannah, but his enormous shoulders and that stringy red hair—he had looked for all the world like George McGilvey. Of course, that was patently ridiculous. The renegade was halfway to New Orleans with Dev in close pursuit. Still . . . She turned her mare around the corner of Abercorn Street, then dismounted beneath the shade of an elm tree.

"Bilbo, I feel the need to pay a surprise call on the Widow Fallowfield. Wait here with the horses. I'll not be long."

The youth nodded uncertainly as Barbara disappeared around the high iron fence, thickly vined with bougainvillea. As quietly as possible, she made her way to the side gate and lifted the latch. Was that man McGilvey? If so, even the likes of Serena Fallowfield did not deserve to be menaced by him. Or was he expected?

Absurd as the idea sounded, it was only slightly less believable than the raider's association with Andrew. Looking around the lush spring garden, which Barbara noted was poorly tended and overgrown with weeds, she made her way cautiously toward the house. *What do I do now? Demand that the servants awaken their mistress and tell her a desperate outlaw is prowling in her garden?*

Just then she caught sight of Serena, dressed in a plum silk robe with her long black hair in disheveled tangles about her shoulders. The widow was walking toward a gazebo in the far corner of the yard, hidden from the house by several Chickasaw plum bushes overgrown with morning glory vines and deergrass. Now Barbara was certain Serena had a rendezvous with George McGilvey. But why? She pulled her full riding skirts close about her legs and began to creep closer to the gazebo, where she was certain the marauder waited for the widow.

Dev cursed the blind chance that had caused him to lose sight of his quarry. A large wagon filled with rum barrels had overturned, blocking his way as he followed McGilvey across the city. The raider was on foot, seemingly headed for a specific destination.

Dev had decided to see what it was before stopping McGilvey. But now the hunter was stymied, for when he had detoured around the barricade of broken barrels and terrified horses, McGilvey had vanished.

"He must've slipped into one of these houses." Dev loped Firebrand slowly down the street, looking at the elegant brick homes. "What the hell is a man like McGilvey doing in this part of the city?" Dev pondered as he turned the corner and saw one of Quint's stableboys standing nervously beneath an elm tree with two horses.

"Bilbo. A little early for a ride. What're you doing out here, son?"

"Mastah Devon. I'se sure glad to see you. The mistress, she done gone 'n run off on me. I been powerful worried." His Adam's apple bobbed painfully, and his liquid black eyes looked enormous.

"The mistress? Is Madelyne here in the city?"

"No, suh. It's her friend, the English lady."

"Barbara Caruthers?"

"Yes, suh. She went in that yard, followin' some big, mean-lookin' fella."

Dev sprinted across the street and around the corner, immediately spying the unlatched gate. Dear God, what insane urge had led Barbara to stalk a man as dangerous as McGilvey!

Once inside the yard, he silently made his way around the perimeter. Best to scout out the grounds before entering the house. The sound of whispered voices in a terse, angry exchange floated on the still morning air. He moved closer to the gazebo which was hidden from the house by an overgrowth of vine-covered Chickasaw plums.

The hair on the back of Devon's neck stood straight up. He freed the Kentucky pistol from his belt and checked to make certain it was ready to fire, then walked up to the gazebo where McGilvey was saying, "The Blackthorne warehouse'll be cold cinders by tomorrow night."

"Not if *you* think to put the torch to it, McGilvey," Dev said as he stepped up onto the wooden planking of the gazebo.

Serena clutched her silk robe to her bosom and paled as the half-breed Muskogee leveled his pistol at McGilvey. "Thank heavens you're here, Devon! This filthy brute accosted me as I walked in the privacy of my own yard." She moved closer to Dev, wanting to give McGilvey the opportunity to over-power Blackthorne.

"Don't believe her, Dev." Barbara entered the gazebo from the opposite side, where she had been hiding. "I heard her instruct McGilvey to burn the warehouse because it contains Andrew's records—which implicate her! She's as guilty as your brother was."

"You lying, meddling bitch," Serena hissed as she turned and came at Barbara with her hands curled into claws.

McGilvey took advantage of the women's exchange and lunged for Barbara, seizing her by her hair and pulling her against his chest. "Throw away that gun, you Muskogee bastard." He raised his knife toward Barbara's throat.

Devon threw his gun across the floorboards of the weathered old gazebo.

Desperately, Barbara stomped on McGilvey's in-step with the heel of her riding boot and twisted free.

As Barbara broke free, Dev dove at McGilvey. The two men went down, rolling across the splintering planks, punching and gouging at each other. When they broke apart and stood up, each held a knife in his hand.

"Now I'm gonna lift that yeller hair from your half-breed skin," the renegade said as he circled Devon. "Then I'll have yer woman. Maybe I'll let her keep all that silver hair of hers . . . for a while."

"Keep your filthy mouth off my woman, scum."
Dev's jaw clenched as he circled the hulking ren-
egade. His eyes never left McGilvey as he asked
Barbara, "Did he hurt you?"

"No, Dev, he didn't hurt me," she replied, warmed
by his words, *my woman*. She stood well to the side
as the two men lunged and parried.

Dev drew first blood, slashing the raider's
shoulder. "This time we're evenly matched,
McGilvey. I haven't been gutted by one of
your renegades. Let's see how you fight against
a Muskogee." He feinted high with his blade, then
moved in low with lightning speed and grazed
McGilvey again, this time on his forearm.

As the men continued to fight, Serena edged slowly
around the vine-covered gazebo, intent on reaching
the pistol Dev had thrown away. Barbara had the
same idea and the two women came at the weapon
from opposite sides, kneeling to reach for it at the
same time.

Serena cursed as Barbara's hand knocked the gun
from her grasp, then fastened in her ebony hair
with a hard yank, cracking her head on the wooden
floor.

"I think not, you silk-clad viper." Barbara pinned
Serena to the plank floor, trying desperately to hold
her down, out of the way of the men engaged in
lethal combat.

By now, both Devon and McGilvey were sweat-
soaked and breathing fast in the sultry morning air.
Blood smeared their bodies, and their clothing hung
in tatters, slashed by the keen edges of honed steel
they wielded with ruthless intent.

Dev saw Barbara struggling with Serena for the
gun and prayed his brother's accomplice would not
harm his love. McGilvey, too, noted the women and
smirked. "This time the Englishwoman won't sink
a blade into me before I finish you." He waited for
Dev's eyes to flicker to Barbara and Serena for an

instant, then lunged for the kill.

But Devon sidestepped just as the bigger man's blade sliced through his rifle shirt. His own knife came up from McGilvey's blind side, and sank into his lower abdomen, left to right, gutting him.

McGilvey let out a gasp of agony and surprise as he staggered free, but Dev's blade flashed again, this time finding its mark for a quick, clean kill, under the breast bone and into the renegade's heart. Dev watched as the brute fell to his knees, eyes already glazed in death. Then he toppled face forward, clutching his belly and landing in a lifeless heap on the floor.

Barbara punched Serena on her jaw, knocking her back into the railing where she collapsed, unconscious. Seizing the gun, she scrambled up and raced into Devon's arms.

"How, by all that's holy, did you stumble on McGilvey? Didn't your first encounter with him teach you anything?"

"Yes. That I'm your woman. And you just repeated it," she said as her hand caressed his face, wiping a smear of blood from one cheek. "Oh, Dev, hold me." She wrapped her arms tightly around his waist.

"I thought you sailed with your brother. You were mad to stay behind."

"So Monty told me. But you see, I don't ever again intend to live as I did in London. Madelyne and Quint have opened their home to me—while I decide what to do for the future."

"And what will you do?" His hands tangled in her silver-gilt hair, stroking the silky masses, reveling in the sweet, feminine smell of her skin.

She looked up at him. "As Alastair Blackthorne's heir, you could make his estates profitable with work and time. And I'm learning to be a very hard worker, Dev. We can do it together . . . if you'll have me." She hesitated, but he didn't reply. "If not, well, I shall open a shop for ladies. After all, who knows fine fashion better than an Englishwoman?"

He felt the warm, pure joy welling up inside him, flowing over him in waves, leaving him speechless with the bliss of the moment. He held her fast and nuzzled her neck as she babbled on about her modiste's shop until he could recapture his voice. "And how will you finance such a venture?"

"Cousin Quint will make me a loan, I'm sure. Madelyne will see to it," she couldn't resist adding.

"I rather imagine he does owe you, considering you were willing to wed Leicester to save him from the firing squad." He felt her shudder in revulsion.

"I'll never wed a man I don't love."

"Won't you, now? Ah, your ladyship, I guess that means I'll have to marry you to save you from spinsterhood."

She squealed in joy and raised her lips to his for a deep, devouring kiss. Neither of them noticed or cared when Serena crawled from the gazebo and fled to her house.

Blackthorne Hill

Quint scanned the hurried note from Devon as Madelyne sat across from him at their dining room table. The courier had interrupted their evening meal with the news of McGilvey's demise. He had no more than scanned it when Madelyne snatched it from his hands and read.

"I suppose I'd better ride for the city to act as intermediary with the authorities. Things are pretty much in flux. With Dev being a King's Ranger and Barbara English, they just might find themselves at odds with the likes of Able Kitchner or Adam Mansell." He put down his napkin and started to rise, but Madelyne placed her hand over his, staying him.

"I suspect the worst they have to fear now is that Serena Fallowfield will sneak into our city house and try to bludgeon them."

"I'm sure we've seen the last of Serena. Dev says she's fled without a trace. Took her jewelry and left behind a fortune in unpaid bills. Every dressmaker, chandler, and cobbler in the city is ready to lynch her on sight. She had family in South Carolina. I'd wager they'll shortly find themselves saddled with a most unwelcome houseguest."

"Then there's no immediate danger. The authorities haven't indicated to Dev that he and Barbara are in any trouble. Lord knows the rebels hated McGilvey just as much as the loyalists. Let's give them privacy tonight, Quint. Tomorrow is time enough to return to the city."

"I suppose we could do that," he said with a blinding smile. Then he shook his head in amazement. "Who'd ever have believed it—my wild Muskogee cousin with an English noblewoman."

"She adores him, Quint. Above all, that was why I couldn't let her marry Weymouth to free you."

"I'd say Dev had a bit of vested interest in getting her out of that bargain as well. Needless to say I'm grateful to Barbara and Dev—and to you. Most of all to you, Madelyne." He raised her hand and pressed it to his lips.

"I think we might find similar occupation to Dev and Barbara's tonight . . . if you're agreeable."

He rose, shoving back his chair, and whisked her from hers in a rustling swish of petticoats. Madelyne wound her arms around his neck and kissed him as he carried her from the room, up the stairs to their waiting bed.

Savannah

Dev sat on the bed and watched as Barbara brushed her hair, then started to plait the gleaming silver-gilt mass. "Please leave it free," he said, rising and reaching out for the brush. She handed it to him and he ran it experimentally through the shiny curls. "You are so perfect, your ladyship," he whispered as he set the brush down and turned her from the dressing table to face him. The look of love glowing from her eyes robbed him of breath.

She shook her head as she stood up and came into his embrace. "No, not your ladyship any longer. I'll soon be a Savannah merchant's wife, Mistress Blackthorne, a title I far prefer."

He rained kisses on her throat, cheeks, and eyelids as he whispered, "You'll always be your ladyship to me, my darling."

"I'll be Dawn Woman to the Muskogee, and plain Barbara to your mother. You must write and send for her, Dev. I so hope she likes me."

"She'll adore you just as I do, never fear." He continued kissing her, holding her like a piece of fine china. "I still can't believe . . . you're here with me . . . or"—He grinned ruefully—"that I'm here in Robert Blackthorne's house, taking his proper English niece to bed with me, in the master suite, no less."

Barbara chuckled. "Robert's ghost won't haunt us or Quint and Madelyne any longer. And they'd want us to use this room and this bed," she added, drawing him to it.

"Then by all means, let us make use of the facilities." He reached for the drawstring of her gauzy nightgown and pulled it loose.

As he bared her shoulders, sliding the gown lower, she ran her fingers through the golden pelt of his chest hair and then reached for the buttons of his fly. He pulled the gown down, trailing soft, wet kisses over her breasts; she shoved his buckskin pants past his narrow hips. They both grew breathless as the excitement of the moment built, but this time the moment was different from all the others before it. The lovers knew they would be together for the rest of their lives. No more stolen, secret trysts, no more heartbreak.

Soon their garments lay at their ankles and they

caressed each other's bare, warm flesh. Kicking away the last remnants of their clothing, Devon parted the mosquito netting on the bed and Barbara climbed up onto the big soft mattress and beckoned him to follow her.

"Come love me, Devon Blackthorne, love me well and long as you always have. But this time, I want you to give me your babe, the first of many, many children."

"Your every wish is my command, your ladyship," he replied. He covered her and thrust into the wet heat of her body as she clasped her arms and legs tightly about him. The first time they crested swiftly, their flesh so long denied this sweet surcease of union. Then they lay, not sated but resting, reveling in the warmth and wonder of holding each other quietly.

Soon the fires of passion rekindled and they began again to ascend the heights, but this time Dev moved slowly, gliding in long, languorous strokes, pausing whenever he felt them nearing the brink of release, until at last Barbara arched her body and imprisoned him with her long, silken legs.

"Greedy witch." He murmured the endearment. Then they exploded over the brink once more.

Throughout the night they alternately slept like two spoons, then awakened to love yet again. Dawn came and went, and they slept at last, in exhausted, blissful oblivion.

Devon awakened first and saw the arc of the sun high in the sky. For a few moments, he simply sat up and watched Barbara sleep. Then she stirred and opened her eyes. Bright noontide light quickly caused her to squeeze them closed.

"We've slept to a shameful hour."

"You don't sound a whit disturbed," he replied.

She rubbed her eyes and chuckled. "Back in London, I never arrived home before dawn nor rose for the day until mid-afternoon. I think we've spent the night a deal more enjoyably than ever I did then."

"You're certain you'll never miss all the glitter of London society? Here I'll just be a merchant—not even a rich one for now. I can rebuild, but it'll take some time—and Quint's good offices. After all, as a loyalist I'll not be easily welcomed in the American business community—not to mention the matter of the feelings about my Muskogee blood."

"You'll succeed—for yourself and for your mother's people," she replied with blind devotion, dismissing all obstacles with an airy wave of her hand.

"Don't forget we've lost the war, your ladyship."

She kissed him lightly. "Yes, but we've gained each other, and that's a victory above all others."

They sealed their pledge of love with a kiss.

Epilogue

September, 1782, Blackthorne Hill

The words of the priest echoed across the warm
air as he closed the graveside service with an
eloquent benediction. The group gathered for the
solemn occasion was small. Noble Witherspoon
and Solomon Torres stood to one side flanking Polly
Bloor, who shed a tear or two surreptitiously. Dev
and Barbara, joyous with the news of their expected
child, held hands and exchanged warm glances as
Charity Blackthorne beamed on her son and new
daughter-in-law, Dawn Woman.

Quint held James, who seemed to understand
the gravity of the circumstances and was silent.
Madelyne smiled wistfully. Even Gulliver, standing
next to his mistress, was subdued, save for his
thumping tail. The freshly dug grave was at the center
of the Blackthorne family plot, beside Robert's final
resting place. The newly carved headstone's inscrip-
tion had been ordered by Quintin to honor in death

the mother he had never known in life. It read:

Anne Caruthers Blackthorne
Beloved Wife of Robert
Beloved Mother of Quintin
b. April 18, 1731 d. November 15, 1753

"Now she can rest in peace, here beside her Robbie, where she always deserved to lie, not hidden in the brambles at the back of the family plot," Madelyne said softly as she knelt and laid a bouquet of pink and purple asters on the grave.

Quint knelt beside her, holding their son between them, and replied, "She owes you a debt from beyond the grave for erasing the stain of dishonor from her name. I shall gladly pay it for her, for the rest of our lives."

Author's Note

The American Revolution was the nation's first civil war. Approximately a third of the colonists supported a break from the mother country, a third were indifferent, and fully another third were fiercely loyal to the king. Even for the patriots, the English parliamentary system of government provided the basis for their protest. After all, they fought for "the rights of Englishmen." No place suffered more devastation because of divided allegiances than Georgia. Thus was born the idea for a dual story with two heroes, one a patriot and the other a loyalist.

In my preliminary reference work on the southern theater of the Revolutionary War, I relied heavily upon *From Savannah to Yorktown* by Henry Lumpkin. This thorough chronicle of all the major battles fought in the South is a brilliant analysis of the British southern strategy and of the American and French countermaneuvers which narrowly ensured its defeat. Also useful for military information and anecdotal material about the war is

Robert S. Davis, Jr.'s *Georgia Citizens and Soldiers of the American Revolution*. From it came the idea for my composite villain, George McGilvey. Lumpkin's work gave me an excellent chapter on the Swamp Fox, Francis Marion, and bibliographic information to further pursue this elusive military genius. Two highly informative biographies of General Marion are Hugh F. Rankin's *Marion: the Swamp Fox* and Robert D. Bass's *Swamp Fox*. A first-hand account filled with fascinating details is Brigadier General P. Horry's *Life of General Francis Marion*, written in collaboration with M. L. Weems.

General reference works on the Georgia Colony during the Revolution are extensive. Among those I found particularly useful are *The Fledgling Province*, by Harold E. Davis; *Forty Years of Diversity*, by Harvey H. Jackson and Phinizy Spalding; and *A History of Georgia*, edited by Kenneth Coleman. Books with a wider scope outside Georgia include *The Americans of 1776*, by James Schouler; *The Women of '76*, by Sally Smith Booth; and the excellent *American Heritage Book of the Revolution*, edited by Richard M. Ketchum.

Drugs and . Pharmacy in the Life of Georgia 1733–1959, by Robert Cumming Wilson, gave me a wealth of information to help make Dr. Noble Witherspoon's medical practices realistic. *Slavery and Freedom in the Age of the American Revolution*, edited by Ira Berlin and Ronald Hoffman, provided me with insights into the life of Southern blacks, and *Recollections of the Jersey Prison-Ship*, edited by Henry B. Dawson, was filled with vivid if horrifying details about the lot of rebel prisoners during the war.

The Creek Indians, or more properly, the Muskogee People, were fascinating to research. One of the best primary sources is Louis Le Clerc Milfort's *Memories*, edited by Ben C. McCary. In J. Leitch Wright Jr.'s *Creeks and Seminoles*, I found an excellent description of the Green Corn Ceremony which I used in *Love A Rebel. The Creek People,* by Donald E. Green, is a fine account of the life and customs which have been carried through to the present. For a most comprehensive account from an anthropological perspective, John R. Swanton's *Social Organization and Social Usages of the Indians of the Creek Confederacy* is unmatched. He recreates in infinite detail Muskogee life and customs in the late eighteenth century.

Carol and I hope you have enjoyed our tale of the exciting and harrowing era of the Revolution in the South and that we have portrayed all sides involved in the conflict sympathetically—patriots, loyalists, and Muskogees.

We love hearing from readers. Please enclose a self-addressed, stamped envelope for a reply.

Shirl Henke
P. O. Box 72
Adrian, MI 49221

A FIRE IN THE BLOOD · SHIRL HENKE

Bestselling Author of *White Apache's Woman*

When half-breed Jess Robbins rides into Cheyenne to chase down a gang of cattle thieves, he is sure of three things. The townsfolk will openly scorn him, the women will secretly want him, and the rustlers will definitely fear him. What he doesn't count on is a flame-haired spitfire named Lissa Jacobsen, who has her own manhunt in mind.

Dark, dangerous, and deadly with his Colt revolver, Jess is absolutely forbidden to the spoiled, pampered daughter of Cheyenne's richest rancher. But from the moment Lissa stumbles upon him in his bath, she decides she has to have the virile gunman. Pitting her innocence against his vast experience, Lissa knows she is playing with fire…but she never guesses that the raging inferno of desire will consume them both.

___3601-0 $4.99 US/$5.99 CAN

SHIRL HENKE

WHITE APACHE'S WOMAN

By the bestselling author of *Terms of Surrender*

Running from his past, Red Eagle has no desire to become
entangled with the haughty beauty who hires him to guide
her across the treacherous Camino Real to Santa Fe.
Although Elise Louvois's cool violet eyes betray nothing,
her warm, willing body comes alive beneath his masterful
touch. She will risk imprisonment and death, but not her
vulnerable heart. Mystified, Red Eagle is certain of but one
thing—the spirits have destined Elise to be his woman.

__3498-0 $4.99 US/$5.99 CAN

"HISTORICAL ROMANCE AT ITS BEST!"
—Romantic Times
Discover the real world of romance with
Leisure's leading lady of love!

SHIRL HENKE
Winner of 6 *Romantic Times* Awards

Terms of Surrender. Although gambler Rhys Davies owns half of Starlight, Colorado, within weeks of riding into town, there is one "property" he'd give all the rest to possess—'the glacially beautiful daughter of Starlight's first family. To win the lady, the gambler will have to wager his very life—and hope that the devil does, indeed, look after his own.
_3424-7 $4.99 US/$5.99 CAN

Terms of Love. Cassandra Clayton doesn't need any man to help her run her father's freighting empire, but without one she can't produce a male heir. When she saves Steve Loring from a hangman's noose, she thinks she has what she needs—a stud who will perform on command. But from the first, Steve makes it clear that he wants more than silver dollars—he wants Cass's heart and soul too.
_3345-3 $4.99 US/$5.99 CAN

LEISURE BOOKS
ATTN: Order Department
276 5th Avenue, New York, NY 10001

Please add $1.50 for shipping and handling for the first book and $.35 for each book thereafter. PA., N.Y.S. and N.Y.C. residents, please add appropriate sales tax. No cash, stamps, or C.O.D.s. All orders shipped within 6 weeks via postal service book rate. Canadian orders require $2.00 extra postage and must be paid in U.S. dollars through a U.S. banking facility.

Name _____

Address _____

City _____ State _____ Zip _____

I have enclosed $_____ in payment for the checked book(s).
Payment <u>must</u> accompany all orders.□ Please send a free catalog.

"STRONG CHARACTERS, EXOTIC SETTINGS, AND A WEALTH OF HISTORICAL DETAIL....IT SWEPT ME AWAY!"

—*Virginia Henley*

RETURN TO PARADISE

Bestselling Author of *Paradise & More*
Winner of 5 *Romantic Times* Awards

Separated at birth and raised in vastly different worlds, the sons of the House of Torres could never know that fate would cast them into a hell of their own making.

RIGO — A half-caste mercenary with a temper as black as his raven locks, he had built his formidable reputation on the battlefields of his emperor and in the bedrooms of countless courtesans across Spain and France.

BENJAMIN — The golden son who could do no wrong, he was a healer with a talent as bright as the future he planned on his father's New World plantation.

Like mirror images — one dark, one light — they pursued the same woman and damned each other to heartbreak. Yet in the end, the power of love would redeem their past sins and destine them for a glorious return to paradise.

_3263-5 $4.99 US/$5.99 CAN